Toni Talk

A Story of Love, Ambition, Commitment, and Betrayal

By

Lurma Swinney, PhD

Toni Talk
A novel published by SD Publishing House
ISBN 978-1-63752-304-9
Copyright © 2021 by Lurma Swinney

www.sdpublishinghouse.com
Printed in U.S.A.

Cover designed by Jay Swinney
Edited by Jeanette O'Dell

To my BFF Divas:

Audrey Davis, Bernice Mitchell, Carnetha Dunham,
Francine Gasque, Roena McCall, Rosa Frederick, and
Leslie Moncur.
Love you, my Sistahs!

Acknowledgements:

I give God all the praise and honor that is due to
His Holy Name.
Thank everyone for supporting me by purchasing my
books over the years.

Part One

Chapter 1

"How could you have done something like this, Toni?"

"Done what, Ron?"

"You *know* what!" he snapped. "How could you have ruined me like this?"

"*Ruined* you?" she pondered. "Ron, what are you talking about?"

"You know what I'm talking about!" he insisted. "Does winning a Pulitzer mean that much to you?"

"Ron…"

"I have lost my job! I am facing a multimillion-dollar lawsuit! I am probably going to be disbarred!" he raged but still remained even-tempered. "*Everything* I've worked all my life to accomplish is *gone*! You are my *wife*! How could you have ruined me like this?!"

"You lost your job?" she asked, puzzled.

"What did you *think* would happen?" he retorted then threw up his hands. "I've got to get out of here!"

"Ron, where are you going?"

"Anywhere! Away from *you*!" he snapped. He turned to leave, and she jumped to him, grabbing his arm.

"Ron, baby, please…"

Jerking away, he snarled, "Don't, Toni!" He turned and exited quickly.

"Ron!" she yelled after him, running to the open door, but he didn't stop. "Ron!" Toni took a deep breath then walked back into the huge, three-story, brick house and closed the sturdy, wooden, double doors. She focused on a news magazine laying on the table and picked it up. She shuffled through the pages quickly. She stopped suddenly and began reading. Shock overtook her and she gasped, covering her mouth. "Oh, my God!"

Part Two

Two Years Earlier

September

Chapter 2

"So, Toni, who did you interview to get such intimate details about the Gambino crime family?" a lady asked, sitting across from Toni and another man in front of *'on the air'* cameras and an enthusiastic live audience.

Toni crossed her smooth, silky legs, exposing a little of her thighs in a deep purple, two-piece suit, with tiny sequins around the lapel, collar, and cuffs. Her electrifying smile was accented on her almond tan, round face by her short, dark-auburn colored hair with upturned curls in a Halle Berry style. Her makeup was immaculate. Two diamond stud earrings decorated her ear lobes. At five feet, six inches and a hundred and thirty-five pounds, Toni was beautiful, confident, and witty, and she knew it as she smiled politely and replied, "Veronica, you know I can't divulge my sources."

"I doubt very seriously if you *have* any," the man in the tailor-made, expensive, black two-piece suit snarled.

"And why would you say that, Mr. Kennedy?" Veronica, the talk-show host, curiously probed.

"Because, Veronica, that column *Ms*. Melton wrote is pure fabrication," he added, emphasizing her title.

"She named some highly important people in her article, Mr. Kennedy, including *you*, most of whom have already been indicted by her allegations," Veronica fueled. "So, if the DA thinks the article Toni wrote in her column, *Toni Talk*, warrants attention enough to go after those people, why do you say the article was fabricated?"

"*I* haven't been indicted," he smugly stood his ground, pushing his designer, wire-framed eyeglasses up on his nose, as Toni just smirked, slightly shaking her head sarcastically. Simon Kennedy was tall and distinguished looking with his deep-chocolate tan, smooth skin, low neat wavy haircut, and a small mustache.

"Toni, what about what Mr. Kennedy is saying. Is the article fact or fiction?" Veronica wanted to know.

Toni slid to the edge of her seat and faced the man head on. "Simon, let's examine the facts," she suggested, thumbing through

13

her iPad. "Did you represent Mr. Antonio Marinara on a murder charge?"

"Yes, but…"

"Isn't he a *known* mobster, directly associated with the Gambino crime family?" she charged. Simon just dropped his head, smiling sheepishly. "Isn't he, Simon?"

He lifted his head to face what he considered an arrogant, little know-it-all! "No, that wasn't proven," he answered directly, as Veronica geared up to hear more.

"Well, let's deal with something that *was* proven," Toni continued. "A month after Mr. Marinara was acquitted by your *brilliant* defense, was he not picked up again for raping yet *another* fifteen-year-old girl and bashing her head in, which was *identical* to the case in which *you* had defended him and won an acquittal the first time?"

****

"What're you looking at, Bev?"

"Ron, look! Your *friend*, Mr. Kennedy, is on *Veronica Live* getting creamed by *my* hero, Miss Toni Melton," the secretary replied, focusing on the small television set on her desk.

"Simon Kennedy is a snake in the grass! It's about time someone expose him for what he is," he replied, focusing on the television screen with her.

Ron Joyner was six-feet-two-inches of masculinity, and his two-piece, dark gray suit caressed his lean body to perfection. His handsome, pecan tan face was outlined with a small, neat mustache, encircling his mouth, tying in with a low, thin, neatly trimmed beard. His low haircut was neat and wavy. Pearly white teeth accented his serious, chiseled features. To say he was handsome was a gross understatement.

Beverly was short and round at five-feet-three-inches, two hundred and five pounds. She wore her long hair pulled back into a ponytail around her light-brown African American features. She

14

wore little makeup on her plump face. She could be cute if she were to lose about seventy-five pounds, but she was comfortable with her weight and did little to improve it.

Beverly focused back on her television screen to watch how Simon Kennedy floundered like the fish that Toni was transforming him into, as Ron smiled, feeling extremely happy that Simon was receiving a savor of his own distasteful medicine.

****

"*Everyone* deserves representation, Ms. Melton!" Simon grunted, growing agitated at this smug newspaperwoman. Who did she think she was, accusing him of catering to criminals?

"Yeah, I guess if the *money* is right, everyone *does*," Toni answered dryly, and he grew so angry at this arrogant woman, he seemed to turn another color.

"I don't have to take *this* from *you* or anyone else!" he announced, struggling to remove his microphone.

"No, I guess you don't," Toni continued sarcastically. "I just wonder how you can sleep at night, Simon, knowing that you are putting *criminals* back on the streets daily, just to line your pockets with *money*!"

"If these accusations continue, Ms. Melton, I *will* see you in court," he concluded. "I *am* protected by the *law* against *slander*!"

"And I, Simon, am protected by the United States Constitution. It's called freedom of the press. You *have* heard of it, haven't you?" she retorted confidently. "So, I'm afraid, if you sue, you won't get very much." She smiled slightly, and Simon wanted to knock her teeth down her throat! "So, you've better stick to your *thugs*. At least you *know* you'll get paid!" He shot her one final leer before stomping off the platform.

****

"Yeah!" Beverly yelled in laughter. "She put him in his place!"

Smiling also, Ron agreed, "Yes, she did. Who did you say she is?"

"Toni Melton of *Toni Talk*."

"*Toni Talk*?"

"Yes, she's a free-lance columnist in *The Weekly Herald*. The magazine comes out every Friday. I don't miss it," she replied. "You better get out more, boss!" She burst into laughter, while he just chuckled with her before exiting back into his office.

****

Toni walked into a busy newsroom, and everyone stood, exploding in applause. She laughed and bowed graciously. "No applause. Just throw money," she joked.

"You were great, Toni," one person remarked.

"You put Simon Kennedy in his place," another person echoed.

"Thankyouverymuch," she laughed. "Where's Bill?"

"In his office," another voice replied. "He was *very* pleased."

Toni walked into her office and dropped her purse on the desk as a perky Caucasian lady entered in a simple knee-length, flare, plaid skirt and a navy-blue, silk blouse, with her curly, permed, blonde and brown, shoulder-length hair surrounding her small, tanned face. "Here's the star!" she beamed, exposing all thirty-twos.

"Angel, how was I?" Toni excitedly asked. They grabbed hands and screamed together.

"You were great! Simon Kennedy didn't know what hit him!" Angel yelped.

Angel Rider-Scott and Toni Melton had been friends since junior high school, when Angel moved there from California. They took a liking to each other right away. Toni wouldn't let the other

16

black girls bully Angel, and Angel taught Toni how to play the piano. They were a perfect match, each about the same height and weight. When Toni decided she needed an assistant, she thought of her friend right away. Angel's African American husband, David, owned his own insurance company and made a decent living for them. When Angel was a freshman in college, she met David, who was a senior, and found herself pregnant shortly after. They were married when she was five months along, and she never did get a college degree. A year and a half ago, when Toni asked Angel to help her in the office until she found a permanent replacement, Angel immediately accepted. She was bored being home alone all day when their two children, Ricky, six, and Sammie, seven, were at school and David was at work.

"I gotta see Bill," Toni announced.

"Okay," Angel acknowledged. "You have some messages, but they'll keep." Toni nodded as she left.

She strolled down the hall to an office labeled, *William Hurley, Chief Editor* and knocked on the door. "Come in," a gruff voice from inside called. Toni opened the door and entered. A short, white man in his sixties, with thinning gray hair, rosacea red face, and a round belly jumped up to greet her. "Toni," he admired, giving her a kiss on the cheek. "You were great!"

"You think so."

"I *know* so."

"If we don't get sued," she chuckled.

"Who cares? If we do, it'll still increase circulation three times, just to read about what we're doing to counteract it," he hypothesized, as the door flew open, and another man walked in. He was a five-eleven, well-built, Caucasian man, with short, dark brown, wavy hair, a clean-shaven, bronzed face, and a winning smile. He was stunningly attractive in his expensive two-piece dark suit.

"There is our star!" he raved, clapping his hands.

"Thank you! Thank you!" Toni accepted, smiling wide, curtsying to the floor.

"You were great, Toni."

"Thanks, Mason," she replied, beaming as he planted a soft kiss on her cheek.

Mason Whittaker was another columnist at the news magazine. He was twenty-nine years old and had been around this establishment all his life. His father, Ted Whittaker, the founder of *The Weekly Herald*, had hoped that Mason would take over for him one day, but he had other plans, so his father promoted his friend, Bill Hurley, when he decided to retire. Bill had started at *The Weekly Herald* from the beginning. He was, at one time, the only editor, and he loved the job.

Toni and Mason were the most valuable people at the news magazine. They were both household names. Mason's column was called *Mason on the Move*. *The Weekly Herald's* circulation was statewide in Georgia, although they were based in a large city called Greenleaf, a little north of Atlanta, with a population of over one hundred thousand people. They were respected all over the city, state, and the major cities in the country. Both of their columns were syndicated in major magazines all over the continental United States, but Mason's exceeded Toni's circulation since he had been at it a little longer than she had, thanks to his father's ownership of *The Weekly Herald.*

Everyone speculated that Toni and Mason were more than just working bullies, and the truth of the matter was, they had briefly dated years ago, but when it didn't work out, they managed to remain friends. Since then, Mason reluctantly married Becky Ward, the daughter of the former mayor because he thought she was pregnant.

"Bill, how is Rita?" Toni inquired.

"The chemo is making her so weak; she's getting to the place where she doesn't want to take it anymore. It's a battle."

"I'm sorry," Toni sympathized. "Tell her I'm coming to see her soon, okay?"

"She'll like that."

"Have you thought about a bone marrow transplant?" was Mason's question.

"They're looking into it," answered Bill dryly.

"Well, keep us posted," Toni concluded, and he nodded.

"Mason, how's the Sanchez research coming?" Bill asked, changing the subject, sitting back at his desk.

Holding out a chair for Toni in front of Bill's desk, Mason replied, "Not too good, Bill. Sanchez is nowhere to be found, except through his lawyer. I intended to meet with his lawyer, but I haven't been able to catch up with him either."

"What about today?" Bill asked.

"I've got an appointment with the new mayor in half an hour to discuss the water treatment story," answered Mason.

"Yeah, that's important. We all want to know if we're drinking polluted water or not," acknowledged Bill.

"What is the Sanchez case?" Toni asked.

"The man who is accused of murdering his wife by dropping a radio into her bathtub," Mason shared.

"Ouch!" Toni chuckled. "Oh yeah, I remember hearing about that."

"What about you, Toni?" Mason asked. "Do you have anything pressing today on your agenda?"

"Not right now, but I'm following up on the electric company's lawsuit."

"Do you think you could run and get an interview with Sanchez's lawyer for me?" Mason inquired.

"But that's *your* story!" Toni rejected.

"I'll owe you," he smirked with his sparkling teeth exposed. She couldn't resist. Mason was so good looking and charming that no one could refuse him.

"All right," she gave in. "But you're going to owe me *big* time!"

"Thanks, sweetie," Mason winked.

"Who is his lawyer?" Toni wanted to know.

"He's some big, hotshot associate with Schuster, Collins, and Ballentine Law Firm," Mason replied.

"If he's such a hotshot, why isn't he a partner?" Toni sneered.

"Oh, it's coming," Mason assured. "He handles almost all of their high-profile criminal cases now."

Toni took out her iPad and asked, "What's his name?"

19

Mason answered, "Ron Joyner."

****

"I can schedule you for four o'clock," Beverly said on the telephone, as Toni walked into the office, and Beverly's eyes widened as her mouth dropped open. As Beverly hung up the telephone, she jumped up to greet her unexpected visitor. "Toni Melton of *Toni Talk* up close and personal, as I live and breathe!" Beverly exploded in laughter.

"How do you do?" Toni graciously accepted, smiling sweetly.

"I just saw you on television a couple hours ago, and now you are *here*, standing right in front of me. Oh, be still, my heart!" she raved. With all the attention Toni usually got, she still wasn't used to it. She felt like just plain ole Toni Melton, not a famous, journalistic icon! "Ms. Melton, may I have your autograph?" Beverly reached on her desk to retrieve her recent copy of *The Weekly Herald*, and immediately flipped to Toni's column. "Here, sign right here on your picture."

"And you are…?"

"Beverly, your *biggest* fan," she chuckled.

"Thank you, Beverly. I appreciate that," Toni acknowledged as she signed.

"You are so *beautiful*. The television and magazines really don't do you justice."

"Thank you. You're sweet," Toni replied as Ron's door opened, and he walked out with a client.

"Boss, look who's here!" Beverly raved.

"Toni Melton!" his client exploded. "May I have an autograph, Miss Melton?"

"Sure," Toni agreed, as the lady took out a note pad.

"Susan Cockfield," the elegant lady spoke. "You are so beautiful."

"Thank you," Toni replied, signing the paper. "Here you are, Susan."

"Thank you," she accepted, then turned to Ron. "I'll see you next week, Mr. Joyner." He nodded and she left.

"Excuse me," Ron focused on Toni, extending a hand. "I'm Ron Joyner. Are you here to see me or to sign autographs?" Beverly silently snarled at him.

Receiving his strong hand in a firm handshake, Toni chuckled, "Yes, as a matter of fact, I *am* here to see you." She didn't know this lawyer would be so good-looking. He left her almost breathless.

"Do we have an appointment...ah...Miss...?"

"Melton," she finished.

"Right," he replied sarcastically as if he really didn't care what her name was or whom she was. She had no right barging into his office unannounced just because she considered herself to be somewhat of a celebrity.

"Ron, Mr. Peterson postponed his appointment until four, so you're free right now," Beverly spoke up quickly, not wanting to disappoint Toni. Ron threw her an annoyed glance then focused back on Toni and extended his hand towards his open office door.

"This way, please," he led, glaring back at Beverly, who simply smiled wide and hunched her shoulders slightly.

Ron closed the door and offered, "Please, have a seat, Miss Melton."

"Thank you, Mr. Joyner," she accepted, planting herself in front of his desk. He couldn't help but to notice her gorgeous, silky legs as she crossed them, taking out her iPad. He sat behind his desk, so he wouldn't have access to look at those killer legs and lose focus.

"What can I do for you, Miss Melton?"

"*Toni*, please," she offered, and he nodded his acknowledgement. "My colleague, Mason Whittaker, is doing an article on your client, Mr. Thomas Sanchez. Mason is tied up today and asked me to conduct an interview with you." She noticed his blank leer, and it confused her because it was more like an annoyed smirk. He straightened in his seat and focused on her face long and hard.

"Miss Melton, I'm going to tell you what I told your colleague," he stated firmly. "I don't *talk* to *reporters!*"

"You've talked to Mason already?" She was confused. Mason led her to believe that he hadn't contacted this lawyer.

"Yes, and I made it perfectly clear to him that *anything* my client and I talk about is confidential, especially since I *know* how *reporters distort* the truth."

"But I'm not a *reporter*," she stated matter-of-factly, growing annoyed with this man. "I'm a *journalist*."

He smiled with a sarcastic smirk then conveyed, "Same difference. *All* of you just want a *story!*" He stood. "So, Miss Melton, I'm sorry but you have wasted your time in coming here."

She stood and confronted him, "Mr. Joyner, a *story* is not my main concern here. I pride myself on getting the *truth*."

"Yeah, right!" he sarcastically chuckled then moved from around his desk. "I have nothing to say."

"Is your client guilty?" she retaliated, exposing her fangs now. She was tired of playing footsy with this arrogant attorney, no matter how drop-dead *gorgeous* he was!

His dazzling, hazel eyes widened, and she assumed that she had touched a nerve in him, but he simply stated, "I don't defend *guilty* people."

"Does your client stand to inherit sixty million dollars from his wife's estate?" she pressed, and he remained silent. "Does he?"

"Miss Melton…"

"*Toni*, please."

He eyed her long and seriously, ignoring her friendly gesture, then insisted sternly, "*Miss Melton*, what part of *no* don't you understand?! I *cannot* and *will* not discuss this case with *you*, *Mason Whittaker*, or *anyone else* he sends to try to ambush me!"

"Mr. Joyner, your client had motive and opportunity," Toni continued to lean on him. "And I hear that he has a mistress. Is that correct?" He stared at her long and hard. He couldn't believe that this beautiful, *unbelievably beautiful*, woman had such mitigating gall as to badger him like this. He was through trying to be nice to her! He calmly opened the door, although he wanted to yank it off the hinges and ram it down her persistent, arrogant throat!

"Good day, Miss Melton," he finalized, escorting her out of his office. "It's been... *real*!" He motioned to Beverly. "Beverly, show Miss Melton out, please!" He quickly retreated into his office and it took all he had to close the door civilly without slamming it. Toni took a long, deep, and concentrated breath.

Beverly smiled shyly, a little embarrassed, and made known, "He's really very nice."

Toni took another deep breath and replied sarcastically, "Sure can't prove it by *me*!" Beverly burst into laughter as a tall, dark man entered in an expensive, tailor-made, hunter-green suit with a tan shirt, tie, and handkerchief in his pocket. His hair was in tiny, neat twists, and his deep, coffee complexioned face was outlined with a neatly trimmed mustache but no beard. He stopped when he spotted Toni and a shy smile covered his face as he leaned against the doorpost.

"Toni Melton," he acknowledged.

"Travis Bland," Toni countered sheepishly, meeting his gaze.

He took a few steps towards her and inquired, "How've you been?"

"Fine, thank you," she responded, as Ron opened his door again then froze solid. He wasn't expecting to see Toni still there.

"We have nothing else to talk about, Miss Melton," he made known.

"I'm leaving *now*, Mr. Joyner," she retorted. He gave her a dubious look before focusing on his colleague.

"Travis, I've been waiting for you," Ron added then walked back into his office.

Travis smiled then focused back on Toni and replied, "His bark is worse than his bite."

"Oh, so he *bites* too, huh?" Toni chuckled sarcastically, and Travis burst into a soft laughter joined by Beverly.

****

23

"Hello, Melissa."

"Hi, Simon," the pecan tan lady responded, with her hair pulled back and secured in a neat bun with a gold barrette, as she stood behind a bakery counter with a white apron covering her green slacks and green rayon blouse. "May I have your autograph?"

"*Funny*, Melissa."

"She clobbered you on TV today, Simon," she laughed. This exposed a dimple on each side of her face. Her other employees continued to work around her, waiting on customers.

"She didn't *clobber* me, Melissa. Toni Melton is an arrogant, nosy, newspaper woman who will get just what's coming to her one day."

"Well, she certainly *didn't* get it *today*," Melissa continued to laugh, and he just stared at her. Then, he had to laugh also. He slowly reached up and brushed her cheek lightly with his fingers.

"You are so beautiful," he announced softly, and she sobered quickly, staring deep into his sincere, dark brown eyes.

"Thank you, Simon," she replied shyly. "What can I get for you today?"

"*You* would be nice," he whispered in her ear.

"But *I'm* not for sale," she made known.

"But are you available for dinner, or wouldn't big brother approve?"

"No, I'm not available for dinner, and *no,* Ron *wouldn't* approve," she giggled. "And *you* know he's my *little* brother. I have him by a couple of years, same as you."

Simon leaned away from her a bit. He positioned himself so that he could keep his arms on the counter as he asked, "Ron and I used to be friends. Why does he hate me so much?"

"He doesn't hate *you*. He just hates what you *do*."

"And what is *that*? I do the *same* thing *he does*. I *defend* people."

"*Criminals*!"

"But that's for the *jury* to decide, not *me*," he defended. "*Everyone* deserves representation."

24

"We're not going to see eye to eye on this, Simon. I happen to agree with my brother. You defend people even when you *know* they're guilty." She paused, her smile turning into a small frown, "Why do you do that?"

"If a person comes in here and you know they sell drugs, would you allow them to buy anything?"

"That's different!"

"What's different about it? We both provide a service. Yours is bake goods and mine is legal. *Money* is *money.* You would still take their money, wouldn't you?"

"But *I* don't put them back on the streets. *You* do."

"The *jury* puts them back on the streets."

"With your *brilliant* defense."

He sobered, smiled seductively, and added, "You think I'm *brilliant*?"

Their eyes locked momentarily. Then she looked away shyly, took a deep breath, and answered, "You *are* in *court.* You *must* be, to keep putting criminals back on the streets."

"*I* don't. The…"

"Yeah! Yeah! Yeah! The *jury* does. That's a thin line, Simon," she held. "I have children. I wouldn't want them to meet up with those *criminals* you *help* put back on the streets."

"I could protect you *and* your children if you'd let me," he suggested softly, and she just stared at him. "What about dinner tonight, Melissa? I want you to get to know *me* again. Not the *monster* Ron has convinced you I've become."

She glared at him momentarily then answered, "I can't, Simon."

"What are you afraid of? You *know* me. I'm the same guy who used to hang around your house when we were kids. What is the problem? You've been by yourself a long time. What has it been? Two years since your husband's death?"

"About that."

"You've done well to keep this business going by yourself."

"Thank you," she accepted.

"So, what do you say? What about dinner tonight?"

"I'm really not ready yet."

He nodded with a slight smile, gazing at her long and hard then finalized, "I'll be here when you are, Melissa. My office is right next door." She nodded with a shy, childlike smile, and then he decided to change the subject because he could see the hurt in her eyes at talking about her dead husband. "I'll take a dozen cake squares. My secretary loves those things."

****

"You dirty rat! You set me up!" Toni charged into Mason's office. He was on the telephone and hung up quickly then jumped up to meet her. "You *knew* that attorney wouldn't talk, and you *deliberately* sent me into the lion's den!"

Laughing, he defended, "I'm sorry! I thought since your legs were better looking than mine, he would respond to *you* better."

"Well, you were *wrong*," she made known. "*Very* wrong!"

"Did you get *anything*?"

"*Nothing!*" she yelled. "That man is as cold as ice!" Then she added in a mocking tone. "Because he doesn't talk to…"

Mason finished with her, "*reporters!*"

"And you *knew* it!" she raged as Bill entered.

"What's going on here?" he inquired.

"Mason set me up!" Toni continued to rage. "Mr. Joyner is not going to talk to *me* or *anyone* else from the *press*!"

Bill smiled and made it known to her, "Well, honey, if *anyone* can get him to talk, *you* can."

"That's what *I* figured," Mason added, and Toni just frowned at him with squinted eyes and a curled-up mouth.

****

"Why was Toni Melton here?" Travis asked Ron, entering his office.

26

"Miss busy-body had the *audacity* to question me about my client!"

"Mr. Sanchez?"

"Yes. Can you believe it?!" Ron confirmed. "That woman made me so mad, I wanted to throw her out on her bony little behind!"

"And what a *pretty* little behind at that," Travis gloated, smiling slightly, and then Ron stopped and glared at his friend.

"What do you know about her," Ron settled.

"Nothing, except that she's an ice queen."

"Why is that?"

"I took her out once."

"You *did*?"

"Uh huh."

"How did you get her *huge* ego into your *small* Corvette?"

Travis laughed and replied, "Man, I was all tuned up to hit that, and she turned as cold as ice on me."

"Oh, you say she's cold because you didn't get to first base with her?" Ron laughed.

Travis laughed as well, "My man, I didn't even get in the *game*!"

****

"Are you going to see it through for me, honey?" Mason asked Toni, lifting her chin with his finger when they were alone again. "You know I would do the same for you."

"Yeah, right!" Toni spat, and then their eyes locked, and he bent down to give her a kiss, but she immediately turned away from him. "How is Becky?"

He exhaled deeply then replied, "Fine." He went to her. "I'm sorry."

She smiled, but kept him at a small distance, "It's okay. We're friends, right?"

"Yeah, we are."

"Well, I don't know if we're *that* good of friends for me to be humiliated by Attorney Ron Joyner again," she acknowledged, turning to leave.

"Toni, please give it one more shot."

"Mason, that lawyer isn't going to talk to you, me, or anyone else in the press," she insisted, opening the door. "He made that perfectly clear!"

"Use that *womanly* charm."

"Go to hell," she sarcastically snapped, walking out as he burst into laughter.

****

"Rita," Bill called, walking into the two-story house from the garage. "How are you?" Stepping into the living room, he focused on his frail wife, sitting on the couch, with a scarf tied around her baldhead, looking so pale and weak.

"Hi, honey," she replied weakly.

He planted a kiss on her forehead, sat beside her, and asked, "Feeling any better today, honey?"

"Not much," she made known.

"I'll get us something to eat."

"Okay," she acknowledged as he got up. "Jill said she's coming home tomorrow."

"What about her job?"

"She said she'll take a leave of absence, so she can help you with all the chores."

"What about Bob and the kids?"

"They're not coming. The kids are in school."

"Bob is all right with that?"

"She says he is," Rita confirmed. "She's only going to stay a week."

"Have you heard from Carol and Billy today, too?"

"Carol called, but Billy didn't."

"Is everything all right with Carol?"

"Yeah, she's fine."

"No more complications with her pregnancy?"

"I don't think so."

"Good," he recognized. "Toni said she'll stop by to see you soon."

"Okay," she accepted. "She was good on television today."

"Yes, she was. Toni's a real trooper," he agreed. "Well, let me fix you some dinner, honey." She nodded. Bill walked into the kitchen and burst into tears. It was so hard for him to see his once vibrant wife wither away to nothing right before his eyes.

****

"Mom!" Toni called, entering a medium-size, ranch style, brick house with steep steps in the front.

"In the kitchen!" a woman's voice called back. Toni walked into the kitchen and found her mother at the stove, stirring in an open pot. Mrs. Melton was barely five feet tall at one hundred eighty pounds with her hair pulled back out of her round, milk-chocolate tan face in a neat bun. Toni planted a kiss on her forehead.

"Hi, Mom."

"Hi, honey," her mother responded, pulling Toni's jacket together at the collar. "Toni, you really shouldn't show all your chest like that."

"What *chest*, Mom?" Toni laughed, opening the refrigerator, taking out a carrot, and biting it. "I only have *one* button loose!"

"Which is *too* many," her mother countered. "God isn't pleased with a woman exposing herself like that." Toni took a deep breath then decided to change the subject. She wasn't up for a sermon.

"Did you take your insulin today?"

"Um hum," her mother groaned, still pacing around the kitchen, preparing her dinner. "Don't spoil your dinner," she added, indicating the carrot Toni was chewing.

"I won't," she frowned behind her mother's back. "Did you see the show?"

"What show?"

"*Veronica Live*. I told you I was gonna be a guess on her show today."

"Oh yes. I remember," her mother acknowledged. "No, I missed it."

"Why?" Toni asked, sitting at the small, wooden kitchen table.

"I had to wash clothes," Mrs. Melton answered nonchalantly, stirring the contents in another steaming pot.

"Mom, the show was *only* thirty minutes. You couldn't take *thirty minutes* out of your day to watch your *daughter* on TV? Don't you have a television in the laundry room anyway?"

"You always do fine, honey. What's the big deal?" she defended, and Toni just blew hard. She couldn't believe her mother! She was the only daughter of three and her mother acted as if she had the plague or something. All her life, she could never remember her mother supporting her in *anything*. It hurts. Mothers and daughters are supposed to be close, especially when there was only *one* daughter, and she was the *baby*. She understood that her mother was bitter with her father for leaving her, but it wasn't *her* fault.

Toni knew in her heart that her mother had run her father away, with all the talk about his going to hell for taking a drink every now and then. She just wore him down. So, one day he said he couldn't take it anymore and left. Three years later, he remarried a nice lady named Juanita. Toni's mother could never forgive Toni for not hating her father for leaving them, but Toni knew why he left. She left herself as soon as she was old enough. She could *never* stay with her mother again.

Despite her ill feelings and frustrations towards her mother's actions, that didn't stop Toni from visiting daily, and her mother always made dinner for them. The main reasons Toni came was to make sure her mother was taking her insulin for her diabetes, and to make sure her mother was eating right. Her brothers, on the other hand, never visited. They weren't saved and they weren't trying to get saved, and they were tired of their mother condemning them to hell, so they just stayed away as much as possible. Nevertheless, Toni loved her mother and wished her mother would love her back.

****

"Hi, baby," a lady singsong into the telephone.

"Vickie?" Ron asked, sitting on his sofa, reading over some papers in black silk pajama bottoms and a bare chest.

"Who else?" she purred, lying on a king-sized brass bed in a yellow lace short teddy.

"I didn't know you were in town."

"I am *tonight*. We have a layover. I'll be flying out in the morning to Japan," she shared. "Can you come over?"

"*Tonight?*"

"Yes," she chuckled.

"We haven't seen each other in over a year. Why tonight?"

"Why *not* tonight?" she cooed, pushing her long, black, straight hair behind her golden, bronze face. "Maybe it's time for us to change things."

"I don't think so," he disagreed.

"Why not, Ron? I've missed you," she purred softly.

"I couldn't tonight even if I wanted to, Vickie. I'm working on an important case right now."

"*All* of your cases are important," she pouted.

"Yes, they are."

"You can't spare a few minutes of your time for me, Ron?"

"I'm sorry."

"I remember when you thought I was *worth* it."

He smiled, thinking of the wild sex he had experienced with sexy Vickie. It was hard saying no, but he had to. "Maybe another time, sweetheart."

"Are you sure, baby?" she purred. "I really, *really* miss you."

Ron had to laugh at her seductive tone. She usually got her way, and she knew it. "I'm sure," he hesitantly concluded.

"Ron, I'll be gone for a long time," she continued.

"Vickie, I thought we had agreed to end this a long time ago."

"*I* didn't."

"Well, it's hard to have a relationship with someone who's always gone."

"I'm here *now*, baby." she cooed. "And I'm ready, willing, and *able*."

"I know you are," he chuckled. Vickie Barber was a twenty-five-year-old stunning, biracial flight attendant, the product of an African American army lieutenant and a Filipino mother, whom he brought back with him when he was stationed there because she was pregnant. Vickie was used to traveling because she was an army brat, so her profession did not bother her a bit. They had dated off and on for two years, and then about a year ago, Ron decided it wasn't working, so he broke it off. For good.

"Then will you come? I promise you won't be sorry."

Ron cleared his throat and reluctantly rejected, "I'm sorry, Vickie. I can't tonight. I'm in court tomorrow. I have to prepare." He knew he could've gone to see her if he wanted because his case was really finished. All he was doing was putting the finishing touches on it, and he could've done that at any time, but the truth of the matter was that Ron really didn't want to start a relationship back up with her. She was a spoiled, little daddy's girl, and he didn't want to deal with that drama again. Dating Vickie was no picnic to begin with, so he *definitely* could live without it.

"Are you sure?" she cooed, pushing her hair out of her face again.

"Yes, I'm sure."

"Your loss, baby."

Ron smiled and responded, "I *know* it is!"

****

"Mason, is that you?"

"Yes, Becky, it's me," he called back, removing his jacket. Becky entered the den where Mason was untying his tie and they kissed shortly. It was cold, void of any emotion.

Becky Whittaker wasn't what one might call pretty by any stretch of the imagination. She was a pale, redheaded, freckled faced, skinny, thirty-year-old Caucasian woman. Her hair was long, thin, and stringy. She was so pale she almost looked albino. She smoked like a chimney and exercised to exhaustion. She was from a prominent family. Her father is now a wealthy rancher, but once a federal judge, and most recently, the mayor of Greenleaf for twenty years. Her mother died when she was young, and her father never remarried. Becky lived with her father on his ranch until she married Mason, but she still visited him quiet often.

"How was your day, honey?"

"It was all right," he answered. "I met with the new mayor and I think I have the makings of a good article."

"He's a nice man. When my father retired, he recommended him highly."

"Yes, he seems nice."

"What about the Sanchez's case?"

"I asked Toni to talk to Sanchez's lawyer today."

Her eyebrows rose as she spat, "*Toni*?!"

"Yeah. I couldn't get anywhere with Mr. Joyner, so I thought maybe Toni could."

Obviously annoyed, Becky replied, "Did she?"

"Did she what?"

"Did Toni get anywhere with Sanchez's attorney?"

"Not yet, but she's going back."

"Mason, why do you *always* need *Toni* to help you?" she charged, and he took a deep breath. He knew his wife was jealous of Toni. He should've never told her about their past relationship, which ended because of Becky's so-called pregnancy. Becky still didn't believe he had gotten over Toni, and she *definitely* didn't believe that they never slept together like he claimed.

Mason has never been in love with Becky, but he respected her. So, when she told him she was pregnant, he felt it was his duty to marry her, although he and Toni were getting extremely close.

Reluctantly, he and Toni had ended their budding romantic relationship when he decided to marry her. Becky never felt Mason had let go of Toni in his heart, and it scared her that, one day, Toni would reclaim him, and she would lose Mason forever.

"Toni is a big help to me, Becky," he answered flatly. "Where's Amy?"

"She's asleep."

"So early. It's only six o'clock."

"She doesn't feel well."

"Did you take her to the doctor?"

"No, she isn't *that* sick. It's just a cold," she explained.

"I'll go and check on her," he said, exiting.

"I'll fix your dinner, honey. Cecilia cooked lasagna tonight," she called, and he nodded.

Mason entered his six-year-old daughter's Barbie doll decorated bedroom and sat on her canopy bed. "Hi, Princess," he singsong. She rolled over to face him.

"Hi, Daddy," she answered weakly. He pulled her up and hugged her closely. No matter how Mason felt about his wife, he loved his little girl unconditionally.

"How's daddy's little princess?"

"I don't feel good, Daddy," she whined, lying down again.

"What's wrong, honey?" he asked, feeling her forehead with the back of his hand.

She sneezed then replied, "I have a cold."

"Did mommy give you some medicine?" he asked, and she nodded. "Well, you'll feel better soon. You don't have a fever." He pushed her shoulder-length black hair out of her cute little oval face and planted a kiss on her cheek. Amy inherited her dark complexion and good looks from Mason, and he was pleased with that. "Daddy will check on you later. Okay, Princess?"

"Okay."

"I love you."

"I love you, Daddy," she squeezed out weakly then smiled slightly. He kissed her forehead again before he left.

Mason walked downstairs where Becky had already put his plate of food on the table. He washed his hands in the kitchen sink and sat at the table with her, where she was finishing a cigarette and stubbing it out.

"Becky, why do you insist on smoking in the house?!" he snapped. "You know that isn't good for Amy!"

"I'm sorry. I forgot," she retorted.

He ordered, "If Amy isn't better by tomorrow, take her to the doctors." She nodded.

"So, *Toni* is going to do the story on Mr. Sanchez?"

"No, Becky. She's just helping me do some research."

"Why?"

"Because I *asked* her to."

"Mason…"

"Please don't start," he insisted. "I don't feel like this tonight. Toni and I are just friends, and we will *always* be friends. Nothing more and nothing less! So quit sweating Toni, Becky!"

"I'm not *sweating* Toni!"

"Yes, you are! You always do! I can't mention her name without you flipping out, so just stop it!"

Becky's jaw clenched a bit. She didn't like this feeling, but instead of responding, she stood and stormed outside. She needed another cigarette. *Badly.*

****

"Hello."

"Toni, I was gone when you got back. I wanted to know how your meeting went with Mr. Joyner," Angel said on the other end of the telephone.

"Girl, let me tell you!" Toni begin to share, sitting up in her bed in a pink nightshirt. "That man is a stone *trip!*"

"He wouldn't talk to you?"

"Not a word!" Toni chuckled.

"Is he as good-looking as I heard?"

"He's *gorgeous!*" Toni burst into laughter.

"That's what I heard," Angel laughed with Toni.

"Well, you heard right, girlfriend. The man is simply gorgeous with stunning hazel eyes," Toni snickered again but sobered quickly. "But his arrogance takes away from his good looks."

"He's arrogant?"

"Honey, that man puts the *A* in arrogant!" she laughed again.

"You just keep working on him. You'll get through."

"I don't know."

"Toni, I've seen you get interviews that I would've sworn on my children's lives that you couldn't get. Mr. Joyner is no different."

Toni took a deep breath. "And why am I doing this? For *Mason Whittaker*! I'm getting my feelings hurt for *him*! Mason was good to me when I first came to the magazine, but what has the brotha done for me *lately*?" Toni burst into laughter.

Angel joined in on Toni's laughter as she observed, "Toni, you're just too nice for your own good."

"I'm *insane*!" Toni concluded still in humor.

"No, you're not," Angel finalized. "Well, I better go and get the kids in bed. I just wanted to check on you since I heard that Mason set you up."

"Well, you heard right," she concurred. "But I must say, I am curious about this case, but I can't get this Joyner to budge. I must be losing my touch!"

"I don't think so," Angel laughed with her friend as her tall, dark-chocolate tan, baldheaded, one-hundred and ninety pounds of pure muscle, husband entered the bedroom in boxers only and settled into bed with her. "Listen, honey, I'll see you tomorrow."

"All right," Toni agreed. "Tell that hunk of a husband hello."

"I will," Angel said as they hung up. She slid down in her husband's arms.

"Toni?"

"Yes, she said to tell my hunk of a husband hello."

"Hello, Toni," he chuckled in his deep baritone voice, and she smiled with him. They kissed lovingly.

Their kissing grew wild and untamed as he quickly slipped off his boxers and pulled her teddy off her shoulders. Angel groaned aloud, surrendering to his affection. Just as their passions soared, they heard one of their children yelling, "Mommy!" David froze and took a deep breath and Angel followed. He planted a kiss on her forehead and rolled off her.

"I'm sorry," she smirked.

"Tell me again why we had children," he laughed as she sprang from the bed.

Chapter 3

Toni walked into Ron's huge, beautiful office calling softly, "Mr. Joyner!" He entered from a small, adjoining stock room, and focused on her. He blew hard.

"What're you doing here, Miss Melton?"

"Beverly wasn't at her desk."

"I know. She had to run an errand," he replied then strolled closer to her. "You didn't answer. What're you doing here? I thought I made myself perfectly clear yesterday."

"I just wanted to ask you about things that are *common* knowledge."

"*Nothing* is common knowledge, Miss Melton, or you wouldn't be here," he made known. "And I really don't have time for this. I'm due in court in about an hour." Her sweet-smelling perfume was doing a number on him, and he had to fight to stay focused. To top it off, that white silk blouse that was tucked securely into a pair of maroon slacks, exposing her shapely curves, was enough to drive a man crazy. Her maroon heels clicked as she walked closer to him, and he had to look away to avoid making eye contact with her beautiful light brown eyes. Her short haircut was sassy and sexy. Her lips were inviting, but he had to keep telling himself that this woman was the *enemy*.

"I won't detain you," she continued. "I'm speaking of the articles that have already appeared in the newspapers. My magazine could give your client good press coverage to even up the score."

"*Good* press coverage!?" he chuckled. "That's an oxymoron isn't it? Those words should *never* be used in the same sentence as press. All the *press* is interested in is a *story!*"

"I beg to differ," she stood her ground, finding it extremely difficult to do so. She couldn't help but smell his clean, fresh aftershave. Looking into his clear, hazel eyes, and focusing on his smooth, succulent lips, as he stood there, so tall and suave in those black trousers, gray shirt and tie, with the matching jacket hanging on a hook in his office, was driving her crazy. This man was simply gorgeous.

39

"I *bet* you do," he chuckled again, and she almost melted, witnessing his beautiful white teeth behind that inviting smile. "As I said, Miss Melton, I can't talk to you about my client's case." He thought that she was much too beautiful to be so irritating!

"Just answer *one* question."

He blew hard. "I won't answer *any* questions!" he insisted. She wondered how someone so gorgeous could be so irritating!

"Does your client have an alibi?"

He chuckled then finalized, "Good day, Miss Melton." He walked to the door and opened it as Beverly was entering. "Beverly, please show Miss Melton out." Her eyes stretched.

"Hi, Toni," she greeted, smiling as if they were old friends.

"Hi, Beverly," Toni responded back in the same manner, then turned back to Ron. "Where is Mr. Sanchez, Mr. Joyner? Why is he hiding?" He just stared at her then she grew forceful. "If you don't cooperate, my magazine will be forced to print the news as we see fit! Don't say you weren't given an opportunity to comment." She witnessed an immediate change in his expression from aggravation to anger.

"If you print *anything* in your magazine that will prejudice the case against my client, Miss Melton, then I will see you in court," he warned forcefully but controlled. "You might have the *Constitution* on your side, but *I* have the *Supreme Court*. So, don't you *dare* threaten me!" With that he turned, stormed back into his office, and slammed the door. Toni and Beverly jumped at the hard sound.

Beverly focused on Toni and jokingly singsong, "Oh! Ohh! You made him annnngry."

"It appears so," Toni giggled.

****

"Mr. Kennedy, Mr. Townsend is on line one," his secretary announced through the intercom.

"Thanks, Lauren," he acknowledged, sitting at his desk, and pushing the button on the telephone. "Ralph, what's up?"

"Hi, Simon, that's what I'm asking you," the man replied. "I have a message to call you."

"Are you sitting down?"

"Yeah, what's up?"

Simon took a breath and announced proudly, "The judge threw it out."

"He threw it out?"

"Yes. He said the DA didn't have sufficient evident for an indictment, so he threw it out."

"Yeah!" Ralph exploded in laughter. "That's the best news I've heard all year!"

"I knew you would be pleased."

"Oh, I am," he replied then sobered. "And what's with you and this Toni Melton of *Toni Talk?*"

Simon's jaw clenched as he replied, "She's just a thorn in my side right now, but she'll soon get what's coming to her."

****

"Hi, Rita," Toni greeted, entering the modestly decorated, two-story, brick house with a basket, and giving the lady a hug.

"Hi, Toni," Rita accepted, forcing a smile in her fragile state.

"My mother fixed you some homemade vegetable soup."

"Thanks," she received, taking the basket. "And thank your mother. Come in." They walked into the den and Rita put the soup on the coffee table then sat on the sofa, and Toni sat beside her. "You were great on television yesterday."

"Thank you."

"You better be careful though, Toni. Those are some pretty powerful people you're messing with."

"They don't scare me," Toni responded then decided to change the subject. "So, how are you, Rita?"

41

"I have good days and bad days. Today is a good day. Thank God."

"Good," Toni recognized. "What are they going to do next?"

"Well, the doctor says the chemo is working pretty well. The cancer cells are minimizing, so they're going to stick with that for a while."

"Bill said you were getting nauseous. Can they give you something for that?"

"Yes. Bill picked up some herb tea for me, and it seems to be working pretty well."

"That's good."

"Enough about *me*. What about *you*?" She probed, smiling a bit wryly, "Have you met a man yet?"

****

"Bev, if that Toni Melton comes back here, have her thrown out!" Ron instructed, as Beverly sat in front of his desk with a dictation pad. A sweet smile suddenly enveloped her face, and he was confused. "What's going on?"

"You like her, don't you?" she questioned, still smiling.

He floundered a bit. "Are you sitting there telling me that you think I like that insufferable pest of a woman who calls herself a *journalist*?!"

"She's pretty," Beverly recognized, continuing to smile.

"She's a *pest*!"

"I know you, Ron. You like her."

"And why on Earth would you say that?"

"I have never seen *any* woman get under your skin as much as she has," Beverly observed. "Go ahead and admit it. You like her. She's incredibly beautiful. She's smart, and she can stand up to *you*!"

Ron threw his hands up exasperated, proclaiming, "You're crazy!"

****

"Simon Kennedy really has the hots for you," a woman remarked to Melissa, standing behind the bakery counter as she replaced some jelly donuts in the case.

"Simon's full of it, Cammie," Melissa chuckled. "I think the only reason he seems to be so interested in me is because he wants to rub it in Ron's face."

"Why?"

"Because Ron doesn't like the clients Simon defends, and they used to be friends *once*."

"They don't like each other anymore?" Cammie asked, lifting an eyebrow.

Cammie was a fifty-two-year-old, almond tan wife with three adult boys. She was only four feet, ten inches and weighed about one hundred and fifty pounds. They had become friends over the years. She was pleasant to be around and kept Melissa laughing when she got depressed. She was the first employee Melissa and her husband hired when they opened the bakery six years ago. She was one of two bakers, as well as counter help with Melissa, and was meticulous in every detail. Cammie's hair was kept back with a hair net, exactly up to code and in a similar fashion to all the other workers in the bakery, including Melissa's.

"Ron thinks Simon is a skunk now because of the people he defends."

"Well, everybody has the right to a defense," Cammie countered.

"You sound like Simon."

"He comes in here every day, and I know he's not eating all those bake goods, as fine as he is, so he must be coming in here just to see you," Cammie laughed.

"He says his secretary likes the cake squares."

"Oh," she pondered with a slight smile. "So, is he getting anywhere with you, girlfriend?"

Melissa laughed, "My brother would pitch a fit if I even so much as *look* at *Simon Kennedy*."

"Your *brother* doesn't have to live with him."

"Who said anything about *living* together?!" Melissa exploded. "You already have Simon and me married off before we've even had a first date!"

"Are you considering it?"

"Considering what, Cammie?"

"That first date with Simon?"

"Not really," Melissa blushed. "I'm not ready."

"Not ready!" Cammie blasted. "Girl, your husband has been gone for almost two years. What are you waiting for?!"

"It's not that easy, Cammie. I thought Kelvin and I would last forever."

"Honey, you couldn't help that he had that heart attack."

"Sometimes I feel responsible."

"Why?"

"For baking all this stuff."

"That's silly," Cammie observed. "The doctor said Kelvin had a heart condition before he married you, but he didn't tell you. So be thankful for those two beautiful children. He could've died at any time. He took a gamble having sex at all."

Melissa stared blankly at the sweets in front of her, "Why did he do it, Cammie? Why didn't he tell me? I loved him so much, I would've married him anyway."

It took her a moment to respond. "I guess he was afraid you wouldn't have made love to him, and honey, that's important to a man. They would rather die than not have sex, especially if they are in love with the woman."

"I think about him often."

"I know, honey, but you gotta learn how to let go and move on."

****

Ron and Simon reached the courtroom exit doors at the same time. Ron slightly frowned and Simon opened the door. "After you, Counselor," he gestured politely.

"Thank you," Ron accepted then walked out, and Simon followed.

"We used to be friends, Ron. Why do you *dislike* me so much now?" he inquired.

"I don't *dislike* you. I just don't like the *company* you keep."

"I *defend* them. I don't *break bread* with them."

"Same thing."

"No, it isn't."

Stopping and facing Simon, who stopped also, he replied, "When I defend a client, I spend almost every waking hour with that client. So, don't tell me that you don't keep company with them."

"It's a *job*."

"I have a job too, Simon, but I don't use it to free *criminals*."

"You and I went to the *same* law school, and if *memory* serves me right, I distinctly remember learning something about *everyone* deserving representation."

"If that helps you sleep at night, Simon, then hide behind it," Ron sarcastically stated then started walking again.

"I don't have to *hide* behind *anything*, and I *sleep* just fine."

Stopping and facing Simon again, Ron countered, "I hope so, but I don't see how."

"I have nothing to feel bad about, Ron."

"As soon as you get your clients out of trouble, they do something *worse*. One day they just might rape your mother or sister, or *wife*, if heaven forbids anyone ever marries you," Ron stated then started to walk again.

"You might be surprised."

"Meaning?" Ron stopped at his pearl black Lexus to face Simon.

"My office is right next door to your sister's bakery, and I think she's rather hot. You know how I have always felt about Melissa. I just might be your new brother-in-law one day, so you better watch it."

Ron burst into laughter then sobered quickly and spat, "My sister has better taste!"

****

Toni and Angel strolled into a restaurant and the hostess immediately found them a table among the full dining room. "It pays being in public with the famous *Toni Melton* of *Toni Talk*!" Angel giggled and Toni shoved her. As they looked over their menus, Toni noticed that Ron had entered and was seated.

"Don't look now but there he is," she whispered to her friend.

"Who?"

"The renowned Attorney Ron Joyner!"

"He *is*? Where?" Angel replied excitedly.

Pointing slightly, Toni returned, "Over there."

Angel twisted a little in her seat, spotted him and gasped, "Oh, my goodness. He *is* gorgeous!"

"And so *stubborn*," Toni added.

"Are you going to say hi?"

"Do you think I should?"

"Yeah, girl."

"Are you going with me?"

"No, I gotta get some filing done. I got a little behind when I had to leave early to take Sammie to the dentist."

"He'll think I'm a pushy bitch if I go over there."

"You are," Angel snickered, and Toni's mouth flew open.

"I thought you were my friend!"

"I am, and friends tell each other the truth."

"So, I'm a pushy bitch, am I?"

"That's what makes you so good at your job."

"Well, he might think bad of me if I barge in on his meal."

"Since when has that ever stopped you?" Angel charged, getting up. "I'll get take-out." With that, she left quickly. Toni just shook her head at her friend.

Toni took a deep breath, got up, and walked over to Ron's table. "Hello, Mr. Joyner," she spoke politely.

Ron looked up at her, exhaled aloud, and asked, "Are you *following* me now, Miss Melton?"

"Hardly," she smirked. "May I join you?"

"No," he stated matter-of-factly, but she sat anyway, and he sighed deeply. "Are you hard of hearing?"

"Not usually," she confirmed, as a shadow appeared over her.

"Good afternoon," a soft voice greeted.

Toni looked up and a short man was standing there with salt and pepper short hair and a nice gray suit. "Mr. Sanchez," she spoke. "I've been wanting to meet you."

"Miss Melton, I need to confer with my client," Ron spoke up. "Please excuse yourself."

"Miss Melton, my pleasure," the polite man greeted with a slight Spanish accent, planting a soft kiss on the back of her hand. "My goodness, the media circuits don't do you justice. You are absolutely breathtaking!"

"Thank you, Mr. Sanchez," she humbly accepted, and Ron thought he would throw up.

Taking a seat, he offered, "Please call me *Thomas.*"

"Thank you, and I'm *Toni*," she continued. "Thomas, I would love to interview you. My colleague wants to do an article on you, telling *your* side. If you would…"

"Mr. Sanchez, as your attorney, I must advise you not to do an interview at this time. The press just wants a *story*," Ron objected.

"So noted, Ron," Mr. Sanchez acknowledged to his attorney then focused back on Toni. "Who is this colleague?"

"Mason Whittaker."

"I've read his column. I'm *not* impressed."

"Excuse me?"

"Mason Whittaker is too political. I don't think he would be suitable to write my story," Mr. Sanchez explained.

"So, you won't do the interview?"

"Yes, I will. On one condition."

"Name it."

"It appears in *Toni Talk* and not *Mason on the Move*."

"But it's *his* story," Toni defended. "I'm just doing the interview for him."

"It's not negotiable, Toni. I like your style. You always tell the truth. I know exactly what I'm getting. If you do the story, then you have yourself an interview for your column," Mr. Sanchez insisted.

"Well, I guess Mason wouldn't want us to lose this story on a mere technicality," Toni reasoned. "All right, I'll do it."

"Good. Ask your questions."

"*Now?*"

"No time like the present."

"Mr. Sanchez, I must object again," Ron made known, as Toni took out her recorder.

"Ron, you're right here. Anything that you feel I shouldn't answer, just stop me."

"I don't feel you should answer *any* questions."

"Let's be fair to the little lady, Ron," Mr. Sanchez debated then focused back on Toni. "Ask your questions, Señorita. I don't have all day."

"Yes, sir," Toni replied enthusiastically. "Did you kill your wife?"

"No. I loved her."

"Do you have a mistress?"

"Mr. Sanchez, I advise you not to answer that," Ron interrupted.

"It's okay, Ron," Mr. Sanchez opposed. "I have nothing to hide. Yes, Toni, I do have a mistress."

"While you were married?"

"Yes."

"Can you elaborate?"

"Certainly," he replied. "My wife and I had only one child. He was killed in a car accident two years ago on his seventeenth birthday. My wife blamed herself because I tried to tell her he wasn't responsible enough for a fast, sports car, but she bought it anyway because he wanted it. After Nicholas's death, Isabella shut down. She couldn't function as either a *wife or* a *person* anymore. That's when I took up with Rosa. I had needs and my wife wasn't fulfilling those needs."

"Did you fall in love with Rosa?"

"Not really. She was just someone to share my bed."

"Did you compensate her?"

"She wasn't a hooker if that's what you're asking. She's a decent woman who happened to fall in love with me, but I couldn't return that love. I still loved my wife, although I couldn't be intimate with her. I didn't want to push Isabella into intimacy if she wasn't ready."

"Where was Rosa the night your wife died?"

"She was with me."

"Then you have an alibi?"

"A *mistress* is *hardly* an alibi when your *wife* is murdered, Toni."

"So, who found your wife's body?"

"I did," he answered. "When I left Rosa's house, I came home, and Isabella was in the bathtub, already electrocuted. I unplugged the radio, felt her pulse and found that she was dead, so I called the police immediately."

"Has your wife ever tried to commit suicide before, Thomas?"

"Yes, twice."

"Do you think this was an accident or suicide?"

"I don't know."

"Was she on medication?"

"Oh, yes. She was on an antidepressant, and she was seeing a therapist twice a week."

"Then why was she alone?"

"Her nurse became ill and had to leave suddenly. The agency arranged for another nurse to come over, and she was on the way," he explained. "Since I wasn't home, I didn't know she was alone. I *never* left her alone."

"Do you stand to inherit sixty million dollars from your wife's estate?"

"My wife was a wealthy woman. She inherited millions, so yes, I am her only heir, and I do stand to inherit her estate," he explained. "And it's probably well over sixty million, but I do have money of my owe, Toni."

"Is there a reason you're hiding out?"

"Yes. I don't want the hassle from the press," he answered then smiled sweetly.

She smiled also then concluded, "May I take some pictures?"

"I thought you had a cameraman?"

"I didn't know I was going to run into you, but I stay prepared."

"I *bet* you do, Toni," he acknowledged. "Take your pictures." She snapped several pictures of him with her cell phone. "That's all I need to ask. Thank you so much."

"You're welcome," he stated. "But, Toni, one thing." He caught her full attention. "I trust that you will give me fair treatment in your column. If you betray me, you *will* have to answer to me. Do I make myself clear?"

"*Crystal.*"

****

"Is Toni back from lunch?" Mason asked Angel, standing over her desk.

"No, not yet" she responded, but continued typing on her keyboard.

"I want to see how she's coming on the Sanchez case."

"Aren't you putting a little too much on Toni? Investigative work is very time consuming."

"She doesn't mind."

"How do you know?" she snapped.

"Because *she* would tell me," Mason chuckled as Toni entered. "There she is...the woman of the hour. What did you find out? Did the lawyer talk?"

"Mason!" Toni squeaked then took a deep breath. "I talked to Mr. Sanchez *himself*." Bill entered.

"Hi, you two. I need to see you in my office a moment," he announced.

"Wait, Bill. Toni talked to Mr. Sanchez," Mason concurred.

"You did, Toni?" Bill asked and she nodded. "What did he say?"

"He gave me the interview on one condition."

"What's that?" Bill wanted to know.

"That *I* write the article in *my* column," Toni replied softly, and Angel stopped typing abruptly and focused on the group.

"What?" Mason exploded.

"I tried to talk him out of it, Mason, but he wouldn't budge."

"You *stole* my story?!" he shrieked.

"I didn't *steal* it!" she defended. "Mr. Sanchez said he wouldn't do the interview if I didn't write the story myself. I didn't think you wanted us to lose the story, so I agreed."

"I don't believe this. You stole my story!" he repeated. "You had no right, Toni! That was *my* story!" He was yelling now, and Bill intervened.

"Calm down, Mason. It sounds like Toni really didn't have a choice."

"Oh, she *had* a choice all right," he fumed. He just gazed at her for a moment.

"Mason, I didn't. Really, I..." she started, but he threw his hands up and flew out the door.

Chapter 4

"This is a good story, boss," Beverly raved over the telephone as she read Toni's article, sitting at her kitchen table. "She softened Mr. Sanchez and made him appear *human*. She did a great job."

"Yes, I saw it, Bev. It was a surprisingly nice article," Ron agreed, sitting in a recliner in his den.

"So, you aren't mad at her anymore?"

"I still think she's an irritating pest, and I'm glad I don't have to see her anymore," he made known.

"Are you sure about that, boss?"

"Yes, I'm sure," he confirmed as he heard the doorbell. "Bev, someone's at my door. I'll see you tomorrow."

"Okay," she agreed, and they hung up.

Ron was wearing brown, silk pajama bottoms, with his hairy, sexy chest exposed. He went to the door and peeked out then sighed deeply. He yanked the door opened quickly and barked, "What're you doing here?"

"Hi, Mr. Joyner, my name is Toni Melton. I'm a journalist with *The Weekly Herald News Magazine*. I…"

"I *know* who you are, Miss Melton. What're you doing here?" he asked, admiring her classy navy-blue jogging suit with matching navy and white colored sneakers, and a navy sweatband around her head, looking very regular and not like the superstar everyone seemed to think she was.

"We got off on the wrong foot. I just wanted to apologize and start over if that's possible," she suggested with a big smile then continued, "I'm twenty-eight years old. I'm a Virgo. I like all kinds of music. I…"

He smiled wide, shook his head, and cut her off, "Come in, Miss Melton." The woman had guts, he had to give her that.

"Thank you. I thought you would never ask," she countered, entering his immaculate condo.

"How did you know where I lived?" he asked and she just tilted her head to one side, and he chuckled. "Oh, I forgot, you're a *reporter*."

"*Journalist!*" she corrected.

"Same difference," he maintained. "Would you like something to drink, Miss Melton?"

"Yes, thank you, Ron. What do you have?"

"Milk, tea, fruit punch."

She joked, "Ooh, you live dangerously!" He had to laugh with her.

He remembered, "Oh yeah, I do have wine."

"Okay, wine it is," she agreed, following him into the kitchen while silently wishing he would put on a shirt. His gorgeous body was doing crazy things to her body. No man had done that to her in a long time. "You have a beautiful home."

"Thank you," he accepted the compliment, handing her a glass of red wine and keeping one for himself. Then he sat on a stool at the kitchen island and she joined him. Simultaneously, they looked at each other slowly then burst into laughter. "So, why did you say you were here, Miss Melton?"

"To get you to call me *Toni*," she grinned, and he smiled with her.

"That could be arranged," he complied then they clang their wine glasses together.

****

"Daddy, you're going to read me a bedtime story?" little Amy burst into the family room with a book in her hands, where Mason sat looking at a ball game.

"Sure, honey," he agreed, turning down the volume on the television set as Becky entered.

"Honey, you're disturbing daddy," she observed to the child.

"It's okay," Mason interjected.

"Did you read Toni Melton's article?" Becky inquired cautiously.

"Yeah."

"What did you think?"

"It was superb as usual."

"It should've been. She stole it from you!" she snapped.

He sighed, "I overreacted, Becky. I sent Toni to get the interview in the first place because she's a *woman*. It backfired on me because she's a woman and a damn pretty one at that."

Becky's expression turned into a slight frown as she replied, "You never call me pretty."

"Then I'm sorry because you are very pretty, Becky," he lied to keep the peace.

Becky hated Toni Melton. She wished she could scratch her eyes out. She knew Mason still carried a torch for Toni, but he would never admit it. *She hated that woman!*

****

"Ron, did they do an autopsy on Mrs. Sanchez?" Toni asked as they sat on the sofa now.

"No, they didn't have to. She was electrocuted."

"What if Mrs. Sanchez took her own life and when she died, the radio fell in her bath by accident?"

"I thought about that, but the coroner was positive."

"But he didn't look for poison in her body, did he?"

"I don't think so."

"Did they find her pills?"

"Pills?"

"Yes, Thomas said she was on medication for depression."

"The police searched the house, but of course they weren't looking for anything that would clear Mr. Sanchez," he pondered. "That house has been undisturbed since his wife's death. I'll get someone to check it out tomorrow."

55

"Good," she completed, feeling satisfied that he was finally listening to her. Then she focused on his chest again and looked away.

"Do you have a sweet tooth, Toni?" he asked.

"A *sweet* tooth?"

"Yes. My sister, Melissa, owns a bakery on the other side of town, and she's always sending me stuff at work. I have some brownies. Would you like to try them?"

"Oh, I love brownies!" Toni glowed as he stood, and she followed.

When they reached the kitchen, he offered her the tray of brownies and she took one, placing it on a napkin, before taking a bite. "Oh, this is delicious!" she raved.

"Melissa has always loved baking, ever since I can remember," he shared.

"Is it just the two of you?"

"No, I have another sister, Denise, who's a teacher, and a brother, Leroy, who used to be a surgeon, but something happened with a patient dying, and he flipped out. He lost everything in the lawsuit, but he didn't fight back. So, he turned to alcohol, lost his family, and now at thirty-eight years old, he's back home with mom and dad, doing absolutely *nothing* with his life."

"Are you the baby?"

"No, Denise is. She's twenty-eight. I'm next to her at thirty, and Melissa is next to me. She's thirty-two, and then there's Leroy," he explained.

"And you said your brother *used* to be a surgeon?"

"Yeah, a heart surgeon."

"I did a story about an incident like that about five years ago when I was with Greenleaf Daily News. Was that at Mercy Hospital?"

"Yes."

"I never did interview the lead surgeon nor anyone on the surgical team for that matter, so I concentrated on the grieving wife who had filed the lawsuit. That *surgeon* was your *brother*?"

Nodding, he confirmed, "Small world, huh?"

"I could never get in touch with him to hear his side."

56

"He didn't fight at all."

"Why?"

"I don't know. I think he just quit because he felt it was *his* fault that the man died."

"So, do you know what happened?"

"Not to this day. Leroy won't talk about it."

"That's too bad."

"Yes, it is. He was a brilliant surgeon."

"So, your mother and father are still together?"

"Yes, by the grace of God though. My dad used to be somewhat of a lady's man, and my mother endured many affairs during their forty-year marriage," Ron shared, and thinking how easy she was to talk to.

"Why do men cheat?"

"Why does *anyone* cheat?"

"Touché," she agreed. "Do your parents still work?"

"No. Dad retired from the railroad and my mom never worked."

"My father worked at the post office until he retired, and my mother is a retired schoolteacher," she shared.

"That's cool to have a mother who teaches."

"It's *obvious* you didn't!" she exploded in laughter. "Do you have any idea what it's like having your *mother* teach you AP English? It was pure hell!" He laughed with her. "She was harder on *me* than *anyone* just so they wouldn't say she was showing favoritism!"

"I guess she had to be," Ron concluded, continuing to laugh, melting Toni's heart with the masculine sound of his voice. "Apparently, she was a great influence on you though."

"I suppose so," she concurred with a melting smile. "The most devastating time of my life was when my father left." Ron focused in on her to listen. "My parents divorced when I was a senior in high school. My mother is somewhat of a religious fanatic. My father just couldn't take it anymore."

"I'm sorry to hear that," he sympathized, "Are you an only child?"

"No, I have two *crazy* ass brothers who are seven years older than I am. They're thirty-five. They're twins, Walter and Dennis."

"Those are *definitely* not twins' names?" he laughed. "Are they identical?"

"Not at all. Walter is over six feet and Dennis is shorter than *I am*. When I was growing up, they used to beat my butt so much. I learned how to fight because of them. They used to do all kinds of mean things to me, and my mother acted as if she didn't care. If it weren't for my dad, I wouldn't have survived those two brothers," she explained.

"They were *that* bad?" Ron laughed.

"*Were* they ever!" she stressed. "They used to tie me up with a thick rope, nail it to a tree and shoot bb's at me. I used to hang there for hours, bruised and bleeding until my dad came home. They used to put tar in my hair. They once even put a snake in my bed!"

"A *snake*?!"

"Yeah, a *snake* while I was asleep. It wasn't poisonous though, but I almost had a heart attack when I saw it. That's when I decided to get even with those brothers," she shared. "When they were asleep one night, I poured gasoline all around their beds then lit a match."

"You *didn't*!"

"I *did*," she stated proudly. "If it weren't for my dad, they would've died, and let me tell you, at that point, I didn't care. I was tired of their abuse."

"Were they injured?"

"Not injured *enough*. Walter suffered second degree burns on his arm and Dennis had third degree on his leg."

"You're *ruthless*!"

"I *had* to be, living with those two idiots," she confirmed. "But I bet you one thing, they never bothered *me* again after that."

"I bet they didn't," he laughed with her. "What're they doing now?"

"They own a construction business together."

"They're still together, huh?"

"They're *inseparable*," she snickered. "It's a good thing their wives get along with each other. Those brothers are close."

Sobering, he asked, "So, what do you do for fun?"

"I…" she started then stopped abruptly. "You have icing on your face." She dabbed at the icing with her finger. Suddenly, their eyes locked, and Toni leaned forward and planted a kiss on his lips.

"Wow," he responded.

"I shouldn't have done that, should I?" she inquired, and then he leaned forward and kissed her. Their kisses grew deeply passionate as they stood, still entwined. "I've never done this before," she confessed between kisses.

"Done what?"

"Come on to a man."

"Is *that* what this is?" he murmured. "I've been wanting to do this all evening, but I didn't want to run you away."

"Really?" she asked, and he nodded. They continued to kiss deeply.

She started working her way down his smooth, hairy chest, smothering his body with tender, wet kisses. She was taking his breath away and he suggested, "Let's take this into the bedroom." She stood up again and they kissed some more. She removed her jacket and he helped her. "Come on," he whispered.

"Ron," she called softly.

"What is it, baby?" he asked, silencing her with a sweet kiss, so she didn't finish her thought. Then he picked her up and carried her upstairs to the bedroom as their lips were still entwined in hungry, seductive kisses. Their bodies clung together with warm excitement as he laid her on the huge king-sized bed and covered her body with his.

"Ron," she breathlessly called. She hadn't felt this sensation in over five years, and it felt so good. Their lovemaking was tantalizing, explosive, and satisfying. Then when he felt the quivering of her body and the clinging of her nails in his shoulders, he released himself with her and they exploded together in a gropingly, intense, cry of ecstasy. They both screamed with immense pleasure as they clung to each other, fulfilling their every desire. Then when every ounce of pleasure was drained from their bodies, she collapsed against him, and he held her close.

He took a deep breath and blew out, "Wow!"

"Ditto," she concurred.

"Miss Melton, will you respect me in the morning?" he joked, and she burst into laughter. He laughed with her as they met in a soft, sweet, sultry kiss.

Chapter 5

"Honey, what're you doing?" Becky asked, tying her bathrobe together, entering Mason's study where he sat at the computer.

"Getting some work done," he replied, not looking up at her but continuing to work.

"So early? It's a little after six o'clock!" she exploded.

"You know I can't sleep late," he shared.

"Want some breakfast?"

"Is Cecilia here?"

"Not yet, but I do know how to cook breakfast," she defended, and he smiled.

"Not right now. Thank you," he rejected. She came and sat in a chair beside him, and he stopped working for the first time, focusing on her.

"Mason, what's going on here?"

"Nothing. Something just popped into my head and I had to get it down before I forgot it."

"I mean with *us*," she responded. "Do you know we haven't made love in over eight months?"

"No, I hadn't realized that."

"Then *start*," she insisted. "Don't you want me anymore?"

"Of course, I do, honey. I'm just terribly busy right now."

"Too busy to make love to your wife?" she charged, and he took a deep breath. Then he met her with a kiss.

"I'm sorry, Becky. I just need to get to work early today to catch Toni."

"Toni?!" She spat. "Why?"

"So I can apologize to her."

"For what? She *stole* your story!"

"She didn't *steal* my story. I overreacted, and I need to apologize to her."

"Why is your life always centered around her, Mason?"

"What?!"

"It's always *Toni*!"

"That's absurd!"

"Is it?"

"Yes," Mason retaliated. "Toni and I are friends, and I don't know why you insist on making more of it than it is."

"You used to date her."

"You already knew that!"

"Did you sleep with her?"

"For the hundredth time, Becky, *no*! I did *not* sleep with Toni!"

"Then why are you so hung up on her?"

"The only one who's hung up on Toni is *you*!"

"Are you in love with her?"

"No, Becky, I'm not!" he insisted then blew hard. He was tired of this obsession his wife had with Toni. Sure, she was gorgeous, but what woman in the public eye wasn't? He cared for Toni a lot but not like his wife thought. She was his friend. He had to admit to himself that if it were possible for him to sleep with her, he probably would, but that was the curiosity in the cat and a little of the dog in the man. It was *not* because he loved her so much. Not *anymore*! He respected and admired her. She was his friend!

"Look, Becky," he calmed down. "Why won't you believe me when I tell you that there is *nothing* going on between Toni and me but *friendship*?"

"Because she's so beautiful."

"So are you."

"No, I'm not. Don't patronize me."

"Listen, Becky, I'm your husband. I love what we have here. Our home, our daughter, our life together. I wouldn't trade it for anything in this world. Please believe me," he explained, stretching the truth a little. "I love you." Well, he stretched it a *lot*! She fell in his arms and cried. He held her close.

"I love you so much, Mason. I would die if I lost you."

"Does it look like I'm going anywhere?" he neutralized, holding her back a little to face him and she shook her head. "I'm afraid you're stuck with me, kiddo." He smiled then kissed her lips sweetly.

"I'm sorry."

"I'm sorry too. I've just been so preoccupied; I guess I *have* been neglecting you," he explained, and she smiled. He took her hand and stood, pulling her up with him. "Let's go to bed." They hugged close as they walked out, and she dropped her head on his shoulder. It felt so good for her to be in her handsome husband's arms again.

****

Toni awakened first, rolled out of Ron's arms, and focused on him sleeping peacefully. He was so handsome; it brought a smile to her lips. She noticed six thirty AM on the bedside brass clock. She tipped out of bed quietly, slipped on Ron's pajama top that was laying across the chair, and exited into the bathroom. She stared at herself in the mirror then took a deep breath. "Toni, what in the *hell* have you done?" she scolded herself in a whisper. "To throw yourself at a man, a perfect *stranger*, and then not use any form of *protection*! Are you *nuts*?" She splashed some cold water on her face and dried it off with a towel. "What on Earth would your mother say?" she continued to talk to herself. "You know what she'll say. *You're going to burn in hell, Missy!*" She took another deep breath. She thought of Ron. He was so *fine*. He was the best lover she'd ever had in her whole life, but then she only had one before him, Nathan, a research scientist she dated for two years before going on a five-year sabbatical from sex. Ron was so gentle yet so exciting. He also had the biggest....

"Toni," Ron called, interrupting her thoughts.

She took a deep breath then replied, "In here." He entered the bathroom with her, still totally nude, and hugged her from the rear.

"Good morning," he cooed, planting a kiss on the back of her neck.

"Good morning," she responded sweetly.

"How did you sleep?"

"Good."

"Anything wrong?" he asked, and she turned to face him.

"No, I was just thinking about us."

He looked deep into her eyes, smiled, and asked, "Do women *really* do that?"

"Do what?"

"Give a man the greatest night in his life then regret it in the morning?" he grinned, and she dropped her head. He lifted her chin with his finger. "Last night was special to me, Toni."

"The way I threw myself on you...I just don't want you to think I was a floozy or something. I have never done anything like this in my whole life!"

"I know," he made known, and her eyes widened. "Toni, if I thought you were that way, you wouldn't be here. I don't sleep with *floozies*. I don't have casual sex, and I don't do one-night stands!" He planted a soft kiss on her lips.

"Thanks, Ron," she accepted with a sweet smile, and then he pulled her in his arms lovingly.

"Let's go back to bed," he cooed.

"I have a plane to catch."

With widen eyes he asked, "Today?"

"Yes, I'm flying to Houston today to interview some inmates about their prison conditions."

"What time is your flight?"

"Three o'clock."

"Then we have time," he acknowledged, smiling sheepishly, kissing her lips again.

"Ron," Toni called softly as he led her back through the bathroom door. He turned to face her again when they were in the bedroom.

"Yes, baby?"

"Do you have condoms?" she asked shyly, and his eyes widen as his eyebrow tilted.

"Condoms?!" he exploded.

"Yes, condoms," she chuckled.

"Baby, I'm clean. I promise. I..."

"No, it's not that," she cut him off, and he raised an eyebrow to hear more. "I'm not on the pill."

"You're *not*?!" he was shocked. "I thought all women over twenty-one were on the pill or something now-a-days."

"I haven't had a man in my life in five years. I didn't see the need."

"*Five years*?!" he blurted out, and she nodded.

"If you think *that's* something, it was *twenty-one* years prior to that."

"Wow, that *is* something," he agreed. "And I thought I was doing good with my *one*."

"You've been celibate for a year?"

"Yes," he answered. "I'm very picky."

"I didn't know *men* could wait a whole year," she snickered.

"I didn't know *anyone* could wait *twenty-one y*ears and again *five* years in one lifetime," he laughed with her. Then he met her gaze and they sobered and kissed sweetly. "No, baby, I don't have condoms. I didn't see a need." He kissed her again and she felt how excited he was becoming.

"Could you go and get some?" she asked between kisses, and he jerked back to face her.

"Now?!" he shrieked.

"Yes, *now*," she burst into laughter.

"Baby, after last night, if you're not pregnant yet, this morning won't make any difference," he made known, thinking of the many times they had made love during the night. "I mean, between us, we had six years to catch up on." He laughed. "I can see that little sperm now, etching away to enter that egg."

"Would you stop it," she laughed.

"Come on, baby," he cooed, kissing her face and neck with soft, wet kisses. He guided her to the bed, and they laid down, still entwined in kisses. "Um, you smell good."

"I *do*?!" she asked, knowing she hadn't taken a shower yet.

"Um hum," he purred, sliding on her.

****

"Sweetie, are you all right?" Bill asked his wife through the bathroom door as he tied his necktie.

"Yes, I'm okay."

"I'll see you at lunch," he called again. "Jill said she would be here around noon."

"Okay. Goodbye."

"Bye."

Rita heard him leave and she dropped to the floor, sitting near the toilet. She didn't want Bill to know that she was throwing up blood. She knew he would worry, and she didn't want that. She knew the cancer was getting worse and she would be gone soon. She prayed that Bill would be able to handle her death. She started throwing up again. She felt so weak. She was tired of fighting this long two-year battle with cancer. One minute it was gone, the next it was back. She was tired. She was just ready to go home now. She prayed that she had done all the right things so the good Master would welcome her into His Kingdom. She closed her eyes to relax in God's peace. Bill didn't understand why she was so peaceful and ready to die, and she couldn't explain it either. All she knew was that the peace of God does surpass all understanding. One day, Bill *would* understand. *One day*!

****

"Wake up, sleepyhead," Ron called. Toni opened her eyes, and he was bringing in a tray of food to her.

She yawned and asked, "Where did you get this?"

"My dear, I have been a bachelor a long time. I *do* know my way around the kitchen," he boasted with a big smile then bent down and kissed her lips. She sat up and he sat beside her, positioning the tray in front of them. She observed eggs, hash browns, bacon, toast, strawberries, and orange juice on the tray.

"Wow, this is a full breakfast!"

"For *you*," he made known, kissing her again. He placed a strawberry between her lips and bit the piece hanging out of her mouth, and they ended in a sweet kiss.

"I could get used to this," she cooed.

"So could I, pretty lady. So could I," he agreed, kissing her again.

"What time is it?"

"You have plenty of time. It's only nine thirty."

"I have to go to the office before I leave to pick up my tickets. Then I have to go home to get my suitcases."

"Are you packed already?"

"No."

"Then you better hurry," he suggested. "How long will you be gone?"

"Three days. I'll be back Thursday night."

"I'm gonna miss you."

"I'm gonna miss you, too," she replied, and they kissed again. "What time do you go to work?"

"Usually around eight thirty or nine."

"Beverly is going to wonder what happened to you."

"I called her."

"Did you tell her I was here?"

"No. Did you *want* me to?"

"No!" she exploded.

"Why not?" he chuckled.

"You don't kiss and tell, do you, Ron?"

"Not usually, but baby, I want you to be around for a long time. I don't want to hide our relationship."

"Oh, so we're in a relationship already?" she joked.

"After last night, my queen, I would say we are."

"But we hardly know each other. Give it some time."

"Baby, we know each other in *every* way that *counts*," he smirked then kissed her lips again.

"Other people might think we're moving too fast."

"The hell with *other* people. The only two who matter are *you* and *me*," he insisted. "How do you feel? Do you want *this* to go anywhere?" She looked deep into his clear, hazel eyes then smiled.

"Oh, yes!"

"So do I," he concurred then kissed her again. He guided a forkful of hash browns to her mouth, so she opened and received it. Then he bent down to her and cooed, "Share." She opened her mouth, and he met her with a kiss as they shared the food together.

****

Becky felt so good being intimate with her husband again. When he left for work, he kissed her again like he hadn't done in a long time. She loved him so much. He took Amy to school on his way, so she was home alone, curled up on the couch and dreaming about her charming, handsome husband.

Suddenly, her thoughts fell on Toni. She jerked up on the couch and lit up a cigarette. She *hated* that woman. She knew Mason still carried a huge torch for her. She didn't know how she could break the hold Toni had on her husband, but she knew one thing, she *had* to find a way.

****

Toni stood with Ron at his door ready to leave, dressed back into the warm-up suit she had arrived in the night before, while he stood in his pajama bottoms only, as they held each other close. "Call me when you get there?" he suggested between kisses.

"I will," she promised. "And if *you* call *me*, and I don't answer, that means I'm at the prison. No cell phones allowed. I'll call you back."

"Okay," he acknowledged. "Um, I hate to let you go."

"I hate to go," she cooed. "But I have to." She reluctantly broke away and turned to leave. "I'll call you." He nodded as he watched her walk to her bone-colored Jaguar. Toni felt so warm inside. She had a man who cared for her so much he didn't want to let her go…a virile, handsome man at that. For the first time in her life, she didn't want to go to work. She wanted to stay with her handsome lover and cuddle up with him forever. She waved to him as she drove off. She wondered if it was really possible to be in love so quickly.

As Ron closed the door, his thoughts still lingered on the beautiful woman who had entered his life so quickly and stolen his heart. He wanted the time with her to last forever, but he knew life goes on, and Toni's life was *definitely* full. He hoped they could manage two careers and still have time for each other. He *certainly* wanted to spend time with her. He wondered if it was really possible to be in love so quickly.

****

"Is Toni in yet?" Mason asked Angel.

"No, not yet."

"She *is* coming in before she leaves for Houston, isn't she?" Mason inquired, standing at her desk, looking so suave in his striped gray and black cardigan pullover sweater, gray shirt, black necktie, and black slacks.

"Yes, she *has* to. Tyler is meeting her here, and their tickets are here."

"What time does her plane leave?"

"Three o'clock," Angel replied, looking up at him with her blonde hair pulled back in a neat ponytail, looking very stylish in a baby-blue silk blouse, short, tight-fitting navy-blue skirt, and six-inch, navy-blue, knee-length boots. "What's the problem, Mason?"

"I wanted to apologize to her," Mason made known. "I know Toni, of all people, would *never* stab me in the back."

"I'm glad to hear it."

"Well, when she comes in, will you tell her I would like to see her before she leaves," Mason concluded, turning to leave and Angel nodded.

****

"Huh hum!" Beverly cleared her throat, looking at her watch when Ron entered. He smiled at her politely.

"Good morning, Bev."

"Good *afternoon*, boss," she sarcastically replied with a smirk on her face

"It's only eleven thirty," he chuckled, still moving towards his office.

"What happened?"

"Nothing," he called back, entering his office, but she jumped up and followed him.

"Don't give me that!" she exploded in laughter. "You've *never* come in this late in the three years I've been working for you!"

"I had a guest. That's all."

"A *guest*?!" she exploded, then softened and smiled. "A *woman* guest?"

"Maybe," he met her glare, hanging up his tailor-made, navy-blue, pinstriped suit jacket.

"Who?" she asked. "That stewardess…ag…Vicki, I think?"

"You sure are nosy," he jeered in humor. "No, not Vicki."

"I bet I can guess," she singsong.

"I bet you can't," he mocked.

"Toni Melton?" she inquired, and his hazel eyes widened.

"How did you know?"

"Are you kidding! The way you two looked at each other, I knew it was a matter of time," she giggled.

"Was it that *obvious* that we were attracted to each other?"

"To *me* it was," she sneered.

"I didn't know I was so transparent. You're too smart for your own good," he observed, and she turned to leave.

"I know," she teased.

"Did you rearrange my schedule?"

"Yes, I did," she confirmed with a sistah-girl attitude and he smiled. "And Mr. Sanchez called."

"Okay," he responded, looking through his files. "Oh, Bev, do me a favor and get Mark Taylor on the phone."

"The coroner?!" she gasped.

"Yes," he established. "I want to ask him something about Mrs. Isabella Sanchez's case. Toni suggested something last night that I need to check on again."

"Oh, it's *Toni* now? Yesterday it was *Miss Melton*," she joked in a singsong tone of voice.

"Get outta here," he joked. She exited, still laughing.

****

"Toni, where have you been?" Angel asked, jumping up from her desk and following her into her office. Toni closed the door and smiled.

"You're not gonna believe this."

"What?"

"I went to see Ron Joyner last night to let him know there were no hard feelings, and…"

"And?"

"And I left this *morning*," Toni squeezed out, and Angel screamed, grabbing her, and hugging her tight.

"I knew it! I knew you were attracted to him!"

"Well, you should've let me know," she laughed with her friend. "Really, Angel, I didn't go there to *sleep* with the man."

"How was it?"

Toni inhaled deeply then exhaled with a smile and added, "Incredible!" Angel screamed again. "Angel, he was so gentle and so, ah…I don't know how to describe it."

"Well, your five-year draught is finally over."

"Is it ever!" Toni confirmed.

Angel soon sobered, locked eyes with her friend and asked very softly, "Is it love, Toni?"

71

Toni took a deep breath then replied, "I don't know. It's so soon, but it certainly does feel like it." A tear trickled slowly down her face and Angel pulled her into her arms.

"I'm so happy for you, girlfriend."

"Thanks, Angel," Toni reacted, holding off her friend and grabbing a tissue from her desk.

"Oh, I almost forgot. Mason is looking for you."

"He is?" Toni asked. "Why?"

"Toni, you finally made it in, huh," Mason blurted out, entering her office.

"Hi, Mason," she acknowledged.

"We'll talk again before you leave," Angel finalized then left, as Toni nodded, moving behind her desk to sit.

"Where've you been?"

"I had something to do," she responded. "What's up?"

He sat in front of her desk and offered, "I just wanted to apologize for my behavior when Mr. Sanchez chose you to write his story."

Toni focused on him hard then accepted, "Thank you, Mason."

"I know you better than that," he went on. "Forgive me?"

She confirmed, "Of course." They both stood, met each other, and hugged lovingly.

"We've been friends much too long for any kind of petty stuff."

"I agree."

"By the way, your article was great yesterday," he admired.

"Thanks," she accepted graciously. "So was yours."

"Thank you," he recognized. "I tried calling you several times yesterday, but you weren't home, and you weren't answering your cell phone."

"No, I was out all day yesterday," she answered shyly.

"Toni Melton, do I see a *man* in those eyes?" he inquired, smiling big, and she burst into laughter.

"What're you talking about?"

"You *know* what I'm talking about. Who is he?" he asked, and she dropped her head. He walked closer to her and lifted her chin with his finger. "Who is he?"

She took a deep breath then admitted, "Ron Joyner."

"Ron Joyner! The *attorney*?!" he exploded, and she nodded. "Well, I guess my setting you up wasn't such a bad thing after all."

"I guess not," she agreed, smiling with him.

"That's great, honey. I couldn't be happier for you."

"Thanks, Mason."

"You deserve to have someone in your life other than this damn job!"

"I agree," she chuckled.

"So, when is the big day?"

"What day?"

"The *wedding* day?"

"Whoa! Not so fast," she snickered, and he laughed with her, as her door opened and Becky walked in, and she immediately felt a knot in her stomach, seeing her husband laughing so joyously with his ex-lover...*her* rival! Becky thought Toni looked so beautiful, standing there in her stylish, designer, silver and burgundy warm-up suit, burgundy sneakers, and a burgundy and silver baseball cap on her head. She was beautiful without even trying to look beautiful. She hated her!

"Becky, honey, hello," Mason greeted her.

"Hi," she spoke softly.

"How are you, Becky," Toni greeted her warmly.

"I'm sorry to barge in. The receptionist wasn't at her desk."

"No problem," Toni replied. "How is Amy?"

"Growing like a weed," Becky answered, forcing a smile while blushing her long, straight, lifeless, red hair behind her ear.

"What brings you here, honey?" Mason directed his attention to his wife.

"I was wondering if you'd like to have lunch?" she asked shyly, feeling inadequate in her plain, brown pantsuit, tan rayon blouse and flat brown loafers.

"Sure. Let me go and finish up a few things and I'll be right with you, okay?" he inquired, and she nodded.

"Mason, have you seen Tyler? We have to leave for the airport."

"I saw him a while ago," Mason replied.

"So, he *is* here. I'll call his cell."

"Have a good trip," Mason concluded, planting a kiss on her cheek making Becky cringe with jealousy.

"Thank you," Toni accepted.

"Don't get *locked* up," he joked.

"Oh, no! I hope not!" Toni chuckled then focused on the jealous wife. "It was nice seeing you again, Becky."

"Same here, Toni."

"Ready, honey?" Mason asked his wife, and she nodded. He led her out.

Toni took a deep breath. She didn't know why Becky hated her so much. She had never done *anything* to the woman. She supposed, like everyone else, Becky believed Mason and her brief relationship had elevated into the *bedroom*. But it hadn't! Not *really*…and that was because of Becky!

Nobody ever wanted to believe the truth anyway. That's why *ugly* women shouldn't marry *handsome* men in the first place. They spend too much time worrying about who they're sleeping with, and to her knowledge, Mason wasn't sleeping around on his wife. She had to admit that if Becky would try fixing herself up, she wouldn't look so plain. She needed a good facial, some makeup, and a decent perm in her straight, lifeless hair. Toni wanted to suggest it, but she wouldn't dare. Becky would probably scratch her eyes out. One thing she knew for sure, the sistah *definitely* had issues! But that was *Becky's* problem. She didn't have time to worry about insecure, jealous wives. She had a plane to catch!

****

"You all right, buddy?" Travis asked, entering Ron's office.

"Yeah, why?"

"You came in late today," he observed. "In the two years I've been working here, I have *never* beaten you to work."

"There's a first time for everything," Ron made known.

He probed, "You had a date?"

"And why would you ask me that, my friend?"

"Well, that's the only reason I can think of for you to be so late," Travis hypothesized as Beverly buzzed.

"Yes, Bev."

"Ron, you have a call on line one."

"Bev, I told you to hold all my calls except Mark Taylor. I need to catch up here."

Smiling, Beverly cooed, "I think you'll wanna take this call, boss."

"Have you checked on those items for me yet?" he asked.

"I'm working on them," she replied then clicked him off.

Ron took a deep breath, picked up the receiver and answered, "Ron Joyner."

"Hi, Ron Joyner," Toni purred, sitting on the plane in first class.

He smiled wide and replied, "Hi. Where are you?"

"Getting ready to go up in the friendly skies."

"So, you made your flight all right?"

"Yes, no thanks to *you*."

He laughed then focused on Travis staring at him, and tried to sober, "Can I call you back? I have someone in the office right now."

"Tell Vickie hello," Travis singsong for her to hear.

"Who is Vickie?" Toni grew stern.

"A long story."

"Well, we'll talk about that *long story* later."

"Absolutely."

"Bye, baby."

"Bye, sweetie," he cooed, hung up and focused on Travis. "What're you trying to do, get me in trouble? You know I haven't seen Vickie in over a year."

"You said *flight*. I thought you two had gotten back together."

"Never assume, my man. *Never* assume."

"Then who is this mystery woman who had you three hours late to work today and now has your nose wide open?" Travis laughed.

"I don't kiss and tell."

"Come now, Ron. Who is she? Is she anybody I know?"

"As a matter of fact, you do. You referred to her as the *ice queen.*"

Travis caught on immediately. "*Toni Melton*?!" he exploded. "You're banging *Toni Melton*?!"

"I didn't say that!"

"You didn't have to! Your behavior says it all!" Travis yelped. "I don't believe it!"

"You did say Toni and you never had anything going on, right?"

"Ugh...*nahhh*!"

"Cause, I wouldn't want to step on your toes."

"Man, go for it," Travis urged. "I see you've melted that ice."

"She's very sweet."

"You old sly dog," he admired, extremely impressed. "I have a new level of respect for you, man. Here you go hitting a *home run* with Toni Melton, and I couldn't even get in the *park*!" He burst into laughter and Ron smiled shyly with him.

****

"Toni, we'll be landing in less than an hour," a medium-built, average height, milk chocolate tan man said to Toni, taking the seat beside her.

"Where've you been, Tyler?"

"I met someone," he shared, smiling shyly.

"I see," she joined his smile.

"I think I'm gonna *enjoy* Houston."

"Good," Toni replied, thinking of her sweet Ron and how much she enjoyed being with him. "Just remember, *business* before *pleasure.*"

"I always do, ma'am," he mocked then smiled with his white teeth, although he did have a slight under bite. She had to laugh with him as she settled back in her seat, putting on her headphones to listen to the soft music while her thoughts continued to drift to her new and exciting lover.

****

"Mark, how are you?"

"I'm well, Ron. How's it going?"

"Very well," Ron answered, settling back in his comfortable, soft brown, leather chair behind his desk. "Mark, I need a favor."

"Name it, Ron."

"You were on duty when Isabella Sanchez's body was brought in, right?"

"Yes."

"Was a complete autopsy done on her?"

"No, it was evident that she died from electrocution, and her husband didn't see any need in doing an autopsy."

"Did you save any of her tissue samples?"

"We do save them for a few days. They might still be available since this is a murder case."

"Good," Ron acknowledged. "Mark, I need you to check her tissues for poison."

"Poison?!"

"Isabella Sanchez was taking prescribed medication for depression. If she were to take a bottle of those, could it kill her?"

"Most definitely. Do you know what she was taking?"

"No, but I have Beverly checking on it now."

"Ron, are you suggesting that Isabella Sanchez committed suicide?"

"That's a possibility."

"I'll get right on it."

"Thanks, Mark," Ron finalized as Beverly buzzed him. As he hung up, he buzzed her in. "Yes, Bev?"

"Ron, Isabella Sanchez's doctor is on line two."

"Thanks, hon."

****

"Mom, are you all right?" a skinny woman with long brown hair pulled back in a ponytail asked Rita, as she joined her weak mother on the patio.

"Yes, Jill, I'm fine," Rita replied. She wore a scarf tied around her head and a flowery house dress. Jill, in a pair of black pants, a green blouse, and a white apron, took a seat beside her mother.

"Dinner will be ready soon," Jill made known, and Rita nodded. "Carol called. She said that she and the baby are fine."

"Good."

"Can I get you anything, Mom?"

"No, I'm fine, honey."

"Dad called and said he'll be a little late," Jill explained, and Rita nodded. She hated to see her mother looking so frail and weak. "I'll go and check on dinner." Jill walked back into the kitchen slowly. She leaned against the counter and stared into space. Soon she was bursting into tears.

****

"Hello, Mr. Sanchez," Ron greeted, entering the magnificent mansion.

"Have a seat, Ron," Thomas replied, casually attired in black slacks and a white, soft-cotton, collarless shirt, hanging loosely. "I called you today."

"I was working on something, so I held off calling you back until I had some news for you."

"What kind of news?" Thomas asked as they sat in the huge, spacious living room.

"The DA decided to drop the murder charge against you," Ron announced, smiling wide.

"What?!"

"They found out that your wife committed suicide."

"Suicide?! She was *Catholic*!" he exploded as a Hispanic maid entered with a brass tray containing a brass coffee carafe and two matching cups. "Thank you, Marta." She nodded then left quietly, acknowledging Ron with a slight nod, and he politely smiled at her.

"She wasn't herself," Ron explained. "She was depressed, and she didn't want to live anymore. Simple as that."

"But how did you find out?" he wanted to know, handing Ron a cup of coffee.

"Thank you," Ron accepted, receiving the cup. "I was talking to Toni Melton…"

Cutting Ron off, he acknowledged, "She did a wonderful story on me."

"Yes, she did."

"Anyway, she was the first to approach me with the idea."

"*Toni* was?"

"Yes, and I checked it out."

"How did she do it?"

"We were all looking at the radio, but she was already dying when the radio hit the water. Her doctor said that she called him that day and requested another prescription for her pills. She told him that she had misplaced them. She took all two bottles of pills in a glass of juice."

"My God," he breathed, astonished, "She wanted to end it that badly?"

"Yes, sir, she did," Ron confirmed. "They found the two empty pill bottles under the bathtub. They had rolled under the legs and were hard to see. *Her* fingerprints were the only ones on the new bottle. The glass with the juice in it was beside the bathtub but

79

nobody checked it for poison. It confirmed that the pills were dissolved in the juice. Again, her fingerprints were the only ones on the glass."

"It was that simple?" Mr. Sanchez acknowledged, and Ron nodded. "So, it's *over*?"

Ron took a sip of his coffee and verified, "Yes, it's over."

Thomas Sanchez was speechless as he sat listening to the news that he had being praying for a while. Now that he was hearing this news, he felt numb. He didn't know what to do first. He took a deep breath then focused on his lawyer and smiled big. "Thanks to you *and* Toni Melton," he made known. "You two were the only ones who believed in me. I appreciate that."

Ron was proud to announce, "You're welcome, sir."

"I can't believe it's finally over," he repeated.

"Well, I'll be on my way," Ron acknowledged, getting up. "Thank you for the coffee."

"You're welcome," Thomas stated, rising with him, "I have already paid your law firm what I owe, but I will also express my gratitude to Toni and you very soon."

"You don't have to do that, sir."

"I know. I want to," he insisted. "Thank you so much, Ron."

"My pleasure, sir," Ron concluded, extending his hand, so Thomas accepted his hand and suddenly grabbed him into a big bear hug.

When Thomas finally released him, he asked with tear-filled eyes, "Where is Toni? I want to thank her too."

Ron took a deep breath then shared, "She's in Houston on a story."

"Then why on *Earth* are you *here*?"

"Sir?"

"She's a jewel, Ron. Don't let her get away," he advised. "Texas is only about a four-hour flight."

****

"Hi, honey," David greeted, entering the house, and planting a kiss on Angel's cheek while she stood at the stove in a pair of tight, blue jeans and an off-the-shoulder, hot pink, silk blouse.

"Hi, baby."

"Where're the boys?"

"Looking at TV."

"They've finished their homework?"

"Oh yeah! Hours ago," she replied, looking up at him. "Why are you so late?"

"I had to look at some property all the way in the country. It took me forever to get there. I got lost twice. The couple said they just bought the house and they needed insurance, so I had to check it out."

"Where was *Kristy*?"

"She had already gone when I got the call," he shared, removing his gray suit jacket and tie.

"I see."

"I'm beat. I'm going to check on the boys and take a shower, then I'm going to bed."

"Bed! Aren't you gonna eat?"

"I'm too tired," he yawned, exiting.

I bet you are, Angel thought. *You're probably full of Kristy! The no-good, little slut! I'll put a stop to this shit and soon!*

****

Toni laid across the king-sized hotel bed in a white, silk, short nightshirt, thinking of Ron, with soft music playing. She couldn't help but to wonder where he was. He was not answering his cell phone, but she didn't want to be the kind of neurotic girlfriend that didn't trust her man. Her mind was so relaxed, daydreaming about her sweet new love, that she barely heard the knock on the door that soon invaded her thoughts. She went to it and peeked out the security hole, then opened it quickly. "Hi, Tyler."

"Hi. I'm going to the café. Would you like for me to bring you something?"

"No thank you. I'm not hungry."

"Hey, love can't fill an empty stomach," he smirked, looking stylish in a pair of black pants and a gray and black button-down shirt, hanging loosely.

"And who says I'm in love?"

"*You* do, by your actions, sweetheart," he replied. "Call me if you need me."

"Thanks, Tyler," she accepted, and he walked away.

Toni closed the door and laid back on the bed as she picked up her ringing cell phone. "Hello?"

"Hi, beautiful," Ron responded on the other end.

"I was just thinking about you!"

"All good, I hope."

"You better know it."

"How are you?"

"I'm great now," she cooed. "I miss you."

"I miss you too," he concurred. "What're you wearing?"

She chuckled, "What am I *wearing*?!"

"Yeah."

"Just an old white night shirt. Why?"

"Any panties?"

"What is this, a *perverted* call?" she grinned.

"Huh hum," he purred.

She played along, "I'm wearing *no* panties at all. I'm thinking about how I would *love* to *lick* you all over."

"Oh, baby, you're killing me," he tutted. "Do you have any condoms?"

"I don't need any *tonight*."

"You never know what might come up," he tittered as a knock came to her door.

"Hold that thought. Let me get rid of Tyler again. I know that's him," she walked to the door and yanked it open. Instead of her expected guest, Ron was standing there with his cell phone in his hand, looking so handsome and radiant, still in his navy-blue, pinstriped suit. "Ron!" she yelled.

"And *who* is *Tyler?*" he sneered, and she exploded into his arms, kissing him all over his face and neck as he laughed. "I missed you."

"This is so sweet," she laughed and cried at the same time. He picked her up around her waist and carried her inside, closing the door with his foot. "I'm so glad you're here."

"So am I, baby. So am I," he acknowledged, kissing her passionately. He held back and wiped her tears with his finger. "You're going to spoil me. No one has ever been this happy to see me." She burst into laughter, jumping into his arms again for a long, sultry kiss.

Chapter 6

"Are you going to be late tonight?" Angel asked David over breakfast.

"I shouldn't be," he answered, taking a mouthful of eggs. "Why? You got something planned?"

"No, I just would like to know," she countered.

"Are you guys finished?" David asked the two little curly headed, biracial boys. The oldest was a little darker than the younger one, but it was still obvious that he too was a product of a mixed couple, because of his curly, silky hair. The boys jumped up from the table together and kissed their mother.

"Bye, Mommy," seven-year-old Sammie verbalized, and Ricky, his six-year-old brother, echoed.

"Have a great day," Angel glowed, giving her boys many hugs and kisses. Then she stood and received a kiss from her husband. He patted her behind and smiled.

"See you, baby," he promised then winked, and she nodded, and then the males left, leaving Angel with her thoughts. She wondered how she could catch David with his little *plaything*. She wanted to bury her foot up the little slut's behind so far, it would take a pair of pliers to get it out. What audacity she had to grin in her face and sleep with her husband behind her back! They think they have fooled her, but she had news for them! *She doesn't fool very easily!*

****

"Wake up, sleepyhead," Toni entered the bedroom with a tray of food, where Ron lay on his stomach, still asleep. She bent down and planted a kiss on his bareback and he smiled.

"What're you doing up so early?" he moaned.

"I have to be at the prison at nine o'clock *sharp*," she shared, slipping into bed with him in her white nightshirt. He turned over and she positioned the bed tray in place and put the food on it.

"*You* cooked?" he teased, sitting up and meeting her with a kiss.

"I'm not as handy as you are in the kitchen. I cheated. I ordered room service," she chuckled.

"Whatever works, baby," he smiled, breaking off a piece of toast and putting it in his mouth.

"Share," Toni cooed, and he opened his mouth and they ended in a kiss as she bit off a piece of the toast in his mouth. "Um, breakfast is beginning to be my most favorite meal of the day."

"Mine, too," he agreed, and they kissed again before breaking apart. "So, what's on your agenda for today?" She fed him a spoonful of oatmeal, and then ate the remainder off the spoon that he had left.

"I have an appointment with three inmates at the prison at nine."

"What's going on at the prison?"

"The inmates are claiming that they are being mistreated, and that when they are in bed at night, they are being raped," she explained, feeding him again.

"Oh, you're going to see *women*?"

She met his gaze and replied sternly, "No. *Men!*"

"You're kidding!"

"I kid you not."

"Who's raping them?"

"Guards…other *men!*"

"Now that's *sick!*"

"Yes, it is," she agreed as he lick some eggs off the side of her mouth, and then they ended in a sweet kiss.

She pushed a grape in his mouth with her finger, and he sucked her finger deeply as she pulled it out slowly. Then she pressed her lips against his, in a long, sweet kiss. "I hate to leave you, baby, but I gotta get ready. If I'm late I won't be able to get in."

"It's okay. I'll be here when you get back," he acknowledged, receiving another kiss from her.

"Tyler will be knocking soon."

Raising an eyebrow, he questioned, "Now, who in the heck is *Tyler*?"

She laughed, "My *photographer*."

"And how does this *Tyler* look?" he pretended to be upset.

"Oh, he's *very* handsome," she teased.

"He is, huh?"

"Oh yes," she played along.

"And how long has he been your photographer?"

"About two years now. He goes *everywhere* with me."

"Has he made a pass at you?"

"No."

"Why not? Is he *crazy*?"

"No, I'm just not his type."

"Then what's his *type*?"

"*You* are."

"*I* am?!"

"Yes, darling. You are *exactly* what Tyler likes," she snickered then burst into laughter, falling back on the bed.

"You..." he exploded, taking the tray off the bed, and diving on her, tickling her severely.

"Oh no, Ron!" she laughed hard. "No!" Soon they sobered and kissed long and enthusiastically. He started raising her nightshirt. "No, baby, I gotta get dressed," she murmured between kisses.

"Um hum," he groaned, sliding on her.

"Ron..." she started but he silenced her with a kiss.

"A quickie."

****

"Becky, I'm leaving," Mason called, standing at the door in khaki pants, collarless brown shirt, and a brown blazer.

Running to catch him in red, silk pajamas, she asked, "Don't I get a kiss?"

"Sure," he acknowledged, planting a kiss on her cheek.

"Is that all?" she frowned, and he kissed her lips this time, more committedly.

"See you later," he finalized, turning to leave.

"What's the big hurry? *Toni Melton* will be there when you get there."

"What is this damn obsession you have with *Toni*?!" he snapped.

"Don't curse at me, Mason Whittaker!" she retaliated.

"I'm sorry, but I'm sick and tired of your obsession with Toni! Toni and I are friends! Nothing more!" he stressed then blew hard. "Besides, Toni is in Houston all week."

"She isn't in the office today?"

"No," he confirmed. "So, please stop it. I hate this shit!" He turned and walked out quickly.

As Becky closed the door a few tears fell from her eyes and trickled down her cheeks. She grabbed a cigarette from the table and lit up. She didn't want to drive Mason crazy. She just loved him and didn't want to lose him. He was right. She had to get over her obsession about Mason being in love with Toni Melton just because they once dated, but how? Toni was so beautiful. She hated feeling this way. She took a long draw from her cigarette and filled her lungs deeply before letting it out. She *hated* her jealousy!

****

Ron sat in bed and watched Toni sitting in a chair, tying the strings in her white sneakers. Her turquoise and white warm-up suit looked so cute on her. He liked everything about her. Could he be falling in love? She looked up at him and he smiled at her, and she returned it. "What're you gonna do today?" she asked, coming, and sitting on the bed.

"I might go sightseeing a little. It's been a while since I've been in Houston."

"It's a beautiful city."

"Yes, it is."

"So, I forgot to ask you about this *Vickie*."

He smiled and teased, "Jealous?"

"Should I be?" she smirked.

Shaking his head, he answered, "Not at all." He took a deep breath then confided, "Vickie was a lady I dated over a year ago."

"What happened?"

"I don't believe in long distance relationships. She's a flight attendant, and she was gone more than she was home."

"A flight attendant! I bet she's pretty."

"She's okay," he answered.

"How long did you two date?"

"About two years, off and on."

"It must've been *serious*."

"Not really," he replied nonchalantly. "Vickie is a spoiled little daddy's girl, and she was looking for *another* daddy. End of story."

"You haven't heard from her in over a year?"

"As a matter of fact, she called last week. She said she was on her way to Japan and wanted to know if we could get together."

"What did you tell her?"

"No thanks. That part of my life is over, and I want to keep it that way. It wasn't *that* good when we were at our peak," he explained. "And you? Since we're airing out our dirty laundry. Are there any lost lovers in your life that I should know about?"

"Well," she began. "I started dating this research scientist when I was in college. He was a lot older than I was. We dated a little over a year and a half."

"What happened?"

"He was going through a messy divorce, and his wife killed him."

"What?!! That's terrible!"

"Tell me about it," she added. "Anyway, she's doing life in prison."

"Did they have any children?"

"No," she explained. "He said that's why he married her in the first place. She told him she was pregnant, and then later he found out she wasn't."

"That's wanting someone *bad*."

"Yes, it is."

"Was her name Adrienne Black?"

"Yes, and his name was Nathan. Do you know them?"

"I know the case," he recognized. "My firm turned it down. The woman had no remorse."

"She felt she had done the right thing. They were already in the divorce proceedings when I met him, but when she found out he was dating me, it sent her over the edge."

"Did you love him?"

"I did. He was so smart. I was impressed."

"I'm sorry, baby," he declared softly, touching her face gently.

"Thanks, honey, but it's okay. I survived."

"And that's why you went on your five-year celibacy?"

She pondered, "I guess so. Nathan was also my first and *only* lover...until *you*." His eyes widened, but he didn't respond. He knew she didn't sleep around, but he had no idea just how little. Right now, Ron respected Toni even more.

"Oh, baby, I forgot to tell you," he decided to change the subject. "You were right about Mrs. Sanchez. She *did* commit suicide."

"How did you find out?"

"I took your advice and asked the coroner to check for poison. She had told her doctor that she had misplaced her medicine, so he wrote her another prescription. She took all the pills."

"What did the DA say?"

"They dropped all charges against Thomas Sanchez. The story hasn't been published yet. We want *you* to do it. An exclusive for you since you're responsible for breaking the case."

"You're *kidding*!"

"No."

"Oh, baby, that's great! Thank you!" she exploded. "Why didn't you tell me last night?"

"Baby, when I got here and saw you in that little nightshirt, Mr. Sanchez was the *farthest* thing from my mind," he made known, and she laughed as a knock came to the door.

"That's Tyler," she hypothesized, jumping up. "Ron, will you get that, honey? I gotta put on some make up."

"Sure," he agreed, getting up and slipping on his pajama bottom, as she ran into the bathroom.

"Put on your top," she called from the bathroom. "I don't want you to upset Tyler. He's gotta stay focus today." Ron smiled as he slipped on the pajama top and then went to the door.

When he opened the door, Tyler's eyes widened. "Is this *Toni Melton's* suite?" he inquired cautiously, admiring this handsome man.

"Yes," he confirmed. "You must be Tyler."

"Yeah," Tyler replied, standing there in a pair of skinny blue jeans, a light blue, button-down, loose hanging shirt, and a matching light blue baseball cap.

"Hi. Ron Joyner," Ron introduced, extending a hand.

"Of course. How are you, Mr. Joyner," he greeted, taking his hand in a firm shake. "You're handling the Sanchez case."

"Yes," he acknowledged. "Would you like to come in? Toni will be out soon."

"No, thank you," he declined. "Tell Toni I'll meet her downstairs in the café."

"All right."

"It was nice meeting you."

"Same here," Ron proclaimed then closed the door as Tyler left. Toni came out in a turquoise baseball cap.

"Where's Tyler?"

"He said he'll meet you downstairs in the café."

"Oh, okay," she responded, going to him. "It's funny but he doesn't look gay."

"What does *gay* look like?" Toni joked, then she and Ron simultaneously burst into laughter.

"Okay, I get the point."

"Well, Tyler is *definitely* gay and proud of it," Toni added then planted a kiss on his lips. "Wanna meet me for lunch?"

"Yeah, that would be great."

"I'll call you, okay?"

"Okay," he agreed, and they kissed again before she rushed out the door.

****

"David, do you have those quotes for Mrs. Gray?" a short, almond-tan, young lady asked as she entered his office. Her hair was long and done in cornrow braids that reached down to the middle of her back. Long, gold earrings hung from her earlobes, beside her oval face, which had a little too much makeup on it. She wasn't a pretty woman, just very flashy in a body-fitting red dress, which hung four inches above her knees, barely covering her protruding, round behind. Her short, brown legs ended with six-inch black pumps on her small feet.

"Yes, Kristy, I have them right here," David replied, taking a folder off his desk. Kristy was twenty-one and had just graduated from college. He was impressed with her interview, recommendations, and her grades, so he hired her immediately. His business was doing so well he had to hire an assistant, and *Kristy* was it. He felt she could bring in a lot of male clients with her flair for style as well as being easy on the eyes.

Receiving the folder from him, she uttered, "Thanks." Then she winked at him. He laughed, thinking that Kristy was such a tease. He knew Angel thought he was sleeping with her, but he wasn't. He didn't say he didn't *think* about it, but he *could* exercise some control when it came to women coming on to him, which Kristy did often. He knew it was just innocent flirting. He figured if he were to respond to her teasing, she would run like a scared little rabbit. He might just put Kristy to the test one day!

****

"There she is, the lady of the hour," Tyler raved when Toni stepped into the busy café.

"Hi, Tyler."

"Come on, what gives?" he inquired. "Weren't you the one who told me *not* to mix *business* with *pleasure*?"

"Yes," she laughed, taking a seat at the table with him.

"Well, judging from the hunk who opened your door, I'll say you've changed your mind."

"I'm *here* aren't I?" she laughed again.

"And I know it was *hard* pulling yourself away from *him*!"

"Yes, it was," Toni sneered. "Did you call for the car?"

He answered with a very efficient, "Outside."

"We better go. We can't be late," she made known, getting up.

"Well, I guess your *dry* spell is over!" Tyler whispered in her ear, and she jovially shoved him.

****

"Hi, I'm here to see Mr. Ron Joyner," a tall, light brown man asked, standing over Beverly's desk, dressed in a casual pair of black khaki pants, a white dress shirt, and a black tie.

She looked up, smiled, and replied, "He isn't here today. Do you have an appointment?"

"I spoke to him a couple weeks ago about a job."

"You did?" Beverly asked, searching Ron's appointment book. "What's your name?"

"Jamie Heard," he answered, smiling behind sparkling white teeth and a winning smile with a dimple on the left side of his face. Jamie was an incredibly attractive young man with an innocent glow about him, with neat, short cornrow braids. Beverly liked him immediately.

"I don't see you in his appointment book. Are you a lawyer?"

"Yes, I teach at the college."

"Where did you meet Ron? At the college?"

"Yes, as a matter of fact, I did. He spoke there a couple weeks ago."

"And he told you to come by?"

"Yes, I told him that I was thinking about going into private practice again and giving up teaching. He said his law firm would be hiring in a couple of weeks and to come by, so here I am," he explained.

"Well, he didn't write it down. Let me send you to personnel to fill out an application. Tell them that Ron told you to come by."

"All right. And which way is personnel?"

Pointing, she instructed, "When you go out of this office, make a right and go all the way down to the end of the hallway and make another right. Then go straight down and you will see the personnel office."

"Okay, thanks," he acknowledged, thinking that he hoped everyone here was as nice as she was.

****

"Angel, have you heard from Toni?" Mason questioned, entering Toni's office.

"Not today. She called last night. Why?"

"I wonder how she's making out at the prison?" he pondered. "It's hard to get a good interview at a place like that, especially when it's a *negative* report about the guards."

"Toni's pretty resourceful," she smiled as a pecan tan young lady entered in a nice two-piece casual, silk, light pink pantsuit.

"Hello," she spoke softly with some folders in her hand. Mason's eyes bulged at seeing the shapely woman.

"Hello," he responded, smiling wide.

"Mason Whittaker, Brandy Sears," Angel introduced.

"How do you do?" Mason greeted, extending a hand.

94

"Hello," the woman spoke, taking his hand. When they released, she pushed her neat, shoulder-length, micro-braids out of her face.

"I haven't seen you around here before," Mason made mention.

"Brandy's been here a week. She was in the temp group that Bill hired," Angel explained.

"How many did he hire?"

"Four," Angel revealed. "They were all Journalism students at the University."

"So, you're a journalism major?" Mason examined the pretty young lady.

"Yes."

"Well, if I can be of any assistance to you, let me know," he offered.

"Thank you. That's genuinely nice of you," she accepted, then handed Angel a folder. "Angel, Mr. Hurley said to give you this to hold until Miss Melton gets back."

"What is it?"

"Her article for next Friday."

"Okay. He's already looked at it?"

"Yes. He said she needs to change a few things when she gets back. He made notes."

"Oh, okay," she acknowledged.

"It was nice meeting you, Mr. Whittaker," Brandy alleged sweetly. "I love your column."

"Thank you," Mason accepted. She turned and left.

"Close your mouth, Mason," Angel ordered then burst into laughter, and he laughed with her, feeling his face getting very warm.

"She's pretty."

"Yes, she is, and *young*!"

"How young is she?"

"Twenty-two. Fresh out of college."

"Wow, that *is* young," he chuckled. "How does someone get that beautiful in only twenty-two years?" Angel just glared at him and he smiled. "I can *look*, can't I? I don't intend to *touch*."

"You just keep it that way," Angel warned, as the telephone began to ring. Then she murmured under her breath, "Dirty old man!"

"I heard that," he hooted.

Giggling also, she reached for the telephone, "Excuse me, Mason."

"I'll talk to you later," he concluded as he left, and she nodded, picking up the telephone receiver.

"Toni Melton's office. This is Angel. How may I help you?"

"Is Toni there?"

"No, ma'am, she isn't. May I help you?"

"Did you say this is Angel?"

"Mrs. Melton?"

"Yes," Toni's mother disclosed.

"How are you, Mrs. Melton?"

"I'm well. Thank you. Toni didn't come for dinner last night. I was wondering if she was all right."

"Mrs. Melton, Toni's in Houston. Didn't she tell you?"

"She probably did. I guess I forgot," she answered.

"Did you call her cell?"

"Yes, but she's not answering."

"Would you like her hotel room number, so you can leave a message for her?"

"All right."

"Hold on. Let me get it for you."

****

"Good morning, Ron Joyner's office, this is Beverly speaking. How may I help you?"

"Hi, good-looking," Ron joked, holding the hotel's cordless phone to his ear, sitting back on the sofa in the hotel suite.

"Boss, how's it going?" she beamed with excitement.

"Great!"

"She was happy to see you, right?"

"Yes, she was, Bev. Thank you for helping me to get a flight out so quickly."

"Anything for *love*, boss," she beamed.

"How is everything there?"

"Fine. You have another case Mr. Ballentine wants you to look at, but it can wait until you get back," she advised. "Oh, a new lawyer came in today. He said he met you at the college when you talked to a group of law students."

"Is he the law professor that's looking to go into private practice?"

"That's the one."

"Yeah, I did tell him to come by. I forgot about that. What did you tell him?"

"I sent him to personnel to fill out an application."

"That's good," he affirmed. "I don't really know him, but I'm sure personnel will check him out."

"Okay," she concurred. "Hey, how is Houston?"

"I haven't seen much of it yet. I arrived late last night."

"I understand," she acknowledged. "Tell Toni hello."

"I will," he agreed. "She's not here right now. She had to go to her interview."

"Well, bring me back a souvenir."

"I'll do that," Ron settled. "Well, take care of everything there. I'll see you Thursday."

"Okay, boss."

"Gotta go, honey. A call is coming in. It's probably Toni."

"Okay. Bye."

"Bye," he concluded then clicked over. "Hello?" There was no answer. "Hello," he repeated.

"Is this *Toni Melton's* room," her mother hesitantly replied on the other end.

"Yes, it is."

"Is she there?"

"No, she isn't. Who's calling?"

"Her mother. Who are you?"

Ron wanted to hide under a bush or something. He took a deep breath then replied, "I'm Ron Joyner, ma'am."

"Are you *staying* there with Toni, Mr. Joyner?"

"I'm just visiting," he reluctantly replied, gluing his eyes shut, wondering if that sounded dumb. How do you *visit* someone in a *hotel*?

"Tell Toni to call me," she snapped then slammed the phone down in his ears. Ron shook the phone in frustration before he hung up.

"Damn!" he spat, remembering how religious Toni said her mother was. Well, what's done is done. He couldn't dwell on that now. To ease his frustration for that situation, he focused back on Beverly's call. He couldn't help but wonder why a law professor would seek employment at a law firm, to start at the bottom again, when he probably already had tenure at the college.

****

"Take your time, Raheem," Toni coaxed as she and Tyler sat in a small room with a young African American man, while a guard looked on, standing at the door.

"Can we talk alone?" the young man asked, indicating the guard with a slight nod of his head.

She focused on the guard and inquired, "Is it possible for us to talk alone?"

"No, ma'am," he retorted sternly.

"He's only in here for a misdemeanor, right?"

"No, ma'am. He's in here for a felony."

"*Selling weed* isn't like assault or murder," Toni reasoned. "I'll take full responsibility for my safety."

"I'm sorry, ma'am, I can't do that."

"That's because he scared what I'm gonna tell you cause *he's* one of them who's *raping* people!" the young man blurted out, and the guard jumped to him, and whacked him over the head with a club.

"That isn't even necessary!" Toni yelled as the guard blew a whistle for help, and within moments, four other guards rushed in, seizing the young man, and carrying him away, while Toni screamed, as Tyler took pictures with his concealed camera.

****

Ron looked up from his newspaper, sitting on a bench in the park, and a lady was staring at him with a fixed smile on her face. He smiled shyly at her and that was her cue to approach him. "Hello," she greeted. "I'm Deborah."

"Hi, Deborah. I'm *attached*," he replied.

"That's a shame," she muttered, strolling pass him, licking her lips seductively, and he had to laugh. She was the fourth woman to approach him today. He didn't know men were that hard to come by. He just shook his head then thought about Toni. She was so sexy and strong. He could *never* cheat on her. He lo...*no*...he *refused* to say that four letter word. What was he thinking? It must be the weather. He smiled, wondering what Toni's mother was thinking. He knew Toni was in for it tonight with her, but that seemed to be the norm with them. Another lady was approaching him with that big, come-hither smile. He didn't want to be bothered again, so he got up and left before she reached him. It was about time for him to meet Toni for lunch anyway. When had the rules changed? When did *women* become the *chasers*?

****

"That was totally unnecessary!" Toni screamed in the warden's office. "And if I'm not allowed to talk to Raheem and all the other men who have similar complaints against your staff, Warden Pike, then I will be forced to print what happened here today!"

"Miss Melton, after lunch, I will have Raheem and all the other men on your list brought up here immediately. If what you say is going on here, *I* want to know who is behind this also."

"Thank you, sir," Toni finally calmed down. "Are those young men safe in here, Warden?"

"Of course, they are," he insisted. "What are you implying, Miss Melton?"

"These inmates are making serious allegations against your staff. I just wouldn't want anything bad to happen to them."

"I can assure you that they are safe. Come back at one o'clock, and I will personally see to it that you get your interviews."

"We'll be here," she confirmed. "Thank you, Warden Pike. Raheem had better be *all right*!"

****

"David, where's Ernestine?" Kristy asked, entering his office.

"I sent her to the bank."

"Oh. Then you want me to answer the phones?"

"No, I can get them," he clarified, standing, and walking to the file cabinet.

"Mrs. Gray is all signed up!" she beamed.

"Good," he approved then started to pass her, but stopped in front of her, focusing on her double-D cups in that tight, low-cut tan dress. Their eyes locked and he shook his head and started to pass her again, but she stepped in front of him. "What?" he chuckled. She took his hand and placed it on her chest. Then she reached up and he met her in a soft kiss.

"I've been wanting to do that for a long time," she breathed.

"Kristy, I think you're so sexy, but I'm married with two kids."

"I know, but can't you have some fun on the side?"

He took a breath, and she took his hand and slid it inside her bra, and he thought he would melt. His body immediately responded, and he could hardly contain himself. He grabbed her and kissed her hard. Their kisses grew wild and gropingly. Then she dropped on the floor and unbuckled his pants. He dropped his head back in anticipation of what was to come. When his pants and briefs dropped to the floor, he stepped forward and left them in a heap on the floor. She then wiggled out of her dress. He focused on the young woman, standing there, dropping her black lace panties to the floor with her dress, and he wanted her. He wanted her *bad*. They slowly strolled into each other's arms and began kissing fervently. Like in the movies, with one hand he swished the contents on his desk onto the floor and replaced it with Kristy's warm, desiring, soft body. He covered her body with his, as they kissed wild and uninhibited. Suddenly, they heard someone enter and they both froze. David looked up and focused on the door and squeezed out breathlessly, "Angel!"

****

"Hi, baby," Toni addressed, meeting Ron with a kiss in the restaurant as he stood from the chair at the table, with Tyler behind her.

"Hi."

"Have you been waiting long?"

"No, I just got here," he made known then focused on Tyler and extended a hand. "Nice to see you again."

"Same here," he accepted, shaking his hand as they sat at the table.

"How did things go?"

"Not too well," Toni shared as the waitress approached their table.

"Hello, Miss Melton, it's a pleasure serving you today," she acknowledged, smiling wide.

"Thank you," Toni accepted, returning her smile.

"I hate to bother you, but may I please have your autograph?"

"Sure," Toni agreed, receiving a paper menu from the lady.

"My name is Carolyn," the waitress shared, and Toni nodded, beginning to write.

"I didn't know your column was in *Texas*!" Ron admired.

"Toni's column is syndicated in magazines around the globe," Tyler spoke up while she signed the menu. Ron was impressed.

"Thank you," the waitress responded, still smiling when Toni handed her the signed menu. "Thank you so much." She tucked the menu in her pocket and took out her pad. "What can I get you to drink?"

"Iced tea please," Toni replied.

"Same for me," added Tyler.

"Same," echoed Ron.

"I'll be right back," she made known then almost skipped away full of excitement.

"So, what happened at the prison?" Ron wanted to know.

"Toni Melton!" a voice shrieked, and two women rushed over to their table with magazines for her to autograph. Ron didn't know he was involved with a woman so famous. Toni was a real trooper. No one would ever guess she was as successful as she was by the way she acted. When he first met her, he thought she was a little egotistical, but he soon changed his mind. She just wanted a story. Now he saw why she worked so hard to get a good story and more importantly, to get a *true* story. People believed in her, and she couldn't let them down. Tyler focused on Ron and smiled. He seemed to know what was going through his mind, and Ron confirmed it with a slight nod of his head and a smile.

****

"You son of a bitch!" Angel spat and David jumped to find his clothes. He pulled on his pants quickly as she entered the office slowly, while Kristy slipped back into her dress.

"How long have you been fucking this little whore?!" she spat.

"Angel, I know you think this has been going on a long time, but it hasn't. I swear," he spoke quickly.

"I'm not a whore," Kristy spat, standing behind David.

"Shut up, Kristy!" he demanded.

"How could you do this to our family?" Angel raged.

"Baby, listen to me," he started. "I..." Before he could finish, Angel had dropped her purse and was attacking both Kristy and him with her fists, while Kristy screamed.

****

"Raheem, when did the assaults begin?" Toni urged the young man, while the Warden and his assistant stood by as Tyler took pictures.

"The first night I got here," the young man of eighteen replied with tears running down his dark face. "It was late. I was asleep. Then I heard my cell door open, and before I could get up, four of them pinned me down while..." he stopped and closed his eyes. "Jesse...he *raped* me." Tears were flowing down Toni's face as she listened to the young man's story, how night after night, guards came into his cell, and all five would take turns holding him down and robbing him of his dignity. Her heart went out to him. She knew he would never be the same, but she had so much respect for him for being brave enough to step forward, to put an end to his abuse. She later interviewed three other young men with similar stories about the same five guards. The Warden was outraged. He sent for the proper authorities and had the five guards arrested immediately. For the first time in Toni's career, she didn't need an award for her story. She just wanted to help these young men, and it felt good. She didn't even want to *write* the story since justice had already been served, but she knew she had to, so laws could be changed, so that nothing like this would ever happen to young people again just because they had made mistakes in life. She always thought of prison as a way of *helping* people to get back on the right track, not *destroy* their futures, which is what those guards were doing to those young men. She only felt outraged.

****

Angel sat, curled up on the sofa weeping softly, when she heard the front door open. David walked in slowly and focused on her. "Angel, honey…"

Throwing up an open hand, she demanded, "Save it, David! Just save it!" He dropped his head and she sniffed. "Just get your things and get the hell out!"

"Angel, baby, please don't do this," he begged. "I made a mistake. Please don't destroy our family over *one* mistake!"

"*You* destroyed our family…not *me!*" she hissed. "You destroyed our family the minute you started sleeping with your little whore! Now get out!"

"Angel, I swear to you, that was the first time. I swear," he insisted. "I love you."

"You don't know what love is!" she yelled, throwing a chair pillow at him. "Now get the hell out before I have you thrown out!"

****

"Hi, honey," Ron met Toni at the hotel door with a kiss.

"Hi," she responded, smiling slightly.

"Tired?"

"*Drained* is more like it," she answered, dropping her head in his chest. He pulled her close.

"What's wrong?"

"Let me take a shower, and I'll tell you all about it," she promised, and he nodded. When she walked into the bathroom, followed by Ron, he had already run a nice hot bubble bath and she smiled, dropped her head back on him. He hugged her from the rear. "How did I get so lucky?"

"*I'm* the lucky one," he recognized then kissed the back of her neck. "Come on."

Ron removed every stitch of Toni's clothes, then he removed his and they submerged into the bathtub full of bubbles together, and she sat in front of him and relaxed back in his loving arms. He sponged her off softly as she glued her eyes shut to bask in his tender loving care.

"Your mother called today. I answered because I thought it was you. I'm sorry."

"It's okay," she responded, turning to face him. They kissed softly, and she leaned back into his arms again.

"I don't want to cause problems between your mother and you."

"Honey, problems existed between us long before I met you," she divulged.

"She said for you to call her."

"I'll call her tomorrow. I can't take my mother's drama tonight."

Chapter 7

"You can't fire me, David!" Kristy raged in his office.

"I have to," he countered. "I've got to make things right with my wife."

"The hell with your wife! I *need* this job!"

"I will write you a good recommendation," he promised.

"No, David! I want to stay *here*!"

"Kristy, I can't do that after what happened. Angel has put me out. The only chance I have of getting her back is if you're not working here anymore. Please understand."

"I understand that you're a *coward*."

"Say what you want, but you can't work here anymore."

"I'll sue you, David. You have no cause to fire me just because your wife caught us in a compromising position."

"Kristy, please..." he started but was silenced by her kiss.

"You don't need *her*, baby. You have me."

"I do need her, Kristy," he countered. "We have two sons. I can't leave them."

"If you fire me, David, you're gonna have to take care of me until I find a job," she insisted, kissing him again. "I'm crazy about you." He felt his nature rising and he kissed her back. "Will you, David, take care of me until I get a job?"

"Yes," he agreed then picked her up and sat her on the desk. He dropped his pants quickly. He lifted her and pulled her panties off swiftly.

"Yes, David, yes," she breathed. Then he stopped suddenly, and she focused on him. "What's wrong?"

He tipped to the door, locked it, and then strolled back to her, stepping out of his pants on the way.

****

Ron kissed Toni's lips and she opened her eyes. "Good morning," he whispered.

"Good morning," she purred.

"Feeling better?"

"Yeah," she yawned.

"Don't you have to go back to the prison this morning?"

"No, I finished yesterday," she made known.

"You did?"

"Yes, we have the whole day together in beautiful Houston."

"That's great!" he concurred then kissed her again. "What'd you want to do?"

"Be with you," she purred, and they kissed again, as the telephone started ringing. "Go away!" Toni gasped. He picked up the telephone and handed it to her. "Hello?"

"Toni, why is a man staying with you?!" her mother immediately charged.

"Good morning to you, too, Mother."

"Toni, I thought I raised you better than that. Shacking up with a man! It's disgraceful! It's sinful!"

Toni ruffled her short hair hard, took a deep breath, and stated, "He's only *visiting*, Mom. We're not *shacking* up together." Ron looked at her, planted a kiss on her cheek then walked into the bathroom.

"I hope not, Toni. I would hate to see you burn in hell."

Ignoring her mother's comments, Toni continued, "How are you, Mom?"

"Why didn't you tell me you were going to Texas?"

"I did, Mom. I told you I was going to a prison in a town outside of Houston to interview some inmates," she nonchalantly explained as Ron reentered, laid beside her, and started nibbling on her ear.

"You should've reminded me."

"I thought I had, Mom. I'm sorry," she accepted, squirming under his tender touch. "Listen, Mom, I'm on my way out the door. I have an early appointment." Her breathing grew more pronounced.

"Yeah, I bet!" her mother snapped, then slammed the telephone down.

Toni replaced the telephone receiver in its cradle and focused on Ron. "What're you trying to do, get me into more trouble?" she chuckled.

"That was the idea," he cooed, kissing her hard as he slid on top of her.

"She is pissed!"

"She'll get over it."

Toni shook her head and stressed. "You don't know my mother!"

****

"Mommy, where's daddy?" Sammie asked as he burst into the kitchen with his brother following behind him.

"Daddy's not here," Angel answered, sitting at the breakfast table with them.

"Where is he?" inquired Ricky.

"Daddy had to leave for a while," she explained, fighting her tears back as hard as she could.

"Who's taking us to school?" asked Sammie.

"Keith's mother," she answered, trying to force a smile.

Noticing her bathrobe, Sammie asked again, "You're not going to work today?"

"No," she squeezed out, finding it difficult to hold back her tears. She jumped up and retrieved the orange juice from the refrigerator, so she could wipe her face without her children seeing her tears.

As soon as she returned to the table, Ricky immediately wanted to know, "When is daddy coming back?"

"I don't know, honey," Angel responded. "Hurry up and eat your breakfast before Keith and his mother come."

****

"So, what would you like to do today, Miss Melton?" Ron asked Toni as she sat back in his arms while they still rested in bed.

"It doesn't matter as long as it's with you," she verbalized, and he planted a kiss on the back of her head.

"We could just stay in here all day and relax," he proposed softly.

"That sounds good to me."

"Cause, if I take you anywhere, I'll have to share you with the world."

She turned around in his arms and made known, "You *never* have to share me with *anyone*." They kissed lovingly. She turned back around and rested in his arms again.

"I didn't realize you were so famous, Miss Melton."

"Does it matter?"

"I don't know," he emphasized then laughed softly. "Do I have to carry your shoes?"

"Only if you want to," she chuckled.

"I've never dated a rich woman before. All the women I know are out to see what's in it for them."

"That surprises me."

"What does?"

"That *you're* rich and you've never dated a rich woman before."

"But I'm not *famous!*"

Toni laughed and made known, "I'm just like all the rest."

"My dear, you are a cut *above* all the rest," he stressed.

"Oh, that's sweet," she purred, turning into his arms and they ended in a long kiss. "Sorry to disappoint you, baby, but I'm not rich."

"Neither am I," he laughed.

****

"Hello," Mason spoke to Brandy as she sat at Angel's desk.

"Hi," she responded, smiling sweetly.

"Where's Angel?"

"She took a few days off."

"Is she sick?"

"I don't know. Mr. Hurley said she called and told him she was taking a few days off and to see if I could fill in for her."

"I guess she's taking advantage of Toni's trip." he hypothesized then focused on the pretty lady in the tight low-cut Angora sweater. "So, how are *you* doing? Are you finding everything all right?"

"Yes, I'm fine."

You sure are, he thought, admiring her braids pulled back in a nice ponytail. He added, "Let me know if you need any help," as he thought again, *A back rub, a massage, or a good lay!*

"I will. Thank you, Mr. Whittaker," she replied in her sultry, throaty Jaclyn Smith voice.

"*Mason*, please," he offered.

"Mason," she complied as he walked off.

Brandy couldn't help but to admit that he was a good-looking man, standing there so tall in that expensive, off-black suit, and a bold lavender necktie with a matching handkerchief peering out the front pocket. She could tell that he was interested in her.

A thought crossed her mind the more she thought of him. Didn't she remember hearing that he was *married*? Maybe he was the kind of man who fooled around. Lord knows she's had too many of those types. *My wife doesn't understand me. I'm leaving her just as soon as little whoever graduates. We don't have sex anymore...* and then the wife comes up pregnant. She had heard them all. She wondered what Mr. Mason Whittaker's story was. They *all* had one! The ringing of the telephone invaded Brandy's thoughts and she picked it up quickly.

"Toni Melton's office. This is Brandy speaking. How may I help you?"

"Who?" Toni asked on her cell phone, sitting on the bed in a pink lace teddy, while Ron showered.

"Brandy Sears."

"Brandy?"

"Yes."

"Where's Angel?"

"Who's speaking please?"

"Oh, I'm sorry," Toni apologized. "This is Toni Melton."

"Oh, Miss Melton. I didn't recognize your voice. Please forgive me."

"It's okay. Where's Angel?"

"She called in and told Mr. Hurley she needed to take a few days off."

"Is she sick?"

"I don't know."

"Are you one of the temps Bill hired last week?"

"Yes, ma'am."

"Well, thank you for helping out while Angel's away."

"You're welcome."

"Do I have any messages?"

"Yes, ma'am, you have a few, but Angel said they could wait until you returned."

"Okay. Angel would know," she pondered. "Brandy, you can drop the *ma'am* and *miss*. We are all on a first name basis there."

"Yes, ma'...I mean, *Toni*."

"That's better," Toni confirmed. "Brandy, would you please put me through to Bill?"

"Yes, Miss....agh...*Toni*. Hold on please."

"Thank you." Toni wondered who Brandy was. She sounded like a nice kid...sweet and pleasant. She hoped Mason or any other hounds at the office wouldn't corrupt the child.

"Mr. Hurley's office. Joanne's speaking. May I help you?"

"Hi, Joanne. It's Toni."

"Hi, Toni. How are you?"

"Fine."

"Are you back?"

"No, not yet."

"How is Houston?"

"It's great," Toni acknowledged, then thinking of Ron she added, "better than I imagined."

"Is the weather good?"

"It's fabulous!" Toni answered. "Is Bill in?"

"I'm sorry, Toni, but he went home to take his wife to the doctor's."

"Is she all right?"

"I think it's just a checkup. He said they might try something new with her treatments."

"Oh, I see," Toni understood. "Well, tell him I called, and I'll see him tomorrow."

"I sure will."

"Have a nice day, Joanne."

"Thank you, Toni. You too."

When Toni ended the call, she went into a deep thought and didn't even hear when Ron entered the room wrapped in a towel. "What's wrong?" he questioned.

"Angel took a few days off," she shared. "It's not like her to take time off when I'm not there. She knows how much I depend on her."

"You think she's sick?"

"I don't know. I better call her."

****

Angel sat, curled up on the couch, weeping softly. She sniffed, blew her nose, picked up the telephone and dialed David's work number. "David Scott Insurance Agency," a voice said.

"Ernestine, this is Angel Scott."

"Oh hi, Mrs. Scott. How are you?"

"I'm okay. Is David in?'

"No, Mrs. Scott. He had to go and look at a property," she answered. "Kristy is here. Would you like to talk to her?"

Angel felt a knot churn up in her stomach. Kristy was still there. David was obviously involved with the slut. She knew then that her marriage was over. "No, I don't wanna talk to *Kristy*!" she answered sternly. "I'll talk to you later, Ernestine."

"Would you like for me to ask Mr. Scott to call you?"

"No, thank you. That won't be necessary. I'll try his cell," she sadly returned. "Goodbye." She hung up quickly and burst into tears. The ringing telephone brought some control over her, and she looked at the caller ID and noticed Toni's cell phone number. She picked it up quickly. "Toni?"

"Angel, what's wrong?" Toni questioned, and Angel burst into tears again. "Angel?"

She sniffed. "Toni, I caught David with...with *Kristy*!"

"Oh, my God, Angel. You're *kidding*!"

"They were in his *office*!" she cried.

"Angel, hold tight. I'm gonna see if I can change my flight from tomorrow to today, all right?" Toni made known, but Angel was crying too hard to answer. "Angel, calm down, honey. I'll be there as soon as I can."

"Toni, don't cut your trip short. I'll be fine," she finally squeezed out.

"Are you sure?"

"Yes. I'll see you when you get back tomorrow."

"Don't worry, honey. Everything will be all right," Toni hypothesized, then hung up as Ron focused on her.

"What's wrong?"

"Angel, my best friend, caught her husband cheating with his assistant," she answered. "Oh Ron, why do men cheat?"

"*I* don't!" he defended.

"I'm sorry, honey. I didn't mean *all* men," she apologized, going into his arms. Then she held up and added, "I've never heard Angel so upset. Honey, would you mind too terribly if we cut our trip short?"

"Of course, I would, but I understand," he expressed then planted a kiss on her forehead.

"She said for me not to come home today, but I'll feel better if I were there with her," she declared. "When Nathan died, I would have gone crazy if it weren't for Angel."

"Baby, you don't have to explain. I understand."

She stared deeply into his caring, hazel eyes and squeezed out softly, "Thank you."

"I'll call and see if we can change our reservations."

114

"Thanks, honey. I'll make it up to you."

"Hey, you don't have to thank me. Your friend needs you. Where else would you wanna be?"

"I better call Tyler first to see if he wants me to change his reservations, too," she suggested.

"Hello," Tyler groaned sleepily, sitting up in bed as a man lay beside him, still asleep.

"Tyler, it's Toni."

Tyler yawned, "Hi, Toni. What's up?"

"Listen, honey, I gotta go back home today?"

"That hunk isn't satisfying you?" he joked.

"Funny, Tyler," she chuckled. "Angel is having problems. I gotta go and see about her."

"Oh, I'm sorry."

"I just wanted to know if you wanted me to change your reservations also."

"No, darling. I'll leave tomorrow as planned."

"Okay," Toni confirmed. "See you tomorrow then."

"Chao, sweetie."

****

Ron and Toni settled back in first class, awaiting their departure. They were both dressed casually in wind suits, Toni's tan, and Ron's brown. The flight attendant entered and stopped at their seats. They looked up together. "Hello, Ron," she spoke softly.

Ron found his voice and greeted, "Vickie, hello. I thought you were in Japan."

"You know I don't stay anywhere long," she replied then focused on Toni. "Toni Melton, my pleasure. I love your column."

"Thank you."

"Vickie Baker," Vickie introduced herself. "I will be taking care of you today. If you need anything, just let me know." *Cyanide maybe?* she thought to herself. *The nerve of this little newspaper woman with my man!*

115

"Thank you," Toni accepted graciously.

"I'll check on you later," she finalized, smiled sweetly then walked off.

Toni punched Ron on his arm. "Ouch!" he yelped. "What's that's for?"

"*Okay*?! You told me she was *okay* looking!" Toni jeered. "If she's *okay* looking then what do you call *beautiful*?! The woman is *gorgeous*!"

"*You're* gorgeous!" Ron cooed, kissing her lips.

"Blow it out your ear, Ron!"

He burst into laughter and added, "Toni, Vickie's *just* a woman!"

"Ron, I'm *just* a woman! *Vickie* is *gorgeous*!"

He turned to her and took her chin between his thumb and index finger and professed sincerely, "You are all the woman I need, Toni Melton. Other women don't even phase me anymore. I always look *forward* to seeing *you*." Toni smiled, and then they met each other with a sweet kiss, just as Vickie walked pass them. She frowned to herself and continued her stride.

****

"Hi, baby," Kristy cheerfully saluted, entering David's office.

"Hi," he welcomed, meeting her with a kiss.

"My offer is still open for you to stay with me until you find some place."

"Thank you," he accepted. "It's expensive staying in a hotel. I think I'll take you up on that offer."

"Really?" she exploded, and he smiled. She walked into his arms and they kissed long and passionately. "I'll fix you a great dinner tonight." He nodded and they kissed again.

"I gotta go and get some more of my things from home."

"Want me to go with you?"

"No," he chuckled. "Angel might shoot both of us."

"I'm not afraid of your wife!"

"It has nothing to do with being *afraid*, Kristy. It has to do with *respect*. I would *never* disrespect Angel like that, by flaunting *you* in her face," he clarified. "Okay?" She just pouted, dropping her head. He lifted her head with his fingers. "Okay, Kristy?"

"Okay," she accepted. "I'll be waiting for you at home." He kissed her again.

****

Angel opened the door and immediately fell into Toni's arms, crying hysterically. "Thank you, Toni. Thank you for coming."

"You don't have to *thank* me, silly girl," Toni tried to console her friend, but tears were stinging her own eyes too. She was still in the tan wind suit she had worn home on the plane. It was tearing her up inside to see her friend in so much pain, and there wasn't a thing she could do to make her feel better but offer her a shoulder to cry on.

When Angel finally released her caring friend, they entered the house and sat on the sofa together in the huge family room. "Where're the boys?" Toni inquired.

"My parents took them for a few days," she answered, blowing her nose, trying to calm down.

"Do they know what happened?" Toni probed, blowing her nose also.

"Not yet. I told them I would explain later," Angel shared, unable to stop the tears. "Toni, why did he do it? I tried to be *everything* David wanted in a wife. When we were first married, I didn't even like some of the things he liked, but I learned to enjoy what *he* liked. Why would he need to have another woman?"

"I don't know, sweetheart," she responded, taking a deep breath. "I don't know."

"I'm sorry about not working while you were gone."

"It's okay, honey. Don't even think about it."

117

"Why did he do it, Toni? Why?" she cried, but Toni didn't have an answer for her distraught friend, so she didn't even try to speculate. Toni just pulled her friend in her arms and let her cry.

Toni often wondered why men cheat herself. She realized that Angel didn't need advice right now anyway. All she needed was someone to release herself to, so Toni just let Angel cry it out on her shoulders.

When Angel settled down again, she was ready to talk, and Toni was there to listen. Angel talked, raged, and shouted her frustrations out while Toni just listened in silence. She knew Angel needed to get all the hurt out of her system. Maybe in time, Angel could accept new things and move forward, whichever direction it was.

****

"Hi, Mom," Ron spoke into his cell phone.

"Ron, where have you been?" she exploded.

"I went to Houston Monday night."

"*Houston*?!" she yelped. "Why did you go to *Houston*? And more importantly, why didn't you tell me?!"

"It was a spur of the moment trip, Mom."

"Oh," she sobered. "How are you, son?"

"I'm fine."

"What do you have planned for Sunday? I was wondering if you could come for dinner. Your sisters and their families are coming. You know it's your father's sixty-third birthday?"

"Yeah, I know," he recognized. "I'll be there."

"Good," she received. Mrs. Joyner was an attractive woman for sixty years old. She had a lovely almond tan face with wire-framed eyeglasses, with her hair pulled back in a neat French roll. She was still small and neat in her black pleated slacks and crème-colored silk blouse. "I'll see you then, sweetheart."

"Ah, Mom, I might bring someone with me if she can make it."

Smiling wide, Mrs. Joyner questioned, "Oh, you have a friend?"

"Yes, she's a friend," Ron concurred.

"Good. Bring her," she agreed. "Is she the reason you went to Houston all of a sudden?"

He chuckled, "Yes, she is, Mom."

"I can't wait to meet her."

"And tell your daughters to be nice," he added. "Every time I bring someone over, they give her the third degree, especially *Denise*!"

She sniggered, "I'll talk to them."

"Should I bring anything?"

"No, honey. Melissa and Denise are helping me."

"All right. I'll see you Sunday," Ron finalized then hung up. He went into thought. He hoped Toni was ready to meet his family. He didn't want her to think he was moving too fast. Following her all the way to Houston had already been a big step and he didn't want to run her away. She is just the woman he had been looking for all his life. Oh, what the heck, he *loved* her. Yes, he said it. Ron Joyner is in *love* with Toni Melton. He just hoped she felt the same.

****

"What'd you want?" Angel hissed at David when he entered the house with his key.

"I came to get some of my things."

"Well, get them and leave!"

"Hi, Toni," he spoke softly.

"David." Toni responded dryly.

"Where're the boys?" he questioned.

"None of your damn business!" Angel flared. "Now, get your things and get the hell out! If I had my way, you'd never see those boys again for as long as you live!" She turned and stormed into the kitchen. He started to follow her, but Toni stopped him.

"David, give her some time."

"I want to see my boys, Toni."

"And you *will*. She didn't mean it. She's just upset. Give her time to calm down. Please! Don't add fuel to the fire. I know Angel. She'll cool down," she pleaded, and he took a deep breath and nodded.

"Where *are* the boys?"

"With Mr. and Mrs. Rider."

"I guess my name is mud around that house."

"Angel hasn't told them yet."

Shocked, he queried, "She hasn't?"

"No, she hasn't."

"Well, that's good," he acknowledged, sighed deeply then locked eyes with Toni. "I'm sorry about all of this, Toni."

"Then why did you do it, David?"

"I don't know. Stupid, I guess."

"Angel said Kristy is still working for you."

He nodded and alleged, "I had no grounds for firing Kristy. She could've sued me broke."

"I don't think so. It's *your* business. You have a right to hire and fire anyone you chose," Toni described. "Could it be that you just don't *want* to fire Kristy?"

"I don't know. I guess so. I feel responsible for her. After all, she's young and it was *my* fault. I can't stand to see her out on the street without a job because of me," he explained, and Toni nodded.

"So, whatever happened to your *wife* and *children* coming *first*?"

He took a deep breath to ponder what she had said. Then he came back with, "I messed up, Toni. Pure and simple. I messed up, and Angel can't forgive me."

"Were you seeing Kristy for a while?"

"No, I swear, but Angel thinks so. When she walked in on us… that was the first time."

"What about *now*. Are you seeing her *now*?" she searched, and he dropped his head but didn't answer in words. Toni understood. "I see." There was a long silence. "Do you want your family back, David?"

"Of course, I do."

"And you also want *Kristy*?"

He sighed deeply and retorted, "Well, I can't have *Angel*."

"So, you're *settling* for *Kristy*?"

"I guess so."

"Do you still love Angel?"

"With all my heart."

"Then search your heart. When you're ready, clean up your act, and come and get your family back. Angel still loves you, and you said you still love her. Kristy is young and sexy, and she has entered your head and confused you. Don't let her enter your *heart*. As I said, when you're ready, come and get your family back. But not until *you're* ready. Just don't wait too long though. Your kids will grow up much too quickly, and you can't get those years back; and your wife might just get tired of waiting. She's a beautiful woman. Men finding her attractive has *never* been her problem," she expounded, and he nodded. David had a lot of respect for Toni. She was Angel's best friend, but she didn't down or judge him. She actually seemed to understand. She was truly a friend to Angel! She was a friend to them both!

****

"Mom!" a voice called, entering Mrs. Joyner's kitchen. She walked into the kitchen and focused on her son Leroy, dirty and stank, with long, nappy, uncombed hair, an unruly mustache, and straggly beard, searching the refrigerator.

"Leroy, where have you been? I've been worried sick! We haven't seen you in *four* days!" she spat.

"I'm okay," he countered, sticking a cold chicken leg in his mouth. "Where's dad?"

"He's upstairs."

"Mom, may I get a loan?"

"And how are you going to pay me back with no job?"

"I'll pay you back."

"You never do, Leroy."

"Please, Mom."

"Go and take a shower and put on some clean clothes," she ordered.

"Then you'll give me twenty dollars?"

"No, Leroy. I will give you no money!"

"Dag, Mom, it's *just* twenty dollars. It ain't like it's hundreds!"

"Go, Leroy, and wash!" she insisted.

"All right already!" he groaned, storming out the kitchen. Mrs. Joyner just dropped her head. She couldn't believe that after all the sacrifices they made to send Leroy to medical school, that he turned out like this. He was such a brilliant surgeon. People came from all over the world to get under Dr. Leroy Joyner's knife. Now, look at him. A drunk, a *bum*! She wished that he had had enough balls to fight for his life. When they suspended his license, he just gave up. The funny thing was that they only suspended his license for three years. It's been five years now, and he was getting worse by the day. He could've fought for his job. Ron was going to help him. He didn't care to fight for either his job or his life. He just rolled over and died, and it seemed that he was *never* coming back. Mrs. Joyner surrendered to a wail of tears.

****

"Is he gone?" Angel asked Toni who came into the kitchen with her.

"Yeah," Toni confirmed, then Angel strolled slowly back into the family room and Toni followed her. They sat on the sofa again. "Are you all right?"

"No, but I will be," she revealed as uncontrollable tears rolled down her face.

"Wanna talk?"

Angel took a deep sigh then focused on her friend. "You are a good friend, Toni."

"So are you."

"Yes, but not many people would've dropped everything miles away and come running to a friend's rescue."

"Oh, I know a friend who would," Toni emphasized, remembering her own ordeal. "I remember when Nathan died, you were in New York, but you dropped everything and came home. I never forgot that."

"You were hurting. I *had* to come."

"Same here, my friend. Same here."

She sniffed, "Thanks, Toni."

"You're welcome."

Angel wiped her tears, blew her nose, and added, "I'm tired of talking about my *pathetic* life. Let's talk about you. How was Houston?"

"Great in some ways and depressing in others."

"What was depressing about it?"

"Interviewing the inmates," Toni shared. "No one should have to endure what they're going through."

"What happened?"

"Young boys, eighteen, nineteen years old, being sodomized by five guards."

"You're kidding!" Angel challenged and Toni shook her head. "And they talked to you about it?"

"Yes, they were very brave," she answered. "They just want it to stop."

"Wow, I thought it was just a myth about prison life."

"It's not. It really happens."

"What happened to the guards?"

"They were all arrested."

"Now they might get a taste of their own medicine."

"I hope not. No one deserves to be treated like that, no matter what they've done," Toni rationalized. "A lot of those young boys are in there for just selling a little weed. I just wish young people would learn to just get an education, so they won't be forced to break the law and risk going to prison or an early grave, but you can't tell them anything."

"I know. It's sad."

"Yes, it is. My heart went out to those young boys. Their manhood was stripped from them. They will never be the same. They all told me that if they could do it over, their lives would be a lot different. They found out that *nothing* is worth their freedom, including *money*."

"That's the truth," Angel agreed. "What about the guards? Are they going to be locked up with the prisoners they assaulted?"

"I don't know. Maybe I'll go back and do a follow-up later," Toni enlightened her friend. "And the sad thing about this is that all of those guards have wives or girlfriends. They don't even claim to be gay. They just assaulted those boys to degrade and belittle them."

"That *is* sad," she whispered. "You know rape is never about sex. It's *always* about control and power."

"That's exactly what the guards intended to do, control those young boys, and now they have changed their lives forever," Toni finalized, and she and Angel just sat there for a while, speechless.

Angel decided to break the silence, "So, what was *great* about Houston? I need some *good* news."

Toni inhaled deeply then exhaled slowly, smiling sweetly, and answered, "Ron came."

"Came where?"

"To Houston," she beamed.

"What?!" Angel screeched. "Ron Joyner came all the way to Houston to see you?!" Toni nodded, and Angel screamed. "The brotha is *serious*! That's *great*!" She jumped and grabbed Toni in a big embrace. "And you left *early*?!"

"It's okay."

"Now I *really* feel bad, you crazy gal."

"No! Don't, Angel!" Toni ordered.

"Are you in love with him, Toni?"

She thought for a moment then blurted out, "Yes! Oh, yes I am!" Angel grabbed her friend in a loving hug again.

"I'm happy for you, honey."

"But I haven't told *him*."

"Why not?"

124

"Because it's so quick. We haven't known each other long. He hasn't said he loved me, and I don't want to run him away with all this love stuff."

"Silly girl, he told you he loved you when he flew to Houston," Angel insisted then burst into laughter. "What more does the man have to do?" Toni giggled with her.

"A girl likes to *hear* the words."

"Trust me, it's better for them to *show* you than to *tell* you."

"I guess you're right."

"I *know* I'm right."

"He also gave me a key to his condo."

"What?!"

"Well, it's because he took my things on to his house from the airport because I wanted to come straight here."

"Girl, a man doesn't give you his key unless he's serious about you," Angel assumed then screamed, "what in the hell more does the man have to do, Toni?! He *loves* you! He *loves* you!" Toni laughed with her friend as her cell phone began to ring. "There he is."

She looked at her caller ID and Angel was right. It was Ron's number. She grinned at her and concurred, "You're right."

"I'm going to make us some coffee," Angel announced, getting up and leaving.

"Hi, baby," Toni said into her cell phone, smiling wide.

"Hi, sweetie," he replied. "How are things?"

"A little better," she answered. "As a matter of fact, we were just talking about *you*."

"Um, that sounds dangerous."

"All good, I assure you," she snickered.

"Are you going to be there the rest of the night?"

"I think so."

"You need me to bring you anything?"

"No, honey. Thank you. I can wear something of Angel's, and in the morning, I'll come by your place and get dressed before I go to work if that's okay."

"That's fine, sweetheart. But if you change your mind about needing anything, call me."

"I will. Thanks."

He paused for a moment. "How would you like to go to my parents' house for dinner Sunday?"

"Sunday?"

"Yes, it's my father's birthday."

"Sure," Toni responded, barely able to contain her excitement. "Does this mean I'm *in*?"

"The votes are still out," he chuckled.

"You're going to pay for that," she seductively tittered.

"Ooh, I can hardly wait," he purred then laughed and she laughed with him. "Well, I don't want to keep you from your friend. I'll see you in the morning."

"Okay."

"Come early so we can have *breakfast* together before we go to work," he cooed.

"I will," she rebounded. As Toni hung up, Angel came back in with a tray containing a coffee pot, two cups, sugar bowl, nondairy cream, and spoons.

"Ah, a woman in love," she observed jovially, and Toni smiled with her. "Or *lust*." They burst into laughter together.

Chapter 8

"What're you doing back?!" Beverly exploded when Ron entered.

"We came back last night."

"But you weren't supposed to come back until tonight," Beverly countered. "You didn't have a fight, did you?"

"Oh, no!" he laughed. "We had a wonderful time. Toni just had an emergency with a friend."

"Here are your messages," she said, handing him a stack of notes. "Welcome back."

"Thanks," he accepted, walking into his office.

"So, how was Houston?" Travis asked, entering after him.

"Great!" Ron answered.

"Or did you get to see any of it?"

"I saw enough," he chuckled.

"Hey, that law professor you recommended is doing fine."

"Good, but I really didn't recommend him. He told me he was looking for a job, and I told him we were hiring," Ron explained. "I forgot his name."

"Heard. Jamie Heard."

"Oh yeah," he remembered. "So, Phillip hired him, huh?"

"Yes, and he's smart as a whip."

"Good."

"Did you know he is married to Taffy Hines?"

"*The* Taffy Hines, the richest black woman in Greenleaf?"

"The one and only."

"No, I didn't know that."

"He *is*."

"Wow! He married into great wealth," Ron observed. "How old is he? Taffy Hines is in her fifties, isn't she?"

"Closer to sixty," Beverly laughed, entering Ron's office, and handing him a folder. "He's thirty. Same as you."

"Wow!" Ron acknowledged. "Thank you." She nodded and left.

"I agree. I don't want money that bad!" Travis laughed.

Ron countered, "Have you ever thought that maybe he *loves* her?"

"No," Travis stated matter-of-factly then burst into laughter again. "I wonder why I can't get that lucky."

"There's still time. You're not married yet."

"You got that right, and I don't plan on either!" Travis declared in laugher. "As much as I love Malik, if I didn't marry *his* mother when she had *him*, you *know* I ain't marrying nobody else."

"Who're you kidding?" Ron jeered. "Wanda wouldn't have married you if you had *paid* her."

"Which was *fine* with me!" Travis laughed with him.

Ron added, "When you meet the right one, you'll change your mind."

He sobered and asked, "Do I hear wedding bells tingling around *you*, old buddy?"

"You never know, my friend," he affirmed. "You never know."

****

"Hi, I'm Toni Melton," Toni introduced herself to Brandy.

"Yes, I know who *you* are, Miss...ag...*Toni*," Brandy acknowledged.

"I hear you're doing a great job."

"Thank you," the lady accepted with her braids coming together in a neat single braid down the middle of her head, hanging down her back, and secured with a purple barrette. She wore a body-fitting two-inches-above-the-knee purple skirt and a white silk blouse tucked securely in it, finishing off with six-inch dark gray pumps. Toni couldn't help but to imagine Mason and the other men at the office drooling over this exotic-looking, young woman with the big behind and small waist.

Brandy admired the lovely journalist in her elegant two-piece, hunter-green, knee-length, flare skirt suit, with fine embroidery on each lapel. Brandy knew the suit was expensive because she had seen it in one of those expensive stores, but it was too much for her budget. It looked classy on Toni. "Any messages for me?" Toni asked.

"Yes. I put them on your desk."

"Thank you," Toni accepted, smiling sweetly, then exiting into her office. Her mind couldn't help but to think about Becky as she sat at her desk. As jealous as Becky was of *her*, she wondered what she would do if she got a glimpse of Brandy, who was stunning, *young*, and seductively dressed. Poor Becky would flip out. She knew that Mason had *definitely* checked *Brandy* out. She was *sure* of it! Speak of the devil....

Mason galloped into Toni's office gaily, "Hi, my lovely," he greeted her with a kiss on her cheek.

"How did you know I was back?"

"I didn't. I came to see how Brandy was doing, and she told me you were back."

"That figures," Toni giggled.

"What?"

"Oh, nothing," she smirked sarcastically. "Do you check on Brandy *often*?"

"What're you trying to say?"

"Oh, nothing!" she continued to laugh. "I don't remember you being so helpful to Angel is all."

"What're you trying to say?" he repeated.

Toni sarcastically added, "I'm sure you know."

****

"Jamie, how are you?" Ron spoke to the young man who sat at his cubicle in the open space with Billy Johnson, the other newly hired lawyer, who hadn't made it up the ladder to having a closed office and a secretary yet.

"Mr. Joyner, my pleasure," the young man acknowledged, standing to shake Ron's hand. They stood at about the same height, but Jamie was a little bit wirier than Ron, whereas Ron's body was athletic and toned. Jamie looked younger than his thirty years because of the neat cornrow braids in his hair, surrounding his boyish, light brown face.

"Is everybody treating you all right?"

"Yes, sir. Everybody is just fine."

"Good," Ron established. "And call me *Ron*. We're all family here."

"Thank you, Ron," he accepted.

"So, you're giving up teaching all together?"

"I'm thinking about it."

"I hear you're married to one of our clients," Ron inquired, wondering what Jamie's story was. Although he was nice, Ron couldn't help but get an eerie feeling about the young man. He didn't know what it was. All he knew was that it was a feeling he couldn't shake. He wondered if it was all in his mind. He hoped so, but usually when he got a feeling about a person, he was usually right.

Chapter 9

"You're nervous?"

"How can you tell?" Toni asked Ron as they walked to the front door of his parents' spacious, two-story, brick house, while he carried a wrapped gift for his father's birthday.

"You're not talking."

"What're you trying to say? I'm a blabbermouth?!" she joked, and he laughed, pulling her close with his free arm.

"Never," he confirmed, then planted a kiss on her forehead. "My family is genuinely nice. I promise."

"How do I look?"

He stood back and focused on her flower printed flair skirt, her fuchsia satin blouse, and her stylish three-inch pumps, smiled, and responded, "Beautiful as always." Their lips met in a sweet kiss. Toni's breath just seemed to leave her body every time he held her. He was so tall and handsome in those loose-fitting blue jeans, gray polo shirt, and sneakers. "Are you ready?" She nodded and they kissed again just as the door flew open, and his mother was standing there smiling. He strolled to his mother and hugged her.

"Hi, Mom."

"Hi, son," she greeted, smiling wide. "How is my handsome baby boy?"

"I'm fine, Mom," he beamed, planting a big kiss on her cheek. He took Toni's hand and started, "Mom, this is…"

"*Toni Melton*!" his mother exploded. "Oh, my God! Why didn't you tell me that you were dating *Toni Melton*?" She grabbed Toni and hugged her tight. Ron just stood back and smiled as his mother swished Toni inside to meet the family, leaving him behind. He walked in while his mother and her daughters were raving over Toni. He went to his father.

"Hey, Dad," he spoke, handing his father the wrapped gift. "Happy birthday."

"Thank you, son," his father responded, receiving the gift, and then they hugged while the ladies led Toni into the kitchen, talking and laughing gaily, raving about her clothes, her short Halle

Berry hair style, her beauty, and her everything else that entered their minds. Ron focused on his brother, standing by the fireplace in a pair of nice brown slacks and a tan, button-down, loosely hanging shirt. His hair was cut short and neat atop of his clean-shaven face. Leroy and Ron were about the same height, but he was a little darker than Ron with a slight receding hairline. Leroy had become thin and wiry because of the alcohol abuse causing him to lose a lot of weight so quickly. Ron walked to him.

"What's going on, big brother?" Ron acknowledged, extending a hand to him.

"You," he countered, and they grabbed hands and pulled each other close in a manly embrace, just as the ladies entered back into the living room. Ron took Toni's hand and they sat on the sofa together.

"Ron, you certainly are full of surprises," Denise raved. "Why didn't you tell us you were dating Toni Melton? You know how much we love her column."

"I wanted to surprise you," he admitted, as Leroy slowly walked into the kitchen.

"Well, you certainly did," Melissa added, pushing her shoulder-length, wavy, black hair out of her face.

"Denise, where's Barry?" Ron asked.

"He had to go out of town," she replied.

"Where's the baby?"

"Upstairs. He's asleep," Denise answered. She was about two inches shorter than Melissa at about five feet four inches. Denise was also about twenty pounds heavier than her sister at about one hundred and forty pounds. Her skin was darker than Melissa's with a milk chocolate smooth coat, but she was decent looking, not a striking beauty, with her short, bouncy, skull-filling straight, Toni Braxton style hair.

"How old is he now?"

"Eighteen months."

"Is he walking?" Ron asked, still holding Toni's hand.

"Not yet. He's lazy!" Denise screamed in laughter.

As they laughed, he looked at Toni and said, "I'll be right back."

"We'll take care of her," his mother made known. "Toni, tell us about all the stars you've met."

As Ron left, he saw his mother take his seat beside Toni on the sofa. He was happy that his family had received her so well. He exited into the kitchen where Leroy was downing a bottle of water, with the refrigerator door still open. "How's it going, man?" Ron asked his brother.

"All right," Leroy nonchalantly replied, closing the refrigerator, and dropping the empty plastic bottle into the trashcan.

"Wanna talk?" Ron asked, sitting on the barstool.

"About what?" Leroy responded, sitting at the table.

"Anything."

Leroy took a deep breath then charged, "Why did you bring her here?"

"Who, Toni?"

"Yes, Toni Melton!" he spat. "The bitch who ruined my life!"

****

Simon Kennedy entered his huge, two-story, stucco-built house and dropped his briefcase on the floor. He yawned as he walked into the kitchen and opened the refrigerator. There was nothing in it but a piece of dried out, brown apple and some bottled water. He made a mental note to buy groceries. Then he thought of Melissa. She was so charming and smart. He knew he could get used to a woman like that. Her skin was so soft. Her eyes so clear. He dropped on the couch, picked up the remote and turned on the television. Wouldn't you know it! One of Melissa's commercials was on. At the end of it, she invited everyone to try her catering service. She was so wholesome and pure. He needed a woman like that in his life. He wanted her bad, but there was one little problem; she thought he was scum. That was *Ron's* fault. He didn't know why Ron insisted on belittling him. He would have to do something to change Ron's mind about him, so he could get to first base with Melissa.

"This is crazy!" he scolded himself aloud. "The woman is off limits!" He kicked off his shoes and removed his tie and jacket, and then settled back on the couch. He couldn't get her off his mind. Even when he, Ron, and Travis were inseparable in high school, he admired Melissa, but she thought they were kids just because she was a couple years older than them. She had always been pretty. It broke his heart when she got married. Although he was sorry what happened to her husband, he knew it was his chance to finally get the woman of his dreams, and he would not stand idly by this time and let some other joker steal her away again. He had to do something about Ron, though, so he could get Melissa, but what? He would think of something! Something really *good*...and *soon*!

****

"Are you all right, baby?" Kristy questioned David while he sat on the sofa staring at the television set wearing gray, silk pajamas.

He half-heartedly smiled and replied, "Yeah. I'm fine." He didn't want to tell her that he was really wondering what his wife and children were doing at the moment.

She sat beside him in her little see-through, red, lace, short negligee and leaned back on him. "What're you looking at?" she cooed.

"Sports highlights."

She placed her hand on his crotch and his body jerked to attention. Kristy smiled. She was glad she could make him respond with a simple touch. She rolled over and straddled his lap and met his mouth with a wet kiss. Their breathing became elevated, and he soon forgot about his family. "Let's go to bed." He whispered in her ear. This young woman was incredible. He had never experienced sex like this in his whole life, not even with Angel, and he loved her with every fiber of his being. How could he break it off with Kristy when she awakened every emotion in his soul and then some?

****

Angel sat in the family room, watching her boys play video games on the television set. "Mommy, when is daddy coming home?" Ricky asked.

"I don't know, honey," Angel replied, trying to force a smile. "But if he doesn't, you still have *me*, right?"

"But I want daddy to come home," he whined.

"Can we call him?" Sammie asked.

Angel didn't want to call David at Kristy's apartment, but a mother would do anything for her children. "Sure, honey," she agreed.

****

David's ringing cell phone brought his and Kristie's explosive excitement to a gradual halt, and their drained bodies collapsed into each other's arms. She lay lifeless on him as he kissed her shoulder tenderly. David took a deep breath and asked, "Is that my cell?"

"Huh hum," Kristy breathed.

"Can you reach it?" he asked, and she reluctantly lifted off him and rolled beside him on the bed, grabbing his cell phone off the nightstand. She handed it to him, and he sat up.

Breathlessly, he answered, "Hello?"

"Daddy, when are you coming home?" Ricky blurted out.

"Daddy, I made an A on my spelling test," added Sammie.

Hearing his boys' voices brought tears to David's eyes, and he wanted to go to them and squeeze them tight, never letting them go. "That's great, Sammie," he forced out, fighting back his tears. "How are you boys doing?"

"Okay," Ricky answered. "Daddy, mommy said she didn't know when you were coming home. When, Daddy?"

"Honey, mommy and I have to work some things out first, okay," David explained, and Kristy saw him wipe a tear from his face, so she slipped on a housecoat and left out.

"Daddy, don't you love us anymore?" was Sammie's question.

"Of course, I do. I love you with all my heart," David insisted. "I'm so happy you called."

"Do you love mommy, too?" Ricky wanted to know.

He took a deep breath and replied, "Yes, I love mommy, too."

"Then come home," Sammie begged. "Mommy is sad, Daddy. She cries all the time. She wants you to come home, too."

"Mommy cries?" he asked for confirmation.

"Yes, all the time," Ricky added. "We think she misses you too."

He felt like his heart had dropped three feet when he heard that Angel was hurting because of him. She turned against her family to marry him. Angel's family didn't come around until Ricky was born. He felt lower than he had ever felt in his whole life. He knew he had to make it right again with her. "I'll call you soon, okay?" he promised.

"Okay, Daddy," Sammie concurred.

"Aren't you coming home?" Ricky cried, and David couldn't hold back his tears any longer. He sniffed hard so he could finish his conversation with his boys. He knew what he had to do. He couldn't go another night without trying to reconcile his marriage.

"Soon, okay," he squeezed out. "Ricky, don't cry. Be a big boy for mommy. I'll see you soon. I promise."

****

"What'd you mean Toni ruined your life?" Ron finally asked his brother.

"The board wasn't going to suspend me. They were going to handle the lawsuit quietly…until she wrote that article. Then they were forced to deal with me publicly."

"She said she tried to interview you."

"I *couldn't* talk to reporters!" he insisted. "They were going to settle the lawsuit privately until her article came out. Then they had to make an example of me and my entire surgical team, just so the hospital wouldn't look bad."

"Why wouldn't you talk to *me*, Leroy?"

"I *couldn't*!" he insisted. "That was part of the settlement. I couldn't talk to *anyone* about what happened."

"You can *now*," Ron demanded. "Tell me what happened."

"I don't *know* what happened," Leroy stated. "All I know is that the man was fine after the surgery and a second later when we started to close, he went into cardiac arrest, and I couldn't save him."

"You should've fought."

"I had *nothing* to fight with," he insisted. "Your *girlfriend* ruined me, and I will *not* sit at the same table with that woman!" Mrs. Joyner entered the kitchen.

"We're ready to eat," she announced proudly.

****

Kristy walked into the bedroom and David was coming out of the shower. "Why didn't you wait for *me*?" she cooed.

He took a deep breath then came back with, "Kristy, I don't want to hurt you, but I've made a terrible mistake."

"I don't think I want to hear this."

He went to her and took her hands. "My place is with my family," he announced, and tears immediately started running down her face. "I'm sorry." He pulled her in his arms.

"I love you, David," she confessed, pulling away from him gently to look in his face.

"It means a lot to me, but I can't stay here anymore," he explained. "Thank you for being there for me. I will always cherish our time together, but I can't continue to hurt my wife and boys. I love them. When I married Angel, it was for better or for worse, and I broke that vow when I found myself being attracted to you. It should've never happened. I'm sorry." He paused. "Angel and I have gone through a lot together. She was a virgin when I met her, and she gave her virginity to *me* and trusted that I would do right by her. I can't forget that. I love her." He paused again. "I will continue to pay you a salary for six months. By that time, you should be able to find something, and I will give you a letter of recommendation, but I can't hurt my family anymore. I hope you understand."

"I do understand, but I love you so much, David," Kristy cried.

He pulled her into his arms again and hugged her lovingly. "Kristy, you're young, smart and beautiful. You deserve better than I can give you. You'll find someone wonderful," he explained.

****

"What's going on?" Mrs. Joyner asked.

Ron sighed deeply and answered, "Leroy says Toni ruined his life."

"What?!" she exploded. "How did *Toni* ruin your life?"

"I don't wanna talk about it, Mom," Leroy insisted, heading for the door. "I gotta go."

"Leroy!" his mother called, and he stopped. "Don't you walk out that door!" He turned to face her just as Toni walked in.

"Is anything wrong?" Toni asked.

"Tell her, Leroy," Ron urged.

"*You* tell her. I'm outta here," he barked then started for the door again.

"Leroy, if you walk out that door, don't you bother to come back," Mrs. Joyner warned.

"Mom, I can't stay in the same room with this woman," Leroy insisted, going to his mother. "She *ruined* me!" Toni's gaze found Ron's for clarification.

"Leroy said the hospital was going to settle the lawsuit privately until your article was published. Then they had to deal with him publicly, so that's why he was fired."

"I didn't know," Toni finally replied then turned to Leroy. "I tried to talk to you, but you wouldn't talk with me."

"I *couldn't*," he insisted. "The hospital forbad me to talk to *anyone* until they settled. But after your article, they *couldn't* settle."

"I'm sorry," Toni breathed softly.

"It's a little late for that," Leroy countered.

"If I had known, I wouldn't have written the article."

"Yeah, right!" Leroy spat. "Mom, I need to go."

"No, you don't," Mrs. Joyner hissed. "You stay here and let's all eat. Toni didn't know the hospital was negotiating for you. It is unfair to blame her. It was her job to report the news."

"That's the story that earned you an award, your own column and opened the door for worldwide recognition, right?" Leroy asked Toni.

Toni dropped her head and confirmed softly, "Yes."

"Well, I'm glad *you* benefited at *my* expense!"

"Leroy, that's not fair," Ron defended. "She didn't know."

"Well, now she does," he finalized then flew out the door before his mother could protest any further.

****

David didn't know what to do first. He checked into a hotel to gather his thoughts. He wanted his family back, but he didn't know how to do that. Angel was definitely not going to easily forgive him, especially after he had moved in with Kristy those few days. He laid on the bed and before he knew it, tears were rolling down his face. He felt so alone and so ashamed. He hated to hurt Kristy, but he had to admit that he didn't love her. He just loved her *body* and the incredible sex! But *that* wasn't enough to leave his family because he loved *Angel's* body also. Sex with his wife was pretty good too. After all, he taught her everything she knew, and she learned very well over the years. She would do anything to please him and that was rare now-a-days with women trying to prove something all the time. He had never really cared much for white girls until he met Angel. Then he had found out that there really wasn't any difference between white and black girls, just the skin color. He loved his wife and he prayed that he could make it right with her. He knew Angel was stubborn, and he didn't know if she would *ever* forgive him.

****

"Ron, I'm sorry," Toni announced sadly as they entered his condo. They had remained silent on the drive home, and all during dinner, it was hard for her to keep from crying. She knew the family was sorry that Leroy didn't stay, although they didn't admit it. They acted as if nothing had happened. Then again, no one knew what *had* happened in the kitchen except Mrs. Joyner and Ron. No one could understand why Leroy left, and neither Ron nor his mother offered explanations. They just wanted his father to have a nice birthday.

"Sorry for what?" he asked, closing the door, and turning to her.

"For Leroy."

"That wasn't your fault."

"Then why do I feel responsible?"

"You shouldn't."

"Building *my* career ruined *his,* and I didn't know. When he wouldn't talk to me, I thought it was because of guilt. I didn't know he *couldn't*," she said as a single tear escaped from her eye and rolled slowly down her face. Ron went to her and pulled her in his arms.

"Toni, Leroy is a grown man. He made his decisions. He'll have to deal with them."

Pulling back from him to look in his face, she asked, "Do you hate me, Ron?"

"I could never hate you," he made known, then planted a kiss on her salty, wet lips. "Let's go to bed."

"I can't stay tonight. I've got to be at work early in the morning. I hate leaving here in the morning and having to rush home, get dressed and run to work."

"Then move in," he suggested softly, and her eyes widened.

Chapter 10

"Good morning, Ms. Washington."

Melissa looked up from behind her bakery counter as Simon Kennedy was entering. "Good morning, Mr. Kennedy," she replied. He took her breath away, looking so handsome in that black two-piece suit, with the white shirt, and the red tie around his neck and matching handkerchief extending from his pocket.

"How are you this wonderful morning?"

"I'm fine. Thank you."

He thought, *I know that's right.* Out loud, he said, "I'll take a bagel and a cup of your delicious cappuccino."

"All right," she concurred, fixing it for him.

"Are you by yourself this morning?"

"Cammie called and said she'll be running a little late, but she's on the way," she answered, handing him the bag. "Court today?"

"Not today," he acknowledged, touching her hand. He let his hand linger on hers a little longer than necessary when receiving the bag. After a moment, she gently pulled away.

"You look nice," she observed.

"You think so?" he beamed.

"Yes."

"Good because I'm on a mission."

"What kind of mission?"

Pushing his wire framed eyeglasses up on his nose and gazing deep into her eyes he made known, "To capture the heart of the woman I'm crazy about." She stared into his eyes long and hard, and then she suddenly looked away and focused on the cash register.

"That's four thirty-eight, Simon," she decided to change the subject.

He brushed her cheek lightly and whispered, "What are you afraid of? I don't bite."

"I'm not afraid of *anything*," she spoke sternly, but feeling a warm sensation from his touch. "I've told you. I don't like your ethics."

143

"I'm a nice guy. *Really*," he made known, handing her a five-dollar bill. He saw her making change and added, "Keep it." She dropped the coins, closed the cash drawer, and focused back on him. "I give thousands of dollars to charities every year, such as the Boys and Girls Club, Cancer Society, Women and Children' shelters, and so on. I take pro bono cases on a regular basis. I also defend *innocent* people. However, the only thing that people focus on are the few cases that I took where the clients were rich and guilty, got out and repeated the crime, all because of an arrogant, loud-mouth journalist!"

She was impressed. "I didn't know you did so much."

"It pays to ask," he countered then shot her a million-dollar smile. "Does it matter?" She took a deep breath but didn't answer as he focused on her. He placed his hand on hers, picked it up, and kissed the back softly. Melissa's heart seemed to melt at his gentle touch. She knew she would have to go home, when Cammie came in, to take a cold shower. Simon Kennedy was so sexy, and she fantasized about being in his bed, making beautiful love to him. This had never happened to her before, not even when she met her husband. What was funny was that she had known Simon almost her entire life when he used to hang with Ron in school. She never thought of him as a lover…until *now*. Melissa pulled her hand away gently and decided to change the subject.

"What journalist are you talking about, Toni Melton?"

"Who else?"

"She's dating my brother, you know," she shared, and his eyes widen.

"*Ron* is dating *Toni Melton*?" he probed, and she nodded. "How can two such large *egos* fit into the same bed together?" He laughed and she smiled with him. "I didn't know they made a bed *that* big!"

"Stop it," Melissa laughed. "My brother isn't conceited."

He chuckled and added sarcastically, "Baby, those two *deserve* each other."

****

"Toni, I need someone to go to Iraq. Do you want it?" Bill asked as he, Toni, and Mason sat in his office.

"Are you serious?!" Toni went ballistic with excitement.

"Yeah. I know you've been itching to go over there," Bill joined her enthusiasm. "Do you still want it?"

"Are you kidding?! Of course, I want it!" she exploded. "Thank you, Bill!"

"You can't take many people with you because of the danger, but I think we can let a three-team crew go with you. All of you will be able to fit into a chopper," he went on. "I'll make the arrangements."

"I smell *Pulitzer* already," Mason hypothesized.

Sobering to focus on him, Toni inquired. "You don't want it?"

"Are you kidding? I'm a family man. Becky would have a fit."

Still beaming, Toni acknowledged, "I guess so."

"I don't want you taking any chances over there, Toni," Bill warned. "If you even *think* you're in danger, retreat! I want *all* of you to come back in *one* piece!"

****

Angel sauntered out of her house in her short pajamas and housecoat to get the newspaper. She spotted David's black BMW parked at the end of her driveway. She strode slowly over to it, and David was sitting in his car asleep. Angel knocked on the window and he jumped. He opened the door yawning. "What're you doing?" she snapped.

"Hi," he responded, exiting the car to examine her.

"What're you doing here, David, and why are you *sleeping* in the driveway?"

"I just wanted to be near you and the boys," he admitted.

145

"And where is *your teenaged slut*?" she spat.

"At her apartment I guess," he retorted. "I'm not with Kristy anymore. I left. And she doesn't work for me anymore." Angel's eyes expanded to hear more. "I messed up, baby. I admit it. I messed up! I wish you could please find it in your heart to forgive me." She didn't answer, but he could tell she was considering his offer. "I love you and I love the boys." He exhaled slowly. "I have no excuse, but I found myself falling into a rut, and I didn't realize it at the time. It seemed like all I did was go to work, come home, sleep, and start over again." He paused. "I love you so much. I never meant to hurt you." He sniffed back his own tears as he witnessed tears rolling down her face. "Kristy was just a *break* in my routine."

"Do you love her?" Angel finally solicited.

"No, of course not. I have never loved *anyone* but *you*," he made known. "Would you please forgive me? I'll spend the rest of my life making it up to you."

"How can I trust you again, David? How can I trust that another *Kristy* won't come along and *break* your *routine* again?"

"Because I'll never let our lives become a *routine* again. I'm going to cut down on working so much, so we can do more things as a family," he promised. "From now on, it's going to be nine to five, and if an emergency arises, I'm hoping the boys and you could come with me to keep from losing quality time." He stared deep into her sad blue eyes. "What do you say, honey? Will you forgive me and let me come home?"

"Dad!" Sammie and Ricky exploded simultaneously, dashing out of the house and into their father's arms. He picked them up together and hugged them tight as they flew into hysterical laughter together.

****

"Lois, would you have the florist send a dozen yellow roses next door to KM Bakery Shop?"

"Sure thing, Simon," the secretary agreed, grinning sheepishly. "Taking it to another level?"

"I'm trying," he glowed.

"How should they sign the card?"

"Thinking of you, Simon."

"I assume this is going to Ms. Washington?"

"Who else?" he divulged. "Thank you." She nodded as he withdrew back into his office. He had to put things in motion, and *Ron* be damned.

****

John Schuster, Blake Collins, Phillip Ballentine, Ron, Travis, and two associates, Carol Greene, the only woman in the law firm, and Thomas Bailey sat at the long oak table in the conference room. "Ron, that was great work on the Sanchez' case," Phillip Ballentine remarked.

"Thank you," Ron accepted.

"I hear Miss Melton is going to do the entire story this weekend?" inquired Blake Collins.

"Yes, she is," Ron confirmed. "She was the driving force into finding the truth."

"What is your relationship with Miss Melton, Ron?" requested John Schuster, the chairman of the board and moderator of the meetings.

Ron smiled and responded, "Very close." John shared his smile.

Carol surprisingly included, "You're dating *Toni Melton*, Ron?"

"Yes," he answered proudly.

"Congratulations," added Thomas Bailey. "You saw how she creamed Simon Kennedy on *Veronica Live*? She's a tough one."

"Not with my man," added Travis. "Ron turned that little lioness into a kitten." Everyone burst into laughter while Ron felt a little embarrassed but smiled anyway.

"So, Carol, how is your case coming with the Chases?" Phillip asked, changing the subject.

"The mother has agreed to let the father see the children every other weekend, so we don't have to go to court for that," she explained.

"Good," added John.

"John, we need to delegate some of those domestic cases to the two new associates," Blake suggested. "Carol's case load is tremendous."

"Yes, we'll start them out slowly," John agreed. "Ron, that was a good call on Jamie Heard. He's doing an excellent job, and his wife is well pleased at his decision to join us."

"Thank you," Ron responded, "but I really didn't do anything. I just informed him of an opening here. I can't vouch for him. I don't know him." John nodded his understanding.

"Who is his wife?" was Thomas Bailey's question.

"Taffy Hines," John answered.

"*The* Taffy Hines?" Thomas wanted clarification.

"The one and only," inserted Phillip.

"In talking to his colleagues at the college, he's quite talented," remarked Blake.

"What about the other new lawyer, Billy Johnson? Is he all right, too?" Travis inquired. "Because he can have the Carmichael case if you think he can handle it."

"Yes, I think that would be a good case for him right now," John answered. "You can go ahead and start the transfer." Travis nodded.

They continued their meeting. John Schuster, the founder of the law firm over thirty years ago, at sixty-one was still highly active and knowledgeable. He was Caucasian, medium height and well-built with a full head of wavy gray hair. He was still married to his high school sweetheart, and to his disappointment, none of their four children went into law. Blake Collins was the second one to make partner. He was sixty, rather short and bald in the top, but concealed it with a well-placed hairpiece. His wife of twenty-five years died the previous year with breast cancer, and they had only one grown daughter. Phillip Ballentine was the third partner. He was fifty-seven, tall and still very good-looking with his dark brown hair, tanned face, and winning smile. He has been married for the past five years to a twenty-nine-year-old former *Miss Greenleaf* pageant queen. They have one set of four-year old twin boys, and he has one other grown daughter from his first wife, whom he divorced for his present wife. His daughter never forgave him and could care less if she ever saw him again. Then Ron was the next to join the illustrious firm, being the first African American. They hired him straight out of law school five years ago, and he had been there ever since, being their lead criminal defense attorney. Next, they hired Travis when he returned to Greenleaf three years ago, after living in Delaware right after graduating from law school. The partners were reluctant to hiring Travis with the short twists in his hair. They didn't want him to portray the wrong image to incoming clients. But as soon as they saw him in action in the courtroom, they decided that taking a chance with him *and* his hair was the right thing to do. Next, Carol Greene and Thomas Bailey were hired about the same time two years ago. Carol was forty-seven and moving from Los Angeles with her husband, who had a job transfer. She was plain looking with her white skin and dyed blonde thinning hair, and her wire-framed eyeglasses didn't help, but she was an exceptionally good lawyer and came highly recommended. She and her computer engineer husband never had children. Thomas was a big man, tall and at about three hundred pounds. His hairline had deeply receded in his light brown hair. He was thirty-nine and married to a little one-hundred-and-ten-pound gourmet cook. They were a strange looking pair. They had two children still in high school. The Firm was highly respected.

****

"That man is *committed*!" Cammie beamed, looking at the bright yellow roses that were just delivered to Melissa.

"He's *crazy*!" Melissa smirked.

"He just knows a good woman when he sees one."

"I just wonder how sincere he is."

"What'd you mean?"

"I just wonder if this has anything to do with his trying to make a point to my brother."

"I don't think…" Cammie started but was stopped by Ron entering through the door. The two ladies' eyes locked momentarily. "Hi, Ron."

"Hiya Cammie," Ron greeted, and Cammie just melted with his strong, handsome smile. She had never seen a dark gray suit with the burgundy bowtie and handkerchief look so good on any one person. "How are the husband and boys?"

"Fine, but I'll give them all up for *you*, baby," she joked.

"You flatterer you," Ron chuckled, and she laughed, walking away. He focused on the roses.

"Wow, someone has a sweetheart," he observed then focused on his sister. "*You?*"

She sighed slightly then answered softly, "They're from Simon Kennedy."

"*Simon Kennedy*?!" he exploded, trying to keep his voice low from the room full of people seated at the tables in the brightly colored decorated bakery. "Why would Simon Kennedy send you roses?"

"I don't know, Ron," she answered flatly, handing him a cup of coffee and a bagel. "He says he wants to take me out."

"Take you out?!" Ron blasted again, still trying to keep his voice at a minimum level. Melissa took a cup of coffee for herself and led him to a table in the back corner with two chairs. They sat and he focused on his sister. "Are you seeing *Simon*?"

"No."

"Do you *want* to see him?"

"Ron, I'm over twenty-one. I think I can make my own decisions."

"Because you know he's only using you to get to *me*."

"So, you don't think a man could find me attractive unless he has an ulterior motive?" she grew defensive.

"I didn't say that," he countered. "But with Simon, it's different." He blew hard then took a sip of his coffee. "He made some comment one day about being my brother-in-law."

"He *did*?"

"Yes, so be careful, honey. That's all I'm saying," he warned, placing his hand on hers. "You've been through too much to let some snake in the grass hurt you!"

****

David and Angel kissed long and hard, lying on their spacious, king-sized bed. The boys had already gone to school, and they decided to spend some quality time together. He helped her removed her nightgown. It felt so good for him to be in bed with his wonderful wife again. "I love you, Angel," he breathed.

"I love you too," she replied breathlessly. Then he pulled his shirt off over his head quickly, as Angel massaged his face and neck with hungry, wet kisses. She opened her eyes momentarily and froze solid when she focused on a large hickey on his shoulder. Angel took a deep breath and dropped on the bed, motionless.

"Baby, what's wrong?" he asked, then noticed tears forming in her eyes.

She motioned her head towards his shoulder and asked, "Kristy?" He looked down, and although he couldn't see it, he knew what it was. He remembered the explosive sex he had had with Kristy, but he didn't think much about it because he thought he was much too dark to get a bruise. Obviously, he was wrong. David took a deep breath.

"I'm sorry, honey."

"So am I, David," she declared, getting out of bed, and pulling her gown back on. He sprang up with her.

"Honey, you knew about Kristy and me."

"*Knowing* it and seeing *evidence* of it are two different things!" she snapped.

"I want to make love to you," he pleaded.

"I'm sorry. I'm just not in the mood anymore," she made known, then stormed out.

David took a long, frustrated breath then pondered aloud, "And women wonder why we cheat!"

****

Toni was so happy. She left work early and hired some movers to move all her clothes and accessories to Ron's condo. She could've done it herself, but she would've had to make more than one trip. She looked around the condo when all her stuff was in place, and she felt an overwhelming sense that she *belonged* there. Her life was perfect. She now had the man of her dreams, and she was going to get the story of a lifetime. What more could any *one* person wish for?

Toni called Melissa and asked how to cook a roast, and she talked her through it. Now it was almost ready for her potatoes and carrots. She had showered and turned on soft music. Candles were on the table with an arrangement of fresh-cut flowers she had picked up from the florist on the way home; and now, all that was left was for her man to come home. When she heard the door open, she smiled wide. Toni stepped into the dining room where the only lights that flickered were the ones glowing from the candles on the exquisitely arranged table. "Toni!" Ron called, but she didn't answer.

When he stepped into the dining room and focused on her, standing there in a see-through, shear pink, lace teddy illuminated by the candlelight only, which also outlined the immaculate table, he smiled and forced out, "Wow!"

"Welcome home," she cooed.

"This *is* home, isn't it?" he chuckled, admiring the dreamlike scenery.

"Yes," she answered, smiling wide, then strolled over to him slowly. He took her into his arms and kissed her smoothly.

"Something smells good. Did you cook?"

"Yes, with Melissa's help."

"Really?"

"Um hum."

"You are something else, Miss Melton," he murmured, then kissed her again.

"Don't you ever forget it, Mr. Joyner," she snickered, and they kissed again. "Go and take your shower and slip into something comfortable, and by then dinner should be ready."

"You did all of this for *me*?"

"Who else?" she announced, and their lips met again.

Focusing on her gorgeous body, he cooed, "May I have dessert first?"

"No," she laughed. "I didn't *slave* over a hot stove for *hours* for you to *miss* the meal!" He laughed with her, and she whispered softly in his ear, "But I'll make sure you get *plenty* of dessert later." A tingle went soaring through his body and he trembled slightly. "Cold?"

"Excited," he cooed, kissing her again.

"Now go!" she jovially demanded, and he stared at her body again, licked his lips, then shook his head, chuckling slightly as he left. Toni burst into a soft laughter. She was so happy that Ron wanted her so much. He made her feel so special.

****

Melissa was about to lock the bakery door when Simon ran up to it. She opened it for him. "Hi," he addressed.

"Hi, Simon," she responded. "I tried to call you to thank you for the roses, but you weren't in."

"Lois told me you called," he acknowledged. "I was in and out all day. Did you like them?"

"Yes, but..."

"But what? No strings attached."

"Ron thinks you're using *me* to get to *him*."

He took a deep breath and recognized, "What an ego your brother has! Why would I do that to you? I've known you much too long to try to play you. Melissa, Ron might be the apple of your eye, but I really don't have time to play childish games with him. *He* doesn't like *me* anymore. *I* have no hard feelings towards *him*."

"Then you're not just using me?"

He looked deep into her clear, light-brown eyes, then slowly planted a soft kiss on her lips, and replied, "What do *you* think?" He paused. "Follow your heart." He kissed her again and this time she kissed back.

****

"How was dinner?" Toni asked Ron as they shared the sofa together. She sat up while he laid down with his head in her lap.

"It was great, baby. You learn quickly."

"Thank you," she accepted, rubbing her fingers across his soft, wavy hair. "I know my mother is wondering why I haven't been over there this week to eat."

"Have you called her?"

"No."

"Why not?"

"I didn't feel like hearing a sermon about my going to hell."

"I would like to meet her."

Chuckling, she assumed, "Honey, *trust* me, you do *not* want to meet *my* mother!"

"I do," he insisted. "Let's go over there this weekend."

"I can't. I'm going out of town the day after tomorrow."

He held up to face her and asked for clarification, "You're going out of town?"

"Yes, honey. I'm so excited," she beamed.

"Why didn't you tell me?"

"I'm sorry, baby. I'm just not used to reporting my every move to anyone. I've got to get used to this. Forgive me?" she

154

solicited, and he just stared at her. Then she planted a kiss on his lips. "Please." He smiled.

"Where're you going?"

"Iraq."

"*Iraq*?!" he flew off the handle, jumping up.

"Yes, isn't it wonderful?!"

"No!" he yelled, shocking Toni to silence. "*Hell no!*"

****

"How was school today, boys?" David asked as they sat at the dinner table.

"We played soccer at recess today," Sammie shared. "Our team won."

"Great," David shared his enthusiasm.

"The teacher wouldn't let us go out for recess today," Ricky frowned. "We had to finish our math."

"Well, your teacher knows best," David concurred then he focused on Angel. "How was your day, honey?"

"It was all right," she answered dryly. "I cleaned out some closets."

"Are you going back to work?"

"Yes, I'm going back in a couple of days."

"I know Toni will be glad."

"I guess so," she agreed with such sadness that his heart went out to her. He hated himself for what he had done to his once spirited wife. She didn't deserve that. She had always been so full of life. Now, she seemed so empty, and it was all *his* fault.

"I signed on a new client today," he made known.

"Good," Angel acknowledged nonchalantly, and David knew he had a lot of work to do with his marriage. A *lot* of work!

****

"Ron, what's wrong?" she demanded, springing to her feet also.

"Toni, people are getting *killed* over there!"

"I'll be safe!"

"And what makes *you* immune to bullets and explosives?"

"Ron, I've *got* to go. Plans have already been made."

"Then *unmake* them, Toni!" he insisted. "I don't want you going to Iraq!"

"Why? This could be the biggest story in my career! It has Pulitzer written all over it," she defended. "Give me one good reason why I shouldn't go?"

Calming down, he asked very sarcastically, "Besides the fact that you could get *killed*?" She stared at him long and hard with a smirk on her face.

"Yes," she retorted just as sarcastically.

"Because *I* don't want you to go. Isn't that reason enough?"

"No, I'm sorry but it isn't."

"What about the fact that I don't want to lose you, damn it?!" he shouted again. "What about the fact that I'm in lo..." He stopped suddenly and their eyes locked. Then he sobered and added very softly, almost a whisper, "I'm in love with you." Toni's eyes immediately swelled up with water. She felt that he had loved her but hearing the words from his own lips had more impact than all the actions in the world.

"I love you, too," she whispered softly. Then they strolled into each other's arms and held close.

"I love you so much," Ron confessed with all his heart now. "I love you, Toni. I've never felt this way before."

"I love you, too," Toni cried and laughed at the same time, feeling so secure in his arms.

Chapter 11

"Hi," Mason spoke to Brandy as he entered the office.

"Hi," she replied, glancing at him and stopping her typing to surrender her attention to him.

"Is Toni in yet?"

"Yes, but she went to see Mr. Hurley."

"Oh, okay," he acknowledged, then smiled wide. "How are you today?"

"Fine," she answered sweetly as Toni entered and noticed Mason drooling over Brandy.

"Do you wanna see me, Mason, or did you come here for *another* reason?" she smirked.

"I came to see *you*," he countered, feeling a little embarrassed, emphasized by his blushing. Toni proceeded to her office and he followed her. "What was *that* about?"

"What?" she smirked, exposing all thirty-twos.

"You know what."

"It seems that you're spending an awful lot of time here since Brandy started filling in for Angel."

"That's not true," he chuckled.

"Yes, it is," Toni refuted.

"Well, she *is* pretty," he admitted.

"And *you're* married!"

"Yeah," he retreated dryly, and Toni laughed.

"So, what do you need?" she asked. "From *me* that is."

"Funny, Toni," he chuckled.

"I thought so," Toni giggled.

"I was wondering when you were leaving for Iraq?"

"Oh, I'm not going. That's what I was just talking over with Bill."

"You're not?"

"No."

"Why? You were so excited about going."

"I was, but I can't go now."

"Do you mind telling me why not?"

"For the same reasons *you* can't go. *Ron* doesn't want me to."

"Ron!" he exploded. "Oh, so it's *that* serious now?"

"Yes, I guess it is," she made known. "I moved in with him."

Struggling to find words, Mason reacted with a small wave of jealousy, "So quickly?"

"When it's right, it's right!"

"I guess so," he agreed. "That's great, honey. Congratulations."

"Thank you."

"Do I hear wedding bells?"

"Why do people always assume that when two people are dating, it automatically leads to marriage? I am perfectly happy the way things are. Thankyouverymuch!"

"Well, marriage is usually the next step when two people fall in love."

"Who said I was in love?" she teased.

"*You* did," he held. "I mean your *actions*. Your whole demeanor when you're talking about him."

"Well, you *are* right. I *am* in love with him," she admitted, and Mason felt a kick in his gut. He didn't know why he felt that way. He didn't even feel about Toni in that way anymore. He supposed it was just knowing that an end to an era has passed. "But that doesn't mean I'm ready to get married."

"Good."

"Why is that *good*?"

"You don't need to rush into anything."

"I won't."

****

"Hi, baby," Simon saluted, entering Melissa's bakery.

"Hi," she responded and met him with a kiss.

"Want to take in a movie tonight?"

"Sure," she agreed, handing him a cup of coffee and a bagel.

"Thanks," he accepted, and she walked from around the counter and met him at a table where they sat together.

"Are you in court today?"

"No, not today," he replied, taking a bite of his bagel.

"Simon, would you like to meet my kids?"

"I would love to," he approved. "Would you like to take them to the movies with us tonight?"

"No," she rejected, looking deep into his eyes. "*I've* gotta get used to this dating thing first before I include my kids."

"Okay, whatever you say," he understood. "But if you're trying to see if we're going to last, I got news for you. I'm not going anywhere."

****

"What're you doing today, honey?" David inquired of his wife at the breakfast table with their boys.

"I want to finish cleaning the closets before I go back to work tomorrow," she made known, while David's cell phone began to ring.

"I left my cell phone on the counter behind you. Would you get it, honey?" he asked, and Angel reached back and picked it up.

"Hello?" she answered, but there was no response. "Hello?"

"Is David there," she recognized Kristy's voice. Angel didn't respond. She just extended the phone to David.

"It's Kristy," she shared, and he froze then took a breath.

"Hello," he said into his cell phone.

"David, I need to see you."

"For what, Kristy?"

"I miss you," she cried, sitting on her bed.

"I'm sorry," he responded. "But *that* is not possible."

"David, please," she begged.

"Are you boys finish?" Angel asked and they both nodded. "Go and get your book bags." They jumped up and ran out.

Angel started to get up too, but David stopped her by placing his hand on hers. "Kristy, Angel is giving me another chance. I'm not blowing it this time for you or anyone else. So, you've got to let go." He focused on Angel's glassy eyes and then he witnessed a few tears roll down her face. He wiped her tears with his fingers and continued talking to Kristy. "I love my wife. What you and I had is over. I'm sorry. So, anything else that you have to say to me, you'll have to say it to my wife." He handed Angel the phone.

"Hello," Angel spoke, and Kristy just hung up. Angel wondered if Kristy would ever be completely out of their lives.

****

"Good morning," Beverly beamed as Ron entered the office.
"Good morning."
"How's it working out with your new roommate?"
"Terrific!" he glowed.
"Excellent!" she approved. "Mr. Sanchez wants you to call him."
"Okay," he acknowledged. "Would you get him on the phone please, Bev?"
"Sure thing, boss," she agreed, and he winked at her as he entered his office. Ron took off his suit jacket and was loosening his tie when Beverly buzzed.
"Yes, Bev. Is Mr. Sanchez on the phone?"
"No, Mr. Sanchez is *here*."
"He *is*? Thanks, hon," Ron recognized then opened the door. "Mr. Sanchez, please come in."
"Thank you, Ron," Mr. Sanchez accepted, entering Ron's office.
"May I get you something?"
"No, as a matter of fact, I came to bring *you* something."
"Really?"
"Yes indeed."

"Please, have a seat," Ron offered. "Mr. Sanchez, how have you been?"

"Great," he answered. "How was Houston?"

"Fabulous!"

"Good. Glad to hear it," Mr. Sanchez supported. "Ron, my wife's estate has been settled, and I would like to offer you a wedding gift."

"A *wedding* gift?"

"Yes, for you and Toni."

"Mr. Sanchez, I think you're mistaken. Toni and I aren't getting married."

"I say you *are*," he chuckled. "You might not know it yet, but it's coming." Ron laughed with him. "I just wanted to give Toni and you this to say thank you for helping me, and most importantly, for *believing* in my innocence." He handed Ron an envelope.

"Thank you, sir, but as I said, you really don't have to…"

"I know, but I *want* to. Please accept my gift for you and Toni. Let her know how much I appreciate the second article she did also, clearing my name for the public."

"I will," Ron concurred. "Thank you, sir. I know we will put this gift to good use."

"Open it. I want to see what you think," he urged. "I'm going abroad in the morning on vacation, and I didn't want to leave until I gave you this. I hope it will be all right."

"Anything you give to us is fine," Ron assured the man, opening the envelope. Then he focused on the check in the envelope and his eyes broaden. He scanned back at Mr. Sanchez and the man smiled. "Mr. Sanchez, this is very *generous*."

"Is it adequate?"

"This is *too* much."

"No. It is not enough," the man retorted. "But I wanted to do something nice for you two."

Ron took a deep breath. "This is more than adequate, sir. Thank you."

"You are most welcome," Mr. Sanchez grinned. "Give Toni my best."

****

"Toni, hello!" Angel exploded at her door.

"Hi, Angel. I came to check on you."

"Come in," she offered, and they hugged lovingly.

"Are you all right?" Toni asked, sharing the sofa with her friend. "I miss you."

"I'm coming in tomorrow."

"Good," Toni acknowledged. "So, how are things?"

Angel took a breath then shared, "Although David is back, I'm still hurting."

"It takes time, honey."

"But I think David doesn't really understand. He says he does, but I don't think he really does."

"Why not?"

"He keeps wanting to make love to me and I'm not ready."

"I know it's hard on both of you."

"You have no idea," she surrendered. "Kristy called this morning."

"How did that go?"

"David told her that what they had is over and that he loves me. Then he gave me the phone, but she hung up."

"Hey, that's a step in the right direction."

"I guess so," Angel agreed. "But, Toni, what if I can never make love to my husband again?"

"Angel, you will. You're just hurting right now. Once the hurt wears away, you'll be able to respond to your husband again."

"But what if I don't."

Toni patted her friend's shoulder lovingly and declared, "You *will*!"

****

Bill entered his house calling, "Rita, are you all right, honey?"

"In here, Bill," she returned, and he walked into the bedroom, and she was surrounded by pictures all over the bed.

"What're you doing, sweetheart?"

"I want to remember everything about our life together before…" she cried.

"Oh, sweetheart."

"Bill, tell me again why you married me."

"Because you are the prettiest girl in town," he beamed, and she smiled with him. "You touched my heart the moment I laid eyes on you." He sat on the bed and pulled her in his arms. "I love you, Rita. I would gladly trade places with you if I could."

"I wouldn't want you to," she made known. "I've enjoyed every day of our life together, Bill."

"Me too, honey. Me too," he agreed, and she dropped her head onto his chest and relaxed in his loving arms. As he cradled his wife in his arms, he knew he had to be strong for her.

****

Ron entered the kitchen where Toni was taking out pots to cook. "Hi, darling."

"Hi, baby," he welcomed, giving her a kiss. "What're you doing?"

"Getting ready to cook. I'm sorry I got home late. I stopped by to see Angel."

"How's she doing?"

"Not too well, but she's trying."

"That's a shame," he sympathized. "Honey, you don't have to feel pressured to cook every night. I didn't ask you to move in to make a slave of you. I know how hard you work."

"You are so sweet," she admired. "But I want to do it…for *now* anyway."

"Okay," he gave in as he removed his suit jacket and laid it across the chair. "Honey, Mr. Sanchez came to see me today." She focused on him.

"Is everything all right?"

"Yes, everything is fine. He's going on vacation in the morning but wanted to give us this first," he shared, extending the envelope to her. She took it and sat, still staring at Ron.

"He gave us a gift?" she asked puzzled, and he nodded.

"He says it's a *wedding* gift."

"A *wedding* gift," she snickered. "Who told him we were getting married?"

"No one. He says he knows it's coming," Ron confirmed. Toni opened the envelope then jerked up to look at Ron.

"He gave us *this*?" she examined, and he nodded. "But it's *two million dollars*!"

"He wants us to have it."

"Can we accept it? I mean, is it ethical?"

"Sure. It's no bride or anything like that!" Ron chuckled. "The case is closed."

"Wow, he's very generous."

"He said we believed in him and it meant a lot to him."

"Yeah, but two million dollars is a lot of money."

"I guess it isn't to him," Ron expressed. "He's worth over five hundred million."

"I thought he only inherited sixty million from his wife."

"That was *her* money, but he had a lot more before he married her. That's one reason I knew he didn't kill her for her money."

Smiling big, Toni inquired, "What're we gonna do with it?"

"I don't know. We'll have to decide together."

Chapter 12

Toni finally, after two months, decided to break down and let Ron meet her mother. It was Thanksgiving Day, and she hoped her mother would be too thankful to pick on her. Besides, her brothers and their families would be there too, so maybe that would soften her mother's blows. She and Ron both were dressed in casual wind suits, hers peach and his royal blue. "Are you ready?" she questioned, standing in front of her mother's house.

"Yes," he confirmed.

"Don't say I didn't warn you," she chuckled then unlocked the door with her key and entered. "Mom!"

"In the kitchen," her mother called. She led Ron in that direction. When she opened the kitchen door, her mother was setting the hot turkey on the counter.

Toni closed the oven door for her, planted a kiss on her cheek and greeted, "Hi, Mom."

"Hi, honey," her mother reacted, glaring at her daughter. "Toni, what did I tell you about those pants?" She charged right in. "A woman is *not* supposed to wear clothing pertaining to a man."

Ignoring her mother's comments, Toni introduced, "Mom, this is Ron Joyner. Ron, this is my mother, Effie Melton."

"Pleased to meet you, Mrs. Melton," Ron extended a hand, which she never took.

She just leered at him then asked, "When are you going to purchase the cow, Mr. Joyner?"

"Excuse me?" Ron queried, being totally taken off guard as he retreated his hand.

"I don't like my daughter living in sin," she stressed, and he smiled shyly, as Toni dropped her head in total embarrassment. "If you want the milk, you need to purchase the cow."

"Mom, please," Toni interjected softly.

Ron smiled again and confessed, "I love Toni, Mrs. Melton. When *we're* ready, we will make that decision together."

"Seems to me you should be ready *now*. You're shacking up together, living in sin," she came back with and Ron was speechless.

He had never known anyone so direct and straightforward like this woman. "What kind of love is it that you have for my daughter to risk her burning in hell?!"

"I don't desire that, Mrs. Melton," he made known.

"But you're allowing it," she countered. "If you continue this lifestyle with my daughter, she *will* burn in hell, right beside *you*."

"Well, at least we'll still be together, Mom," Toni joked then burst into laughter, and Ron laughed with her, but her mother didn't think it was funny. She was still glaring at Toni when they heard the front door open.

"Mom!" a man's voice called.

"Ron, come and meet my crazy brothers," Toni erupted, taking his hand, and leading him into the living room.

"There's my baby sister," Walter laughed, grabbing Toni into a big bear hug. Then Dennis got in his hug. Although Walter was about five inches taller than Dennis, they were both overweight with protruding bellies, shaved baldheads, and a pecan tan color. Walter's attire was a pair of black jeans and a pullover white shirt, while Dennis wore a deep burgundy warm up suit. Walter's wife, Mia, was an Asian woman with long, straight, black hair, wearing a loose fitting knit dress that reached almost to her ankles. They had one seven-year-old little girl named Katelyn, who resembled her mother more than Walter, with a blue-jean skirt on and a turquoise silk blouse. Dennis's wife, Joyce was an inch taller than he, with a smooth, dark chocolate complexion, shoulder-length braids in her hair and a simple, straight dress that reached almost to her ankles. The daughters-in-law were no fools. They knew better than to wear either pants or short dresses around their mother-in-law. Dennis had two children, a nine-year-old son named Cory, who seemed to be glued to his game on his iPad and a six-year-old daughter named Chelsie, who wore a blue jean skirt as well and a baby blue silk blouse. They all hugged and greeted Toni and Mrs. Melton while Ron looked on.

Toni took Ron's hand and introduced, "Ron, this is my brother Walter, his wife Mia, and their daughter, Katelyn. Walter, Mia, and Katelyn, this is Ron Joyner." They welcomed him fondly. Then she went to her other brother. "Ron, this is my brother, Dennis, his wife, Joyce, and their children Cory and Chelsie." They extended friendly greetings to Ron as well.

"Ron, I hope you never make her mad. Hell hath no fury," Walter laughed. "She almost burned us to death when we were kids."

"You two were rotten to me," Toni laughed.

"That was still no reason for you to allow the devil to use you to try to kill your brothers!" her mother added sternly, silencing everyone.

"Well, we had it coming," Dennis broke the cold silence in laughter, and everyone joined him, except their mother.

****

"Mommy was scared to ride on the roller coaster," Melissa's little five-year-old daughter, Alexandria, laughed while she knelt in front of Simon, looking at pictures in the photo album of their trip to an amusement park.

"Remember the drop zone, Allie?" Melissa's seven-year-old son, Keith, added, giggling wildly. "I thought mommy would scream herself to death." They all laughed.

"You didn't get on the roller coaster, but you got on the *drop zone*?" Simon snickered.

"They tricked me," Melissa made known, hearing the doorbell ring.

"That's Aunt Louise!" Alexandria yelled, jumping up with Keith following her. Soon a tall, elegant looking lady entered with three other children, two boys and a girl, about the same age as Melissa's children.

"Hi, Louise," Melissa spoke.

"Hi, Melissa," the lady acknowledged in a sophisticated, northern, *Helen Willis* demeaner.

"Simon, this is Louise Canfield, my sister-in-law. Louise, this is Simon Kennedy," Melissa introduced.

167

"My pleasure," the lady spoke, extending a hand to Simon, and he stood to receive it.

"The television didn't do you justice, Mr. Kennedy," Louise stated, admiring his strong, handsome body in those blue jeans and maize polo shirt.

"*Simon*, please, and thank you. I think," he chuckled.

"Oh yes, Simon. It's *all* good," Louise snickered. "Are you kids ready?"

"Yeah," Keith answered, retrieving his overnight bag while Alexandria started to seize hers, but her male cousin helped her.

Keith walked to Simon and inquired, "You'll be here when we come back?"

"I don't know, buddy, but I'll certainly see you later, okay?"

"Okay," the boy beamed then hugged Simon.

"Bye, Simon," Alexandria added then received her hug.

"Bye, sweetie," Simon finalized. "Have a nice time." She nodded then ran to catch up with the other children.

"I hate to rush, but Hunter is waiting for us at home," Louise announced.

"All right," added Melissa, walking her to the door. She kissed her kids, and they ran to the white Rolls Royce.

"It was nice meeting you, Simon," Louise concluded.

"Same here," Simon acknowledged, and she walked out, followed by Melissa.

Turning to Melissa, Louise whispered, "He's a keeper."

"We're taking it slow."

"Honey, your kids like him. I wouldn't take it *too* slow, before someone else snaps him up," Louise suggested. "My brother would approve."

"You think so?"

"I *know* so," Louise confirmed. "See you tomorrow." They hugged then Louise turned and left. Melissa stayed on the porch until the car was out of sight, and then she walked back into the house where Simon was putting up the photo album.

"You seemed to have made a good impression on my sister-in-law. She likes you," Melissa shared.

"She's nice," he accepted then focused on her. "What about *you*? Do *you* like me?" She smiled and they walked slowly into each other's arms, ending in a long, passionate kiss.

"Very much," she admitted, and they kissed again.

"I love you, Melissa," Simon confessed, and her eyes stretched. "I know we haven't dated long, but I have always loved you, even when we were kids. You don't have to respond. I just wanted you to know."

"Simon, that's so sweet," she pondered. "I care very much for you, but…"

"No buts," he cut her off. "That's enough for now."

****

"I don't know about you, but I feel like I need a shower after being dumped on all day by your mother," Ron laughed, entering his condo with Toni.

"I'm sorry," Toni chuckled.

"It's not your fault."

"I told you she was a trip. That's why my brothers don't go over there much."

"I can see why," he recognized. "She certainly doesn't bite her tongue."

"Are you mad?"

"No, honey," he settled, moving to her, and putting his arms around her waist. "Your mother can't run me away. I love *you*. I want to live with *you*, not *her*."

"I'm glad," she announced, and they kissed.

"I'm thirsty," Ron cooed. "Let's go to bed so I can get some of that *free* milk." Toni burst into laughter.

Chapter 13

"Honey, I'm leaving," Ron called to Toni, who was still in the bathroom, but she didn't answer. "Toni?"

"I'm coming," she returned weakly, standing at the bathroom sink, holding on to keep from falling. She felt so dizzy and nauseated but didn't know why. She rinse her mouth, took a deep breath then walked out the bathroom.

"Are you okay?"

"Yes, I'm fine," she answered with a sweet smile, then he planted a soft kiss on her cheek.

"What're we going to do for Christmas? It's in a few days."

"Your mother asked us to come there for dinner, and my father asked us to come there, so I don't know what we should do."

"We can go to your father's house for dinner and see my parents later that evening. We gotta deliver our gifts to everybody anyway."

"Yes," Toni agreed, holding on to the dresser chest for support to keep from falling. She didn't want to tell Ron how she felt. She knew he would worry.

"Are you sure you're okay, honey?" he inquired, and she nodded, forcing a smile. "You don't look like yourself."

"I'm fine. Go ahead and get outta here. This is your last day at work until after Christmas."

"Okay," he concurred, kissing her lips. "See you tonight and we can wrap gifts, okay?" She nodded. "Love you."

"Love you, too," Toni replied, and he left. Toni dropped on the bed the minute he walked out. She felt awful. She dialed Angel's number.

"Hello," David answered.

"Hi, David. It's Toni."

"Hi, Toni. How are you?"

"Fine. Has Angel left for the office yet?"

"No, not yet," he revealed. "Hold on." She waited a few minutes.

"Hello," Angel answered within minutes, but it seemed like hours to Toni.

"Angel, I don't feel well. Can you come over and take me to the doctor?"

"Sure, honey. What's wrong?"

"I don't know," Toni replied with tears stinging her eyes. She didn't want to be sick, just when everything was going so well in her life.

"Don't worry. Everything will be all right," Angel consoled her friend. "I'm on the way."

****

"There's Simon!" Keith yelled in his mother's bakery, looking out the window. Before Melissa could react, he had opened the door and he and Alexandria were jumping on Simon, as he laughed, enjoying the attention.

"Are you ready?" he asked the excited children.

"Yeah," Keith answered quickly.

"You have your skates?" Simon asked.

"Yeah," added Alexandria. "There're in the backroom."

"Go and get them and we can go," he advised, and they ran out.

"Hi," Melissa saluted and met him with a kiss.

"Hi."

"You're brave."

"I'm going to enjoy this," he welcomed.

"Can you skate?"

"I was the skating champion three years in a row in high school," he laughed as the children ran out, kissed their mother, and flew out the door.

"Come on, Simon," Keith called.

"See you later," Simon finalized to Melissa as he ran to catch up with the children.

"Bye."

"And loves children too," Cammie joked. "I would say that you have found yourself a winner, Ms. Washington."

****

"What did the doctor say?" Angel ran to Toni when she came from the back of the doctor's office.

"Let's go," Toni retorted blankly, not stopping her stride, and Angel had to trot heartily in her six-inch heels to catch up with her.

"What's wrong?" Angel requested when they reached the car. Toni burst into tears. "Oh, honey, what is it?"

"Angel, I...I..."

"What?"

"I'm *pregnant*," Toni squeezed out and Angel's mouth spread into a smile.

"You scared the hell outta me. I thought you were *dying* or something," Angel yelled. "Pregnant! Is that all?"

"Is that *all*?" Toni sniffed. "Ron is gonna flip. We didn't plan on having a baby right now!"

"Some things are planned for you," Angel countered, and Toni shot her a smirk. "I think he's gonna be thrilled."

"But how can I be pregnant? We use condoms."

"*All* the time?"

"Yes, "Toni insisted then pondered. "Well, *almost* all the time."

"Didn't you notice your period wasn't coming?"

"My periods have never been regular. You know that," Toni clarified. "Angel, I have my career. I don't have time for a *baby* right now."

"Well, you better make time, girlfriend" Angel insisted. "A *baby*!" She grabbed Toni and hugged her tight. "I'm so happy for you!"

****

Brandy was making copies in the workroom when Mason entered. "Hello."

"Hi," she responded.

"You're back *here* now that Angel's back?"

"Yes, getting my hands dirty," she laughed.

"Well, my secretary will be out this week if you want to help *me*."

"Is it *safe*?" she singsong jokingly.

"How *safe* do you want it to be?" he cooed back, moving remarkably close to her.

"Safe enough to avoid angry *wives*," she stressed.

He brushed her cheek slightly with his finger and whispered, "I'm *very* discreet." He locked eyes with her. "Are *you*?"

"When I *have* to be," she countered, still smiling sweetly. Her perfume was driving him wild, and she knew it by the bulge that had ignited in his crotch. He couldn't resist this voluptuous woman any longer, so he bent down and planted a soft kiss on her lips, and she kissed back.

"Could I come by your place tonight?" he breathlessly inquired.

"What time?"

"What about now?"

"*You* might have it like that around here where you can leave anytime you want, but unfortunately, I don't."

He winked and shared, "I'll arrange it."

****

Toni entered their condo and Ron was putting up a Christmas tree. "Sweetie, you bought a tree," she observed, smiling wide.

"Yeah. I thought we needed a little bit of Christmas cheer in here."

Looking at the ceiling-high tree, she remarked, "It's beautiful!"

"Want to help me trim it?"

"Sure," she agreed. "But what are you doing home so early?"

"You didn't look like you felt well this morning, so I came to spend some time with you," he shared, meeting her with a kiss.

"Oh, that's so sweet," she cooed.

"So, are you all right?"

"Sort of."

"What do you mean, *sort* of?" he chuckled, and then focused on her walking away to take off her coat. He left the tree and went to her. "Sweetheart, what's wrong?"

"Ron, I…"

He lifted her chin with his finger and asked, "What is it? Are you sick?"

"No," she answered softly. "Just pregnant."

Ron thought he hadn't heard right, and she met his gaze as he repeated, "Pregnant?" She nodded slowly, and a big smile spread across his face. "Pregnant?!" He picked her up and spun her around, laughing hysterically. "Oh, honey, that's wonderful!"

Laughing with him, she asked, "You're *happy* about this?"

Putting her back down, he acknowledged, "Are you kidding?! I couldn't be happier." He kissed her lips hard. "I love you."

"I love you, too," she assented, and they kissed again.

"How far along are you? When is it due?" he wanted to know.

"I'm about two months, but I have to make an appointment with an Obstetrician to know when it's due."

"*I'm* going to be a *daddy!*" he exploded, kissing her again. "So, when are we getting married?"

Toni's eyes stretched wide, and she challenged, "*Married*?! Who said anything about getting *married*?!"

"*I* did," he insisted. "Toni, I want my child to have a *real* family. I don't want to raise a child in a household where his parents are just *shacking*. What kind of morals would that be teaching him?"

"Ron, I don't want you to marry me just because I'm *pregnant*."

"It's not *just* because you're pregnant. It's because we *love* each other."

"We'll see, honey."

"*Toni!*"

"We'll see!" she concluded, and he just stared at her.

****

He bathed her face and neck with soft, wet kisses. Brandy gasped with pleasure as Mason explored every inch of her body. Mason had never had sex with a black woman before and this was new to him, so he took his time. He wanted to please her. Brandy surrendered herself to him completely as they settled on her soft, queen-sized, gold, satin sheets. He whispered in her ear, "Are you on the pill?"

"Yes," she breathed, and he knew that was his cue to have his way with her openly and completely.

"Good," he cooed, covering her mouth with his. Their passion was wild and untamed. She didn't know anyone could make her feel so good. She tasted so sweet to him. They clung to each other's body tightly to make an exchange that was filled with pure unadulterated, satisfactory desire. Brandy had never known any man to satisfy her so completely. Mason had never known any woman to bring out so much of himself. When it was over, she collapsed on his strong body and he held her tight. He kissed her moist forehead and exhaled deeply.

"That was wonderful," he finally breathed.

"I could get used to this."

"Good," he replied. "I ain't going nowhere."

She held up and focused on his handsome face and asked, "You promise?"

"I promise," he confirmed, and they met each other with a soft, sweet kiss. He pulled her down on him and held her close.

****

"Angel, we need to talk," David announced, entering their bedroom where Angel sat on the bed in a green, cotton nightgown, reading a book.

"About what?" she asked, laying her book on the nightstand.

"Angel, you *know* what," he stated matter-of-factly, joining her on the bed.

"Are the boys asleep?"

"Yes," he answered then took a deep breath. "Baby, I know I messed up. I admit that, but I love you and I want to be close to you." He paused and sighed deeply. "We haven't made love in over two months. It's killing me."

Angel sighed deeply then confessed, "I'm sorry. I just haven't been in the mood."

"Then when, baby?" he wanted to know. "Are you going to punish me for the rest of my life?"

"I'm not trying to punish you. I just haven't felt like having sex lately."

"Angel, I know I hurt you. I know I did a terrible thing, but I thought you had forgiven me. I thought we were gonna try to work on our marriage?"

Angel took a deep breath then inquired cautiously, "David, did you marry me because I was pregnant or because you loved me?"

"I married you because I loved you. I still do," he proclaimed. "I explained to you what happened with Kristy."

"Does she still call you?"

"No."

"Do you still pay her?"

"Yes, I owe her that much. It wasn't all her fault what happened. I promised to pay her a salary for six months, and then she's on her own. I think that's fair," he explained. "I don't see Kristy. Ernestine mails her checks to her each week." He paused, feeling so awful that he had hurt his wife so deeply. "Angel, you know if I could undo what I did, I would. I swear on my mother's grave I would." She didn't answer. "I love you so much."

"I love you, too, David," she sniffed. He gently pulled her in his arms, and they kissed lovingly. "Come to bed." She pulled her gown off over her head and David's eyes twinkled at seeing his wife's luscious body for the first time in two months.

****

Mason planted a kiss on Brandy's forehead, and she opened her eyes. "I've got to go, sweetheart."

"So soon?" she cooed, snuggling up closer to him.

He squeezed her tight, took a deep breath and replied, "I'm afraid so. I like to spend time with my daughter before she goes to bed."

"How old is your daughter?"

"Six."

"I bet she's beautiful."

"Yes, she is," he acknowledged, smiling proudly. "If I do say so myself."

"Does she look like you or her mother?"

"I think she looks like me, but then again, I could be prejudice," he chuckled, and she laughed with him, and then he grew serious. "I enjoyed today."

"I did too," she agreed, and their lips locked in a soft kiss.

"I've really got to go, though," he repeated, and she nodded, moving out of his arms. He kissed her again before getting up.

Brandy sat up, watching him getting his clothes together. "What in the hell am I doing?" she spat and drew his attention.

"What're you talking about?"

"I'm talking about *us*! You're a *married* man. There's no future in dating a married man!" she explained. He came back to the bed and sat on the edge. He lifted her chin with his finger.

"You're very special to me," he announced. "I don't want you to think I'm using you. I want to continue seeing you."

"You do?" she was surprised.

"Of course, I do. You can't get rid of me that easily," he shared then kissed her lips again.

"I've never dated a married man before, Mason. This is so new to me."

"Then we're even. I've never cheated on my wife before."

"Never?"

"Never!"

"That's hard to believe."

"Why?"

"A good-looking, successful man like you. I would think the women would be all over you."

"I didn't say I didn't get offers. I just never saw anyone that was worth risking my family over."

"Then why *me?*"

"I told you, you're special to me," he cooed and touched her chin with his finger. "Come on. Shower with me?"

****

"Mommy, when is daddy coming home?" Amy whined to Becky while they sat in the den, working a jigsaw puzzle together in their nightgowns.

"Soon, sweetie," Becky hypothesized, looking at seven thirty on the clock.

"Can we call him?"

"He might be on a case, darling," Becky tried to explain to her daughter, but her thought was that her husband was probably with some bimbo. She wondered if it was Toni Melton. She hated that woman. She saw how Mason looked at her, like he could eat her alive! Mason had better pray to his maker if he was with another woman. She would not stand for that. She would see him in hell first! *And* his whore!

****

Mason stood at Brandy's door, about to leave, and they kissed long and aggressively. "I'll see you tomorrow, okay?" he made known. She nodded. He focused on her face, and she didn't have any make-up on, but she was still incredibly stunning and sexy. He kissed her again. "You are so beautiful." She smiled sweetly. Then he reached into his pocket and handed her a stack of folded bills. "Buy yourself something nice." She frowned and threw the money on the floor then stomped away from him.

"I'm not a *whore*, Mason!" she spat.

"Wait! Wait! Wait!" he called, catching her hand. "I didn't mean to…"

"Just get out!" she insisted.

"Brandy, I didn't mean to imply that you were a whore. I told you, I've never done this before. That's what they usually do in the movies," he spurted then smiled, and she burst into laughter. "I'm sorry. I really am. I know you're not a whore. I would *never* insinuate that. If I thought you were a whore, I wouldn't be here." He lifted her chin. "Forgive me for being stupid?" She didn't answer. "Please," he whined, and she smiled again, then he pulled her in his arms and took a deep breath. "I don't want to lose you. I've never had any woman to make me feel like this." They kissed lovingly then he picked up the money and stuck it back into his pockets. "See you tomorrow." She nodded and he kissed her one more time before leaving. Brandy watched Mason get into his black Lamborghini and wondered just how rich he really was.

****

"Are you cold?" Ron asked Toni cuddling on the couch together.

"No, I'm fine," she answered, leaning back on him between his legs in his arms. He placed his hand on her stomach.

"You okay, little man?" he joked, and Toni laughed. "I sure hope you're not as stubborn as your mother."

"*And* your father," Toni added.

"Hey, baby, I've been thinking. Why don't we buy a house in the country with the money Mr. Sanchez gave us?"

"Oh, honey, that's a terrific idea," Toni agreed, turning to face him.

"I want our child to have a lot of room to run and play."

"So do I," she glowed. "Want me to call a realtor tomorrow?"

"Yeah, that would be great."

"David's a realtor."

"David?"

"Angel's husband."

"Oh yeah."

"I'll call him tomorrow."

He looked deep into her eyes. "I love you."

"I love you, too," she accepted, and they met each other with a kiss, and he squeezed her tight.

"I'm going to be a *daddy!*" he exploded in laughter, and she laughed with him.

****

Mason walked into the house and was met by an angry Becky, standing at the door, frowning with one hand on her hip and the other one surrounding a cigarette. "Where in the hell have you been? It's almost *eight thirty!*" she raged.

"I had a late appointment," he lied. "Is Amy asleep?"

"No, but she's in bed. She tried to wait up for you," she replied, not believing him. "Who is she, Mason? Toni Melton?"

"Toni?!" he blasted. "Why are you so jealous of Toni? I told you, Toni and I are just *friends*!"

"Yeah, I bet."

"Listen, Becky, Toni is dating Ron Joyner! So please stop accusing me of sleeping with her!"

"Ron Joyner, the *attorney?*!"

"Yes," he answered. "She moved in with him and they are *very* happy."

"I bet that broke your heart," she spat sarcastically.

"And why would that break *my* heart?" he countered then heard a loud...

"Daddy!"

Mason turned around and Amy was running into his arms, so he swooped her up and held her close. "How's daddy's girl?"

"Fine," she beamed. "Why are you so late?"

"Daddy was detained, honey. I'm sorry," he explained. "Come on, let me go and put you back into bed."

"What de...ta...?" Amy stammered.

"Detained means I was held up because daddy was meeting with a client," he explained.

"This conversation isn't over, Mason," Becky made known.

"Yes, it *is*," he stressed, piggyback riding his little laughing daughter back up the stairs.

Chapter 14

Ron strolled into the office and handed Beverly a cigar, with another unlit one hanging out of his mouth. "Good morning, beautiful!" he radiated.

"What's going on?" she asked, then froze and covered her wide-opened mouth. "No!" she screamed, and Ron nodded his head enthusiastically. "Toni's pregnant?!" she exploded, jumping up as he continued to nod. Beverly sprang from behind her desk and grabbed him in a big cuddly hug, screaming hysterically. "That's great, honey!" Travis walked in and froze.

"What's going on? You got a raise or something, Beverly?" he laughed.

"Here, Travis, my man, have a cigar," Ron offered proudly, handing him a cigar, and Travis focused on the smiling duo, and then he caught on.

"Toni's pregnant?" he questioned, and both Ron and Beverly nodded fervently. Travis smiled wide. "Well, congratulations, man. Put it there." He grabbed Ron's hand and they hugged while Jamie entered.

"I see I'm just in time for Christmas presents," Jamie joked.

"I got *mine* early," Ron boasted, handing Jamie a cigar.

"Who's pregnant?" Jamie inquired.

"Toni, silly," Beverly jeered.

"Toni?" Jamie was confused.

"Yes, Toni Melton," added Beverly.

"The *journalist*?" Jamie asked and Beverly nodded. "Then who...?" He was confused.

"Ron!" Beverly exploded, still smiling.

Jamie focused on Ron. "You're married to *Toni Melton*?"

"Almost," Ron revealed. "If she wasn't so stubborn."

"I didn't know you were seeing Toni Melton," Jamie responded. "Congratulations!"

"Thank you," Ron accepted, unable to contain his excitement.

****

Mason walked into Toni's office and heard her in the adjoining bathroom in her office. "Toni," he called, but she didn't answer, so he walked in the direction of her painful groans. "Toni, are you all right?" he called in front of the closed door.

"Be out in a …" she started but stopped suddenly, heaving another round of vomiting in the toilet. Soon she opened the door, looking weak and exhausted.

"Hey. What's wrong? Are you sick, honey?" Mason was concerned, looking at her, and she shook her head. Then he smiled. "Pregnant?" She took a deep breath then nodded with a slight smile. "Congratulations!"

"Thank you," she accepted, moving slowly to her desk, and sitting.

"It'll go away in a couple of months," he hypothesized, sitting in the chair in front of her desk.

"If I *survive* a couple of months," she yelped and he laughed, as Brandy entered.

"Oh, I'm sorry, Toni. I didn't know you had someone in here. Angel told me to come on in," she apologized.

"It's okay. Mason isn't *somebody*," Toni joked, and Mason directed a smirk at her then stood and went to Brandy.

"How are you this morning, Brandy?"

"Fine," she answered shyly. Toni's gazed caught Mason's and he smiled sweetly at her.

Handing to Toni a manila envelope, Brandy shared, "Mr. Hurley said to give you this. He's made some corrections."

"Thank you," Toni received it. "Good ole Bill refuses to come into the twenty-first century. Still does everything on paper when it would be so much easier to edit on the computer."

"Well, he's from the old school," Mason chuckled then caught Brandy's focus.

"Have a good day," she concluded sweetly, and he nodded, then she left.

184

"Mason, you *didn't*," Toni spurt.

"Didn't *what*?"

"You know *what*?" she assumed, then he sat and took a deep breath.

"She's *hot*!"

"And how do *you* know?" she spat, and he met her gaze and chuckled shyly. "You dirty dog!"

"It's not like that," Mason defended. "I care about Brandy."

"Hum um."

"I'm serious," Mason maintained.

"And what about *Becky*?"

"Toni, you know I've never loved Becky. I married her because she said she was pregnant," he defended and noticed Toni's far-a-way look. "What did I say?"

"Ron wanna get married, but I don't want him to marry me just because I'm pregnant, but he can't understand that," she explained.

"Honey, your situation is a *lot* different from mine," he hypothesized. "You and Ron are in love. I *never* loved Becky. She tricked me. I met her at a party. You know the story. I was drunk and she took me home. She said we had sex, but I didn't even remember it. The next thing I knew she said she was pregnant. Then to keep my reputation, I agreed to marry her and get divorced as soon as the baby was born. Then later I found out that she didn't get pregnant until *after* we were married." He paused and smiled. "But when I saw my little girl, I *had* to stay."

"That's sweet, Mason."

"But I've never been happy," he added. "Brandy makes me happy."

"*In* or *out* of bed?"

"Both," he laughed. "She just seems to push all the right buttons in me."

"Sounds like you're falling in love with this girl," Toni observed, and he pondered.

"I think you're right."

"Be careful, Mason. Hell hath no fury like a woman scorned. Trust me. I'm speaking from experience."

Chapter 15

"Merry Christmas, darling," Ron gleamed, handing Toni a big, wrapped box, while they sat on the floor in front of the huge Christmas tree.

"Wow!" Toni sparkled, sitting in his black, silk pajama top while he wore the bottoms. She opened the present slowly and focused on a beautiful, dark-chocolate brown, leather coat. "Oh, honey, this is beautiful!" she exploded into his arms, giving him a big kiss.

"I didn't know what to get a woman who has *everything*, then I remembered you said you wanted a coat," he explained.

"It's beautiful," she admired, trying it on. "Perfect fit!"

"For now," he laughed. "I'll have to get you another one in a couple of months."

"A couple of months?!" she exploded in laughter. "My clothes are getting too small *already*!"

"That's good," he laughed with her. "You're beautiful."

"Thank you, honey," she accepted. "Here, baby, this is for you." She handed him a small, wrapped box. He ripped it open and focused on a beautiful, gold, Rolex watch.

"Oh, honey, this is so nice!" he glowed then met her with a kiss. "Thank you."

"I looked at your other watch, and I felt you needed something with a little more *flair*."

"This certainly *does* have flair," he chuckled then kissed her again. "I love you."

"I love you too."

"This is our first Christmas together."

"Yes, it is."

"Merry Christmas, baby."

"Merry Christmas, sweetheart," she replied, and they kissed again.

****

"It's Simon!" Alexandria shouted in hysterical laughter, looking out the window while standing on the couch. Then she jumped down and opened the door. "Hi, Simon. Merry Christmas!" She jumped in his arms, and he put the packages that were in his hands on the floor to better hold her, and then he squeezed her tight.

"Merry Christmas, sweetie."

"Hey, Simon," Keith yelped, jumping to his feet, giving him a hi-five.

"What's happening?" Simon joked with giggling Keith.

"Merry Christmas," Melissa added as he put Alexandria down.

"Merry Christmas," he acknowledged.

"Come on. Let's open our gifts," Keith suggested, helping Simon pull off his coat.

****

"Merry Christmas, Mom," Toni established, entering her mother's house, followed by Ron, with an armful of gifts.

"Merry Christmas," her mother replied rather nonchalantly, as Toni planted a quick kiss on her cheek.

"Merry Christmas, Mrs. Melton," Ron added, following Toni and her mother into the den. They removed their coats and Mrs. Melton focused on Toni long and hard in those tight blue jeans.

"You're gaining weight, Toni," she observed.

Toni smiled and admitted, "No, Mom. I'm pregnant." Ron took her hand and they sat on the couch together.

"Pregnant!" Mrs. Melton spat, and Toni nodded. Her mother took a long, deep, and concentrated breath. "That's the devil's child, Toni!"

"What?!" Ron spat.

"That child will never be blessed!" she raged. "It was conceived in sin! Toni, how could you do such a thing to a child? It will hit hell wide open, just like the two of you!"

Ron bit his bottom lip to stay calm. He was not going to stand by and let this bitter old woman dictate his child's future. He looked at Toni and suggested very quietly, "Let's go, honey."

"Mom, apologize to Ron," Toni insisted.

"Apologize?!" she exploded. "I will *not* apologize for telling the truth! That baby is cursed, and so are *you* and so is *he*!" Ron took a deep breath and stood. He was so angry he didn't want to respond. He didn't know if he could contain his temper, so he yanked his coat off the chair and flew out the door.

"Mom, how could you?" Toni spat. "I'm your *only* daughter. Why do you hate me so much?"

"I don't hate you. I love you. That's why I've got to tell you the truth. I can't stand to see you bound for hell."

"It's *my* life, Mom," Toni stressed with tears running down her face. "I love Ron, and I love this baby. My baby is not cursed! It's *already* blessed because it has two parents who love it and love each other!" She paused as she cried, "Why do you treat me like this? What have I ever done to you but tried to love you?"

"You are a sinful child, Toni. First it was that married man, and now it's this sinner. And you see what happened to the first one," she explained. "Nothing good ever comes from the devil."

A pang of sadness shot through Toni's entire body. She felt... *numb*. "I made a mistake with Nathan. I'm not a bad person because I made a mistake. We *all* make mistakes. It's called being human. Maybe if you'd just try to talk to me in a Christian way, you could've won me over by now. But I refuse to end up like you. And if being mean and hurting your children to the point that they can't stand to be around you is being a Christian, then you can have it!"

"That's blasphemy, Toni, and you will burn in hell for it!"

"Then I'll see you there, Mom," Toni finalized then turned, grabbed her coat, and ran out. When Toni jumped into the car with Ron, she couldn't stop crying. He pulled her in his arms and held her close.

"Toni, I know she's your mother and you love her, but I can't come back here anymore," he admitted. "I've tried to get along with her, but I refused to continue to endure this kind of abuse from *her* or *anyone* else." Toni focused on Ron.

"I don't blame you," she wept. "If she weren't my mother, I wouldn't come back either."

****

Angel watched David sit on the floor, playing with the brand-new train set with their boys. They were laughing so happily, she was glad she had taken him back, if not for *herself*, for her *children*. Boys really *do* need their fathers. It's a pity too many were growing up without a father in the house. She was willing to bet everything she had that if things turned around and there were more fathers in homes…*good* fathers, the government could stop building so many jails and prisons and start building more colleges and universities. David looked at his wife curled up on the couch and winked at her, and she smiled. Then he mimed, *I love you* and kissed at her. She felt so warm inside that she had her husband back and they were genuinely happy. Angel tilted her head towards upstairs and stood. David's eyes widen then he stood quickly. "Hey, boys, I'll be right back. Go on without me for a while." They continued as if he wasn't even missed.

David walked into the bedroom and Angel was standing in the middle of the room, completely nude, and his body responded immediately. He dropped his pajama bottoms on the floor, and she swallowed hard. Then he removed his pajama top and let it drop to the floor.

"Lock the door," Angel breathed, and he did. He went into his wife's arms and they hugged lovingly, kissing smoothly and zealously. David was so thankful to have his family back, and he knew in his heart that he would let nothing ever come between them again.

****

"Mason!" Brandy exploded, jumping in his arms at her door. He smiled, picking her up and carrying her through the door and closed it with his foot.

"You're happy to see me, I assume."

They kissed extensively and fanatically then she beamed, "Oh, yes. I didn't know I would see you today."

"It's Christmas, isn't it? You *know* I had to see you today," he proclaimed.

"I'm so happy to see you," she cried. "How long can you stay?"

"Long enough to wish you a Merry Christmas," he made known, kissing her again.

****

"There's my baby girl!"

"Hi, daddy," Toni welcomed, receiving a gigantic hug from her father. Then he extended a hand to Ron.

"Merry Christmas, Ron," Mr. Melton acknowledged, smile still widening. Toni's father had a light brown complexion, was five feet ten inches, with a protruding belly and a bald spot in the top of his head, surrounded by thin, graying, black hair.

"Merry Christmas, sir," Ron acknowledged, handing him some wrapped boxes. "These are for you and Juanita."

"Thank you, son," he accepted. "Juanita has your gifts under the tree somewhere. "Juanita!" he called. "The kids are here!" A short, fat, pecan-tan, *Aunt Bea type* lady entered with her hair pulled up in a bun on the top of her head. She was a plain, homely type, wearing a straight, flowery housedress.

"Toni!" she exploded in a very pronounced southern drawl and hugged her tight.

191

"Hi, Juanita," Toni addressed.

"Ron," Juanita greeted with a hug also.

"Hi, Mrs. Melton," Ron received.

"Come on in, you two," she urged friendly, and Ron could see why Toni's father preferred this woman to Toni's mother. Although Toni's mother could wrap rings around Juanita in the looks department, their attitudes were complete opposites. "Pete, take the kids' coats. Dinner is ready." Mr. Melton took their coats while Juanita grabbed Toni's arm and guided her into the den. She patted Toni's stomach. "How're you two?"

"He's fine. I'm a mess," Toni laughed.

"The first few months are the hardest."

"Tell me about it," Toni agreed, while her father and Ron went into a conversation about football.

Chapter 16

Toni dragged into the office, sticking out a little more at four and a half months pregnant now. "Hi, Angel," she spoke.

"Hi, honey. How are you?" Angel responded.

"I'm okay," she replied, her face a little bit fleshier from her pregnancy, and her hair a little longer, but not near shoulder-length yet, and still in upturned curls.

"Here are your messages," Angel acknowledged, handing Toni a stack of notes.

"Thanks."

"How's the house coming?"

"Great. Ron hung the drapes in the living room last night. He wouldn't let me help."

"Can you blame him?"

"I guess not," Toni agreed. "He treats me like I'm going to break."

"Enjoy it," Angel laughed. "Cause when that baby comes, all the attention will be focused on him."

"*Her.*"

"You know what it is already?"

"We think so. They weren't sure because it was turned the wrong way when I had an ultrasound done, but they think it's a girl."

"Oh, that's sweet. *I* wanted a girl."

"There's still time," Toni chuckled.

Angel jovially made known, "Not hardly! David goes ballistic when I even *mention* having another baby."

****

Mason tipped up behind Brandy in the copy room and planted a kiss on the back of her neck. "Hi."

She turned and they ended in a sweet kiss. "Hi," she cooed.

"I have to do an interview at four. I'll see you about five thirty," he revealed, and she nodded.

"Want something to eat when you get there?"

"Other than *you*?" he purred, and she smiled.

"Yes, other than *me*."

"Hum um," he murmured then kissed her again. "Want to take in a movie?"

With widen eyes she replied, "Sure, but don't you have to rush home?"

"Amy's spending the night with my parents."

"What about *Becky*?"

"We can take in the six o'clock movie and I'll be home by nine."

"All right," she agreed.

"See you later," he whispered in her ear and she nodded. Just as he was leaving, Becky was entering, and Mason drew in a breath.

"Becky, what are you doing here?" he charged.

"I can't come to see my *husband*?" Becky inquired sarcastically then focused on Brandy in that short, body-fitting knit red dress and six-inch tan heels and extended a hand. "Hello, I don't know *you*. You must be new. I'm Mrs. Mason Whittaker."

"How do you do, Mrs. Whittaker?" Brandy accepted her hand in a shake. "I'm Brandy Sears. It's nice to meet you." Brandy's heart seemed to drop two feet just as Toni entered.

"Becky, hello," Toni accosted Becky with a wide smile.

"Hi, Toni," Becky accepted, staring at Toni's protruding stomach. "I didn't know you were expecting. Mason didn't tell me."

"Yeah, four and a half months now," Toni beamed proudly.

"Congratulations," Becky recognized, smiling slightly, feeling extremely happy that she didn't have to worry about *Toni* anymore.

"Thank you," Toni acknowledged. "It's nice to see you."

"Thank you," Becky received.

Feeling the need to rescue Brandy out of a bad situation, Toni suggested, "Brandy, would you bring me those files from Bill's office, please?"

"Sure, Toni," Brandy agreed. "It was nice meeting you, Mrs. Whittaker."

"Same here," Becky established, then watched the pretty woman walk away quickly.

"Becky, it's nice seeing you again," Toni finalized.

"Likewise," Becky replied as Toni exited behind Brandy. Becky wondered if this young woman, *Brandy*, was Mason's *latest* crush. She knew someone was occupying her husband's concentration lately, and after seeing this new little bimbo, it *must* be her. She *would* find out and let the chips fall where they may!

****

When Toni returned to her office, Brandy entered slowly. "Hi, Toni," she spoke.

"Hello, Brandy."

"I came to thank you."

"There's no need to thank me," Toni confirmed.

"Oh yes there is. I didn't know how to leave. You know a wife can pick up on things very quickly."

"I know," Toni agreed. "Brandy, if you don't mind my asking, why do you sleep around with a married man, knowing there's no future in it? You are a beautiful young woman. Mason is nice, good-looking, and rich, but he's *married*. I don't think he's going to leave his little girl for you or anyone else."

Brandy took a deep breath and answered, "There's only one answer. I love Mason."

"And I love you," Mason proclaimed, entering quietly, and the two women simultaneously focused on him. "Thanks, Toni, I owe you one." Toni nodded with a slight smile, and then he went to Brandy. "I do love you. I'm sorry about this whole situation, and I don't want to lose you." He planted a kiss on her lips, and then pulled her in his arms.

"I love you, too," she concurred, and they kissed again.

"All right, you two, get a room!" Toni laughed, and they burst into laughter with her.

****

Simon entered Melissa's bakery and she smiled wide. "Hi," he addressed her from across the counter.

"Hi," she acknowledged, walking from around the counter and leading him to a table.

"Hello, ladies," he spoke to the other counter help.

"Hi, Simon," they answered in unison, admiring this handsome man in the dark gray suit, accented by a maroon tie and handkerchief.

Sitting at the table with Melissa, Simon shared, "I'm on my way to court, and I couldn't leave without seeing your beautiful face."

"That's sweet," she whispered, and he touched her hand lovingly.

"I love you," he confessed.

"I love you," she accepted, and they kissed just as Ron entered. Ron stood at the door and took a deep breath then he walked to his sister and Simon.

"You're fogging up the windows," he spoke with a stern voice and an annoyed smirk on his face. Melissa and Simon broke apart, smiling shyly.

Simon stood and extended a hand to Ron, "How are you, Ron?"

"I was good until I came in here and saw you fondling my sister."

"Ron!" Melissa exploded.

"Just kidding," Ron countered, smiling slightly, and taking Simon's hand, but he really wasn't kidding. He didn't know what his sister saw in this slick, sorry excuse for a lawyer. "I just stopped by to pick up some brownies for Bev and Toni."

"How is Toni?" Simon asked.

"Do you *really* want to know," Ron jeered sarcastically. "Or are you just making conversation?" Melissa dropped her head in embarrassment.

"I *want* to know," Simon retaliated. "I wouldn't have *asked* if I didn't."

"Then in that case, she's great! Thank you for asking."

"And when is the blessed event scheduled?"

"In about four and a half months."

"I know you're excited."

"Yes, we are," Ron confirmed. "Well, I gotta get back to work." He cocked his head to the side to finalize their visit. "Simon, it's been real."

"For sure," Simon acknowledged, then Ron strolled to the counter. Simon sat beside Melissa. "That was an experience."

"I'm sorry, Simon."

"There's no need to apologize for Ron, honey. Ron and I grew to be mortal enemies *long* before you and I became friends," he explained then smiled, as Ron left with his box of brownies. "Well, I guess I better get going." He stood and she stood with him. "I'll see you tonight." She nodded and he kissed her again then left. Melissa felt so torn between her brother, whom she loved and respected unconditionally, and the man she loved and respected unconditionally. She didn't know what to do to bring them closer, but she knew she had to try something. But what?

****

"Toni!" Ron called, entering their enormous, newly built, magnificent, three-story, six-hundred square feet, brick house, wearing a black pinstriped suit with a white shirt, red necktie, and handkerchief.

"In the nursery," Toni called back.

Ron trotted up the brass spiral staircase, taking two steps at a time in the direction of her voice and spotted Toni standing on a step ladder, and his breath ran out. "Toni, what're you doing?!" he gasped, jumping to her, securing his hands around her waist, and taking her down.

"I was just hanging these curtains," she admitted, standing in a lavender colored, cotton sweat suit and a lavender hair band outlining her face to keep her hair back. "Aren't they cute, honey?"

"Yes, there're very nice," he concurred, looking at the little musical notes on the yellow, lace curtains. "But, honey, this ladder is unstable. If you need something reached, let me do it for you."

She cheerfully agreed, "Okay. I wasn't thinking." Then he placed his hand on her stomach.

"How are you, little lady?" he cooed, bending down to put his ear to Toni's stomach. "Oh, she's very active."

"Yes, she is," she agreed. "What'd you want to eat tonight, honey?"

"We can order take-out."

"Chinese?" she asked.

"That's good."

"Okay, I'll call."

As he exited the room, he pointed and ordered, "Don't get back on that ladder." She willingly nodded.

Chapter 17

"Mom!" Toni rushed into her mother's house. "Mom!"

"In here," she called. Toni followed the sound of her mother's voice into the kitchen.

When she entered, her mother was stirring contents in a boiling pot on the stove. "Mom, I received a message that there was an emergency with you. What is it?"

"I'm fine, Toni. I just called because I hadn't heard from you in a while."

"Then why did you say it was an *emergency*? I was worried that it was your sugar!"

"Because I wanted to show you something, and I didn't know if that man would let you come if it weren't an emergency."

"Mom, that *man's* name is *Ron*, and he doesn't *control* me. I *do* have a mind, you know."

"Then why haven't I seen you?"

"Because I didn't think you wanted to see me in *this* condition," Toni referred to her protruding stomach. "Now what is it you wanted to show me?"

Mrs. Melton took the Bible off the table and instructed, "Look right here, Toni, in Galatians 5:19-21, it reads that the work of the flesh like adultery, fornicators, uncleanness will not inherit the kingdom of God." Toni took a deep breath.

"Mom, is this what you tricked me to come over here to see?"

"Toni, you, your baby, Ron, you're all under the curse. You *must* repent! You must turn your life over to God before it's too late!" she begged, grabbing Toni's hands.

Jerking away from her, Toni shouted, "Mom, stop it! Please, just stop it!" But her mother kept on.

"Toni, the day of judgment is near! You must surrender your life to Christ before it's too late. That baby is of the devil! He's a devil child, Toni!" she raged, and Toni turned and ran out in tears. Her mother ran after her. "That baby could be the antichrist! He's coming, you know! The antichrist is coming! The Bible will be fulfilled! Your baby, Toni, *could be* the antichrist!" Toni covered her ears and ran out the front door.

Toni was so upset; the tears blinded her vision. Just as she was about to go down the steep steps, she missed one, sending her tumbling down screaming to the paved walkway below.

Moments later, there was only silence and her body laid lifeless.

****

"Hi," Mason spoke to Brandy sitting at the desk, outside of his office.

"Hi."

"I'm going to Chicago in two days. How would you like to come with me?"

"Chicago?!" she exploded, jumping up.

"Yes," he shared her enthusiasm.

"But I have to work."

"You *will* be working. You'll be with me as my assistant."

"Will Mr. Hurley go for that?"

"I'll make sure he does," he assured her, and she jumped to him and hugged him tight.

Sobering, Brandy inquired, "But will I get paid? I need to work, you know. I have bills."

"Of course, you'll get paid," he promised, still hugging her around the waist. "Won't it be great, spending two nights together? I won't have to get up and rush home."

"Oh, yes," she cooed. "That would be fantastic." Brandy couldn't help but wonder how Becky would take this news. She could tell that Becky wasn't a force to reckon with.

****

Ron tore into the hospital rapidly. He walked to the nurse's station and asked, "What room is Toni Melton in?"

"Are you a relative?" the lady inquired, admiring the handsome man in the expensive, tailor-made brown suit with the tan, collarless shirt, and a tan handkerchief in his pocket.

"Yes, I'm her husband!" he shouted, losing all patience with this woman.

Looking at her charts she revealed, "Room 103." He didn't hear anything she said after that. He just started in that direction. He knew the hospital well because he used to spend a lot of time there with Leroy.

When Ron opened Toni's door, she was lying with her eyes closed and her mother was sitting in a chair by the window. "What happened?" Ron asked Mrs. Melton.

"She fell down the steps," she answered, getting up, and Toni, hearing Ron's voice, opened her eyes and focused on him.

"Ron," she called weakly as tears immediately started flowing down her face.

"Yes, honey, I'm here," he spoke softly. "How do you feel?"

She started crying even harder as she squeezed out, "I lost her, Ron. I lost the baby." She cried hard as Ron pulled her in his arms, crying with her.

"God took that devil child," Ron heard Mrs. Melton say. He straightened up, sniffed, and focused on her. "That child was the antichrist. That's what I was trying to tell Toni. God took that child. He couldn't let another demon come to this Earth." Ron just stared at Mrs. Melton as tears ran down his face. He couldn't believe her. He couldn't believe that this crazy old woman was standing there saying that *his* child by the woman he loved was a demon child.

"Get out of here!" Ron demanded through clenched teeth, still holding Toni's hands.

"God took that child. He couldn't let that child…"

"Get the hell outta here!" Ron yelled. "And don't you *ever* come back!"

"Toni is *my* child. She is no relation to you! You can't put me out!"

"The hell I can't!" he insisted then started towards her, but Toni jerked him back.

"Mom, please leave," Toni insisted through tears.

"Are you turning your back on your mother for *him*, Toni?" she hissed.

"Mom, I don't feel like dealing with this today. Please, just go," Toni squeezed out again.

Mrs. Melton picked up her purse and concluded, "I can't believe that you would turn on your own mother for a *man*!"

Ron spat, "Just get the hell out!" He turned back to Toni and Mrs. Melton walked out slowly. Just as she did, she almost bumped into Mr. Melton and Juanita.

"Effie, how is she?" Mr. Melton asked.

"Ask her yourself," she spat. "You'll all burn in hell together!" Then she walked out. Mr. Melton and Juanita looked at each other then entered Toni's room slowly.

"Toni," her father called. Ron stood up and walked to him. "How is she?"

"She's going to be okay," Ron sniffed, wiping his face with his hand. "She lost the baby though." Mr. Melton dropped his head as Juanita took Ron's hand. Then Mr. Melton walked over to Toni's bed and took her hand. She opened her eyes and focused on her father.

"Hi, honey," he spoke with tears swelling up in his eyes, and Toni burst into tears again.

"Daddy, I lost the baby!" she cried.

"I know, sweetie," he sympathized, cuddling her in his arms as they cried together. "I'm so sorry."

Chapter 18

Mason walked into Bill's office asking, "Where's Toni?"

"She's in the hospital. Didn't you hear?" Bill shared, sitting at his desk, taking off some plastic framed eyeglasses and focusing on his visitor.

"What's wrong?"

Bill sighed deeply then announced, "She lost the baby."

"Oh, no!" Mason sympathized, dropping in a chair. "When?"

"Yesterday afternoon."

"After she left work?"

"Yeah. She went by her mother's house and apparently fell down the steps."

"Fell down the steps!" Mason exploded. "How did she do that?"

"I don't know all the details yet. I just got that little bit of info from Ron."

"Are they very upset?"

"Oh, yes," Bill verified. "Ron could barely talk when I spoke with him."

"Did you send flowers?"

"Yeah, I sent some from all of us here."

"Good," Mason settled. "Hey, where's Brandy? I haven't seen her today."

"Oh, she called. She's having car trouble."

"Where is she?"

"At home. She said a mechanic was on the way."

"I'll go and pick her up," Mason offered, standing, and heading for the door.

"Mason!" Bill called, and he stopped and turned to face the elder man. "How serious is it with Brandy and you?"

Taking a deep breath, Mason answered, "Oh, you know?"

"You would have to be blind *not* to know, the way you two play googly-eyes with each other," Bill chuckled. "You don't want to lose your family over *hormones*, Mason."

"It's more than *that*, Bill," Mason stated then blew hard. "I love her." Bill's eyes stretched then he smiled shyly. "I know what you think, but it's more than just *sex*." He paused to sit in front of Bill's desk again. "I don't know. When I'm with Brandy, I come alive. I've never felt like this with *anyone*."

"Even *Toni*?" Bill asked and Mason's eyes widen.

"Toni was special to me at one time, but it's been over with her for a long time. We were able to remain friends. I cherish my friendship with Toni."

"So, you are *not* redirecting the love you had for *Toni* to *Brandy*?"

"Absolutely not!" Mason insisted. "I love Brandy for *Brandy*. What Toni and I shared briefly is over, and we *certainly* never fell in love. I'm sure if we had had more time, we would have, but *Becky* ended that with her lies."

"Mason, you *did* marry Becky, so please don't disrespect her. No matter how it came to be, Becky is still the mother of your child," Bill advised.

"I don't disrespect Becky. She wouldn't let me even if I tried," Mason chuckled.

"Just be careful. You wouldn't want to jeopardize your career over a scandal, with your column going so well," Bill warned. "You know three more magazines have just picked you up?" Mason nodded.

"I'll be careful," Mason accepted. "Thank you, Bill"

****

Angel, dressed in a pair of black leggings with a huge, loose pink blouse, and a ponytail in her hair, opened Toni's hospital room door slowly with a huge, picturesque green plant in her hand and saw that Ron and Toni were both asleep. She went to him, touched him lightly and he opened his eyes. "Hi," she whispered.

"Hi, Angel," Ron spoke softly, wiping his eyes.

"How is she?"

"Upset," he answered, standing.

"That chair isn't the most comfortable bed," Angel noted. "Go home and get some rest. I'll stay with her."

"I don't want to leave her," Ron rejected.

"I'll be fine," Toni responded, and he walked to her bed.

"Good morning, honey," he spoke, planting a kiss on her forehead.

"Hi," she responded, forcing a slight smiled then focused on her friend. "Hi, Angel."

"Hi, honey," Angel greeted, putting the plant on a table among the many other plants, flowers, and balloons, and then going to the bed, she focused on Ron again. "Go ahead, Ron. Get some rest. I'll be here until you come back."

"Yes, honey, go," Toni urged. "I'm fine."

"Okay," he finally agreed. "I guess I do need to shower and change." He focused on Toni again. "I'll be back as soon as I can." She nodded. Then he turned to Angel. "Thanks, Angel. I won't be long."

"Take as long as you need," she insisted. He kissed Toni again then left. Angel pulled the side rail down and sat on the edge of Toni's bed.

"Do you need anything, honey?" she asked, and Toni shook her head. Angel took a deep breath. "Toni, what happened?"

****

"Mason, what're you doing here?" Brandy asked at her door, stepping aside so he could enter.

"What's wrong with your car?"

"I don't know. It's old," she answered with frustration. "The mechanic couldn't get it cranked, so he's gone to get a tow truck to pull it to the shop."

"Come on. I'll take you to work."

"I'm waiting on the mechanic to come back."

"Call him and tell him you're going to work and to do whatever he needs to do."

"All right," she agreed.

"Why didn't you tell me you needed a car?"

"Why?"

"Sweetie, I want to take care of you."

"Mason, I don't need you to *take care* of me."

"I know you don't, Brandy, but I don't want you breaking down on a deserted street either."

She laughed, "My old clunker isn't *that* bad."

"I'm *serious*," he made known, and she knew that he was, so she sobered.

"Mason, I don't want you to think I just want you for your money!" she announced, and he walked so close to her she could feel his warm, minty fresh breath.

"Brandy, I know you don't, but I can help you," he insisted. "I was reluctant to offer help after the way you went off on me for giving you money before." She smiled. "But, honey, I don't want to see you struggling when I'm in a position to help."

"Okay," she agreed then joked. "Then buy me a Lexus, my dream car." Then she burst into laughter and he laughed with her, pulling her into his arms. They ended in a sweet kiss. Brandy couldn't help but to wonder how she would get out of this situation with Mason when... She didn't even want to think about it. She didn't want to hurt him, but she knew he would be. There was no way around it.

****

"I can't believe your mother would do such a thing!" Angel spat. "But I don't know why I'm surprised. She did me the same way when I got pregnant, but *you're* her *daughter*! Her *only* daughter! How could she upset you like that!" Angel was so mad, she was fuming.

"Ron put her out of here yesterday."

"Good for him."

"Angel, what if she's right?"

"About *what*, Toni?!" Angel spat, surprised.

"That God took my baby as a punishment for my sins."

"Toni, that's stupid! Don't even go there! *God* is *love*. He wouldn't punish an innocent little baby because of what the parents do!" Angel hypothesized. "Look at all those teenagers out there having babies from two and three different men. If God was gonna take *anybody's* babies, it should be *theirs*! At least you and Ron can *support* a baby. Those teenagers have to go on government assistance! So, you stop that crazy talk!" Angel witnessed tears roll down Toni's face and her heart went out to her friend.

"Angel, I miss my baby already."

"I know, sweetie," Angel understood, pulling Toni in her arms. "I know."

****

"Hello?"

"Ron?"

"Hi, Melissa," Ron recognized into the telephone receiver, sitting on the couch, sniffing back his tears.

"Hi, honey. How is Toni?"

"How did you know?"

"It's in all the newspapers."

"It *is*?"

"How did *they* know?"

"Ron, you're forgetting that Toni is a celebrity," she laughed. "Someone at the hospital must've leaked it."

"News travels fast."

"Especially *bad* news," Melissa agreed. "How is she?"

"She's taking it hard."

"I'm sorry, honey," she sympathized. "How are *you* holding up?"

He took a breath and admitted, "I'll be okay."

"Need anything?"

"No. Thanks."

"Well, know that we're here for you, sweetie."

"Thanks, Melissa."

"Who's with Toni now?"

"Angel. I just came home for a few minutes to shower and change."

"That's good. I'm glad she's not alone," she made known. "Ron, I mean it. Call if you need *anything*."

"I will."

"Have they said anything about when she'll be able to go home?"

"The doctor said something about in the morning."

"Okay. I won't hold you. I know you need to get some rest," she finalized. "I'll bring Toni and you some lunch and dinner today. So, don't get anything."

"All right."

"And I know Toni would much rather have *my* food than that *hospital* food."

"I'm sure you're right," Ron agreed.

"See you later, honey."

"All right, Melissa. Thanks."

****

"Hey! Hey! Hey!" Mason laughed, entering Toni's hospital room with Brandy trailing behind him. Toni smiled because she always opened her column with *Hey! Hey! Hey! America!*

"Hi, Mason," Toni responded, continuing to force a smile. "Brandy."

"Hi, sweetheart," Mason greeted, moving to her bed as Angel stepped back. "Hi, Angel."

"Mason," Angel spoke then focused on Brandy. "Hi, Brandy."

"Hi, Angel."

"Hi, Toni," Brandy added. "How are you?"

"I'm here," Toni responded.

"Where's Ron?" Mason asked.

"I *made* him go home and get some rest," Angel answered. "He was here all night, and I know that chair isn't comfortable."

"I *know* that's right," Mason agreed then focused back on Toni and whipped out a newspaper. "You made the headlines, gorgeous!"

"What're you talking about?" Toni chuckled, receiving the newspaper from him.

"Front page," he added.

Toni's eyes stretched when she silently read the huge headlines on the front page of the newspaper, *Award-winning Journalist Toni Melton Miscarries Criminal Defense Attorney Ron Joyner's Love Child!* "*Love Child*," Toni shrieked. "How did *this* get out?"

"You're famous, darling," Mason gleamed. "People talk."

"The *hospital* staff," Toni stated matter-of-factly.

"It's no big deal," Mason added. "When you're in our line of work, *any* press, good or bad is beneficial, just as long as it's *printed*!"

****

"How is Toni?" Rita asked Bill when he entered the house.

"Sad."

"Did you go by the hospital?"

"Yeah, I went by for a few minutes on my way home."

"I feel so sorry for her. I remember when we lost our first child. We were devastated," Rita recalled.

"I remember," he acknowledged, sitting on the couch beside her. "How are *you*?" He planted a kiss on her forehead.

"I'm okay," she replied. "They haven't found a bone marrow donor yet."

"I know. I called," he returned. "Let's just keep praying, honey. Everything will be all right."

As Rita sat with her husband, she couldn't help but feel sorry for him. She had made peace with dying, but he had not. He was such an optimist; she prayed that he would be all right when the time came for him to finally say goodbye to her.

****

Mason and Brandy pulled up to her small, rented, ranch-style, three-bedroom brick house in his Lamborghini, and a beautiful, brand-new, black Lexus, trimmed in gold was parked on the street between her house and her next-door neighbor's. "Wow, my dream car!" Brandy beamed. "I wonder who it belongs to." When they exited Mason's car, Brandy was still looking at the Lexus. Mason walked in front of her, took her hand and dropped some keys in it.

"Some dreams do come true," he admitted, smiling wide. Brandy's eyebrow raised and he nodded.

"Mine?" she asked cautiously, and he nodded again.

"You needed a *car*."

"You're kidding," she breathed, still not believing that he had actually bought her a brand-new car. He took her hand and walked her to the car.

"Get in," he coaxed, but she was still in shock. He took the keys from her and clicked the locks open with the remote then opened the door for her.

"Mason," she breathed. "You bought me a *car*?!"

"You *needed* one, baby."

"But a *Lexus*?!" she stressed.

"That's what you wanted, right?" he inquired.

"No one has ever done anything so nice for me before," she announced weakly.

He planted a soft kiss on her lips and declared, "I love you, Brandy. I would do *anything* for you." She grabbed him and hugged him tight, laughing and crying at the same time.

"I love you. I love you!" she chanted, smothering his face with wild, wet kisses while he enjoyed the attention.

****

Ron sat on Toni's bed, massaging her feet. Toni was glad visiting hours were over. She was delighted that so many people thought so much of her to stop by, but she was tired of putting on a brave front for them. Ron and Angel were the only two people with whom she felt she could be completely herself.

"That feels good," she cooed.

"Good."

"Did you see the article in the newspaper?"

"I saw it," he chuckled. "*Love* child."

"I'm sorry, honey."

"It's my own fault," he joked. "With all the women in the world, I had to fall in love with a *celebrity*! Now my life is an open book!" He laughed and she joined him.

"I'm sorry," she continued to laugh.

"It's all good, honey," he confirmed. "Sweetheart, would you like to get away for a while? We can go to my beach house in Hilton Head. We would be alone. Hardly anyone would be around in February."

"That's sounds great. Can you get off?"

"Oh, yeah. *You* come before *anything* or *anybody*."

Chapter 19

"Brandy!" Mason called, walking into her house with his key.

"In the kitchen," she called back.

He strolled in and put his arms around her waist from the rear while she stood at the sink. He planted a kiss on the back on her neck. Brandy had taken the braids out of her hair and it hung about an inch below her shoulders in a soft, silky wrap with short bangs in the front. "Hi again. Are you packed for Chicago?"

"Yes," she murmured, leaning back in his arms. "Are you just leaving work?"

"Yeah," he replied as she turned around in his arms and they kissed lovingly. "What're you cooking?"

"Lasagna. Can you stay for dinner?"

"Sure," he agreed, kissing her again. He then removed his expensive suit jacket and laid it on a chair at the table, and then sat in a different chair. Mason looked around the small sized, well-decorated house and thought that Brandy had great taste. "Do you like it here?"

"In this house?" she asked with a raised, inquisitive eyebrow.

"Yes."

"Oh, yes. It's great here. The neighbors are great. They stay outta your business. I like that more than anything," she chuckled.

"Would you like something bigger?"

"Honey, I can't afford anything *bigger*," she laughed.

"I didn't *ask* you that," he stressed, and she caught his gaze.

"No," she replied, looking at him. "This is more than adequate for me."

"Are you sure?"

"Yes, honey, I'm sure. It's just *me*. I don't need a big ole *mansion* like you have," she insisted, smiling, and he shared her smile.

"Didn't you tell me that you were renting this house?" he asked, and she nodded. "Who's the owner?"

"Why?"

"Since you like it, wouldn't you like to *own* it?"

"It's not for sale."

"Baby, *everything* is for sale if the *price* is right," he insisted.

"Mason, you've already bought me a car. It's too much," she observed, sitting in his lap at the table and he wrapped his arms around her waist.

"Brandy, *nothing* is too much for you. I don't want you worrying about bills. I want to take care of you," he explained.

"I'm not used to anyone taking care of me," she confessed softly. "I lived in a foster home for a while after my mother died until I was adopted. This is all so new to me."

"I'm in a position to help you. Let me!"

"I keep forgetting you're *rich* because I didn't fall in love with your *money*. I fell in love with *you*."

"I know that, and that's why I want to take care of you. You don't ask for anything. I admire you for that," he stated then smiled. She smiled back just before she jumped up to check on her food in the oven. Mason focused on Brandy's shapely body in those tight green slacks and his body responded immediately. He stood and walked behind her, and she could feel him pressing against her backside.

"Let's skip dinner," he cooed, kissing her neck, grabbing a handful of her soft, but also firm, behind.

"But I want you to taste my lasagna," she laughed.

"I'd rather taste *you*," he moaned, unbuttoning her pants. She surrendered to his passion and let him help her step out of her pants. He then dropped his own pants while still devouring her neck and face with tender, wet kisses. Then he picked her up and sat her on the table and snatched off her lace panties quickly. Suddenly, his cell phone began ringing.

"You're going to get that?" she cooed. He took a deep breath, released her, and stood. Mason pulled his jacket off the chair and yanked his cell phone from the pocket. He looked at the caller ID and noticed his home phone number.

"It's Becky," he breathed then took another deep breath before answering it. "Yeah, Becky!"

214

"Mason, when are you coming home? You know Amy is in that recital tonight."

"That's *tonight*?!" he exploded.

"Yes."

"What time?"

"Seven."

"Where, at the school?"

"Yes."

"Go ahead and I'll meet you there."

"Why can't you come home, and we go *together* as a *family*?"

"I'm busy right now, Becky," he hissed as Brandy slid on her knees and took power over his emotions. The pleasure ripped through his body so severely he gasped, and Becky grew annoyed.

"What're you doing?"

"I…" he was so short of breath he could barely speak or *think* of anything to say. "I'm doing an interview, Becky. I'll meet you there." He hung up quickly and pulled Brandy up. "What're you trying to do, get me in trouble?" She laughed and their lips met in a long, intense embrace.

"You gotta go?" she breathlessly asked between kisses.

He swished her up in his arms and declared, "Wild horses couldn't drag me away right now."

****

"Are you cold, honey?" Ron asked, bringing in a blanket and joining Toni on the couch in front of the fireplace in his beach house.

"No, not really," she answered, shaking her head. He sat behind her and pulled her back in his arms, covering both of them with the blanket. He was wearing the brown, soft cotton pajama bottoms that Toni wore the top to, so she could feel his erection pressing against her backside. She looked back at him and smiled. "Don't even *think* about it, buddy!" she laughed.

215

"What?" he chuckled. "I didn't say anything." She laughed with him. "Just an involuntary reaction at being so close to you." He squeezed her close in his arms.

"Ron," she called softly, growing serious. "Do you blame me?"

"Oh no, honey. It was an accident."

"But I shouldn't have let my mother get me so upset."

"Toni, you couldn't help it. She was saying some awful things."

"I wonder why she hates me so much."

"She doesn't hate you. She's just confused."

"It hurts to know that my own mother hates me."

"Toni, she *doesn't* hate you," he stressed. "She's just one of those people who thinks it's *her* way or *no* way!"

"Ron, you even said yourself that you didn't want our child to be raised with parents who were shacking up."

"I just want the best for our family. I *certainly* don't believe God took our baby because she was a *demon*!" he insisted. "Your mother was out of line. If she's such a Christian she should be showing love and the *goodness* of God, not trying to *badger* people into getting saved. I don't even believe *that* is of God. Do you?"

Chapter 20

Mason held Brandy close on the dance floor in the dim light, while a band bellowed one of Billie Holiday's jazz classics. He held back a little and kissed her lips then squeezed her close to him again. Brandy felt so secure and loved by him. "This was a good idea," he whispered in her ear.

"Yes, it was," she agreed. "I love Chicago. It's such a beautiful city."

When the music stopped, he took her hand and they headed back to their seats. "Mason Whitaker!" a lady shrieked in laughter. "It *is* you!" Then she turned to two other women and waved them over.

"How do you do?" Mason welcomed the attention, smiling wide as Brandy slowly backed out of the way.

"May we have your autograph, Mr. Whitaker?" another lady asked.

"Sure," Mason agreed.

"My goodness, you're more good-looking in person than in the magazines," another lady observed, admiring him in his casual, dark slacks, expensive designer sweater, and casual sports coat.

Focusing on Brandy, the first lady asked as he signed his autograph on their pads, "Is this your wife?"

Mason pondered momentarily then quickly came back with, "No, this is Brandy Sears, a colleague. We're doing a story here and decided to take in some sights in your lovely city."

"Oh," the lady's smile melted a little but soon returned. She didn't care whom he was sleeping with as long as she got his autograph, and more power to the pretty sistah in her body-fitting, whine colored, silk dress and six-inch black heels. If she herself could get *Mason Whitaker* in her bed, she would too.

When the ladies had gone, Brandy looked at Mason and laughed, "Bad idea!"

"No," he chuckled. "I had a good time, but it *is* time to leave. My interview is early in the morning." They walked towards the door.

"Do you think our pictures will be plastered all over the front-page news in the morning?"

"No, I didn't see any paparazzi, only *fans*."

"Thank you, Mason," she acknowledged, looking deep into his eyes. "I had a wonderful time."

"So did I," he concurred, feeling a strong urge to grab her and kiss her, but thinking better of it. "Ready?" She nodded. Brandy's love for Mason grew even more that night, but she couldn't shake the feeling of a knot in the pit of her stomach at what's to come.

****

"Toni," Ron called, entering the bedroom where Toni sat at the vanity table crying. He pulled her up gently and held her close in his arms. "It's okay, honey."

"I miss her so much, Ron. I miss our baby."

"I know, sweetie. I miss her too," he made known, holding her close.

"I let you down."

"No, honey, you didn't," he consoled the weeping woman. "Don't even *think* that."

Part Three

Seven Months Later

Chapter 21

"Okay, Toni, what do you have for next week?" Bill asked as he sat in his office with Mason, Toni, and some other magazine employees, organizing the next magazine issue.

"Bill, I'll have to run the story about the contaminated school lunch that hospitalized half the student body," Toni shared. "The one with the rapes at the university isn't finished yet. I need to go back up there to interview some more girls."

"Okay, we'll put the high school's poison in then," Bill agreed. Toni nodded as he went on to Mason. It felt good for Toni to be back in the swing of things. It had been over seven months since she had lost her baby, and although she still thought of her little girl often…well, time was a slow healer.

****

"Mrs. Sanders, tell me what happened," Ron urged, sitting in a small room across from an average looking woman at a prison. She looked drained and sad. Ron's heart went out to her, and he didn't even know her situation.

"I told you what happened! I killed the son-of-a-bitch! I told the police! I told the psychiatrist! I told the press! I told *everyone* what happened. I don't need a hotshot lawyer like you. I'm guilty! I'll just take my punishment and be done with it," she barked as if he were aggravating her instead of trying to help her.

"Well, your sister seems to think you need help. She's the one who hired the firm."

"My sister is living in a dream world, Mr. Joyner," she insisted. "Now, you're wasting your time. I don't need a lawyer. All I need is for everyone to leave me the hell alone!"

"Then why don't you tell me *why* you killed your husband?!"

"I don't have to answer that."

"Why don't you want to defend yourself?"

"I told you, I'm *guilty*," she repeated. "And from what I've heard about *you*, you don't defend *guilty* people!"

"That's true in most cases, but there must be a reason *why* you killed him."

Standing, she concluded, "Good day, Mr. Joyner. If you insist on pacifying my sister with this defense, go right ahead, but you'll get no help from *me*!" She nodded to the guard and she led her out. Ron blew hard. He never knew of anyone who refused defense, especially when they weren't paying. Her sister could obviously afford his firm's services. Why was this woman hell bent on receiving a lethal injection from the state? *Why*?

****

"Who in the hell did you buy a Lexus for, Mason?!" Becky charged into her husband as soon as he entered the house.

"What?"

"You heard me."

"What are you talking about?" he chuckled.

"The Lexus corporation called as a follow up survey on how we liked our new Lexus. Who did you buy it for, Mason, and don't you *dare* lie to me!"

"They must have the wrong number," Mason lied. He felt like sure a fool. He forgot to tell them to call his cell phone and not his home phone.

"You lying son-of-a-bitch!" she spat, slapping his face. "I will *not* stand around and let you make a mockery of our marriage. Whomever the little whore is, you better get rid of her, and I mean *fast*! Because if you don't, I'll take Amy and we'll go so far away from here, you'll *never* see her again for as long as you live!" She was fuming and Mason knew it. In all the years they've been married, Becky had never hit him. He had never seen her like this before, and he knew she wasn't just bluffing. Becky's father was the mayor of Greenleaf for over twenty years until he retired to focus on his ranch. Before that, he was a federal judge, and before that a successful lawyer. He knew a lot of powerful people. If Becky wanted to take his daughter and hide out forever, her father could very well make that happen. "Do I make myself clear, Mason?"

"Yes," he finally replied.

"Get rid of the bitch, and I mean *now!*" she fumed. "Or you'll be damn sorry!"

****

Ron and Toni sat in a nice, cozy Italian restaurant eating dinner. "This food is delicious," Toni observed.

"Yes, it is."

"We haven't been here in a long time."

"Well, I thought it was time to take the love of my life somewhere nice, instead of ordering take-out!" he chuckled, and she laughed with him.

"That's sweet, honey," she singsong.

Ron grew serious, looked into Toni's eyes, and announced, "It's coming up to our one-year anniversary."

"You remember."

"How could I forget, the way you barged into my office demanding to know about my client," he laughed, throwing his head from side to side like a black woman with attitude.

She laughed with him and added, "That seems so long ago."

"That's because so much has happened in one year," he recognized.

"I guess so."

"Baby, I love you. I don't want to continue shacking up with you. I want this to be permanent," he announced, taking her hand. "Toni, will you marry me?"

Toni smiled wide then blurted out, "Yes! Yes! Yes!" They jumped up and ran into each other's arms, hugging and kissing as if they were the only two people in the restaurant. The other people enjoyed the show as flashbulbs exploded around them. Toni knew

this would be in the newspapers too, but she didn't care. She loved
this man. She didn't care if the whole world knew it.

Chapter 22

"Hi, Mom," Toni spoke, entering her mother's kitchen, and her mother looked up at her from over the stove.

"So, he *finally* let you come to see me?"

"Ron doesn't *let* me do anything, Mom," she defended then sat at the kitchen table. "I'm my own woman. You know that."

"Humph," she groaned, and Toni ignored the gesture.

"I didn't come here to fight. I just wanted to invite you to Ron's and my wedding next Saturday."

"And you're *just* telling me."

"He just proposed last night, but we didn't see any need in waiting."

"Are you *pregnant* again?"

"No, Mom, I'm not."

"Then why the rush?"

"There's no rush. As I said, we didn't see any need in waiting."

"You're already living together. Why on Earth would you spend good money on a wedding?"

"Ron's family wants to give us a wedding, but they promised they would keep it small with just the family and a few friends. We didn't even *want* a wedding, but we're doing it to appease them."

"Anything for *Ron*," her mother sarcastically remarked.

Ignoring her comment, Toni went on, "Will you come?"

Mrs. Melton took a long and concentrated breath then came back with a soft, "No."

Toni felt her heart drop. She didn't know why she let her mother continue to hurt her. It was obvious that her mother wanted nothing to do with her, but she kept trying. "Mom, why do you hate me so much?"

Mrs. Melton took another deep breath and replied, "That's silly. I don't hate you, so don't start *that* again."

"Mom, I'm your *baby*. Your *only* daughter. We should be *close*, but you don't want that. Why?" Toni asked, but her mother remained silent, so Toni continued. "When I was a child, if it weren't for daddy, you would've let Walter and Dennis kill me."

"Your brothers were *not* going to kill you," she stated matter-of-factly.

"They took me to the top of a tree and tied me there. They were throwing cans and shooting bb's at me. I wiggled loose and fell to the ground, breaking my arm in two places, and you wouldn't even take me to the doctor," Toni explained with a heavy heart.

"I didn't know you were hurt."

"I was hurting, and I told you I couldn't move my arm, and you just said to get out of your face. I had to suffer with a broken arm for two hours until daddy came home and took me to the emergency room." Toni stopped to regain composure. "Why did you let them treat me like that?"

"They were only doing *children* stuff."

"They physically *abused* and *tortured* me, Mom!" Toni yelled. "The only abuse I didn't suffer from those two idiots was *sexual* abuse, but I believe if they had wanted that, you would've looked the other way on that, too."

"Toni, that's sick!" Mrs. Melton spat.

"Is it, Mom?" Toni charged.

Locking eyes with her, her mother insisted, "Yes, it is!"

Toni softened and asked quietly, "Why, Mom? Why did you let them hurt me?"

"They didn't hurt you," Mrs. Melton remained in denial.

"What about the *snake* in my bed?"

"It wasn't *poisonous*," she answered. Toni just stood and turned her back to her mother as Mrs. Melton continued, "And it was *you* who almost burned your brothers to death." Toni couldn't believe her. She spun back around to face this *stranger* she called her mother.

"I *had* to do something to protect myself! You sure weren't going to do it, and daddy worked, so he wasn't there all the time."

"That still was no reason for you to burn your brothers."

"But *there* were reasons for *them* to treat *me* like they did?" Toni asked sarcastically, but her mother didn't answer. "Mom, I have won ten major awards in my career, and you have yet to come to *any* of the ceremonies. Why?"

"I'm not going to sit around with those heathens and make conversation," Mrs. Melton declared, and Toni just dropped her head. "The Bible says separate yourself from unbelievers, Toni."

"You worked for twenty-eight years. Were all of those people saved on your job?"

"That's different and you know it!"

"Is it?" Toni questioned and her mother just glared at her. "Tell me something else, Mom. Does your Bible say anything about *love*?" Toni was adamant but nonchalant, and her mother just continued her leer. "Because you might want to start with your *daughter*!"

****

"Hi," Melissa gleamed, meeting Simon with a kiss as he entered her bakery just as she was locking the door.

"What're the kids doing tonight?"

"Keith's struggling with math, so I guess we'll spend tonight on that."

"I used to be rather good in math. Want me to come over and help him?"

"Would you?!" she exploded.

"Sure."

"Thanks, honey."

"Glad to do it," he established. "I'll run home, shower and change then come right over."

"All right. I'll throw something together for dinner."

"You always do a terrific job cooking."

"Thanks," she replied.

"You're ready?"

"Yes, I just need to make one phone call first. I need to confirm the flowers for Ron and Toni's wedding."

"So, they're finally doing it, huh?" he smirked.

"It's great, isn't it?" she marveled. "Alexandria is going to be in the wedding. You can sit with Keith. I have to…"

"Whoa!" he exploded. "Who said I was coming to the wedding?"

"Aren't you?"

"Your brother can't stand me, and his wife-to-be tries all she can to *discredit* me. Why on *Earth* would I want to go to their wedding?!"

"For *me*," she singsong.

"For *you*?!"

"Yes, I'll be busy with the caterers. I need for someone to sit with the children," she explained.

"Melissa, it's *their* family! It's not like they'll be around *strangers*."

"Please," she cooed, hugging him around the neck. Then she planted a kiss on his lips. "Please, baby. I want you there with me."

He chuckled then gave in, "Fine, but you're gonna owe me *big* time."

****

"Mason, are you avoiding me?" Brandy queried, entering his office.

"No," he retorted quickly then took a deep breath. "Yeah, I guess I am."

"Why? What's wrong?"

"Becky found out about the car."

"What's she going to do?"

"She says if I don't stop seeing you, she'll take Amy and hide out, and I'll never see my daughter again."

"She can't do that!" she shrieked.

"She can do *anything* she wants," he made known. "She and her father have the money *and* resources to make it happen."

"So, what're you saying?" Brandy solicited weakly. "You don't want to see me anymore?"

"No, Brandy, I'm not saying that. I don't know what to do except for us to cool it right now, just until Becky gets over being mad about the car."

"So, what am I supposed to do in the meantime?"

He went to her and pulled her in his arms and promised, "We'll figure something out. Just stick by me, okay? I love you." He held her tight.

Chapter 23

Ron stood beside Travis, his best man, smiling big, and Travis sensed he was nervous. Jokingly, Travis whispered in his friend's ear as Angel entered, smiling wide, "It's not too late, my man. We can make a clean getaway right through that opening behind the roses."

Ron chuckled slightly, trying to look inconspicuous, and whispered, "No thanks."

"Are you sure?" Travis continued, smiling wide as he spoke to shield his conversation.

Ron looked up and noticed Toni entering the magnificent garden on her father's arm, looking so beautiful and happy with a crown of pearls encircling her head like the goddess she was, and he whispered back, "I'm *very* sure."

"I feel you, man," Travis finalized.

Ron thought Toni never looked more gorgeous as she strolled through his parents' wonderfully decorated garden in the beautiful September sunlight, dazzling in a crème-colored, formal dress that rested in an array of lace to the bottom of her calf, ending with satin, crème-colored, three-inch pumps. Her hair was in ringlets around her pretty face under the crown of pearls, with pearl stud earrings caressing her earlobes. Her pearl necklace serenaded her small, exposed neck, and her lace sleeves encircled her elbows. Ron took a deep breath as she walked towards him with a wonderful, bright smile glued to her face.

As Toni walked on her father's arm to the man she loved unconditionally, her heart seemed to skip a beat. He stood there so tall and handsome in a black tuxedo with a crème-colored cummerbund and bowtie. His face was bright with a fetching smile, and his hair, mustache, and beard were trimmed to perfection.

Little Amy and little Alexandria, dressed in crème-colored, formal gowns with their hair pinned up like little princesses, trailed in front of Toni and Mr. Melton, dropping pink colored rose petals, and smiling big. Mason and Becky stood, admiring their cute little girl while Simon stood with Keith smiling at Alexandria.

Mason angled around as if he was focusing on the wedding party, but he really was trying to get a glimpse of Brandy. When he spotted her, standing there with Bill, Rita, on a cane, and other co-workers, his heart almost skipped a beat. Her loveliness swept right through his body, and when she looked at him and smiled, he thought his heart would melt. She was stunning with her hair pinned up and wearing a velvety mint green, sleeveless dress that was outlined with a rounded, sequined neckline that flowed down and caressed her tiny waist. A dainty ribbon, mint green belt accented the top of the skirt which then ballooned out in an array of satin, down to three inches above her knees, and it was all accented by bone-colored, six-inch heels.

Brandy took a deep breath as she noticed Mason watching her. Although she smiled sweetly at him, her heart was breaking. He was standing there looking so debonaire in that expensive, black suit. His wife was looking gorgeous in her Queen Elizabeth-style, baby-blue evening dress, with a neckline that flourished all the way to her chin in lace. Her gleaming, red hair was secured in a stylish bun with her baby-blue earrings setting the tone of her exquisite taste. Mason and his wife both reeked of money. How did she ever think she could compete with that?

Angel smiled sweetly, standing there, serving as Toni's matron of honor in her pink, lace dress, with her hair in a single braid down the center of her back while pink roses and baby's breath encircled it. David stood in the audience with his boys, admiring his scenic wife from afar. He was so happy to have her back. He had truly learned his lesson.

Beverly stood beside her husband, smiling big in her tan, formal, sequined two-piece dress suit. She was so happy for Ron and Toni, two people she thought the world of. Standing beside her was Mr. Thomas Sanchez, who knew this day would come. He just wondered why it took so long to get here. He was extremely happy for the lovely couple. Beside him were other people from the law firm: the three partners, John Schuster, Blake Collins, and Phillip Ballentine with their wives; Carol Greene and her husband; Thomas Bailey and his wife; Jamie Heard with his wife; Billy Johnson and his girlfriend; and some others.

Melissa and Denise stood at the door of the kitchen and watched from afar while Barry kept Denise's and his baby. Both felt they couldn't leave the kitchen completely. They had to make sure everything was going right with the caterers. After all, it was them who had convinced Ron and Toni to have a wedding in the first place and promised they would take care of everything. Melissa and Denise were well pleased. What started out being a small wedding, ended up being about one hundred guests. They were blessed that their parents had this huge, back yard garden. The arch and the chairs fit perfectly. The florists had decorated the already beautiful garden even more beautiful with pink and white roses.

Mr. and Mrs. Joyner sat together with Juanita Melton, wondering where Toni's mother was. Mr. Melton joined them after giving Toni away. Her brothers, their wives, and children were all in attendance, but there was no sign of their mother. They hoped she wasn't ill. They were looking forward to meeting her.

"I now pronounce you husband and wife," the preacher proclaimed. "Ron, you may kiss your bride." Ron and Toni smiled at each other, and then they kissed as if they had never kissed in their whole lives, and the audience applauded in excitement.

****

"Effie!" an old lady called at Mrs. Melton's door as she banged on the door instead of ringing the doorbell.

Mrs. Melton opened the door with knitting materials in her hands. "Hi, Shug."

Wobbling in on a wooden cane, the old lady declared, "I thought you were sick. Why aren't you at your daughter's wedding? It *is* today, ain't it?"

"Yes, it's today."

"I thought so. It's been plastered all over the newspapers and TV all week," she chuckled. "Why ain't you there? I would be there myself if this old knee wutn't acting up." Mrs. Melton sat in one chair and the old lady sat across from her in another.

"Shug, Toni and I don't see eye to eye on things."

"That's no reason to miss one of the biggest days of her life."

"I don't know why they're having a wedding anyway. They've been living in sin for almost a year."

"Well, at least they're making it *right* now, honey."

"I don't even approve of this Ron Joyner."

"Honey, *you* don't have to live with him, *Toni* does. And if she loves him, there's really nothing you can do but keep them in your prayers," Shug defended. "Now, why don't you get dressed and at least make it to the reception?"

"I don't want any part of either that wedding or the reception, Shug. Toni has turned her back on me for that man."

"Now, Effie, you know that ain't true. Toni came to see you almost every single day before her accident here, and she still pays your bills. Honey, you've got something to be thankful for. You have a *good* girl," Shug explained.

"I don't ask Toni to pay my bills. That's *her* choice."

"Effie, you better thank God for that girl every day. Your retirement check ain't that much. You can do whatever you want with your money. Toni takes care of your medicine and all. My kids are in their forties and fifties and are so sorry. I never know from one day to the next if I'll see their names in the paper for robbing or something else stupid," Shug reasoned. "And talk about helping me with my *bills*! *They* still come to *me* for money, and I ain't got nothing but my little retirement check every month. Honey, you're blessed to have a girl like Toni. She's not perfect. *Nobody* is! But she loves you, and I think you should support her!"

****

"You look amazing."

Brandy turned around from retrieving punch from the flowing fountain and focused on Mason, looking so wonderful, smiling at her. "Hey," she responded, smiling slightly.

"Hey," he replied. "You look so beautiful."

"Thank you. You look nice, too."

"Where's your car? I didn't see it when I came. I didn't think you were here."

"I rode with Bill and Rita. I didn't want Becky to see it."

"You don't have to worry about that."

"I just don't want to cause any problems for you," she stated, and he smiled that award-winning smile at her, burning a hole right through to her heart, so she looked away.

"Oh, I have something for you," he revealed, digging into his inner pocket, and handing her some papers.

As Brandy focused on the papers her eyes widen as she squeezed out, "It's the deed to my house." She looked up at him. "You bought the house for me?"

"You wanted it, right?"

She just stared at him as her eyes started filling with water. "This is so sweet." He handed her a handkerchief from his inner jacket pocket and she wiped her tears before handing it back to him. He put it back in his pocket. "Thank you, Mason. It means a lot."

"You're welcome," he responded, feeling a strong urge to kiss her. Unlike Becky, Brandy appreciated *everything* he did for her and that meant a lot to him. They stood, staring deep into each other's eyes, sharing a silent, intimate moment.

"I miss you," Mason whispered, breaking the trance that lay between them.

"Same here."

"I don't even see you at work anymore. Where is Bill hiding you?"

"I'm working in the mailroom now."

"The *mailroom*?!" he exploded.

"Yes," she chuckled. "All that fan mail you get on your desk every morning, I'm responsible for getting it there."

"Do you like it?"

"Sure," she admitted. "It's a job."

"I don't even think I know where the mailroom is."

"No, you *wouldn't*," she responded a little sarcastically.

"And what's *that* supposed to mean, Miss Sears?"

She laughed softly and added, "Just that you big shots don't have any reason to come to the mailroom. We little guys see that the mail gets to you."

"Is that supposed to be funny?" he chuckled.

Sobering, she replied, "No." Looking to the left behind him, Brandy observed, "Your wife is looking for you." He just stared at her, and she soaked in his gaze. Mason wanted to grab her in his arms and never let her go, and she was aching for the same.

"Bye," he finally concluded.

"Bye," she responded, blinking hard to hold back more tears.

****

Simon held his hand out to Ron and offered, "Congratulations, Ron."

Receiving his hand in a shake, Ron replied, "Thank you, Simon."

Then he focused on Toni and added, "Best wishes, Mrs. Joyner."

Smiling wide, she chuckled, "Oh, I like the sound of that. Thank you, Mr. Kennedy."

The receiving line continued as everybody else wished the happy couple well wishes. Simon felt more out of place at this wedding than he had ever felt in his whole life. He looked up and focused on Melissa's smiling face, and he knew he loved her more than words could say. What a person would do for love? Being at *this* wedding, *he* knew better than anyone.

****

"Amy was so tired," Mason laughed, entering their bedroom, wearing brown silk pajamas, as Becky sat up in bed reading a book. "She was so sleepy; she couldn't keep her eyes open."

"So, it's Brandy Sears, right?" Becky stated matter-of-factly, not looking up from her book.

"What?"

"Your *mistress*."

"What are you talking about?"

"You know *exactly* what I'm talking about. Brandy Sears is the one you're having the affair with," Becky insisted, closing the book before getting off the bed and standing in front of him.

"Becky, I..."

Raising an open hand, she demanded, "*Don't* Mason! Don't insult my intelligence by denying it! I saw the way you two looked at each other today. She's the one, isn't she?"

He took a deep breath then admitted, "Yes, she *was*." She dropped on the bed again. "It's over, Becky. I swear! It has been for some time now." Becky remained silent and Mason sat beside her on the bed. "Look, Becky, I know I messed up, but I'm here. I'm with you and Amy. So please, let's move pass this."

"You love her, don't you?" she asked quietly.

"I love my *family*."

"Does she still have that *car*?"

"Yes."

"I want you to take it back."

Mason's eyes stretched wide, then he declared softly, "I can't do that."

"And why not?"

"It was a gift. I can't take it back," he stood firm, and Becky jumped up. He followed her. "Becky, the woman doesn't have nearly what you have."

"She has *you*!"

"*You* have me!"

"No, I have your *body*. Your *heart* is with *her*!"

"How can you say that? I broke it off with Brandy weeks ago because I didn't want to lose *you*."

"You didn't want to lose *Amy*! It had nothing to do with *me*!"

"It has *everything* to do with you!"

237

"Then why haven't you made love to me in *months*, Mason? Does *Brandy* keep you that satisfied, that you can't even make love to your own *wife*?"

"I didn't know you wanted to."

"And why wouldn't I?"

"When you found out about the car, you were so upset, I was afraid to even approach you with sex."

She went to him, stroked his face gently, and announced softly, "I love you, Mason. I have always loved you." They met each other with a soft kiss.

Mason didn't want to make love to Becky, but he knew he had to do his husbandly duty to keep peace. He couldn't even get excited as they kissed hard and zealously. He thought of Brandy. He could smell the sweet aroma of her expensive perfume. He could feel her smooth, soft brown skin. He could...Oh, yes, thinking of Brandy brought on immediate excitement. He closed his eyes to feel her presence as he laid on the bed with his wife. She was unbuttoning his pajama top and he could see Brandy's sweet face, kissing him, teasing him, fondling him, and massaging him. He could... "Oh, Brandy," he whispered. Becky tensed up and froze under his body. Had he called Brandy's name out loud? He opened his eyes and focused on his wife's disappointed frown.

He had.

"Get off of me, Mason!" she demanded.

"I'm sorry," he breathed, rolling off her onto his back.

"I'm not *Brandy*, damn it!" she spat, jumping off the bed and pulling on a housecoat and he sat up, dropping his head. "I'm *Becky*! *Becky*! *Becky*!" she yelled in tears. "Your *wife*!" She started out the room, but Mason jumped up and caught her hand.

"Becky, I'm sorry. It's just that we were just talking about Brandy and...."

"Save it, Mason!" she insisted then stormed out in tears. Mason dropped on the bed and buried his head in his hands. He wondered what she would do next.

Chapter 24

"Good morning, Mrs. Joyner," Ron beamed, focusing on Toni, lying in his arms.

"Good morning," she responded cheerfully. They kissed lovingly. "What time does our plane leave for Jamaica?"

"Ten o'clock," he shared. "We have plenty of time."

"For what?"

"You figure it out, Mrs. Joyner," he whispered, rolling on her.

****

"Toni had a beautiful wedding, didn't she, Pete?" Juanita observed to Mr. Melton over breakfast.

"Yeah, my little girl is all grown up now," he answered.

"I wonder why Effie didn't come."

"Effie's a trip," he stated. "I never understood why she treated Toni the way she did. Those boys almost killed her, and Effie never opened her mouth."

"And you don't know why?"

"I've never been able to figure her out. She claims to be a Christian, but what kind of Christian would treat her only daughter so badly?"

"And Toni's such a sweet girl," she observed.

"Yes, she is."

"Maybe one day we'll know, honey."

"I hope so," he added. "I just hope her attitude doesn't bother Toni too much. She deserves to be happy. It was Effie who caused Toni to lose the baby, but she'd never admit it though."

"That's sad."

"Yes, it is," he pondered. "Maybe one day that woman will come to her senses. Toni does more for her mother than those boys ever even *thought* about doing, and *Toni's* the one she gives her butt to kiss."

****

"So, *this* is the mailroom," Mason smirked as he entered the crowded room where Brandy looked up from her desk and focused on him, looking so out of place in his expensive tailor-made dark suit, gold Rolex watch, and eight hundred-dollar shoes.

"What're you doing down here...*slumming*?" Brandy grinned. Other people spoke to Mason enthusiastically, with him replying politely as they continued their work.

"As I was opening my mail this morning, I thought of you," he replied sweetly.

"Come on," she suggested, leading him into a small room and closing the glass door.

"How've you been?" he asked, stroking her cheek lightly.

"I'm okay."

"Seeing anyone?"

"Why?"

"You know why," he whispered, staring deep into her eyes.

"No, I'm not," she responded, trying not to be hypnotized by his dreamy, brown eyes.

He lifted her chin with his finger and confessed softly, "I love you, Brandy. I hope you know that."

"I do, Mason," she confirmed, dropping her head.

Lifting her head with his finger again, Mason declared, "I'm sorry I hurt you. I never meant to. All I ever wanted to do was to take care of you."

"I can take care of myself."

"I know you can. You're a big girl, right?" he jovially mocked.

"That's right," she confirmed with attitude.

"I *know*," he cooed very seductively, and she had to smile. He grew serious again. "Brandy, I don't know if you can understand this or not, but I need to be there for my little girl. It's not that I'm choosing her over you, it's just that…"

"Yes, you are, Mason."

"What?"

"You *are* choosing your little girl over me," she added.

He blew hard then agreed, "I guess I am."

"Don't apologize for it," Brandy suggested and caught his attention. "You *should*. She's your daughter. You need to make any sacrifice that you can for her. Too many children grow up without fathers in the home, and it sometimes messes up their heads. I applaud you for choosing your daughter's happiness over your own. I *admire* you for that. When I was in foster care, I wished I had a father who cared enough about me to come and rescue me but that never happened."

"I'm sorry," he responded. Mason couldn't believe Brandy was so understanding. His love for her grew even more. He knew he had to do whatever it took to have her in his life.

Chapter 25

Although Toni's wedding was eight months behind her, she still found herself daydreaming about it often. She loved her husband so much. They hadn't been separated since their marriage…until *now*. She was on her way to a city near Columbia, South Carolina to interview some college girls about their date rape by the same guy. Nothing had been done to the rapist because he was a superstar athlete, and his daddy was the mayor in that city. She focused on Ron's picture on her cell phone as she sat back in first class to listen to the music through her headphones. Although she had only left a couple hours ago, she missed him already. Tyler came back and sat beside Toni, spotting the picture on her cell phone.

"Mrs. Melton-Joyner, he'll be there when you return," he stated, and she smiled slightly, taking off her headphones.

"I know," she agreed. "I just miss him."

"Love!" he spat as if it was a dirty word. "Who needs it?" Toni shoved him in laughter as Vickie walked to them.

"Hello, Miss Melton," she spoke sweetly.

Toni looked up at her, smiled, and started, "Hello…ah…"

"Vickie," the lady finished.

"Yes, Vickie. I'm sorry."

"It's okay. I don't expect you to remember flight attendants' names as famous as you are," Vickie replied with a little sarcasm in her tone, and Tyler's eyebrows raised a little, sensing the tension between the two women.

"Tyler, this is Vickie, an old friend of Ron's," Toni introduced. "Vickie, this is Tyler Woods, my friend and photographer."

"How do you do?" Tyler spoke politely.

"My pleasure, Mr. Woods," Vickie responded, forcing a smile. "And how is Ron these days, Toni?"

"He's great. Thank you for asking."

Focusing on the rings that adorned Toni's finger, Vickie added, "Oh, so it's *Mrs. Joyner* now?"

"Yes," Toni announced proudly, and Vickie felt her heart drop.

"I've been out of the country. When did that happen?" Vickie wanted to know.

"Eight months now," Toni answered.

"Congratulations," Vickie offered. "Tell Ron too, okay?"

"I'll do that."

"Well, I've got to serve. I'll see you soon," she replied, and then walked off quickly with a heavy heart. She knew she had lost Ron forever.

"Ooh, I enjoy a good cat fight!" Tyler squeaked.

"Tyler!" Toni exploded.

"So, I gather Miss Vickie was one of Ron's past flames?" Toni nodded. "And from the look on girlfriend's face, she's not quite over your husband, doll."

"Well, *he's* over *her*," she spat.

"I hear ya, girlfriend," he giggled. "But she *is* a looker. Girlfriend's got it going on!"

"Shut up, Tyler!" She shoved him and he burst into laughter.

****

"Mrs. Sanders, if you talk to me, I can promise you that nothing will go beyond these walls except for what *you* agree to expose," Ron explained, sitting on the couch with the woman in his office. Her sister had posted bail and was working hard to make Mrs. Sanders put up a fight. "Please, tell me something so I can defend you. Don't you want to raise your daughter?" She jerked her head to face him.

"My sister can raise Priscilla."

"She's thirteen years old. That's a critical age for girls. They *really* need their *mothers*. Don't *you* want to raise her?"

"We can't always have what we want, Mr. Joyner."

"Why won't you let me help you? Your sister believes in you. She is risking *everything* to save you."

Mrs. Sanders took a deep breath. "Mr. Joyner, if I tell you why I don't want you to defend me, will you let it go?"

"I can't promise that, but I do want to know what happened."

"You can't tell anyone unless I give you permission, right?"

"That's right."

"Even your partners?"

"*No one!*"

She cleared her throat then started, "I had a sorority meeting that morning, which I have every first Saturday of the month. Melvin was going fishing, and Priscilla was going to a neighbor's house to visit a friend." She paused and took a deep breath. "When I got to the meeting, I found out it was canceled because our president was in the hospital, so I went back home." She paused again as tears started swelling up in her eyes. "When I got home, I noticed that Melvin's car was still there." She closed her eyes to hold back her tears, but it wasn't working. They flowed anyway, and her voice cracked so much, she could barely speak. "I walked into our bedroom and he wasn't there. Priscilla likes loud music like all teenagers do, so I heard the music coming from her room, so I went to tell her to turn it down. I thought that maybe Melvin rode with someone else which he sometimes did." She paused again and Ron handed her some tissues from his coffee table. She dropped her head in her hands, and he could barely hear her because of her hysterical tears. "I heard Priscilla say, *you're hurting me. Please stop.*" She paused again to try to regain composure. "When I walked into my daughter's room, Melvin was...." She cried hard again. Ron pulled her in his arms. Then when she finally regained composure, she held off him and tried to continue. "His pants were down to his ankles and he was ... *raping* my little girl!" She burst into a roar of tears. Ron pulled her close again; she cried in his arms for quite a while. Beverly opened the door and he slowly waved her out. She silently pointed to the bank bag in her hand, and he knew she was going to run that errand, so he nodded, and she silently closed the door. After a while, Mrs. Sanders held off Ron. "I'm sorry," she apologized.

"There's nothing to be sorry for, Mrs. Sanders," he consoled her, fighting back his own tears, and handing her some more tissues.

She finally continued. "My daughter was lying helplessly on her bed with no clothes on. He was on top of her, robing her of her innocence. When I entered, he jumped up, pulled up his pants, and I looked at Priscilla and sad tears were rolling down her beautiful little face. She had a questioning look on her face, as to say, *Mom, why didn't you protect me*?" She paused again. "I went into our bedroom, and he followed me with a *pathetic* look on his face, saying nothing, just *staring* at me. I dropped on the bed, crying, and then, when he came near me, I lost it. I remembered the gun in the top drawer, and I opened it and fired. All I remember is my daughter screaming, and when I came back to reality, he was lying in a pool of blood, and the police were knocking on the door. I guess a neighbor heard the shots and called them."

"How many times did you shoot him?"

"I don't remember. The police report said five times," she sniffed. "All I know is that I wanted the son-of-a-bitch *dead*!"

****

"Hi, Angel," Mason spoke, entering Toni's office.

"Hi, Mason."

"When is Toni coming back?"

"In two days."

"That's a short trip."

"She's *married* now," Angel acknowledged.

"Yeah," he chuckled. "So, how is David?"

Her eyes widened because Mason had never asked about her husband. As a matter of fact, he had never asked her about *anything* concerning *her* life. Their conversations always *began* and *ended* with *Toni*. She looked up from her typing and answered, "Fine."

"Good," he responded. "And the boys?"

"Great."

"Why are you surprised?"

"You've never asked me about my family."

"Then I'm sorry. I should have," he declared. "Family is important."

"And…we're…*not*…talking about *me* anymore," she recognized hesitantly. He laughed slightly and she added, "How is Brandy?"

His eyebrows raised slightly as he answered, "Okay, I guess."

"So, you're trying to decide if Brandy is worth breaking up your home," Angel stated more like a statement than a question.

"I can't leave my little girl."

"But you *are* in love with Brandy?" she probed, and he nodded. She smiled and took a deep breath. "You don't love Becky anymore?"

"I've *never* loved Becky," he admitted, sitting in the chair in front of her desk. "Becky tricked me into marrying her. I thought she was pregnant, but she wasn't."

"Mason, I might not be the best person to discuss this with," Angel made known. "A little over a year ago, David had an affair." He looked surprised. "I was devastated. I couldn't even come to work."

"I remember. That was during the time that Toni was in Texas, right?"

"Yes."

"How did David and you patch things up?"

"He quit seeing the lady, but since she worked for him, he had to pay her a salary for six months."

"How did you feel about that?"

"It made me mad as hell, but I knew that was the only way he could get rid of her, so I accepted it."

"But your situation was different from mine. *David* loves you. *I* don't love Becky."

"Yeah, it was a little different," Angel concurred. "But Becky is *still* your *wife*, and until you end your marriage, you have no rights to Brandy." That wasn't what Mason wanted to hear. To be honest, he didn't know *what* he wanted to hear, but he knew *that* wasn't it! More importantly, he knew he had a decision to make. He couldn't go on like this. He was letting the love of his life get away. He didn't know what to do.

****

"Mrs. Sanders, you have a very strong defense if you acknowledge what happened to your daughter."

"I will *not* put my daughter through that," she insisted. "She would be embarrassed, and people would make her feel like it was *her* fault. I can't do that to her. I'd rather die!"

"But I think you could get a jury to understand why you did what you did. You really were temporarily insane."

"I *knew* exactly what I was doing, Mr. Joyner. I told you that I wanted the son-of-a-bitch dead, so I killed him!" She paused then added weakly. "I have no defense."

"But you said you didn't remember anything until your daughter screamed, and the police were at your door. That's temporarily insane."

"But I'm not going to put my daughter through that. She would have to testify, and I will *not* do that to her! She's been through enough!" she insisted. "There's no need to talk. My decision is final!"

"But you could get the *death* penalty."

"So be it."

Ron took a deep breath. This woman had a strong case for murdering her husband and she chose not to use it. "I don't agree with your decision, Mrs. Sanders, but I do respect your right to make it."

"Thank you, Mr. Joyner. So, this conversation will end here?"

"Yes, ma'am, it will," he concurred then smiled at her. "You are a brave woman."

She took a breath then countered, "I feel like a coward."

"No *coward* would make the kind of sacrifice you're making for your daughter," he proclaimed then took a long and concentrated breath. "Mrs. Sanders, I beg you to reconsider."

****

"We were at a party. I was with Lacie and Debra," the young girl spoke with tears rolling down her face as Toni listened attentively while Tyler silently took pictures. "Logan asked me to dance and then he just seemed to stay around me the rest of the evening. I felt special because he's such a popular boy on campus. Everybody is speculating that he will be drafted by the NBA." She paused again and Toni handed her a tissue from the table in the kitchen of the small dormitory.

"Would you like to take a break, Kellie?" she asked softly, and the girl shook her head.

"I need to get this over," she squeezed out in between tears. Toni nodded. "Later when the party was over, Logan asked me if I wanted to go back to his dorm for a nightcap. I didn't think anything was wrong with it because I trusted him. His father is the mayor for Christ's sakes!" She blew her nose. "But he noticed my apprehension, so he said that the others were coming too. By then, Debra and Lacie were both talking to some of Logan's friends as well." She paused again to take a much-needed breath. "So, I said okay. When we got there, no one was there but Logan and me. He said the others were on their way. Then he started coming on rather strong...*really* strong! I told him I wasn't that kind of girl, and he laughed. He said, *All you bitches are that kind of girl!* I was so shocked, I told him I was leaving, but he grabbed me and threw me on the floor. He said no girl ...." She was crying so hard she could scarcely talk, but she pressed on anyway, "He said no girl turns him down. Then he ripped my panties off, and the next thing I knew he...he *raped* me. I screamed for him to stop but he wouldn't." Toni took the girl's hand and squeezed it lovingly, but that didn't soothe her much, so she moved closer to the weeping girl and pulled her in her arms, holding her tight. She focused on Tyler and slightly shook her head. He stopped taking pictures.

****

"Hello, Mr. Wheeler," Simon welcomed, extending a hand to the average height man that just entered his office.

"Hello, Mr. Kennedy."

"Please, have a seat."

"Thank you," the man accepted, taking a seat in front of his desk as Simon sat behind it.

"Now, why don't you tell me why you're here?"

"My brother is accused of robbing a convenient store clerk at gunpoint," he started. "He was at the store about the time that she was closing, and they fingered him."

"What did the store clerk say?"

"She couldn't see his face. He wore a ski mask. Some homeless people saw it."

"And they said it was your brother?"

"Yes."

"Was it?"

"Excuse me?"

"Did your brother do it? Did he rob the woman?"

"No," the man replied.

"Did he *say* he didn't, or do *you* know for a *fact* he didn't?"

"He *said* he didn't. I mean, I wasn't with him or anything, but I believe him."

"Why do you believe him? Is he an honest person?"

"He's my *brother*. Family's got to stick together," the man articulated. "Will you take the case?"

"I don't know. Has your brother ever been in trouble before?"

"Minor stuff?"

"Like what?"

"Not paying child support, traffic tickets, and stuff like that."

"No armed robberies?"

"No."

Simon took a deep breath. This case didn't sound right to him. He was tired of defending criminals, and since falling in love with Melissa, he decided he wasn't going to do that anymore. "I need to talk to your brother and the witnesses before I make up my mind," Simon made known.

"I have the money if that's what you're worried about," the man spoke up quickly.

"No, that's not my main concern."

"But my brother needs you. I heard you were the best, and you never cared if a man was guilty or not!"

"So, Mr. Wheeler, are you telling me that your brother *is* guilty?"

The man took a deep breath, then answered softly, "He might be. I don't know."

Simon closed his pad and stood as he announced, "I won't be taking the case, Mr. Wheeler."

"But why?" The man jumped to his feet.

"I don't defend *guilty* people anymore," Simon stated, and it felt good.

****

"Were you drinking at the party?" Toni asked Kellie.

"No, I don't drink. I only had soda."

"What does the DA say about your case?"

"They won't touch it because of Logan's father."

"And the college? Have you told the Dean?"

She chuckled, "Yes, and it was pathetic. I left his office feeling like the biggest slut this side of the Mason Dixie."

"So, he didn't believe you?"

"That's putting it mildly."

"Are there other boys here at the school you've been intimate with?"

The girl took a deep breath then surprised Toni with, "Mrs. Melton-Joyner, before that night, I was a virgin!" She took a deep breath and exhaled slowly.

"I'm sorry," Toni apologized. "I had to ask."

"I know," the girl understood.

"What about the other girls who were raped by Logan?"

"They won't come forward. They're afraid."

"Of what?"

"Getting the same treatment as I have," she replied. "The boys on the basketball team are harassing me, threatening me, and I can't return to school next semester."

"They put you out?!" Toni exploded.

"Yes, and that was the last straw. My parents are working on getting me a lawyer out of state; someone that won't be afraid of these people. Then my mom told me to call you. She loves your column and she felt you could help."

Toni looked at Tyler with a turned-up mouth and squinted eyes, slightly shaking her head. Tyler knew that look. This was more than an interview now. It was *war!* Toni was furious! "Give me the names of the other girls Logan raped."

"They won't talk."

"Oh, they'll talk!" Toni insisted. "I promise you that! *They will talk!*"

****

Ron sat in his dark office staring into space when Beverly opened the door. "Hi," he responded softly.

"Hi," she replied. "What's going on?" She flicked on the lights and sat in the chair in front of his desk. "Thinking about your wife?"

"Not this time," he chuckled, sitting up straight. "I was thinking about Mrs. Sanders."

"How is the case going?"

"It *isn't!*"

"What'd you mean?"

"How do you *defend* a person who doesn't *want* a *defense?*" he contemplated, and Beverly hunched her shoulders. "Neither do I."

"Why doesn't she want a defense?"

"Personal reasons! *Very* personal reasons."

"But you can't talk about it, right?"

"Right," he concurred. "I'm sorry."

"It's okay," she understood. "But you still want to defend her against her will."

"Yes, the woman doesn't deserve to go to prison for the rest of her life, or worse, but how do I make her see it?"

****

"Good morning, Mrs. Melton-Joyner."

"Don't good morning me, Dr. Brumble!" Toni charged into the Dean's office, followed by Tyler. "I want to know why Logan Kaplansky is still being treated like a superstar after raping at least three girls, while his victims are too afraid to speak because they will get thrown out of this school?"

"We know nothing about Logan raping three girls."

"I have three taped interviews with three different girls who claimed that Logan Kaplansky raped them. Kellie Canty reported her rape and was treated like trash!"

"She *is* trash as far as I'm concerned," the Dean defended. "There are a number of boys who can validate being with Kellie." Toni just stared at the man in total disgust. "I don't know what she told you, but Kellie has been around the block a few times, if you know what I mean." He chuckled and Toni wanted to slap his face. "So, Mrs. Melton-Joyner, you can pack up your little interview and leave now. This institution is prepared to sue you *and* your magazine if you print *anything* you can't prove!"

****

Mason and Amy walked the halls of the mall while she skipped ahead of him into another department store. "Come on, Daddy," she called as he followed her, carrying a lot of packages.

"I'm coming, sweetheart. You're wearing your old man out," he laughed. Amy was very patient when her daddy had to stop several times to sign autographs, so he felt he could be patient with her also.

She headed for the toy department while he followed behind her. "Amy," he called. "Don't go so fast."

"Okay, Daddy," she answered, stopping, and browsing as he tried to keep up with her. Suddenly, Mason looked in another direction and he spotted Brandy at the perfume counter. His heart seemed to skip a beat as he watched her. She looked so elegant in that straight, knee-length, body-fitting, silk, rust-colored dress. Brandy looked up and focused on him staring at her and she smiled sweetly. Her heart seemed to beat in double-time as she stared at the love of her life, looking so tall, successful, and distinguished in his khaki pants and brown polo shirt. She walked to him slowly. Her hair flowed loosely to her shoulders and Mason had to take a deep breath. She looked like one of those models on television, strolling gracefully down a runway.

"Hi," she finally spoke, standing before him.

"Hi," he responded.

"I didn't know you were a fan of the mall."

"I'm not," he shared. "The things we do for our children." He indicated Amy playing with toys and Brandy spotted the enthusiastic child.

"She looks very happy."

"She *should* be. She's spending all my money," Mason chuckled, indicating the many packages in his hand. Brandy laughed with him.

He grew serious and asked, "How are you?"

"I'm fine. Thank you," she answered. "And you?"

"Not that good but I'm coping," he confirmed, as Amy ran to them. The child stopped and focused on Brandy. "Amy, this is Brandy Sears, a co-worker of mine. Brandy, this is my little girl, Amy."

"Hello, Amy," Brandy addressed, bending down at eye level with the child.

"Hi," Amy responded, smiling sweetly. "You're pretty."

"Thank you," she accepted. "You're very pretty too."

"Were you *Miss Greenleaf* one year?" Amy asked, and Brandy's smile widened.

"Yes, I was. How did you know?" Brandy answered and Mason's eyes stretched. He had no idea that she was once a beauty queen.

"I saw your picture in a souvenir booklet that my friend gave me. Her big sister was in that pageant," Amy explained. "She said you were the first African American to win *Miss Greenleaf.*"

"Yes, I was," Brandy verified. "It's a small world, isn't it?"

"I knew you were beautiful, Brandy, but I had no idea you were a beauty queen," admired Mason.

"Yes, I was Miss Greenleaf once," she answered proudly. "It seems so long ago."

"And you work with my daddy?" Amy confirmed.

"Yes, I do," Brandy answered.

"If I get my daddy to bring my pageant booklet to work, will you autograph it for me?"

"I'll be happy to," Brandy agreed.

"Cool," Amy finalized, still smiling wide.

As Brandy continued to talk to Amy about her school, and Amy showing her the toys she was playing with, Mason's heart filled with joy. It was nice seeing the two people he loved most in this world communicating as if they were old friends. Brandy finally stood and focused on Mason while Amy ran back to the toys.

"Well, I better get going," she announced.

"It was nice seeing you."

"Thank you," she acknowledged. "You know where to find me if you want to see me." He nodded slowly, and she added, laughing, "Knee-deep in mail." He laughed with her. Mason didn't know how he would manage it, but he had to have Brandy. After all, he deserved to be happy.

****

"Did you talk to her?" a lady inquired over the telephone in her spacious, immaculate kitchen of her ten-thousand-square-feet, luxurious mansion.

"Yes, Mrs. Whittington," Ron responded, sitting at his desk in his office. "She refuses to put up a defense."

"What is *wrong* with my sister? Doesn't she know she could get the *death* penalty?" Charlotte Whittington snapped. She had married a rich, white television producer.

"She doesn't care."

"Did she tell you why?"

"I can't discuss anything with you that I talked about with your sister, Mrs. Whittington. I'm sorry."

"I understand. I respect that," she finalized. "I guess I've got to talk to her some more."

"Please do that," Ron advised.

****

"I don't print *anything* I can't prove!" Toni retorted to the dean. "So, don't you *dare* threaten me!" Dr. Brumble was surprised at her professionalism. He admired her, but he was not going to let her bully him just because she was famous.

"You have nothing but Kellie's word against Logan's. I don't call that *proof*," he went on.

Toni reached into her bag and retrieved some papers. "I have more than that, Dr. Brumble." She looked over the papers. "I have a sworn statement from Kellie's doctor, stating that when he examined her the day of the rape that she was still a virgin. I have a statement from the attending physician when she was admitted to the hospital after the rape that without a *shadow* of a doubt, in his *professional* opinion, Kellie *had* been sexually assaulted." She paused and focused on the speechless man. "Kellie's grade point average is a 3.95 on a 4.0 scale. What do *you* have to justify her dismissal from this institution?"

****

"Who was the pretty woman Amy and you talked to today?" Becky asked Mason as she entered their bedroom in an olive-green, silk nightgown, where he sat in bed working on his laptop.

"What?"

"Amy said a pretty woman, the former *Miss Greenleaf* talked to her today. She wants her autograph. Who was she?" she wanted to know, and he took a breath. "Brandy?"

"Yes," he admitted, and she exhaled deeply.

"Are you still seeing her?"

"No," he blurted out. "I didn't know she was going to be at the mall! It *is* a public place!"

"But you just *had* to introduce our *daughter* to her?"

"What was I supposed to do, *ignore* her?"

"Yes."

"That's silly," he defended. "What Brandy and I had is over. Why can't you let it go? We all live in this town together. We're going to bump into one another from time to time. Just let it go, Becky!"

"How can I let it go, Mason, when *you* haven't?!"

****

"Hello," Ron answered the cordless telephone, lying on the king-sized bed in his pajama bottom and bare chest.

"You have a collect call from a lonely wife to her incredibly sexy husband," Toni cooed on the other end, lying on the bed in the hotel room in a short, pink night shirt, and he smiled.

"Put her through please," he played along.

"Hi, baby."

"Hi, sweetie," he responded softly with a big smile on his face. "How are you?"

"Lonely. Missing you."

"Me too," he agreed. "Are you finished there?"

"Yes, I'll be leaving out of here in the morning."

"I can't wait to see you."

"Same here," she acknowledged. "So, you miss me?"

"Umm, I didn't know I could miss *anyone* this much."

"I like the sound of that."

"What, me *suffering*?" he laughed.

"No. You *missing* me," she snickered.

Adjusting his body to ease the pressure in his pajamas, he chuckled, "Oh, I *miss* you, Mrs. Joyner." She laughed again.

"So, other than *missing* me, how are you?"

"I'm okay, I guess. This case I'm handling is kind of tricky."

"What'd you mean?"

"Mrs. *Press Woman*, you know I can't discuss my case with you."

She chuckled, "*That* again?"

"Yes, *that* again."

"But I'm your *wife* now."

"Baby, the law didn't change when we got married," he insisted.

"All right, Counselor," she accepted. "Well, my case is heart wrenching."

"Did you dig up all the dirt?"

"Oh yeah," she confirmed. "Now, I've just got to wait and see where it lands." Her phone clicked. "Honey, hold on. I have a call coming in." She clicked over. "Hello, Toni Melton-Joyner."

"Mrs. Melton-Joyner, Mayor Kaplansky here."

"How do you do, Mayor?"

"Very well, thank you," he replied. "Mrs. Melton-Joyner, I'm sure you know why I'm calling. I would like to talk to you about the situation at the college."

"I'm leaving in the morning, Mayor," she made known. "I tried to schedule an interview with your son earlier, but he wasn't available."

"He's here at home," he revealed. "Could you come out to my house tonight? I know it's probably an inconvenience, but I would really appreciate it."

"Sure, Mayor, I'll be glad to come. What time?"

"How soon could you get here?"

"I could be ready to leave here in about ten minutes, but I don't know how long it will take me to get to your home."

"It'll take you about fifteen minutes to get here from where you are," he explained. "Would you like for me to send a car for you?"

"That won't be necessary. I have a driver. Thank you."

"All right, Mrs. Melton-Joyner, I'll see you in about thirty minutes."

"Yes, sir," she finalized then clicked the phone back over. "Ron, are you still there?"

"You better not be making a date, Mrs. Joyner," he joked.

"As a matter of fact, I was. I'm off to see the Mayor."

"Okay, honey. I'll see you tomorrow."

"I'll get in about three."

"Okay. Love you."

"Love you, too," she concluded then kissed at him through the telephone. When Toni hung up, she dialed another number.

****

Tyler lay outstretched on the king-sized bed, watching an athletic-toned man emerge from his bathroom, wrapped only in a towel. He gasped at the well-built man as the telephone rang. He almost didn't answer it as the man dropped the towel exposing a lean, chiseled frame. Tyler took a big breath then yanked the phone up. "Toni, this better be good!" he snapped.

"How did you know it was me?" she laughed.

"Who the hell else could it be?"

"Tyler, get dressed. We're going to see the Mayor."

"Now?!" he almost screamed.

"Yes, *now*."

"Toni, you're killing me!" Tyler shrieked as the man joined him on the bed.

"Sorry," Toni chuckled. "I'll make it up to you."

"I don't think so, Toni," he nonchalantly replied with a little sarcasm.

"Meet me downstairs in ten minutes. I already called the driver."

****

"Daddy, I need batteries for my doll house," Amy whined, entering the family room where Mason and Becky sat watching the television set.

"Honey, it's time for you to go to bed," Becky announced, getting up.

Picking her up on his lap, he suggested, "Daddy will go and get some batteries so you can have them first thing in the morning, okay?" She nodded then he planted a kiss on her forehead. "Good night, Princess."

"Good night, Daddy," she responded, jumping down, and taking Becky's hand, as Mason stood.

"You're going out *now*?" Becky asked him.

"Yes, so she'll have the batteries in the morning."

"Can't you get them in the morning?"

"Honey, you know Amy gets up long before we do on weekends," he explained. "I'll be right back."

****

Toni and Tyler exited the limousine and walked up to the elaborate, twenty-thousand-square-feet mansion. Toni's red silk blouse was tucked securely into her black slacks, accented by a black belt and black heels. Tyler's tan loosely hanging, button-down shirt draped over his brown slacks on top of brown loafers. The door opened immediately and a woman in a maid's uniform showed them into the Mayor's study where he stood to greet them with two other men in suits also present. "How do you do, Mrs. Melton-Joyner?" the Mayor welcomed, extending a hand to Toni. "Thank you for coming at such short notice."

Shaking his hand, Toni acknowledged, "My pleasure, Mayor Kaplansky." Then she focused on Tyler. "My assistant and photographer, Mr. Tyler Woods." The two men shook hands.

The Mayor introduced the two other suited men. "My lawyer, Mr. George Tanner and my assistant, Mr. Tyrone Black." The greetings were extended by all, then they sat, Toni in the chair in front of the Mayor's desk, the mayor behind his desk, the two men stood back on opposite sides of the mayor's desk, and Tyler stood near the door.

"Mrs. Melton-Joyner, we have a very delicate situation here," the Mayor began. "My son is accused of raping this Kellie girl, and he swears she's lying. Now, I'm interested in settling this thing because I don't want an article in *Toni Talk* to ruin my son's college career *and* his future."

"With all due respect, sir, your son ruined *himself* when he decided to take pleasure in degrading young women by violating their bodies," Toni reasoned.

"It's *her* word against *his*," Mayor Kaplansky defended.

"No, sir, it's *their* words against *his*," she shared. "I have the doctor's interview who examined Kellie after the rape, and I'm wondering why your son wasn't charged immediately!"

"The doctor can't be one-hundred-percent sure she was raped. All he has to go on is the girl's words," Mayor Kaplansky insisted, growing annoyed with her. "From what I hear, the girl wasn't as innocent as you claim. My son has friends who can testify to that."

Toni chuckled slightly then stared the man straight in the face and added, "Mayor Kaplansky, before the night that your son so brutally violated that young girl's body, Kellie Canty was a virgin!" Mayor Kaplansky's mouth dropped open.

"You can't be serious," he finally spoke, finding his voice.

"Oh, but I am. Kellie Canty wanted to run track and had to have a physical done. She was examined by a doctor the day of the rape. That doctor will testify that she was a virgin that afternoon." Toni concluded smugly, and she could see the anger building up in the Mayor's red face.

"Go and get Logan!" he ordered to his assistant between clenched teeth.

"He's asleep, sir," the man shared.

"I don't give a damn!" the Mayor yelled. "Get his ass *up* and bring him here! *Now!*"

****

Mason sat in his silver Cadillac Escalade in front of Brandy's house. Her house was dark, so he knew she was probably in bed already. He wanted so badly to see her. He noticed nine thirty on his Rolex. He emerged from his car slowly, and with his key, which she never asked for back, he let himself into her house. Mason tipped slowly into Brandy's bedroom and spotted her asleep in the queen-sized bed. She looked so peaceful, innocent, and delectable lying there. He took his sports coat off and laid it on the chair in her room and walked to her bed. He sat on the bed and she slowly opened her eyes. "Mason!" she gasped.

"Hi," he whispered.

"What're you doing here?"

"I wanted to see you," he revealed, as she sat up a little. Then before she could say another word, he was pressing his lips against hers. She tasted so sweet he couldn't believe how much he'd

262

missed her. He undressed quickly as they kissed passionately. Then he pulled her nightgown off over her head and rolled on her. She received him lovingly with small gasps of desiring breaths. Mason felt like his whole world was perfect as he made love to the woman he loved. She was so sweet and so giving.

Brandy had dreamed of this night for a long time. If she was dreaming, she didn't want to wake up. Then soon their breathing escalated as they exploded into a riveting exchange of love together. He kissed her lips again and slid down on her to relieve her of his weight and rested his head in her abdomen. She rubbed his soft hair lovingly as their breathing returned to normal.

****

"Kellie Canty was a *virgin!*" Mayor Kaplansky snapped to his sleepy son, standing there in black silk pajamas and a matching robe. "Now, you tell me the truth, and you tell me *now!*" The tall, blonde-headed young man burst into soft sobs.

"She wanted it, Dad. She did," he whimpered.

"She was a *virgin,* you moron!" Mayor Kaplansky yelled, losing all patience with his son. "How could you be so stupid as to *rape* a *virgin?!*"

"I didn't know she was a virgin until..." he stopped and cried, and then Mayor Kaplansky turned back to Toni.

"Mrs. Melton-Joyner, I really didn't know. I *believed* my son when he told me he didn't do this."

"I understand."

"What can we do to rectify this situation? Your column could destroy him."

"Mayor, I'm sorry, but my loyalty at this point is to Kellie Canty. She is the one who called me."

"I could make it worth your while if you'd help us."

"I'm sorry, but I print the truth. I can't be bought."

"I'm not asking you to lie. All I'm asking for is a little empathy where my son is concerned."

"Is he willing to give me an interview?"

"Yes, I can assure you."

"Then all I can do is write it," she made known. "Kellie has gone through a lot since she made her claims against your son. His teammates have harassed her. She has been thrown out of school. She is a nervous wreck, and not just her, but I have testimony of two other girls whom your son raped."

"I understand," Mayor Kaplansky replied. "I will see to it that my son gets the help he needs, and the girls get the help they need, both financially and emotionally."

Toni took a breath then added, "Then Logan will soon forget this, but those *girls* will *remember* what he did to them for the *rest* of their lives."

****

Mason exhaled deeply then announced, "I have to get home, baby."

"I know," Brandy understood, and then he planted a kiss on her lips, rolled out of bed, and started exiting the bedroom. He looked back at her, and she had dropped her head, so he walked back to her and sat on the bed again.

"Do you have any idea how much I love you?" he inquired, lifting her chin with his finger.

"Do you, Mason?"

"Yes, I do."

"That's good to know," she accepted, and he planted a tender kiss on her lips. "I can't continue to do this, Mason."

"I know."

"It hurts too much when you leave."

"It hurts me too, Brandy. More than you know," he confessed. "But I just couldn't stay away tonight." He looked into her eyes. "Are you sorry I came?"

"No," she confirmed. "Not at all. I just hate to see you leave."

"I'm sorry," he consoled, then pulled her in his arms and took a deep, frustrated breath. Mason was torn between two worlds, and he didn't know how much more of it he could take without being pulled apart altogether and never recovering.

Chapter 26

Toni entered their house and focused on Ron, standing there all smiles. "Ron!" she exploded. "What're you doing here? I thought you would be at work."

"I missed you."

"And you left work early just to see *me*?"

"Of course," he confirmed then walked to her and kissed her lovingly. "Welcome home, Mrs. Joyner."

"Thank you," she cooed between kisses as he started unbuttoning her blouse.

****

Mason entered Toni's office and focused on Angel who was typing. "Toni isn't back?" he asked.

Looking at the clock, Angel answered, "She should be back in town by now, but she's not coming in today. She'll be here in the morning. Is there anything I can help you with, Mason?"

"No, I just wanted to see if she knew anything about the Sanders' case her husband is handling," Mason shared. "Bill wants me to cover it."

"You're not going to let Toni do another interview for you, are you?" she chuckled.

"After the Sanchez case? Are you kidding?!" he laughed. "I just want to see what she knows about it."

"Probably *nothing* if she has to depend on Ron for the info."

"I guess you're right," he agreed as Brandy entered. "Hi," he spoke to her sweetly.

"Hi," she acknowledged, smiling shyly then focused on Angel. "Here's Toni's mail, Angel."

"Thank you, Brandy," Angel accepted, taking it, and standing. "I'll put it on her desk, so she can get it first thing in the morning." She left them alone when she exited into Toni's office.

"Did you get into trouble last night when you returned home?"

"I *stay* in trouble with Becky," he laughed. "So, what else is new?"

She laughed with him and revealed, "I enjoyed last night."

"So did I," he concurred, touching her face then changing the subject. "You need an alarm system in your house."

"An alarm system?!" she blurted out.

"Yes, I walked right in and you didn't hear me until I was right up on you."

"That's because you had a *key*!" she stressed. "My neighborhood is pretty safe."

"I'm still calling an alarm company today."

"You're too good to me."

"I wish I could do more," he sobered, looking deep into her eyes, and Angel returned, breaking the trance between them.

****

"Wow, that's what I call a real welcome home," Toni breathed, snuggling up close in Ron's arms.

"Want something to eat?" he asked.

"I'm too tired to eat," she chuckled, and he planted a kiss on her moist forehead.

"So, how did your visit go with the Mayor?"

"Actually, very well," she responded, sitting up in bed, facing him as he propped his head on a pillow to listen. "Logan Kaplansky admitted that he raped the girls. His father is going to get help for him and the girls."

"That's wonderful, honey," Ron beamed. "I'm proud of you."

"Thank you."

"So, that gives your story a whole new angle, right?"

"Yes, but as I told Mayor Kaplansky, I still have to print the truth, just in case the DA decides not to press charges against Logan again."

"It seems he doesn't have a *choice* with Logan's confession."

"You would think so," she pondered. "What about your case? How is it going?"

"Slow."

"So, did she tell you why she iced him?"

"Iced him?!" Ron burst into laughter. "You've been looking at too many cop shows on television, baby."

"Well, did she?" Toni wanted to know.

"I can't tell you," he responded.

"Ron, you can tell me *that!*" she exploded.

"No, I can't. I can't tell you *anything* my client and I talked about. I told you that, sweetie."

"What if I guess?"

"I'm not listening, Toni," he insisted, sliding down, and turning his back to her.

"Well, I've been thinking about this," Toni continued anyway as Ron ignored her. "Ron!" She rolled him back over by his shoulders.

"Toni, I can't discuss this with you."

"Then, I'll do the talking."

"I can't tell you if you're right or not."

"The way I figure it...," she started, and Ron just shook his head. "The only thing that would make a woman mad enough to kill her husband is...."

"Maybe she wouldn't quit nagging him," he laughed.

Toni laughed but continued, "Anyway, Mr. Joyner, before I was so rudely interrupted. She has a thirteen-year-old daughter, right?" Ron didn't answer. He just stared blankly at her. "Ron, you can answer that. It was in the newspapers already."

"Then, you don't need for me to answer, do you?" he replied sarcastically, and Toni punched his arm. "Ouch. Husband abuse! You women are lethal!" He burst into laughter and she followed.

"Anyway, I know she has a thirteen-year-old daughter by the newspaper articles," Toni continued. "The only thing that would make a woman mad enough to kill her husband and have no remorse is if he was...*molesting* her daughter." She looked for signs in his expression to tell her more but saw nothing. He maintained a stone face although it was hard for him. Ron couldn't believe how perceptive his wife was. "Am I right?"

"Are you?" he remarked, and Toni went on.

"But why would she not want a defense," she pondered. "Of course. She doesn't want her daughter to testify. She is old enough." She focused on him. "Am I right?" Ron held up and kissed her lips.

"No more talking," he pulled her down on him.

"Ron," she whined.

"Um hum," he cooed.

"Are you gonna tell me?"

"Tell you what?" he purred, nibbling on her ear.

"If I'm right," she pouted, being swept away by his gentle touch. He silenced her with a long, sweet kiss as he rolled over on her, and she finally let the conversation go as her husband brought her to another steaming climax.

"You fight dirty, Counselor," she breathed in his ear, clinging to his warm, moist body, to receive every drop of love he had to give.

Part Four

Four Months Later

Chapter 27

"Ron, Mr. Schuster wants to see you right away," Beverly announced as he entered the office, coming from lunch.

"All right," he answered, turning around to exit the office again.

Ron walked down the long corridor to John Schuster's office. His pregnant secretary said, "Hi, Ron."

"Hi, Katie. When are you due?"

"In three months," she glowingly returned. "Go on in. They're waiting for you."

"Thanks," he acknowledged, then entered the office and came face to face with the stone faces of John Schuster, Blake Collins, and Phillip Ballentine, sitting at the conference room table. "What's up, gentlemen?"

"Sit down, Ron," John spoke first. Ron sat slowly as he observed the solemn atmosphere.

"What's going on, John?" he wanted to know.

"Ron, have you read your wife's column today?" Phillip asked.

"No, not yet," he answered. "The magazine didn't come out until noon, which was an hour ago, and Toni usually brings one home. Why?"

"I think you need to take a look," Blake added, handing Ron a copy of *The Weekly Herald*.

Ron focused on the men hard, and then slowly dropped his head to find Toni's article. As he read silently, his eyes widen. Then he looked up at them. "I don't understand," he shared softly. "I never told Toni *any* of this."

"She named *you* as her informer," Blake charged.

"It's not true," he defended.

"Then why would she name you?" Phillip wanted to know.

"I have no idea."

"So, you *never* told your wife anything about the Sanders' case?" inquired Blake.

"No, of course not."

"Then why would she say you did?" asked Phillip.

"I told you, I don't know."

"Ron, we're trying to understand," John added. "Please give us something to go on here. We're scheduled to make you a partner next week."

"I don't know what to tell you, John. I never discussed *this* case or *any* other case with Toni," Ron defended. The three men looked at each other.

"Ron, Priscilla Sanders tried to commit suicide five minutes after this article was published," John spoke up, and Ron's eyes widened. "A few minutes after that we received a call from Mrs. Whittington. She's filing a multimillion-dollar lawsuit against this firm and you. She is also filing a case against you to have you disbarred."

"But I didn't tell Toni any of this," he repeated weakly.

"Who's going to believe you? She's your *wife!*" Blake commented. Ron didn't have an answer for the man. "Ron, as much as we hate to do it, we have no other choice but to suspend you, without pay, until this mess is cleared up."

"Whatever happened to innocent until proven guilty?" Ron sarcastically inquired.

"We're sorry, Ron," added Phillip. "Mrs. Whittington is terribly upset. If you're not here, then maybe we can get her to back down."

"From the *firm*, not *me*?" Ron asked dryly and they remained silent. "So, I'm alone here." They still didn't answer, so he stood. "Thanks, gentlemen, for your *support*." He turned and walked out, leaving the magazine on a table.

****

"Brandy, is Bill here?" Toni asked, exiting her office with a copy of the new addition of *The Weekly Herald* under her arm.

"He didn't come in today, Toni," Brandy shared.

"I'm going home. I don't feel well."

"Okay," Brandy acknowledged. "Oh, Angel called a few minutes ago. She said for you to call her."

"She's back from her vacation?"

"She didn't say. She said to call her on her cell."

"I'll call her later. I need some rest. I think I'm coming down with a cold or flu or something," Toni remarked. "See you tomorrow."

"Okay, Toni."

Toni walked out of her office, and a lady admired, "Gutsy article, Toni."

"Thank you," she accepted.

"Your article was brave, Toni. Won't he be mad?" another lady added.

"I can't worry about that," she announced, not breaking her stride.

"Toni, some television news reporters are here to see you," another lady spoke.

"Television?" She stopped then took a deep breath. "It's probably about the article. I don't feel like talking to anyone today. I'm going out the back way."

"Okay," she confirmed, then Toni continued to walk. "Have a good day."

"Thanks," Toni accepted, feeling good that everyone loved her article. She hadn't read it yet, but she knew what it was about, and that pleased her. She always brought home a copy to share with Ron. It felt good to be appreciated.

****

"Beverly, where is Ron?" Travis asked.

"He went to Mr. Schuster's office," Beverly answered.

"He left there a while ago," he responded. "They suspended him."

"What?!" she exploded to her feet. "They *suspended* him?! But he's making partner next week!"

"Not anymore."

"But why?"

"Have you read Toni's column today?"

"Not yet. Why?"

"She named *Ron* as her informer to the Sanders' case."

"Ron wouldn't do that!"

"Then why would she say he did?"

"I don't know, but there's something definitely not right about this, Travis," Beverly theorized. "I better call Ron."

****

Ron sat in the dark, family room, hearing the telephone ring, but ignoring it. He couldn't believe Toni could deliberately set out to destroy him like this. Soon he heard the door open, and she turned on the light and jumped. "Ron, you scared me. What're you doing sitting in the dark?" She dropped the magazine, her work bag, and her purse on the table. She realized Ron hadn't answered her, so she turned and focused on him. "Ron, what's wrong? Are you sick, honey?" She walked to him and sat on the couch beside him. She reached to touch his forehead, but he jerked back, and stood. "What's going on?"

"How could you have done something like this, Toni?"

"Done what, Ron?"

"You *know* what!" he snapped. "How could you have ruined me like this?"

"*Ruined* you?" she pondered. "Ron, what are you talking about?"

"You know what I'm talking about!" he insisted. "Does winning a Pulitzer mean that much to you?"

"Ron…"

"I have lost my job! I am facing a multimillion-dollar lawsuit! I am probably going to be disbarred!" he raged but still remained even-tempered. "*Everything* I've worked all my life to accomplish is *gone*! You are my *wife*! How could you have ruined me like this?!"

"You lost your job?" she asked, puzzled.

"What did you *think* would happen?" he retorted then threw up his hands. "I've got to get out of here!"

"Ron, where are you going?"

"Anywhere! Away from *you*!" he snapped. He turned to leave, and she jumped to him, grabbing his arm.

"Ron, baby, please…"

Jerking away, he snarled, "Don't, Toni!" He turned and exited quickly.

"Ron!" she yelled after him, running to the open door, but he didn't stop. "Ron!" Toni took a deep breath then walked back into the huge, three-story, brick house and closed the sturdy, wooden, double doors. She focused on a news magazine laying on the table and picked it up. She shuffled through the pages quickly. She stopped suddenly and began reading. Shock overtook her and she gasped, covering her mouth. "Oh, my God!" She couldn't believe it, so she read it again, this time aloud.

Hey! Hey! Hey! America! This is truly a revelation day. I have the scoop on the story everyone has been talking about: the Sanders' murder case. What would make a woman so angry to kill her husband in cold blood and have no remorse? Only a child. I have it from good authority, Mr. Ron Joyner, Mrs. Gloria Sanders' attorney, that Mr. Sanders was playing house with his thirteen-year-old stepdaughter. Mrs. Sanders caught him in the act and blew his brains out. Now, let's face it, Ladies, wouldn't you have done the same?

Toni didn't want to read any further, so she released the paper, and it fell to the floor. "Oh, my God!" she whispered. She just sat motionless, staring into space. "Oh, my God!" She took a deep breath and glued her eyes shut. Suddenly, she grabbed her purse and dashed out the door.

Chapter 28

Toni sat, curled up on the couch, with puffy, red eyes from crying all night. She looked at the clock again and noticed one o'clock in the afternoon. Ron had stayed out all night and all that Saturday morning. That was not like him, but she understood because she knew he was extremely upset. Suddenly, she heard the door open, and Ron stepped in, same suit from yesterday, but now wrinkled, needing a shave, and focused on her. "Where've you been?" she inquired weakly.

"It doesn't matter."

"It matters to *me*," she insisted. "Where in the hell have you been all night, Ron?! I've been worried sick!"

"I was at a hotel."

"You couldn't come home and talk to me?"

"What is there to say?"

"Whatever happened to innocent until proven guilty, Counselor?" she stressed, throwing his words back at him.

"*Innocent*?" he spat then chuckled. He took a deep breath and remained calm. "I'm moving into the beach house."

"Just like that? You're *leaving*? You're ready to throw in the towel and give up on our marriage just like that?"

"You have ruined me. How can I *ever* trust you again?!" he insisted.

"You *never* trusted me *period*, Ron!" she yelled.

"It's a good thing, too," he spat. "I'm going to pack."

"You're not going *anywhere*!" she countered, and his eyes widened.

"*Excuse* me?"

"You heard me! You're not going any damn place until I tell you *exactly* what I think of you!"

"Don't try to bully me, Toni. You've taken *everything* from me. I just don't give a damn anymore."

"Not even about the *truth*?" she retorted, and he just stared at her. "You have indicted, convicted, and sentenced me without even giving me a trial."

"You want a trial, Toni?" he snapped. "I'll give you a trial!" He was yelling now. "It was *your* column that ruined me! It was *your* signature that sealed the article. It was *you*, my *wife*, who *destroyed* me! And I don't have the energy to stand here and argue with you about it!" He started to pass her, but she grabbed his arm.

She whispered between tears, "I didn't write that article."

****

"Have you talked to Ron?" Simon asked Melissa as they fixed dinner together.

"No, why?"

"Did you read Toni Melton's column?"

"Yes, I did. It was powerful."

"It could get Ron disbarred," he announced, and she jerked to look at him.

"It could?"

"Yes. He divulged confidential information to her about a client."

"Then why would Toni write it?"

"I don't know. I guess a Pulitzer means more to her than her husband."

****

Toni loosened her hold on Ron's arm, and he focused on her. "What do you mean, you didn't write the article?"

"Just what I said, Counselor," she insisted then sat on the couch again. "My article was a follow-up from the Mayor's son's rape crimes of three girls. He was sentenced to five years on probation as long as he stayed in therapy. That's what my article was about. I never wrote that article that was printed."

"Then who did?"

"I wish I knew."

"But it has *your* signature."

"My *signature* is on a *rubber stamp!*" she made known. "And Tyler certainly didn't take those tacky pictures that have his name attached to them! He's pissed!"

"What're you saying, Toni, that the exact conversation that you and I had, when you were speculating about why Mrs. Sanders killed her husband, ended up in your column, but you didn't write it?"

"That's *exactly* what I'm saying," Toni clarified. "Ron, none of those things were validated in that article. I don't work like that. Did you even read it?"

"Yes."

"I mean *really* read it?"

"*Yes.*"

"Then you should know it's not my style. It's not my voice. It's a good copycat, but it's not me," she explained, and Ron just stared into space, and then slowly walked away from her. "Why would I *deliberately* try to hurt you?"

"For a *Pulitzer*, what else?" he countered, facing her again.

"*Seriously*?! I don't give a damn about a Pulitzer if it means hurting *you!*" she insisted. "I love you, Ron. I could *never* hurt you." She grabbed a tissue and blew her nose. "Not only that, but I may be getting sued too. If you think I could hurt *you*, then what about *myself*? My *reputation* is at stake. Why would I hurt *myself*?"

He took a long and concentrated breath then asked weakly, "Who did it?"

"I don't know."

"Why would anyone do such a thing?"

"I don't know that either, but I can guarantee you, I *will* find out!"

****

"Mason, did you read Toni's article?" Becky asked over dinner.

"Yeah, I read it."

"What do you make of it? Why would Toni hurt her husband like that? Didn't she know he could get disbarred for *this*?"

"That article doesn't look like Toni's style."

"What're you mean?"

"I mean, I helped Toni to create her unique style of writing. That was not it. It looks as if someone *deliberately* sabotaged Toni's column."

"But why?"

"I have no idea," Mason stated. "I do know that Toni's pissed off a lot of powerful people, and maybe it's finally caught up with her."

****

"Toni, this is *crazy*," Ron finally responded. "Who would have a reason to destroy us?"

"I don't know, Ron. Not *yet*!"

"But doesn't Bill approve your articles before they are printed?"

"Yes, and his seal was on it."

"Why would he approve something like that?"

"Bill wasn't even there. He's been out of the office for over two weeks with Rita through her surgery."

"So, someone used his seal to authorize the article?"

"Yes."

"But doesn't Gary approve the articles when Bill is out?"

"Not when he sees Bill has already approved them," Toni explained. "Since Bill's seal was already on the article, Gary just pushed it on through. If Bill has already approved an article, there's no need for Gary to approve it too. He thought I had written the article ahead of time, which I sometimes do, and Bill approved it before he took those two weeks off."

"This is insane," Ron pondered. "If someone did this, that means that someone is out to...*destroy* you, me, or *both* of us."

"Yes, it does, and we need to stick together, so we can find out who it is," Toni hypothesized. "Are you with me?"

"Of course," he agreed, then focused on her sad face and took a breath. "I'm sorry, baby."

Toni sniffed and continued, "Ron, whoever is trying to destroy us didn't hurt me nearly as badly as your thinking that I could deliberately try to ruin you. I thought we had more than that in our marriage." Ron sat beside her and took her hands.

He took a deep breath then agreed, "You're right, I should've known better." He paused. "Please forgive me?" Ron wiped her tears with his fingers and planted a kiss on her lips. "Please, baby."

"You hurt me, Ron," she whimpered.

"I know and I'm sorry," he cooed, kissing her again.

"Ron, stop," she purred. "I'm mad at you."

"I know," he groaned, kissing her more passionately. Toni couldn't resist her husband's loving affection, and she felt herself being drawn into his seductive power. He smothered her neck and face with tender, soft, sultry kisses.

"Where've you been? I was worried about you," she cooed between kisses.

"I told you, baby. I was at a hotel."

"Alone?" she asked, and he froze, held back, and stared into her eyes.

"Of course, *alone*," he insisted. "I was hurt, Toni. I thought you had betrayed me. I wanted to be alone so I could think. I'm sorry I hurt you." His soft lips covered hers again in a smooth, moist kiss, and she surrendered to his affection. "Let's go to bed."

"It's in the afternoon," she cooed between kisses.

"I know, but I didn't get any sleep last night," he shared, standing, and gently pulling her up from the chair.

"You want to sleep?" she purred.

"Sure, but not right away." He answered, smiling sheepishly, guiding her into the bedroom with his arms secured around her waist. "I need to apologize to my wife first."

283

****

"Honey, did you read Toni's column?" Mr. Joyner asked his wife as they sat, watching the television.

"Yes," she answered. "I'm surprised Ron is still talking to her."

"I don't know much about the law, but couldn't something like that get Ron disbarred?"

"I should think so," she agreed.

"Did you call him?"

"No, not yet. I was waiting for him to call us."

"Who?" Leroy asked, entering, and sitting.

"Ron," Mrs. Joyner replied. "In Toni's column this week, she stated that Ron gave her confidential information about his client. The little girl mentioned in the article as being sexually assaulted by her stepfather tried to commit suicide."

"Humph," Leroy grunted. "I told all of you that Toni Melton was trouble, but you wouldn't listen." Before he could get the statement out of his mouth, breaking news on television blurted out the details of the story and the lawsuits.

****

David walked into the kitchen and asked Angel, "Who're you calling?"

She replaced the receiver and answered, "I was calling Toni again."

"You still haven't talked to her?"

"No, and I'm getting worried."

"We'll be back in town tomorrow, honey. You can stop by their house then."

"David, Toni did *not* write that article! Toni's article this week was supposed to be the follow up from the college rape cases. I know because I typed it." Angel contended. "And I want to know what the hell is going on, and I want to know *now*!"

****

"The phone is ringing again," Ron breathed, holding Toni in his arms as they lay in bed.

"I don't feel like talking to anyone today," Toni cooed, snuggling up even closer in his arms.

"Me either," he agreed, then planted a loving kiss on her forehead. "Do you forgive me now?" She held up on one elbow over him to focus on his sincere, hazel eyes.

"The jury's still out, Counselor."

"Do I need to resubmit my case?" he cooed then kissed the tip of her nose.

"That would probably be wise," she teased him.

"Then stop the presses, I'm coming in with my summation," he cajoled seductively, pulling her down on his smooth, warm body, ending in a long, sultry kiss.

Ron and Toni's lovemaking knew no boundaries as he kissed and caressed every inch of her desiring, soft skin. Toni moaned with pleasure as her husband had his way with her. Soon their bodies were rocking to the beat of each other, until the everlasting explosion erupted from their inner souls, leaving them drained, fulfilled, and satisfied. Their lips met one last time before he rolled off her and pulled her into his arms.

"The defense rest," he breathlessly announced.

"*Not guilty*," Toni followed his lead, snuggling up close to him while they drifted off to sleep together.

****

"Hi, Effie!" Shug spoke, entering Mrs. Melton's house on her cane.

"Hi, Shug," Mrs. Melton welcomed her neighbor with her knitting in her hand. "Come on in the den."

"Did you see the news?" Shug inquired, dropping in a chair.

"Yes," Mrs. Melton acknowledged, sitting on the sofa.

"What do you make of it? It says Toni published some incriminating evidence against her own husband, and that little girl she wrote about tried to commit suicide."

"I saw it, Shug," Effie retorted a little irritable at her for recapping.

"Well, what do you make of it?"

"Toni is an opportunist. She probably had her mind focused on a Pulitzer Prize, not the *consequences*."

"That doesn't sound like Toni."

"Shug, you have always worn blinders when it came to Toni," Effie insisted. "Toni looks out for only *Toni*!"

"That is *simply* not true. I saw highlights of Toni's wedding on the TV. There couldn't have been two people happier," she defended. "I don't think she would deliberately hurt her husband. You need to call her to see what's going on!"

"It's none of my business."

"Toni is your *daughter*!" Shug insisted. "Of course, it's your business!"

"Toni makes her own decisions, Shug!" Effie made known. "She doesn't want any interference from *me*."

"Effie, why are you so hard on the girl? My God, she is good to you!"

She focused on the concerned lady and announced smugly, "Shug, Toni will be *Toni*, and she *always* survives, so don't waste your time worrying about her!"

****

Toni awakened still in her husband's arms. She looked up at Ron and he was staring into space in the dark bedroom. She looked at two thirty AM on the clock then moved up a little to rest her head in his chest and he pulled her close. "What's wrong?" she whispered.

"Nothing. I just can't sleep."

"Would you like to talk?"

"You need to get some sleep. We'll talk tomorrow."

"Are you worried?"

"Not really *worried*. Just a little *concerned*. That poor little girl." He paused. "What do I say to Mrs. Sanders? My God, what she must think of me! I gave her my word that I would keep her secret completely confidential."

"And you did, honey."

"But no one believes it."

"Right now, they don't, but we'll get to the bottom of this."

"I know," he concurred, squeezing her lovingly, and she welcomed the affection. "I'm gonna have to talk with Mrs. Sanders. She probably won't believe me, but I must let her know that I didn't betray her confidence."

"You might be surprised, honey," Toni hypothesized. "Somehow, people as a whole are very good judges of character."

"I hope you're right, sweetheart," he contemplated, taking a deep breath. "I hope you're right."

Chapter 29

Toni and Ron were awakened by the persistent ringing of the doorbell. "Who could that be?" she groaned, looking at eight AM on the clock. They had talked until the sun rose, and it seemed like they had just gotten to sleep.

"I'll get it, honey?" he offered.

"I'll go with you?" she added as they both got up and pulled housecoats over their nude bodies. They walked downstairs together, and Ron opened the door as Toni stood behind him. Angel exploded into the house waving a copy of *The Weekly Herald*.

"Toni, what in the hell is going on here?!" she demanded. "I've been trying to call you forever!"

"I thought you were still outta town," Toni replied as Ron closed the door.

"We came back early. I was worried about you!" Angel made known. "Toni, what the hell is this in this magazine? You didn't write this! This is *not* the article I typed for this week's column!"

"I know, Angel," Toni took a deep breath. "I'm sorry I didn't answer the phone. Reporters have been hounding us for a story."

"Would you like to have a seat, Angel?" Ron offered.

"No, Ron. Thanks," Angel rejected then focused back on Toni. "*Who* wrote this article? This crap doesn't even sound like you."

Toni blew hard then answered, "We don't know."

"What'd you mean, you don't know?"

Toni glanced at Ron then back at Angel and added softly, "We think we're being set up."

Angel glared at her friend with a slight frown on her face, then in total shock she repeated, "Set up?" Toni nodded. "Who would do something like this?"

"We don't know," Toni replied. "Ron's been suspended from his job, facing disbarment, and a multimillion-dollar lawsuit."

Angel just stared at her friend in total confusion. "Someone *deliberately* set you up?" she finally found her voice.

"Yes. It seems so."

Angel took a few steps, swirled around, and added, "This is unreal." She pondered and Toni walked to her.

"We are going to find out who did this, Angel, and we might need your help. It was obviously someone at the magazine, so I don't know who to trust other than you," she explained.

"You know I'll do anything to help," she agreed, then took a deep breath. "Cause we gonna *find* that snake-in-the-grass!"

****

Toni and Ron sat at their kitchen table together drinking coffee after Angel left, trying to make sense of their situation. They answered all their calls today, including the reporters to say they had no comments. All family members called to offer support. Travis, Jamie, Billy, Carol, and Thomas from the law firm all called as well as Mason and other people at the magazine, and a few other friends, to offer their support. The telephone was ringing again. "Hello?" Ron picked it up.

"Ron, it's Beverly. Where've you been? I called all day yesterday."

"Hi, Bev. I'm sorry. Toni and I just didn't feel like answering the phone yesterday."

"I understand, honey," she replied softly. "What's going on? I know you would *never* betray a client, and that article did not sound like Toni. Are you being set up?"

"Yes, we believe we are," he confirmed, and heard Beverly take a deep breath. "You're right, Toni didn't write the article, and we have to find out who did."

"Are you coming in tomorrow?"

"Just to clear out my office. I'm suspended."

"I heard. I'm sorry," Beverly spat. "Then I'm outta there, too."

"No, Bev. I need you there to keep your eyes and ears open. Someone from the firm had to have leaked that information that was printed."

"All right," she agreed. "I'll see what I can find out."

"Thanks, honey."

"Is Toni all right?"

"We're both coping."

"Call me if you need anything, okay?" Beverly offered.

"I will. Thanks," Ron concluded then hung up and looked at Toni. "She's upset."

"I could tell," Toni acknowledged, then touched his hand as he exhibited a faraway look in his eyes. "What's wrong?"

Ron looked up in her clear brown, sincere eyes and confessed, "It just hurts me that everyone we know automatically knew you didn't write that article...except *me*." They stared long and hard at each other. "I'm so sorry, baby."

"Ron, you were suspended from your job, facing a lawsuit, and disbarment. You were not thinking clearly. Honey, I don't blame you. I probably would've thought the same thing if I were in your shoes."

He looked deep into her eyes and declared softly, "How did I get so lucky to find you?" She smiled sweetly at him and their lips met in a long, gratifying kiss as they heard the doorbell ring. Ron took a deep breath, smiled, and dropped his head. "I'll get it."

Soon Ron returned and Mrs. Melton walked in slowly behind him. "Mom!" Toni exploded, getting up to meet her.

"Hi, Toni," she spoke softly.

"Are you all right?" Toni wanted to know.

"Yes," she answered.

"Honey, take your mother into the den where she'll be comfortable," Ron suggested.

"No, I'm fine right here," Mrs. Melton spoke up. "I heard about your trouble, and I wanted to come by to talk with you for a moment."

"Okay. Have a seat," Toni offered, and her mother sat at the table and Toni sat with her. "Can I get you anything?"

"No, thank you."

Turning to leave, Ron said, "I'll be in the…"

"No, Ron, please stay," Mrs. Melton insisted, and he nodded and leaned against the cabinet at the door.

Mrs. Melton took a deep breath then started, "You two have a beautiful home."

"Thank you," Toni accepted, remembering that her mother had never been in their home.

"Shug said you didn't write that article. Is that true?"

"Yes, Mom, it's true. I didn't write that article."

"I guess Shug knows you better than I do," Mrs. Melton chuckled slightly, and Toni smiled with her. Toni thought of all the times Mrs. Shug ran over to the house to stop her brothers from killing her, while her mother just looked the other way. "I came to apologize to the both of you." Toni's eyes met Ron's, and they shared a puzzled look, and then Toni focused back on her mother. "The Holy Spirit convicted me about the things I said to you two about your baby." She paused. "I was out of line and I was speaking from the flesh and not the sprit. I'm sorry." Toni touched her mother's hand, which lay on the table and smiled sweetly at her. "I said some terrible things about your child, and you had every right to put me out, Ron." She paused again and looked at him. "I didn't approve of your shacking up, so I thought you had produced a demon child. The Holy Spirit helped me to realize that *all* life comes from God. I had no right to judge you. It's my job to tell you the *truth*, not *condemn* you. I'm sorry." She sniffed and wiped a falling tear from her face. Ron handed Mrs. Melton and Toni some tissues from the counter because they were both crying.

"Mom, why do you hate me so much?"

"Toni, I don't hate you. I love you," she answered then paused. "When you were born your daddy made you the center of his universe. I guess I was a little jealous. Then, as you grew up, I realized early that you could take care of yourself. I knew that your brothers' little silly pranks were going to mold you into the wonderful woman you are today. Maybe I let it go a little far, but I really did not think they would physically hurt you."

"But they did hurt me, Mom, and many times, I thought they *were* going to kill me."

"I'm sorry, honey," Mrs. Melton apologized. "I guess you didn't feel safe in your own home, but I do love you, and I'm enormously proud of you. I'm proud that you've found a man who genuinely loves you."

"Thank you, Mom," Toni exploded into her mother's arms and they hugged lovingly.

****

Simon played chess with Keith in the kitchen, while Melissa braided Alexandria's hair in the den, looking at the television. Soon, Simon and Keith charged into the den laughing. "Who won?" Melissa asked, finishing Alexandria's hair.

"He got lucky this time," Simon laughed.

"Keith *beat* you?" exploded Melissa.

"Like a drum," Keith laughed, and then Melissa noticed Keith slightly shoving Simon.

"What's going on, you guys?" she quizzically inquired.

"I have consulted with the highest court in the land on this matter, and I have received its approval," Simon began, and Melissa was puzzled as Keith and Alexandria stood back smiling big, while he knelt in front of her. She gasped.

"Melissa, I love you. I love your children. I don't want to continue to live my life without any of you. Will you marry me?" he asked. Melissa focused on her smiling children then back at Simon.

She took a deep breath then admitted, "I love you, too, Simon." She paused then exploded, "Yes!" He grabbed her in his arms as the children cheered. Then both children ran and sat on each side of their mother as Simon pulled out a small black, velvet box. He opened it, pulling out a magnificent, sparkling, diamond solitaire with small diamonds encircling it, and placed it on Melissa's trembling finger. He kissed her lips softly.

"I love you," he whispered.

"I love you," she returned, and then they kissed again just before the kids jumped on their mother with excited hugs.

****

"So, do we have everybody on the list?" Ron asked Toni when they were alone again, sitting at the table.

"I think so."

"Now, let's go over them."

"Honey, do you remember when I was teasing you about why Mrs. Sanders killed her husband?"

"Yes."

"It seems strange that someone seems to know we had that conversation," she pondered.

Ron looked around and included, "Are you saying that maybe…"

"We might need to call a *bug* exterminator," she finished.

"Let's take a walk," he suggested, taking her hand. They put on their coats and walked outside and proceeded down the sidewalk. "I know a man, Chuck Warren, who went to law school with me. You probably heard me mention him."

"Is he the one who went into investigative work?"

"Yes," Ron confirmed as they walked hand in hand. "He has his own private investigative firm. I'm sure he can send someone to check our house for bugs."

"It's Sunday. Do you think he could send someone *today*?"

"I'll call him and see," he shared, taking out his cell phone.

"Do you have his home phone number?"

"I think I have his cell number saved," he answered, searching the contact list in his cell phone. "I used him for a few other cases for the firm."

"Do you think he could send someone undercover to get into your law firm to check things out?"

"I'll see," he agreed. "Here it is." He punched in the number.

"Chuck Warren," the Caucasian man with short brown hair and horn-rimmed eyeglasses answered on the other end.

"Chuck, Ron."

"Hi, Ron," he greeted. "I read Toni's article. I had a feeling you'd be calling me. How are things?"

"Hectic," Ron acknowledged.

"How can I help?"

****

"All clean," the short, baldheaded Mexican man announced, putting his equipment up after a three-hour search.

"No bugs of any kind?" Ron asked.

"Nope."

"Are you absolutely sure?" was Toni's question.

"I'm positive," he verified in a slight accent. "If any bugs *were* here, they're *gone* now. I checked everything. The phones included."

"Well, it's good to know that no one has invaded our *private* lives," Ron concluded. "How much do we owe you?"

"Chuck will bill you."

"Thank you," Ron finalized, walking the man to the door.

When he left, Ron and Toni focused on each other. "Well, what's next?" she questioned.

"Let's go over our list?" Ron suggested and she nodded.

"It looks like we're dealing with two people, honey," Toni hypothesized. "Unless there's *one* person who has access to *both* our offices!"

Chapter 30

Ron entered the hospital room slowly, and Mrs. Sanders, sitting beside her daughter's bed, looked up at him while her daughter lay asleep. Ron quietly took a seat in a vacant chair near the door.

"I've been set up," he finally made known. "I don't know who, but *I* know I *never* shared the information you gave to me with either my wife or anyone else. Toni didn't even write the article, but we're working to find out who is responsible."

"You never told your wife?" she asked quietly.

"No, I never told *anyone*."

"Do you know how they got the information?"

"No, I don't," he answered. "Not yet."

"Your wife didn't write the article?"

"No, ma'am. Her real article was a follow-up of some rapes at a college," he continued and there was a long silence. Then he focused on the sleeping girl. "Is she going to be all right?"

"Yes, thank God," she recognized.

"Good," Ron breathed, standing. "I know the firm will assign a competent attorney to handle your case if you still want the firm to represent you."

"And *you*? Where will *you* be?"

"I've been suspended until the investigation is complete," he shared. "It's a polite way of saying I've been *fired*. Your sister is suing the firm for millions of dollars and appealing to the bar association for my disbarment."

"My sister makes hasty decisions," she noted nonchalantly.

"Well, take care, Mrs. Sanders. I just wanted you to know that I *never* betrayed you."

Focusing on him, she came back with, "Mr. Joyner, my case hasn't come up yet. When it does, I *do* hope this mess is resolved because I would definitely want *you* to represent me." His eyes widen.

"You do?" he solicited, and she nodded. "But I might be disbarred."

"We'll see," she acknowledged. "I'll talk to my sister."

"Mrs. Sanders, I couldn't give your case the attention it needs right now because I'm trying to resolve my own problems."

"I understand," she validated. "But whoever did it, hurt *my* family as well, and I would like to know who it was too." She paused. "You were so caring when I shared that horrible secret with you. I knew there had to be an explanation. I just didn't believe the man whom *I* had talked with would betray me like that. Thank you for coming here today."

"You're welcome," he accepted. "But, since you don't want representation, *any* lawyer can handle it for you."

"Mr. Joyner, I didn't want representation because I didn't want it to come out what my husband had done to my daughter. Now that it's already out, I'm going to need the *best* representation money can buy because I *can't* go to jail now. I've got to see to it that my daughter is nurtured through this. She's suffered so much. I can't leave her now," she explained then took a breath. "I'll wait for *you*!"

****

"Angel, if any reporters call, I'm not available," Toni announced, poking her head out her office door.

"Got it," Angel acknowledged as Mason entered.

"Hi, beautiful," he spoke, smiling wide at Angel.

"Hi yourself, handsome," Angel played along.

"I didn't know if you were back. I thought Brandy was up here since she wasn't in the mailroom today."

"You're still running that poor girl down?" Angel chuckled, and he just winked at her.

Toni heard Mason's voice and stuck her head out of the door again. "Mason, come here," Toni urged, and he obliged.

"Have you found anything out yet?" he probed, planting himself in a chair in front of her desk.

"No, not yet," Toni answered, sitting behind her desk. "Mason, do you remember if there were any new people in the office in the last couple of weeks?"

"I don't remember. Sorry," he sympathized as Angel buzzed Toni.

Pushing the button, Toni acknowledged, "Yes, Angel."

"Toni, Bill wants to see you and Mason right away."

****

"Hi, Bev," Ron spoke, entering his office.

"Ron!" she yelped, running to hug him. "How are you?"

"I'm all right," he made known. "Anything going on out of the ordinary today?"

"No, same o' same o'," she revealed. "They took your computer."

"*Who* did?"

"Maintenance. They said it was an order from Mr. Schuster."

"It's okay," he expressed. "Don't worry. Everything is going to be all right."

"They were talking about moving the two new guys in your office, Jamie Heard and Billy Johnson."

"Well, it's a shame to leave this office vacant. They'll enjoy it," he verbalized. "I just came by to get a few personal things I left."

"I still can't believe they did you like this."

"Don't be too hard on them. They have to protect the firm."

"That stinks!"

****

"We're getting a lot of heat from your article from last week, Toni," Bill spoke as Toni, Mason, and Gary, his assistant editor, sat in front of his desk. "I wanted you to know that we're pleading the fifth on this right now, until we find out who is behind this. I don't want any of you talking to any reporters." They all nodded their agreement. "Toni, how is Ron taking this?"

"He's okay."

"Toni, I'm so sorry. I feel responsible," Gary spoke up, pushing his eyeglasses on his face. "I should've read the article."

"You had no reason to read it, Gary. It had Bill's authorization stamp on it."

"Who delivered the article that day to the printing room?" Bill asked.

Looking in his notes, Gary answered, "Brandy Sears." Mason's eyes stretched.

Bill pushed a button on his desk. "Yes, Mr. Hurley," his secretary answered.

"Joanne, get Brandy Sears up here please," he ordered.

"Yes, Mr. Hurley."

Then he focused on the group in his office. "I want to know if Brandy let the article out of her sight between my office and your office, Gary." Gary nodded as the secretary buzzed. "Yes, Joanne?"

"Mr. Hurley, Brandy Sears didn't come to work today."

"She called in?"

"No, sir. She just didn't show up."

"Did you check with Lynn?"

"Yes, sir. Lynn said she didn't call in today, and when she called her, there was no answer."

"Thank you, Joanne," Bill replied then noticed a glance between Mason and Toni.

"I can run over to her house, Bill," Mason offered, and Bill nodded.

"Good because I want to talk to Brandy Sears *today*."

"I'll go with you, Mason," Toni suggested.

"That's not necessary, Toni," Mason defended.

"I think it is," she countered.

"Why?" he charged. "Do you think Brandy had something to do with this mess?" They were both on their feet now.

"Maybe."

"That's absurd, Toni. I *know* Brandy. She could *never* do what you're suggesting!"

"How *well* do you know her, Mason?" Toni retorted. "I'm not talking about in *bed*. I'm talking about *really* knowing her!" Mason shot Toni a deep stare and Bill knew he had to interject.

"Mason, let Toni go with you. This is *her* life we're talking about."

He took a deep breath, then waved his hand toward the door and sarcastically remarked, "After you, Mrs. Melton-Joyner."

"Thank you, Mr. Whittaker," Toni mocked, and they left.

****

Ron walked to John Schuster's secretary's desk, but there was a new lady sitting there. She was a bronze, biracial beauty, with long, silky black hair, short and curly in the front and reaching to the middle of her back in an array of waves in the rear. Her eyes were a beautiful radiant light-brown color, and the tight, low-cut, gray sweater she wore left little to the imagination. "Hello," Ron spoke friendly.

"Hi," she answered, smiling back.

"Katie's on maternity leave *already*?"

"Yes, she was having complications," she spoke in a deep, throaty, Kirstie Allie tone.

"I'm sorry to hear that."

"I think she'll be fine. The doctor just wants her off her feet until the baby comes."

"Oh, I see," he understood. "Is John in?"

"Yes, and you are...?"

Ron came back with, "I'm sorry. I'm Ron Joyner."

"Nice to meet you, Mr. Joyner," she greeted, thinking that she had heard about him, but she had no idea he was so fine. "I've heard a lot about you."

"All good, I hope," he chuckled.

"*Very* good," she laughed with him then pushed the button. "Mr. Schuster, Mr. Ron Joyner is here to see you."

"Ron?!" he blasted. "I'll be right there." Ron couldn't tell if John was happy or upset that he was here. Soon the door flew open, and John came out with a big smile, extending a hand. "Ron, how are you?"

Taking his hand in a shake, Ron received, "Fine. Thank you, John."

Focusing on the exotic-looking woman, John inquired, "Have you met Jordan?"

"Yes, briefly," Ron revealed.

"Ron, this is Jordan Curry. Jordan, this is Ron Joyner," he introduced. Ron and the lady shook hands as she stood, exposing a pencil-thin, mid-thigh length, black skirt.

"Nice to meet you, Jordan," Ron greeted.

"Same here," she accepted.

"We were lucky to get Jordan on such short notice. Katie called in today and Jordan walked through the door at the right time," he explained, and Ron was willing to bet her resume didn't get much attention, because the men were probably too busy checking *her* out. "Come on in, Ron?" He led Ron into his office.

"Why did you take my computer?" he started right in.

"Ron, you know it's standard procedure to seized everything when someone is under investigation."

He took a deep breath then frankly inquired, "John, do you *actually* think I betrayed a client by telling Toni that stuff?"

John took a deep breath also then came back with, "No, I don't, Ron, but in order to make it look good, we had to suspend you for a while. Please be patient with us. We're not perfect, but we *do* believe in you."

"You didn't sound like you believed in me Friday when you fired me."

"We gave it much thought since then. We want you back, but *after* the investigation and the lawsuits have been settled."

****

Mason didn't see Brandy's car in the driveway, so he used his key to let himself in and turned off the alarm. "A *key*?" Toni was surprised.

"Just keep quiet," he snarled. She laughed, and he laughed with her.

"It's funny how wives always look in the wrong direction," Toni observed. "While Becky was worrying about *me*, Brandy just moved in and stole your heart right from under her nose."

"You think?" he sarcastically replied, smiling slightly.

They walked into the house and it seemed so quiet. "She's very neat," Toni observed.

"Yes, she is," Mason concurred, walking into the bedroom, followed by Toni. Mason opened the bathroom and Toni opened the closet. Both were bare. Then Toni looked in the dresser drawers and they were empty as well.

"She's *gone*," she was the first to announce.

"She must've gone somewhere for the weekend and didn't get back yet."

Toni blew hard then insisted, "Mason, take the damn blinders off! *Brandy* is *gone*! You don't take *everything* you own on a *week*end trip! The woman is *history*!"

****

"Helloooo," Travis singsong to Jordan, exposing all thirty-twos.

"Hi," she responded, void of any emotion.

"You're new," he recognized. "Because I *definitely* would've noticed *you*."

"Yes, I am," she chuckled slightly this time. "I'm just filling in while Katie is on maternity leave."

"Well, maybe Katie will find herself *another* job while she's out," he joked.

Laughing, she countered, "I don't think it works like that."

"Quit drooling over my help and get in here," John exited his office and ordered jovially.

"I'll talk to you later," Travis made known with a smile plastered on his face, as Jamie and Billy entered.

"Helloooo," it was Jamie's turn to singsong now.

"Hello," Jordan replied. She was used to men noticing her, but this bunch was pathetic.

"Hi," Billy chimed in.

"Jordan, I want you to join us please," John suggested, and she nodded, getting up and grabbing her tablet. John led everybody through another door in his office to the adjoining conference room.

Travis couldn't keep his eyes off Jordan as she entered and sat in a chair away from the long conference room table. John, Blake, Phillip, Carol, and Thomas were already seated. John took his seat at the head of the table. "You all saw Jordan on the way in, but I need to make a more formal introduction," he started. "This young lady is Jordan Curry. She comes highly recommended to us from a law firm in Columbia. She's relocated up here and we were lucky to get her. She will help me out until Katie returns, and I'm sure we will be able to find another position for her when that happens."

"Hallelujah!" Travis beamed, and they burst into laughter.

"Travis, I'm glad you approve," John laughed.

"One more question, married or single?" Travis inquired.

"Single," Jordan answered quietly, and Travis smiled wide at her, and she just shook her head. Travis couldn't detect a positive response from her and that intrigued him. He loved a challenge.

John continued with the introductions, "Jordan, this is Blake Collins, Phillip Ballentine, Travis Bland, Carol Greene, Thomas Bailey, Jamie Heard, and Billy Johnson. You met Ron Joyner earlier today. Hopefully, he'll be back with us soon."

John drew Travis's attention now and he inquired, "Ron was here *today*?"

"Yes," John confirmed. "He came to get a few things out of his office."

"Where was I? In court?" Travis continued.

"I think you were," John concurred. "Anyway, I called this meeting to introduce all of you to Jordan and to let you know that Jamie and Billy will be sharing Ron's office until he returns." A knock came to the door. "Come in."

Beverly walked in slowly and announced, "Mr. Schuster, I just received your message that you wanted to see me. I didn't know you were in a meeting."

"Come in, Beverly. Yes, I sent for you because I want you to know what's going on," John spoke, as Travis pulled out a chair for her and she sat, speaking to everyone, and they responded friendly. "Beverly, we have decided to put Jamie and Billy in Ron's office until Ron returns. I think they will be more comfortable in that office than in those small cubicles." Beverly nodded with a slight smile. "I was hoping that you could stay in there and help them as much as possible."

"Of course," she agreed then added sarcastically. "I'm here to serve…until *I* get ousted out like *Ron*." There was a deep silence at her comment.

John finally broke the silence by saying, "Beverly, Ron is like family. You know we had no choice but to suspend him until the investigation is complete."

"With all due respect, Mr. Schuster, Ron Joyner is the most honest person I know," Beverly retaliated. "And frankly, sir, I don't see much of an investigation going on."

"I assure you, Mrs. James, we are doing everything in our power to clear Ron's name!" Blake spoke up.

"Like what?" Beverly was insistent.

"Like…ah…" Blake stammered.

"I thought so," she spat then added even more sarcastically than before. "I'm sure Ron *appreciates* what you're all doing to help *clear* his name." She stood. "Please excuse me. I've heard all I wanna hear." She walked out, leaving everyone stunned that a mere *secretary* had the audacity to speak to the partners like that.

To ease the tension, Travis scanned over to Jordan, smiled sweetly, and joked, "Welcome aboard."

****

"She's gone, Bill," Toni spoke first when she and Mason entered Bill's office.

"What do you mean, she's *gone*?" Bill exploded.

"Brandy has packed up all her things and gone," Toni repeated then focused on Mason, who hadn't said a word since they left Brandy's house. "I'm sorry." He walked to the window.

"We need to find her," Bill spoke firmly. "If she knows anything about how that article was printed in your column, I want to hear it." He walked to Mason. "Is her car in her name or yours?"

"Hers," Mason responded weakly without turning to face Bill.

"Well, we might can get someone to track her down by either the license plates or OnStar," Bill added.

"I'll see what I can find out," Toni offered, rushing out the door, and Bill nodded.

Bill put his hand on Mason's shoulder and checked, "Are you all right?" Although Mason nodded, the truth was that his heart was breaking.

****

"Hello," Ron answered the telephone, sitting on the couch.

"Ron, Chuck."

"Hi, Chuck."

"Listen. My man is in."

"In *where*? The *firm*?"

"Yeah," Chuck laughed.

"That was quick."

"You know me. I don't dawdle," he boasted jovially. "Listen, all of you need to meet but not in town. What about your lake house near Santee?"

"That would be fine."

"I know it's about a two-hour drive for you, but it's best for all of you not to be seen together."

"Yes, I agree," Ron concurred. "When can we meet him?"

"About eight tonight?" Chuck suggested. "Will that give you and Toni enough time to get there?"

"Yes, we'll be there."

"Good. When you get there, call me and put me on speaker."

"All right."

"Let me get a pen so I can write down the address to text to my contact," Chuck replied. "Carlos told me he didn't find any bugs in the house. I'm glad of that. Now we know that this mess came from either your office, Toni's office or *both*!"

****

Mason walked into his house and Amy ran into his arms. "Hi, Daddy," she shrieked as he picked her up.

"Hi, Princess," he forced a smile. His daughter was the brightest spot of his life, and especially on this day. She was becoming a very tall eight-year-old. He still couldn't believe that Brandy was responsible for setting Toni up. She had no motive.

"Look at what I drew today in school," Amy beamed. showing him a paper in her hand.

"This is great, honey."

"See, this is mommy, this is you, and this is me."

"That's fantastic," he stated, planting a kiss on her cheek as Becky entered.

"You're early!" she acknowledged, stubbing out her cigarette.

"A little," he concurred, putting Amy down and giving Becky a quick kiss.

Becky focused on him long and hard then inquired cautiously, "Anything wrong?"

"No," he answered quickly, removing his jacket while Amy helped him, as a woman entered in a maid's uniform.

"Good evening, Mr. Whittaker," she spoke sweetly.

"Hi, Cecilia," Mason returned. "Something smells delicious."

"Beef stroganoff," Cecilia shared, smiling wide.

"You're going to spoil me," Mason joked, then focused on his wife. "I'm going to take a shower before dinner."

Mason walked into their bedroom, dropped on the bed, and buried his face in his hands. Becky entered slowly and beckoned, "What's wrong?" He jumped and stood.

"Nothing, I told you. Can't I come home early for a change?"

"You're upset. I can tell."

"I'm fine," he insisted. "Just leave me alone please. I don't feel like the hassle tonight."

"Does this have anything to do with Brandy?"

"Brandy?!" he exploded.

"Yes, your *mistress*."

"It's been over between Brandy and me for a long time now, and you know that."

"Has it?"

"Yes," he insisted, taking off his tie. "Now, could I please take my shower in peace?" He walked into the bathroom as Becky walked out of the bedroom. Mason took his clothes off slowly, still thinking about Brandy's disappearing act. He didn't know what he would do without her. He loved her so much. He just wished she would come back and clear her name. According to Bill and Toni, she was *already* guilty. "Where are you, Brandy?" he pondered aloud. Mason took a deep breath then stepped into the shower and let the warm water flow on his nude body. Soon he felt tears burning his eyes and he leaned against the shower wall, letting the tears flow with the water.

****

"How about dinner tonight?" Travis asked Jordan as she sat at her desk, typing.

"I don't think so," she answered dryly.

"I'm a nice guy. Ask anyone."

"Don't ask *me*," Carol interrupted. "He's a *hound*!" She burst into laughter.

"Carol, I can't believe you went out on a brotha like that!" Travis laughed with her.

"Jordan, I need the Roger's case file, honey," she announced.

Standing, Jordan walked to the filing cabinet, with Travis following her every move with his eyes, checking out her every curve in that body-fitting, above the knee, rust-colored skirt, and Carol laughed. "Don't hurt yourself, *brotha*," She joked. Travis licked his lips and smiled.

"Here it is," Jordan offered, handing the woman the folder.

"Thanks," Carol accepted then left, throwing a playful smirk to Travis.

"Well, how about it?" Travis focused back on Jordan. "What about dinner tonight?"

"I don't *know* you," Jordan insisted.

"How else are you gonna get to know me if you don't have dinner with me?"

"I'll see you here at the office."

"You are *very* beautiful."

"Thank you."

"But then I *know* you knew that already," he assumed, and she laughed. "You have a lovely laugh. What nationality are you?"

She raised an eyebrow and sarcastically smirked, "*American.*"

"Nah, you're something more than American!" he yelped.

She took a breath and admitted, "My father is African American, and my mother is Caucasian and Portuguese."

"Travis, are you still bothering Jordan?" John charged, exiting his office.

"No, I'm just conversating."

"Jordan, I'm leaving now. I'll see you tomorrow," John concluded. "If this man doesn't leave you alone, call *security*."

"Now, why are you going out on a brotha like that?!" Travis joked, and Jordan laughed with him. Jordan knew, by the twists in Travis's hair that he was a *true* brotha; his *own* man who didn't care what other people thought. She had to admit that he was also a *fine* one and *very* persistent! It was going to be hard keeping him at arms' length.

* * * * * * * * *

"Ron!" Toni called, entering the house, and Ron met her.

"Hey, honey."

"Hey," she responded, meeting him with a kiss. "Miss me?"

"Always," he cooed, kissing her again.

"I have some news."

"I have some, too."

"Great," Toni continued, dropping her purse on the table nearest the door.

"What did you find out?" Ron asked, walking with Toni into the sunroom.

Sitting beside her husband, she stated, "It looks like Brandy Sears had something to do with the set up."

"*Brandy Sears*?!" he exploded. "*Mason's* girlfriend?!"

"Yes, she's *gone*. Took off without a trace."

"But why? Do we know her? What reason would she have for ruining us?"

"Ambition! Jealousy! Who knows? We're trying to track her down now."

"How is Mason?"

"Not too good," she shared. "But I can't worry about him right now. We gotta get our life back."

"And speaking of that, we have to be at the lake house by eight to meet the man Chuck planted in the firm."

"That was quick."

"Chuck is an awesome guy!"

"Something smells good. What did you cook?"

"I cheated. I had it delivered from the restaurant on Elms."

"They *deliver*?"

"They couldn't resist my charm," he joked, and Toni laughed with him. "Hungry?"

"Starved."

****

Simon tucked Keith into bed and planted a kiss on his forehead. "Simon, when are you and my mommy getting married?"

"We haven't set the date yet, buddy, but I hope soon."

"Me too," Keith agreed. "I like having you here with us. You remind me of my daddy."

Simon took a much-needed breath to absorb what the child said. "That's the nicest thing anyone has ever said to me, Keith. Thank you," Simon responded. "Good night, buddy."

"Good night," Keith replied then turned over to go to sleep as Simon left his room, almost bumping into Melissa.

"Is he asleep?" she whispered.

"No, not yet."

"I'll meet you downstairs. Let me kiss him goodnight," she made known, and Simon nodded.

Simon walked downstairs, fixed two glasses of lemonade, walked back into the family room, and sat. Soon Melissa came and sat beside him. He pulled her into a loving embrace ending in a kiss, and then she leaned her head back in his chest. "I'm ready to set a date, Melissa," he announced softly.

"Soon, honey."

"What're you waiting on, *Ron's* permission?"

She jerked off him to confront him and declared, "No. I just don't want to add to Ron and Toni's confusion right now."

"But I'm ready to be your husband *now*. I'm tired of going home every night, and the children are too."

"The *children*?!"

311

"Yes, Keith just asked me when we were getting married because he likes having me here."

"Keith said that?"

"Yes, and he also said that I reminded him of his father."

Melissa sat back slowly, and Simon held up to face her and vowed, "I love you, Melissa. I love Keith and Allie. I want us to be a family. Why don't you want to set a date?"

She sighed deeply then suggested, "What about March?"

"It's October. What about December?"

"Can we get ready by *December*?"

"Baby, I'm *already* ready!" he declared, pulling her in his arms.

"*December* it is," she agreed.

"We can start tomorrow looking for a house."

"A house?!" she exploded. "I thought we were going to stay here."

"No, baby. This is the house you shared with Kelvin. *I* want to buy you a house. We can get it built or we can buy one already built. We can decide that together," he explained then focused on her. "Okay?"

"Okay," she agreed. "I love you, Simon."

"I love you, baby," he cooed, and they ended in an extended kiss. Simon shifted the bulge in his pants. "I better get the hell outta here before you have to *throw* me out." Melissa burst into laughter.

****

The doorbell rang in the modestly decorated lake house and Ron hypothesized, "That must be Chuck's man." He walked to the door, followed by Toni close behind him. When Ron opened the door, his mouth dropped wide open. "It's *you*!"

"Yes, it's *me*," Jordan Curry confirmed with a wide smile extending across her face.

"Come in," Ron offered, and she entered. "I thought Chuck said you were a *man*."

312

"Chuck said he would like to be a fly on the wall when I met you tonight," she chuckled.

Ron turned to Toni, "Honey, you remember I told you that Katie was already on maternity leave?"

"Yeah," Toni acknowledged.

"*She* took Katie's place."

"Hi, I'm Toni," Toni offered, extending a hand.

"Oh yeah, honey, this is…" Ron started. "I'm sorry. I forgot your name."

"Jordan. Jordan Curry," she finished, taking Toni's hand in a shake. "I love your column, Toni."

"Thank you," Toni accepted, checking the beautiful woman out. "Let me take your coat."

"Thank you," she agreed, giving her coat to Toni.

"Have a seat please," Ron offered, leading her into the cozy living room with the fireplace burning.

Looking around the paneled lake house, Jordan observed, "This is nice."

"Thank you," Ron responded as Toni reentered. "I better call Chuck, so we can get started." He took out his cell phone and dialed while Jordan took out an iPad.

"Ron!" Chuck acknowledged on the other end.

"Chuck, you old rooster. You pulled a fast one on me."

"You like my angel?" Chuck laughed through the speaker on the cell phone.

"Angel?" Ron was confused.

"Yeah! If *Charlie* can have *three*, surely *Chuck* can have *one*." They burst into laughter together. "Toni, how are you, beautiful?" Chuck recognized.

"Hi, Chuck. I'm well. How are you?"

"Great!" he answered. "Hi again, Jordan."

"Hi, Chuck."

"Okay, Jordan, talk to me, honey," Chuck advised.

"Chuck, I didn't find out much today," Jordan started. "Ron, Beverly is your secretary, right?"

"Yes," Ron confirmed.

313

"Mr. Schuster held a meeting today to announce that the two new lawyers, Jamie and Billy, would be sharing Ron's office, and he asked Beverly if she would help them," Jordan explained. "Well, that upset her, and she was rather direct and blunt."

"That's Beverly," Ron added.

"She told Mr. Schuster that she didn't see anything they were doing to clear your name, Ron."

"Beverly did that?" Ron asked.

"Yes, and she also walked out of the meeting, letting them know that she knew she could be *ousted* out just like *you*."

"Beverly is a friend, Ron?" was Chuck's question.

"Yes, more of a friend than I thought," Ron contemplated.

"Do you think she's someone Jordan could confide in later?"

"Definitely," Ron confirmed.

"Good to know. But right now, we don't want *anyone* to know," Chuck continued. "Anything else, Jordan?"

"No, nothing but Travis Bland is a *pest*."

Ron burst into laughter and shared, "You're new meat. Travis is like a hungry blood hound when it comes to new meat."

"Can he be looked at as a suspect?" Chuck wanted to know.

"I don't think so," Ron speculated. "We were friends since elementary school. I don't think Travis would do anything to hurt me."

"He was disappointed to know that you were *there* today, and he missed you," Jordan spoke again.

"He was in court when I came by," Ron added.

"That's what Mr. Schuster told him."

"Chuck, Toni has some news," Ron shared.

"Good," Chuck acknowledged. "Let's hear it, Toni."

"Brandy Sears is missing. She is a young woman who started as a temp but was promoted to a permanent position because of her relationship with Mason Whittaker," Toni explained.

"That's interesting," Chuck pondered.

"Brandy was the one who carried the article down to the print room," Toni added.

"What's her name again?" Chuck asked. "I've got to put a person on this right away. We need to check her background, but more importantly, we need to *find* her."

Chapter 31

"Do you ride?" Travis asked Jordan, leaning over her desk.

"Ride what...*you*?" Jordan answered politely.

He burst into laughter and considered, "Um, that's a thought." She knew by his expression that he was *really* thinking about it, and then he shook his head to recover his mind from out of the clouds. Focusing back on her, he asked, "Horses?"

"Yes, I do," she confirmed, melting his heart with her stunning, bronze face which was exposed with her hair pulled back in a stylish ponytail and straight bangs hanging just above her eyebrows.

"How would you like to go with me to the stables to ride?"

"You have a ranch?"

"No, but my man, Jamie Heard and his wife do, and they have given us full access to it."

"Jamie Heard who works *here*?"

"Yeah. He married an old rich broad," Travis explained. "What do you say?"

"It sounds like fun."

"Then it's a date?"

"Sure, why not?" she confirmed, wondering what information she could gather from this determined man. He pulled a small black address book from his inner pocket.

"Write your address down for me."

"So, they're really *black*," she laughed.

"What?"

"Your little *black* book," she continued, and he finally caught on.

"Oh no, it ain't even that kinda party!" he chuckled, flicking the pages in her face. "See, no stars by any names. I keep *important* numbers in here, like the dentist, my sisters. etc."

"What about your *mom*?"

Pointing to his head, he announced proudly, "I keep hers up here. Now my sisters, I don't call them enough to remember their numbers."

"I see," Jordan understood, still smiling as she wrote her number and address down. "I thought people kept all that stuff in cell phones now."

"That's true, but I like a back-up," Placing his hand over his heart, he cooed, "Yours, I'll keep in *here*." Jordan smiled shyly.

You're such a prick, she thought, then looked back at him, handing him the book, and asked very sweetly, "What time should I be ready?"

"Is ten o'clock good?"

"Yes, that's fine."

"Bring some changing clothes. We can make a day of it," he suggested, and she nodded.

You might be a prick, but I gotta hand it to you, you're a gorgeous prick, Jordan thought again, then nodded, and agreed, "All right." He walked away glowing like the cat that swallowed the canary.

****

"Beverly, could you please get Mr. Marshall on the phone?" Billy asked through the intercom system. William (Billy) Johnson was a sharp dresser in his designer suits and expensive shoes. He was of Italian descent with a Sicilian mother and a Caucasian father. at five-feet-nine-inches tall, muscular built, wavy, black hair, and a winning smile, he considered himself to be somewhat of a ladies' man. He was the youngest associates in the firm at twenty-six years old. He was single but kept steady company with a few women.

Beverly stopped typing, frowned, and replied, "Yes, Billy." Then she thought, *Give a man an office, he thinks he's mightier than God Almighty himself. He probably expected her to call him Mr. Johnson too, but he better not hold his breath. She would quit before she addressed a little snot-nosed kid like him as Mr. Anything!* Travis walked in, invading her thoughts.

"Hi, lovely lady," he flirted.

"Hi, Travis," she acknowledged, picking up the telephone.

"Have you heard from Ron?"

She held up a finger to silence him as she announced into the receiver, "Mr. Billy Johnson is calling for Mr. Wayne Marshall, please." She paused. "Hello, Mr. Marshall." Pause. "Fine, thank you, and you?" Pause. "Good, hold please for Mr. Johnson." She pushed a button and said, "Billy, Mr. Marshall's on line one."

"Thank you, Bev," he replied. And she thought, *Who gave you permission to call me Bev? Nobody did that but Ron.* She looked up at Travis and blew out a frustrated sigh. "Lord, I'll be glad when Ron comes back. I don't know how much more of this I can take!"

He chuckled, "You're not getting along well with your two new bosses?"

"I have *three* bosses, God, Jesus, and the Holy Ghost!" she insisted, and Travis saw that *she* was serious, although *he* was joking. "These clowns around here are *nothing*!"

"Sorry, Beverly. I know it's rougher on *you* than *anybody* around here," he sobered. "Have you heard from Ron? I can't get in touch with him. Every time I call, the voicemail comes on."

"I think they're living low."

"But why? Ron and I go *way* back! Can't he talk to *me*?"

"I'm sure he'll call you soon, Travis."

"Are he and Toni having problems?"

"Why?"

He chortled, "She *did* get him fired!"

Beverly eyed him intensely before slowly warning, "Don't believe everything you hear."

****

Angel walked into Toni's office inquiring, "Where is Brandy?"

"She's not here anymore," Toni answered, looking up from her computer as Angel sat in front of her desk.

"Where *is* she? She got another job?"

"We don't know. She just disappeared."

"Mason doesn't know either?" she pressed, and Toni shook her head. "You're kidding?!"

"No."

"Then I know Mason is going ballistic!"

"I guess he is."

"He was *crazy* about Brandy!"

"Yes, he was and still is."

"Why would she do that?"

"I don't know."

It took a moment, but Angel managed to connect the dots. "Do you think she had anything to do with setting you up?"

"It appears so," Toni confirmed. "She was the one who submitted the article to the print room."

Angel pondered, "Well, I'll be...so what would she gain from ruining you? She's too far down on the totem pole to replace you."

"I don't know."

"Is anyone looking for her?"

"Yes, a *lot* of people!"

"I would sure love to hear what Miss *Thang* has to say for herself."

"You and me both!"

Chapter 32

"Ron, hand me that spatula, son," Mrs. Melton asked as Ron sat on the bar stool in the kitchen while his mother-in-law and Toni cooked.

"Sure, Mama Effie," he replied, getting up and handing it to her.

"Thanks, honey," she acknowledged.

"Mom, did you take your medicine today?" Toni asked, tossing the salad.

"Yes, Toni," she answered, and Toni planted a kiss on her cheek.

"Good," she recognized. It felt so good to Toni that she finally had a mother whom she and her husband could enjoy and not try to avoid. Her mother was completely different towards them. She loved the closeness they now shared. "Have you heard from Walter and Dennis today?"

"No, not today."

"How is their business doing?" Ron asked, dropping a grape in his mouth.

"They say fine," Mrs. Melton shared then went into a chuckle. "Those two are crazy enough to make *anything* work." They all laughed. "How is the situation going with the two of you?"

"Slow, but it's going," Toni stated.

"Well, we'll just keep praying. Everything will work out just fine," Mrs. Melton assumed, and Toni squeezed her shoulder lovingly.

****

"Wait up," Travis called, trailing behind Jordan on his horse as she sailed through the air on her stallion. Soon she stopped under a tree and dismounted, and Travis rode up to her slowly. "You weren't kidding when you said you could ride." He watched her from his horse.

"This is a fine animal," she remarked, rubbing the horse's smooth, light brown coat.

Dismounting his black horse, Travis agreed, "Yes, they are beautiful."

"It's so wonderful out here," Jordan admired, soaking in the large green terrain.

"Yes, it is," Travis concurred. He couldn't believe how lucky he was that she had finally accepted his invitation. She was so beautiful; he could barely take his eyes off her. Malik would like her. He had to admit that although his son was only twelve, Malik took after him when it came to women. They both liked them gorgeous!

Jordan looked just like the riders in the movies with her brown leather jacket, brown riding boots and her shiny black hair pinned back with a barrette, and a brown leather hat covering it.

Travis took a blanket from a bag, hanging on the horse, and spread it on the ground, then sat and reached his hand out to her. She took his hand and allowed him to help lower her on the blanket. He leaned against the tree trunk as Jordan lay down on one elbow. "So, who is Jordan Curry?" he asked.

"Just a girl," she sarcastically answered.

"Come on," he urged. "What's your story, pretty lady?"

"What do you want to know?"

"Everything," he resolved, looking deep into her clear, light brown eyes.

"Well, I'm twenty-eight, single, and free," she chuckled.

"Where are you from? I know you're not from South Carolina with that accent."

"No, I'm not. I'm from Montana."

"Really?"

"Yes, really," she mocked.

"So how did you get *here*?"

"I received a scholarship to the University, fell in love with the South, and decided to stay."

"What does your father do?"

Laughing, she replied, "Believe it or not, he's a lawyer."

"Oh no!" He laughed with her. "You can't get away from us, huh?!"

"I guess not," she admitted, continuing her laugher, while he sobered.

"You are so beautiful," he admired, causing her to sober also. He leaned forward and planted a gentle kiss on her lips, and she indulged him by kissing back. "Wow!" he added, and Jordan snickered. She knew if she played her cards right, Travis could be an asset to what she was trying to accomplish.

****

Angel and David were exiting the movie theater laughing heartily when they spotted Kristy with a man entering the doors. Kristy was wearing her characteristic short skirt, tight blouse and six-inch heels, and her date was tall, very dark, and young. They all froze and stared at each other, while Kristy's date was totally unaware of the situation. "Hello," David finally broke the silence.

"Hi, David," Kristy spoke quietly, trying to force a smile, and then focused on Angel who was not smiling at all. "Angel."

"Kristy," Angel acknowledged dryly.

"Sean, this is David and Angel Scott. David and Angel, this is Sean Battle, my fiancé," Kristy introduced. The three people greeted each other cordially.

"So, when is the big day?" David inquired, trying to break the unbearable tension.

"June," Kristy beamed.

"Congratulations," David offered, spotting the diamond on her finger.

"Thank you," she responded, echoed by Sean.

"Well, don't let us detain you from the movie," David spoke up. "Have a good evening."

"Thank you," she accepted.

"It was nice meeting you," Sean concluded.

"Same here," added David while Angel just smiled sweetly, and then the couple walked away.

David focused on Angel and asked cautiously, "Are you all right?" She nodded quickly. "Are you sure?" She nodded again, and they proceeded out of the movie theater doors. "I'm sorry, honey."

"It's okay," she half-heartedly countered. David stopped and stood in front of her.

"Do you know how much I love you?" he solicited, and she just smiled slightly.

"I know, but it still hurts sometimes."

"I'm sorry," he made known. "I promise I will *never* hurt you again."

"I hope not," she received. "I *truly* hope not." Although David loved his wife unconditionally, he had to admit that Kristy looked good. *Too* good! He hated to admit it, but he felt a little twinge of jealousy seeing her with another man. He knew what a good time she could give a man in bed, and his heart ache a little knowing that he could never have her again...*or could he*?

****

Travis and Jordan sat on his couch in his condo drinking iced tea and eating popcorn. They had already showered and changed and were now relaxing in blue jeans and casual shirts. "Want to take in a movie or something?" he asked.

"No, I'll just wait for dinner," she declined. "So, how long have you been working at the firm?"

"About three years now."

"Do you like it?"

"Oh yeah," he glowed as his cell phone began to ring. Travis looked at the caller ID. "It's Ron, my *man*! Excuse me, honey." He yanked the phone off the coffee table. "Well, it's about damn time! I just called you a million times!"

"Hello to you too, Travis," Ron joked on the other end of the telephone, sitting in the den beside Toni. "I'm sorry it took me so long to get back to you."

"How the heck are you, man?"

"I'm okay."

"Hey, man, why did Toni write that article? She had to know it would get you in trouble!"

"Toni didn't write the article, Travis. She was set up."

"What?!" Travis exploded, springing to his feet.

"*Toni* didn't write the article, and *I* didn't give her that information."

"Wow, that's heavy," he absorbed. "Toni should have known if she messed with big dogs long enough, they were bound to, sooner or later, *bite!*" he chuckled. "What're you going to do?"

"We're looking into it, but we have to take it slow."

"What can I do to help, man?"

"Just keep your eyes and ears open and let me know if you see or hear anything."

"So, you think someone in the firm is in on it, too?"

"Definitely," Ron confirmed. "I didn't give anyone that information about the Sanders' case. It had to come from the firm."

"Hey, man, Jamie and Billy are sharing your office and Beverly is pissed."

"Bev is a good friend."

"She sure is. She told those cock suckers where to go in the meeting!" he laughed. Travis sobered a bit then added a few seconds later, "Hey, man, hang tight. You know I'm with you."

"I know. Thanks."

When Travis hung up, he focused back on Jordan. He sat beside her and shared, "That was Ron Joyner. He's a lawyer in the firm who got a bad deal."

"Yes, I heard. I met him when he came to see Mr. Schuster," she acknowledged. "So, you don't think he's guilty?"

"Heck no! But I had to admit that I thought his *wife* was, but Ron said she didn't write the article. That's a shame that someone would screw around with two good people like them."

"Have you been friends long?"

"Ever since grade school."

Jordan contemplated this for a second before stating, "Well, don't worry. The truth usually has a way of coming out, whether we want it to or not."

Chapter 33

"Honey, we don't have anything to drink here. I better run and get some soda or something," Toni suggested in their lake house.

"I'll go with you," Ron offered.

"No, honey. Jordan might come. One of us should be here when she arrives."

"Oh yeah," he remembered. "Okay, I'll wait for Jordan but hurry."

"I will," she added, meeting him with a kiss. He walked her to the door and watched as she hopped into her car, cranked it up and pulled off. Ron was about to close the door when he saw Jordan pull up from the opposite direction in her fire-red Porsche.

"Hi," he spoke.

"Hi, Ron. How are you?" she responded, getting out of her car with a box from Melissa's bakery in her hand.

"I'm okay," he recognized, closing the door when she was inside. "You visited my sister's bakery, huh?"

"Yeah, it's great!"

"What did you get?"

"Cake squares."

"Ooh, my favorite!" he whooped, and she laughed as they walked into the kitchen. "So, how are things going with my man?" Ron opened the box and took out a small cake square and dropped the whole thing in his mouth.

"Travis?" she blushed.

"No, *Pinocchio!*" he laughed.

"He's a hound."

"Yes, he is, but he's good people," Ron concurred with his mouth full.

"I guess so," she pondered. "Where's Toni?"

"She went to the store to get something to drink."

"She ought to see you now," Jordan laughed. "You have icing all around your mouth." She took a napkin and dapped around Ron's mouth. Suddenly, Jordan stopped and stared at Ron while he

327

swallowed, enjoying his cake square. She lifted his head slowly and planted a soft kiss on his lips before he knew what was happening. Ron's eyes widen as he stared at her.

"Jordan," he finally found his voice.

"I'm sorry," she blurted out. "I shouldn't have done that."

"No, you shouldn't have!" he confirmed. "Toni's the *only* woman for me."

"Hey, hey, hey, you guys!" Toni called, entering the house. When she entered the kitchen, Ron shook his shock off and ran to get the bags from her, and Jordan just dropped her head. "What's going on?" Toni asked puzzled.

"Nothing," Ron answered quickly.

"Hi, Toni," Jordan finally responded, shaking off her disappointment and shame. Toni wasn't satisfied with either of their responses, but she'd let it go...for *now*!

****

"Have you and Simon set a date yet?" Mrs. Joyner asked Melissa as she helped her prepare dinner, while Simon sat in the den with her father and Leroy.

"Yes, December nineteenth."

"A week before Christmas?!" her mother exploded. "We've got a lot to do before then. How are we going to get everything done so quickly? Melissa, we..."

"Slow down, Mom," Melissa laughed. "Everything is taken care of. Cammie is directing the wedding. She's taking care of all the flowers and food."

"What about your *dress*?!"

"I was hoping that you and Denise could go with me to pick one out."

"You know we will," her mother agreed, grabbing Melissa in her arms. "What about Toni? I know she'd love to help."

"I hate to bother Toni with all that they're going through right now."

"Yeah, I guess so, but at least *ask* her, so she won't feel left out."

"Okay, I will."

"Have you told Ron yet?"

Melissa took a deep breath then confessed, "No, I'm afraid of what he might say."

"Honey, Simon is a nice man. Your children love him, and most importantly, *you* love him. You can't go by what either Ron or anyone else thinks. This is *your* future, not *theirs*," her mother explained.

"I know, Mom, but Ron was so supportive of me when Kelvin died. I just don't want to disappoint him."

"I'm sure in time, Ron and Simon will become friends again. They were at *one* time. They *can* be again."

"I hope you're right."

"I *know* I'm right," her mother insisted. "Call your brother." Melissa nodded slowly.

"What about the wedding party?"

"I figured I would ask Toni and Denise to be Matrons of Honor, and I have a few friends I could ask to be bridesmaids."

"Is Simon handling the groomsmen?"

"Yes, ma'am."

"What about his best man?"

"Simon doesn't have any brothers. I'm hoping he will ask Ron."

"Ron?!"

Smiling, Melissa acknowledged, "*Crazy* isn't it?"

"Maybe not."

"What about Leroy?"

Melissa's smile faded as she recalled, "I don't know, Mom. He didn't even come to Ron and Toni's wedding."

"You know why. He just can't forgive Toni, but I say she isn't responsible for his becoming a drunk. He should've fought for his career like Ron tried to get him to do. He can't blame anybody for that but himself," her mother explained.

"That's the problem. What if he shows up *drunk*?"

"I don't think he will, honey. Leroy hasn't had a drink in over three months."

"You're kidding!" Melissa exploded.

"No, I'm not. Don't you see how much better he looks?"

"I thought it was because you made him take a *bath*," Melissa laughed and her mother laughed with her, as her father and Simon entered the kitchen.

"We're starving," Mr. Joyner announced. "Where is that dinner? With *two* of you in here, we still can't get dinner!" He burst into laughter.

"Perfection takes time, Dad," Melissa joked as Simon hugged her lovingly from the rear.

****

"So, what's the scoop on you and *Miss Jordan*?" Toni asked Ron after Jordan had gone.

"What *scoop*?" Ron chuckled.

"Don't play dumb with me, Ron Joyner!" she insisted, and he burst into laughter.

Grabbing her around the waist, he joked, "Are you jealous?" He planted a big kiss on her lips.

"Should I be?" Toni inquired seriously.

"Of course, not," he insisted as he let her go.

"What happened, Ron?"

"It was nothing, Toni. Jordan just kissed me," he nonchalantly announced then turned to leave. "I'm going to take a shower. Are you gonna join me?"

Toni couldn't believe her ears. She definitely couldn't believe Ron's attitude either. How *dare* Jordan kiss *her* husband! "Ron!" she called, and he stopped, turned, and faced her. "What do you mean she *kissed* you?"

"It was nothing, Toni. I had icing on my face and Jordan was helping to clean it off and she kissed me."

"And what did *you* do?"

"Nothing. What could I do? I was surprised," he defended, and she just stared at him and he continued. "Then I told her that *you're* the only woman for me."

"And what did *she* say to that?"

"Nothing because that's when you came home."

"I can't believe it!" Toni was growing angry. "I thought I could trust Jordan!"

"You *can*, but even if you *can't*, you *know* you can trust *me*," Ron declared. "It was no big deal! Don't make a mountain out of a molehill!"

"This *is* a mountain, Ron!"

"No, it *isn't*!" he insisted, going to her. "Toni, I really don't see other women in that way anymore." He touched her face lightly. "I love you, baby. I could never cheat on you. I watched my father cheat on my mother for years. I would never do that to you. I love you too much for that." He planted a kiss on her lips. "I'm a big boy. I can take care of myself. I don't need *you* to fight my battles for me. So please, honey, let it go." She took a breath to say something, and Ron placed his finger to her lips. "*Let...it...go!*" He kissed her again. "Let's go and take our shower." As Toni followed Ron out, hand in hand, her mind was still on the fact that Jordan kissed her husband. It might be over for *Ron,* but it was *far* from being over for *her*...at least...until she could have a woman-to-woman talk with *Miss PI*!

****

"So, you're finally going to tie the knot again," Denise observed as she and Melissa sat in their mother's kitchen, making out the guest list for the wedding.

Melissa took a deep breath, smiled, and answered, "I guess so."

"So, how is he in *bed*?" Denise inquired, smiling wide.

"I don't know."

"You don't know?!" Denise yelped. "You mean you and Simon haven't...?"

"That's right."

"Why?!"

"Because we didn't want to."

"Or *you* didn't want to?"

"Simon agreed we should wait too," she shared. "I was a virgin when I married Kelvin, and I'm going to wait until I marry Simon."

"Excuse *me*, Miss *Thang*!" Denise smirked, and Melissa laughed. "Then how do you know he can satisfy you?"

"He satisfies me just fine," Melissa stressed. "Simon is kind and thoughtful and caring...," she meditated and added, "oh yes, he *satisfies* me *just fine*."

"Have you two finished with the guest list yet?" Mrs. Joyner asked, entering the kitchen.

"Not yet, Mom," Denise giggled. "We're working on it." The young women burst into laughter and their mother simply stared at her daughters.

Chapter 34

"Hi, Beverly," a young, caramel tan woman in a short skirt and tight sweater barely covering her huge breasts greeted, pushing her long, straight, blonde weaved hair out of her face.

"Hi, Felisha," Beverly responded, continuing to type. "What can I do for you? Travis needs something?"

"No. I came to see Jamie."

That got Beverly's attention now, and she froze, focusing on the seductive-looking girl. She knew that Felisha had been Travis's secretary for over a year and had been trying to get him in her bed for most of that time, but he simply wasn't interested. Even the biggest hound in the world had limits. Unlike Ron, *Travis* was certainly a *hound*. Beverly gave the young woman a quizzical look then asked, "Why do you wanna see Jamie?"

"He said he had a sofa for sale, and I wanted to see when I could see it."

Beverly stared at the young woman long and hard, and Felisha looked away. Beverly knew she was lying, but she was too much of a lady to call Felisha on it. "Wait a minute." Beverly pushed the intercom button.

"Yes, Beverly," Jamie answered immediately.

"Felisha's here to see you about a sofa," Beverly announced, then thought, *she probably wants to know which one you're gonna bang her on.*

"Send her in please, Beverly, and hold all my calls," Jamie requested.

Beverly focused back on the young, fidgeting woman, and waved her hand in the direction of the office, with a smirk on her face, giving Felisha permission to enter. "Thank you, Beverly," Felisha replied in her high-pitched, whiny, southern drawl, then clicked away in her six-inch heels.

When she walked in, Beverly heard the door lock. "Rat!" she spat.

"Hi," Jamie purred, taking Felisha in his arms in a long kiss.

"Jamie, this isn't a good idea. I think Beverly knows about us," Felisha protested as he fondled her body, still smothering her face and neck with kisses.

"Who cares?" he barked.

"*I* care!" Felisha retaliated. "I have to *work* with these women!"

"Baby, you don't have to work *anywhere*. I have enough money to take care of you."

"Your *wife's* money!"

"*Mine* too," he insisted. "Now, quit worrying and give me some sugar." They kissed long and passionately.

"Why can't you wait until we get off work and meet me at my place?"

"Because I have to go somewhere with Taffy, and I can't wait another day to see you," he insisted, unbuttoning her sweater.

"Where's Billy?" she asked, being sucked in by his charm.

"In court," he answered, picking her up and placing her on his desk. "He'll be gone all day." He raised her short skirt, still kissing her. She gasped from his affection. She started to relax and reached down to unzip his pants.

****

Beverly looked up from her typing and welcomed with a big smile, "Hello, Mrs. Hines. Excuse me…Mrs. *Heard*."

"Hi, Beverly," Taffy Hines-Heard accepted, returning her smile, looking very elegant in her short black leather jacket with a matching mushroom hat. Although she was in her late fifties, she could give any woman in her thirties a run for her money. Taffy was attractive, sophisticated, and stylish without being beautiful. Her almond tan skin glowed with just a touch of makeup that looked totally natural, and her hair hung a little below her hat, barely touching her shoulders.

"You look very lovely," Beverly admired. Although Taffy Hines was the richest black woman in Greenleaf, she didn't act the part. She was wonderfully wholesome and nice.

"Thank you, Beverly," Taffy received. "You look nice yourself. That color looks fabulous on you."

"Thank you," Beverly acknowledged. "I guess you want to see your husband?"

"Yes, thank you."

"My pleasure," Beverly agreed jovially. She started to invite Taffy to go into her husband's office, but she didn't want to do that to this nice woman. She didn't deserve to be hurt by Jamie and his little plaything, so she buzzed him.

****

Toni walked into Mason's office, and he was reclined at his desk staring out the window. "Mason," she called, and he jumped, turned around and sat up straight.

"Hi, Toni."

"Hi," she returned. "Are you all right?"

"Sure. We have to learn to bounce back, right?"

Toni sat in front of his desk and consoled, "If it's any consolation, I *do* believe Brandy loved you. The way she looked at you, it was evident. I don't think she could've faked that." He just stared at Toni for a while then smiled slightly.

"Thanks, Toni," he received. "But don't worry about me. I'll be all right." He took a deep breath. "Have you heard anything about her whereabouts yet?"

"Not yet," Toni answered. "Do you know where she grew up?"

"In a small town about thirty miles west of here called Burnsville if she was telling me the truth"

"Does she have any family?"

"No, she was adopted. She said both of her adopted parents are dead now."

335

"I see," Toni pondered.

They fell silent until he gathered the nerve to ask, "Do you actually believe Brandy had something to do with that article?"

"Yes, I do."

"But why? What's her motive?"

"I don't know. That's why we must find her."

"It couldn't have been your job. Brandy is at the bottom of an exceptionally long list of successors for your spot."

"That's what Angel said. No, I don't think it had anything to do with my *job*."

"Then what?"

"I don't know," she responded. "I *honestly* do not know. All I *do* know is that *Brandy* was the only one in a position to use Bill's authorization stamp and pass that article on. That's why we have to find her."

****

Felisha was kneeling on the floor servicing Jamie, who sat in his recliner, with her talents of a deep throat impersonator when they heard Beverly buzzed. "Damn," Jamie snapped. "I told her *no calls!*" He fought to catch his breath then answered, "Yes, Beverly. I told you to hold my calls." It was all he could do to maintain a normal level of speech with Felisha buried between his legs, draining the life out of him.

"I know you did, Jamie," Beverly singsong. "But your lovely wife is here."

Jamie almost knocked Felisha on the floor as he jumped to his feet and spurted out, "I'll be right there, Beverly. Thank you."

"You're quiet welcome," Beverly singsong again then focused back on Taffy. "He'll be *right* out, Mrs. Heard."

"Thank you, Beverly," Taffy acknowledged sweetly. "How is Ron? Have you heard from him?"

"Oh yes, we talk often," Beverly shared. "He's okay."

"I can't believe anyone would think that Toni wrote that article. It wasn't her style."

"I know, but some people believe it."

"That's a shame, and I've known Ron for years. He would *never* divulge information like that to *anyone*."

"I agree," Beverly replied as Jamie exploded out of his office, pulling on his suit jacket.

"Honey, I didn't know you were coming down here today," he spoke sweetly, giving her a peck on the cheek.

"I had to run by the accountant's office and decided to come and take you to lunch," she announced. "I didn't know you were so busy."

"It's okay. I'm always happy to see you," he lied, forcing a smile. "I wished you would've called though. I think I have a busy day scheduled. I wasn't even going to take a lunch break." He focused on Beverly. "Beverly, how many appointments do I have today?"

Beverly looked up at him, smiled, and replied sweetly, "None." She refused to cover for him or anyone else who cheated on his wife.

Jamie's eyebrow raised abruptly. "Really?" he countered sheepishly, wanting to strangle Beverly. "Then, I guess I'm free, honey."

"But are you busy *now*?" Taffy inquired. "You didn't want to be disturbed."

"I was just finishing something up," he thought quickly, planting his arms around her shoulder. "Come on, darling, we can leave now."

"Great," Taffy replied excitedly. As they walked out, Jamie darted back an *if looks could kill* look at Beverly and she just smiled sweetly at him.

"Have a nice day, Beverly," Taffy called back.

"Thank you," Beverly concluded. "You too." Beverly didn't even tell Felisha that Jamie was gone. She was just going to let the little slut stay hidden until she realized on her own that he wasn't coming back right now.

****

Ron sat at the computer, in his home office, trying to access the firm's records through a back door. Suddenly, he was in and he blew hard. He searched the receipts, invoices, and upcoming trials. He didn't see anything out of the ordinary. Then he was about to search the employee records and was knocked offline. "Son of a gun!" he breathed just as the doorbell rang. Ron signed out and rushed to the door.

Melissa was standing there with a box of baked goods. "You won't come to *me,* so I'll come to *you,*" she announced.

"Hi, sis," he addressed her, planting a kiss on her cheek. "Come in." She entered, and he closed the door. "What did you bring me?"

"Some brownies."

"Ooh."

"My very own special recipe."

"Thanks," he accepted, opening the box to take one out, and then stuffing it in his mouth. "How are the wedding plans coming?" Her mouth dropped open.

"You know?"

"Of course, I know," he chuckled with a mouth full of brownies.

She took a deep breath then asked, "Are you mad?"

"Why should I be mad?" he questioned, sitting on the couch, and taking a big gulp of bottled water that was on the coffee table. Melissa sat beside Ron and turned towards him.

"I know how you feel about Simon."

"Hey, if he makes *you* happy, then I'm happy for you," he made known.

"Thanks, Ron."

"You don't have to thank *me.* Thank *Simon!*" Ron maintained. "I haven't seen you look this happy in a long time."

"I *am* happy, littl' brother."

"Good," he held. "And I know the kids are crazy about him."

"They *really* are."

"Then that's all that matters," Ron finalized then burst into laughter. "I guess you just see something in the man that *I* don't see!"

"Ron!" she exploded.

Still laughing, Ron added, "But I don't have to live with him. *Thank God*!" Melissa picked up a chair pillow and hit him across the head as they continued to laugh.

****

Jamie walked back into the office and focused on Beverly who ignored him as if he weren't there. "Did you have fun today?" he asked sternly.

"And what are you referring to?" she retorted smugly, still typing.

"You know damn well what I'm talking about!" he snapped, and she stopped, stood, and challenged him eye-to-eye.

"Don't you *ever* curse at me again!" Beverly insisted.

"I didn't curse *at* you," he made known.

"I'm the only one who's here," she stood her ground.

"I'm sorry," he softened, so she stared at him long and hard before taking her seat again and resumed typing. He took a deep breath. "Look, Beverly, I know you don't like Billy and me in Ron Joyner's office, but we are, and you're going to have to deal with it." Beverly didn't answer and Jamie grew upset. "Geese! You act as if Ron Joyner was *balling* you or something!" Beverly stopped typing and focused on Jamie.

"How dare you!" she spat. "Ron and I are *friends*. A man and a woman can be friends without anything *sexual* going on?!" She eyed him. "Maybe you don't know." She shook her head. "You're not fit to tie Ron Joyner's shoestrings!" Jamie grew terribly upset then.

"Listen, Beverly!" he yelled. "Ron Joyner is *out,* and *I* am *in*!" He calmed down quickly. "You're supposed to be *helping* me. I need to know that you're with me."

"I don't help men *cheat* on their wives!" she spat.

He blew hard then came back with, "You're *just* a secretary, Beverly. You can be replaced!"

"And so can you," she remained firm.

"All I have to do is..."

"Then *replace* me," she responded smugly, cutting him off, and he was boiling by now. "I'd like to see you try!" She stood and faced him head-on. "*I will not*! I repeat, *will not* cover for *you* or anyone else. Take your little bimbos to a cheap hotel where all the other whores go!" She grabbed her purse, and before Jamie could respond, she added, "I'm going home. I've had *enough* of this *conversation*!" She stomped out, leaving him so steamed, he had to take deep breaths to calm himself.

****

Beverly walked down the hall so angrily she didn't see Jordan, and they crashed into one another. "Oh, Beverly, I'm sorry," Jordan apologized, picking up the papers she had dropped.

"It was my fault," Beverly acknowledged, helping Jordan seize her papers.

"Are you leaving?"

"Yeah, I *have* to before I say something I'd *really* regret to that arrogant *Jamie Heard*!" she snapped.

"I thought he was nice."

"Huh!" Beverly snapped.

"But he lets everyone here use his stables, right?"

"Yeah right! How many of *us* ride *horses*?" Beverly smirked sarcastically and Jordan chuckled.

"Would you like to talk about it?" Jordan offered. "Mr. Schuster is out for the rest of the day."

Beverly thought for a while, then she answered, "Yeah, sure."

****

"Hi, beautiful," Simon greeted Melissa with a kiss as she opened the locked bakery door for him and then relocked it.

"Hi," she welcomed. "Come into the back with me. I need to number the containers of icing."

Following her, he asked, "Why do you number them?"

"So that they can stay rotated. We want to use the first ones we make first, so they stay fresh."

"I see," he understood, leaning back on the counter, while she labeled the gallon sized plastic containers number one, number two, and number three. "You just make three at a time?"

"Yeah," she confirmed. "This is to start us off in the morning. When the bakers come in, they will make more. We make everything *fresh*." She was proud, and he knew it. He loved that about Melissa. She was such a perfectionist.

"So, how are the wedding plans coming?"

"Slow," she chuckled. "December nineteenth is right around the corner."

Catching her around the waist, he suggested, "Don't let it get to you, honey. I want this to be a *happy* occasion, not a *stressful* one."

"I can't help it," she came back with, wrinkling her face in frustration.

"Oh, it'll be all right," he finalized, grabbing her in a loving hug.

"I talked to Ron today," she announced, and he released her.

"Really?"

"Yeah, and to my surprise, he's okay with us."

Simon chuckled, "Now, that *is* a surprise."

"He says he just wants me to be happy."

"That's good. I know you were worried he wouldn't accept our marriage," Simon made known. "But honey, even if he *didn't*, this is *our* life. We know how we feel about each other. Right?" She nodded and he planted a kiss on her lips. Then he pulled her in his arms. "I love you so much."

"I love you, too."

****

Toni opened the door to the lake house, and Jordan was standing there smiling wide. "Hi, Toni," she greeted.

"Hi, Jordan. Come in," Toni responded, and she did.

"Where's Ron?" Jordan asked as Toni closed the door.

"He went to get a newspaper."

"Oh, okay," she acknowledged, sitting. "Toni, Jamie Heard made Beverly really mad today. She was..." Jordan stopped when she realized Toni wasn't really listening to her. "What's wrong?" Toni just looked up and stared at her, and Jordan caught on and took a breath. "Ron told you about the kiss."

"Was he supposed to hide it from me?"

"Of course not."

"Why, Jordan?" Toni wanted to know. "I was beginning to think you were my friend."

"I *am* your friend."

"And coming on to my husband?"

"I didn't *come on* to him. I just kissed him," Jordan defended.

Toni chuckled sarcastically, "Oh, *excuse* me. Is *that* all?"

"Toni, it was no big deal."

"I think it's a *very* big deal!"

Jordan took a deep breath and continued, "Toni, Ron and I were just talking and eating cake. Then I noticed that he had a big blob of icing on his face and when I started to clean it up, I just kissed him."

Toni took a deep breath then asked softly, "Do you want my husband, Jordan?"

"No!" she exploded.

"Then I can't for the life of me figure out why you kissed him!"

"I don't know either, Toni. I just *did*."

"Do you want to *sleep* with my husband?"

"Of course not!"

"So, you always go around kissing *married* men for no reason?" Toni charged, and Jordan just took another deep breath.

"When I was a child, I had a younger brother. I used to clean cake off his face too, and then I would always kiss him," she explained, remembering with a faraway look in her eyes. "That was our ritual. And for a split moment, Ron reminded me of my little brother when I used to clean him up."

"Where is your brother now?"

Jordan announced with tears staining her eyes, "When he was seven, he ran into the street after a basketball and was hit by a car." She paused. "He died instantly." She took some tissues off the coffee table, wiped her eyes, and blew her nose.

"I'm sorry."

"Thanks," Jordan sniffed again. "That was fourteen years ago, and I haven't thought about him much lately." She paused again. "I'm sorry I kissed Ron." She confronted Toni eye to eye, and Toni could see her sincerity. "I really and truly don't want your husband."

"That's good to know," Toni remained firm. "Because I don't know what we're getting ourselves into here, and I need to know that you're not gonna let me fall just to get my husband."

"I would *never* do that."

"I don't know, Jordan. We really don't know you very well. You see, *you're* licensed to carry a gun. *I'm* not," Toni explained. "When we're out there, I need to know you got my back, girlfriend."

"I gotcha back."

"Are you sure?"

"Yes, I'm *sure*. You don't even have to sweat it. I gotcha back."

Toni chuckled and switched into her impression of a sistah-girl tone, with the neck movement and all, "And keep your damn lips off my damn husband, heifer!"

"Well slut, you shouldn't have married someone so damn fine," Jordan joked back in her impression of a sistah-girl also.

Still in her act, Toni proclaimed, "But he's *my* fine man, Cunt! You don't want me to get ghetto *up in here* on your red ass!"

"I hear ya, heifer, but just make sure when you *jump,* you jump *straight!*" Jordan mocked her, and they burst into laughter together, as Ron entered.

"Sounds like a party," he chuckled.

****

David slid into bed with Angel and pulled her in his arms. "The boys were so tired their heads barely hit the pillows before they were asleep," he chuckled.

"They're very active," Angel acknowledged, sharing his excitement about their children. "Do they have enough blankets on their beds?"

"Oh yeah. They were both kicking the covers off. I had to keep putting them back on," he declared then planted a kiss on her forehead. "Tired?"

"A little."

"How are Toni and Ron doing?"

"They're trying to be brave, but I know they're hurting," she explained. "It's got to be hard on them."

"They haven't found out who's behind their troubles yet?"

"Not yet."

"Well, maybe soon."

"I hope so," she agreed, snuggling up close to him.

"Cold?"

"Uh uh," she grumbled, and he smiled, turned to face her, and pulled her into his arms, kissing her long and fervently. David held up and pulled off his pajama top, exposing his well-built brown body and Angel just gasped, admiring her husband's athletic, strong abs. He laid on her, smothering her neck and face with seductive, wet kisses, and she groaned with pleasure.

"Honey," Angel murmured between kisses.

"Hum um," he moaned, still massaging her neck and chest with tender kisses.

"I want to have another baby," she whispered in his ear, stopping him in his tracks, and then Angel burst into laughter because David acted as if he was frozen solid. "I didn't just *stab* you, David! You can move!" He held up on one elbow over her, half-heartedly smiling.

"Why?"

"I just do. I want a little *girl*."

"What if it's another *boy*?"

"Then we'll try again," she joked, and his eyes widen.

"You can't be serious," he chuckled in disbelief.

"I'm not," she laughed then sobered quickly and cooed. "I'm kidding about a fourth child, but I would like to have just *one* more." She held up and began kissing his neck, and he was being suck into her passion.

"You're fighting dirty," he cooed.

"Is this a fight?" she purred.

"It is if you want another child," he stressed, and she froze then dropped back on the bed.

"Why? We only have *two* kids. It's not like we can't *afford* another child, honey."

"What about your job?"

"I *can* take a maternity leave," she sarcastically revealed.

"Angel, I wouldn't want you *working* with *three* kids," he insisted. "It's bad enough you're working with *two*."

Smiling wide, she pressed, "So, we *can*?"

He took a deep breath then suggested, "Can I think about it?"

****

"Beverly is very upset that Ron isn't there," Jordan explained while Ron and Toni listened from the couch and Chuck on the speakerphone. "She hates Jamie and Billy. She says Billy is an arrogant snob and Jamie is a cheating snake."

"Ron, do you think either one of them would be a person of interest who would want to destroy you?" Chuck asked.

"I don't see why," Ron answered. "I helped Jamie get the job, but I don't know either one of them well enough to be considered enemies."

"Why did Beverly call Jamie a cheating snake?" was Toni's question.

"She says she's fooling around with Felisha."

"Travis's secretary?" Ron inquired.

"Yes," answered Jordan.

"Isn't he the one who's married to Taffy Hines?" Chuck explored.

"Yes," Ron answered. "And she's a nice lady. She doesn't deserve that."

"No, she doesn't," added Toni.

"Beverly said Taffy Hines asked about you, Ron," Jordan added.

"That was nice of her," Ron accepted.

"Chuck, Beverly also said there was an exterminator there before all this happened," Jordan shared.

"They spray periodically," added Ron.

"Ron, you talked to Mrs. Sanders in your office, right?" inquired Chuck.

"Yes." Ron answered.

"Then maybe we need to check the exterminator out," Chuck suggested. "Jordan, text me the man's name. Hey, wait a minute. I have a fax coming in."

"Anything important, Chuck?" Ron inquired.

"I put in a check on Brandy Sears' employment history," Chuck shared. "Ron, when did Leroy go through that trouble at the hospital?"

"Seven years ago," Ron answered.

"Well, I'll be," Chuck pondered.

"What is it, Chuck?" inquired Jordan.

"Brandy Sears was a candy striper at the hospital exactly seven years ago and then disappeared," Chuck responded.

"What?!" exploded Toni.

"Do you think she was involved in setting Leroy up too?" Ron asked.

"It's too much of a coincidence for her *not* to be," Chuck speculated. "Ron, you get a hold of Leroy tomorrow and call me. You can call me from your home. Jordan doesn't have to be there. I want to know what happened at the hospital seven years ago."

"Leroy won't talk about it," Ron made known.

"Well, he just might have to," Chuck insisted. "If your family is a target of some kind, then your *sisters* could be next!"

Chapter 35

Jordan searched diligently in a filing cabinet in John Schuster's office. She knew that if there was anything unethical about this law firm in their treatment of Ron, Mr. Schuster would have access to the evidence. Suddenly, she heard the door open, and she jumped, spinning around to face the intruder. "Hi, beautiful," Travis spoke, smiling wide.

"Hi," she returned, smiling back. He walked to her slowly and she had to breathe deeply. He looked so good in that expensive, black suit, accentuated by a pale gold silk shirt with the matching pale, striped gold and black tie and handkerchief.

Travis walked so close to Jordan she could feel the heat from his gorgeous, masculine, lean, well-built body, and she could smell his minty fresh breath when he asked, "How about dinner tonight?" She was so choked up from his fresh aftershave, his deep, sexy voice, his even white teeth, she couldn't find her voice to utter a single word. All she could do was nod. He smiled sweetly and added, "Seven?" She nodded again, and he planted a kiss on her lips. "See you then." She nodded again, and then he turned and strolled out just as smoothly as he had entered. Jordan was able to breathe for the first time after he left her presence. Was she falling for this man? It was obvious that he was nothing but a womanizer. She couldn't let herself get involved with Travis Bland. He could be a *suspect*. She had a *job* to do! Was she *crazy*?! Oh, he was so sexy and *fine,* her flesh grew warm.

"Snap out of it, Jordan!" she ordered herself. She took a deep and concentrated breath, then went about with what she was doing, but her mind was still on Travis's lean, sexy body.

****

Ron opened his front door and Leroy was standing there, looking normal with his clean-shaven face and a small, neat mustache, low neat haircut, casual khaki pants with a black, pull-over polo shirt, and a short black leather jacket. Ron smiled wide. He was delighted that his brother looked so healthy, almost like his old self. "I'm here," Leroy snapped. "What'd you want?"

"How are you, big brother?" Ron inquired. Leroy had always been impatient. That's one trait that made him a brilliant surgeon. He wanted his patients well, and he wanted them well *now*! So, he did everything in his power to see that they were!

"I'm fine. Why did you want to see me?" Leroy barked. "I told you I have nothing else to say about what happened to me. It's over and done with."

Sarcastically, Ron offered, "Wouldn't you like to come in?" Leroy took a deep breath, shook his head slightly like he couldn't believe his baby brother's nerves, and then entered Ron and Toni's house for the first time.

Leroy looked around in amazement at his brother's exquisite, huge house. It was even bigger than the one he had shared with Sharon, his former wife, and their two children, Leroy Junior, who was now sixteen, and Monica, who was now twelve. He was enormously proud of his little brother, but he *couldn't* say that he was proud of his *choice* in *women*. The bitch had destroyed him. He just couldn't forget that.

"Nice," Leroy grumbled, indicating the house.

"Thanks," Ron accepted. "Come with me into the sunroom." Leroy hesitantly followed his brother, and Ron sat on the couch while Leroy flopped on a chair. "Would you like some tea or something?"

"No."

"OJ?"

"*Nothing!*" Leroy insisted. "What is this all about, Ronnie?" Ron smiled. He hadn't heard Leroy call him *Ronnie* in a long time. Although Leroy entered the house with a major chip on his shoulders, it still felt good to know that a part of his brother's past was still in him somewhere. At least he came so there *was* hope!

"Leroy, you know Toni and I are investigating how that story was published in her column."

"Why? Didn't *she* write it?"

"No," Ron announced, and Leroy's eyes widened. "Toni didn't write that article."

"That's what *she* said!" Leroy barked sarcastically.

"That's what's *true!*" Ron retaliated.

Leroy stared at him long and hard then came back with, "Then what does this have to do with *me*? *I* didn't write it!"

Ron chuckled and continued, "Leroy, do you remember my friend from college, Chuck? Chuck Warren?"

"Yeah," Leroy answered suspiciously. Why was Ron asking him about Chuck Warren? "He was the one who went to law school with you and decided to open a private investigative firm instead of practicing law, right?"

"Yes."

"What about him?"

"Toni and I hired Chuck's firm to investigate this case for us."

"And?"

"And he found some pretty interesting things, not just about *our* case but *yours* as well" Ron announced, and Leroy raised an eyebrow. Ron knew he was finally getting his brother's attention.

"What *things*?"

"I'm gonna call him and let him explain, all right?" Ron suggested and Leroy exhaled then slowly nodded. Ron picked up the telephone, dialed the number and put it on the speaker. They could both hear Chuck's phone ringing.

"Chuck Warren Investigations," a woman's voice answered.

"Hi, this is Ron Joyner. May I speak to Chuck please?"

"Yes, Mr. Joyner. He's been expecting your call. Hold on, please."

"Thank you."

"Ron," Chuck answered immediately. "How are you?"

"Hi, Chuck. I'm fine. I have you on speaker. Leroy is here with me."

"Hi, Leroy. Long time no see."

"Hi, Chuck," Leroy replied solemnly. "What's this all about? Ronnie knows I don't want to stir this thing back up."

"Even if it could clear your name?" Chuck examined.

"What?" Leroy spat.

"Leroy, we have reason to believe that what happened to you was *no* accident," Chuck announced.

"What're you talking about?" Leroy wanted to know. "I was convicted of *negligence*."

"I'm not talking about *negligence*," Chuck clarified. "I'm talking about *murder*!"

****

"Bill, do you have a moment?" Toni solicited, entering his office.

"Yeah, come in, sweetheart," he responded, waving her in.

"How is Rita?" she asked, sitting in front of his desk.

"Well, we finally have some good news," Bill announced. "They think they have found a bone marrow donor for her."

"That's great, Bill!" Toni exploded. "Is she home?"

"Yes, I'm taking her to the medical center whenever they're ready to do it."

"I couldn't be happier for her…and *you*. I know how worried you've been."

"Thanks, Toni," he accepted. "Now, what can I do for *you*?"

"I wanted to ask you something about Brandy Sears."

"I haven't heard from her yet," he shared. "Has Mason?"

Shaking her head, Toni verified, "No."

"She really did a number on him."

"Yes, she did," Toni agreed. "What I wanna know is who hired her."

"She was hired temporarily by HR through a temp service. Then Mason put the screws on me to hire her permanently," he explained. "What's this all about, Toni?"

"Bill, I feel pretty sure that it was Brandy who set me up, but I don't know anything about her, so I don't know *why* she did it."

"Did you talk to Mason? He was closer to her than anyone here."

352

"He doesn't know much about her. He just knows she was a good *lay*," Toni acknowledged then laughed, and Bill laughed with her.

"Why don't you go to the temp service and see what they have on her?"

"Yeah, maybe I'll do that," Toni concluded. "We *have* to find her…to clear this mess up!"

****

"What're you talking about?!" Leroy exploded, sitting on the edge of his chair now. "I didn't *murder* anyone!"

"He's not talking about *you*, Leroy," Ron interjected. "He's talking about someone else at the hospital."

"On my surgical team?" Leroy solicited.

"Yes," answered Ron.

"Leroy, we have reason to believe that someone might have set you up just like they did Ron and Toni," Chuck continued.

"It was the same surgical team I've always used," Leroy insisted. "You are way off base here, Chuck."

"Leroy, tell us everything that happened during that operation," Ron suggested.

"Ronnie, I told you, I don't wanna talk about it!" Leroy insisted, springing to his feet. "It's over and done with!"

Ron jumped up and confronted his stubborn brother, "Leroy, that man was probably *murdered* to destroy *you*. If that's the case, don't you want to know who *did* it?" Leroy stared long and hard at his brother. "Don't *you*?" He didn't answer and Ron sensed something else going on. "What're you hiding, Leroy? Why don't you wanna get the answers you need to get your life back?"

"I *do* have my life back," Leroy persisted.

"In a *bottle*?" Ron countered.

"I'm not drinking anymore," Leroy defended. "I haven't for months."

"Yes, I know and I'm proud of you, but don't you want to practice *medicine* again?"

"Not really," he answered.

"Leroy, medicine is what you spent all your life doing. You were at the top of your profession when it was stripped away from you," Ron explained. "Why don't you wanna know the truth? What happened in that operating room that day, Leroy?"

"I didn't do anything wrong!" Leroy maintained. "I *didn't*!"

"I know, and *we* want to help you," Ron made known. "Please, let *us* help *you*."

Leroy sat again, and Ron followed. "Leroy, there was a candy striper at the hospital during that time," Chuck continued. "Ron, show him the picture and see if he remembers her."

"I didn't see *candy stripers* very often," Leroy chuckled slightly with a little sarcasm.

"I understand," Chuck accepted. "Just take a look at the picture, please."

Looking at the picture of Brandy without removing it from Ron's hand, Leroy stated, "I don't know her. What's so special about her anyway?"

"We think she was behind the plot against you, and not only *you*, but Ron and Toni as well," Chuck enlightened. "Take a good look at the picture, Leroy. *Please!*"

Leroy took the picture this time and studied it, then shook his head, "I don't know her." Then suddenly a flashback of Brandy's smiling face flickered before his eyes. "Wait," he exploded.

"You remember something?" Chuck inquired.

Thinking hard, Leroy pondered, "I do remember seeing her."

*   *Leroy walked down the halls of the hospital, in his blue, surgical scrubs with a white doctor's smock about to pass two women. As he passed them, an envelope fell from one of the ladies' hands. He stopped, picked it up, and handed it to her. "Here you are, young lady," he offered, handing it back to her. He looked in Brandy's good-looking, young face with her long hair pulled back in a ponytail and a striped skirt and top.*

"Thank you, Dr. Joyner," she accepted, receiving the envelope, and handing it to the other woman.

"Hi, Tracie," Leroy greeted the other woman dressed in blue, surgical nurse's scrubs.

"Hi, Dr. Joyner," the blonde-headed lady replied with a dazzling smile on her pretty Caucasian face.

"Thank you for a job well done in there," Leroy acknowledged.

"You're welcome," Tracie recognized.

"I'll see you in the morning, and we'll do it again."

"Yes, sir," the lady agreed, smiling sweetly. "Oh, Dr. Joyner, this is Brandy Sears. She goes to school with my kid brother, and I'm dating her brother. She's the best candy striper here!"

"I bet she is," Leroy settled, extending a hand. "Nice to meet you, young lady."

Taking his hand in a shake, Brandy proposed, "Thank you, sir. Likewise."

"Well, you ladies have a nice day."

*"Thank you, Dr. Joyner," they concluded in unison.   *

"That was the first and last time I remember seeing her," Leroy expounded to Ron and Chuck, coming out of his daydream.

"Who was this nurse?" Chuck wanted to know.

"Tracie Myers. She was on my team a few times," Leroy answered.

"What happened to her when you were convicted?" Chuck continued.

"I never saw Tracie again," Leroy pondered. "As a matter of fact, I don't remember seeing her after the incident occurred at all."

"She wasn't at the trial?" was Ron's question.

"No," answered Leroy.

"I think we need to find Miss Tracie Myers," Chuck replied sternly.

"So, do you think Tracie and this Brandy girl had something to do with what happened in the OR that day?" Leroy probed.

"What *did* happen, Leroy?" Ron asked.

Leroy focused on Ron then took a deep breath and began.

*   *"It went great,"* Leroy announced to this surgical team, standing over a man lying on the operating table, still with their masks on. *"Thank you all for a job well done."*

"That was a magnificent job, Dr. Joyner," another doctor said to Leroy. *"You make it look so easy."*

"Thank you, Jay," Leroy replied, giving the patient on the operating table an injection. *"Let me give him a dose of amiodarone and you can close."*

"Yes, Dr. Joyner."

Leroy stepped back and the other doctor stepped in and suddenly the heart monitor went berserk. Leroy jumped back to the patient and yelled, "What the hell happened?"

"I don't know," Jay responded, stepping back to give Leroy space.

He began pounding into the man's chest. "Paddles!" Leroy yelled. Tracie handed them to him immediately and he began. "Clear!" The man's body did not respond. "Damn it, come on!" Jay reset the machine. "Clear!" Then Leroy threw the paddles down and started a rhythm pounding in the man's chest. Soon, he heard the worst sound of his life...the monitor flatlined and Leroy closed his eyes and dropped his head back. Then he tried one more attempt to save the dying man, but it was no use.   *

"He was gone, and I couldn't do anything else to save him," Leroy announced to Ron and Chuck.

"What was the cause of death?" Chuck asked.

"Overdose of amiodarone."

"How did he get an overdose?" queried Ron.

"They said *I* gave it to him, but I know I didn't," Leroy insisted. "I checked the dosage several times before we entered the OR."

"Why didn't you fight?" added Chuck.

"This is ancient history!" Leroy snapped, jumping up again. "It doesn't matter anymore!"

Ron jumped up behind him, losing all patience with his brother, "This is *not* ancient history! What happened to you may be directly related to what happened to Toni and me. And if that's true, Melissa and Denise might very well be next! Now, you tell me what you're hiding, and you tell me *now!*" Ron grabbed Leroy's shoulders and yelled this time. "What is going on, Leroy? What in the hell are you hiding?! This is our *lives* we're talking about, damn it! Why are you *refusing* to defend yourself?! What *is* it?!"

Leroy locked eyes with his determined brother and replied weakly, "I was having an affair with the man's wife."

Ron's eyes widen as he probed blandly, "The *dead* man?"

Leroy dropped his head and answered faintly, "Yes."

****

"Melissa, we used all three containers of icing already, and the rest isn't ready yet," one of the bakers explained as Melissa walked into the kitchen.

"I think we have enough in the case until the rest of the icing is ready," Melissa made known. "But maybe we better make four or five for in the morning during this busy season."

"All right," the lady agreed. "How are the wedding plans going?"

"Slow," Melissa chuckled. "I'm going to be a nervous wreck before the wedding gets here."

"Don't do that," Cammie added, entering the kitchen. "You want to *enjoy* your *honeymoon*." Melissa smiled shyly. "And speaking of your honeymoon, your *honey* is out front."

"*Simon's* here?!" Melissa blurted out.

"Why are you so surprised? He comes in *every* day," Cammie acknowledged.

"But I thought he was in court already," Melissa replied, exiting the kitchen. She walked from behind the counter and took Simon's hand. "Hi."

"Hi," he spoke, planting a kiss on her cheek.

"I thought you were in court," she continued, walking to a dining room table in the back with him.

"I'm on my way now," he shared. "I just stopped by to ask you something."

"Sure. What is it, sweetie?" she pondered.

"I was just wondering how you'd feel about me asking Ron to be my best man," he considered. "Ron and I used to be very close, and I was wondering…" He stopped when he witnessed a smile spreading across her face. "You like the idea?"

"I think it's a wonderful idea."

****

"You were having an *affair* with the wife of the man who died on your operating table?" Ron asked Leroy slowly, and he nodded.

"Patricia and I met at a medical conference. She was an insurance rep and tried to get me to buy insurance. She was very persistent, so to get her off my back, I agreed to talk to her," Leroy explained. "One thing led to another and we started having an affair." He paused. "No, it was *more* than that! I *loved* her, and I thought she loved me. We had planned to divorce our spouses and marry each other. She said the night she asked Hank for the divorce is the night he had his heart attack."

"And *you* were the *only* surgeon available that night?" Ron searched.

"Yes," Leroy confirmed. "Ken was on vacation in Hawaii and Doug was home nursing the flu. It was *me* or no one! Besides, I didn't know who the patient was until I was in the operating room. It *was* an emergency you know!" Ron walked away and sat again, and Leroy continued. "Patricia even turned against me. That hurt more than *anything*, for the woman I loved and wanted to spend the rest of my life with to believe that I would kill her husband just so we could be together."

"So, that's why you didn't fight?" Chuck inquired.

"Yes. If the affair had gotten out, no one would've ever believed I did all I could to save Hank's life. *Patricia* didn't even believe it, and she was supposed to have been in love with me. Why would anyone else?" Leroy explained. "So, it was better to be charged with negligence than *murder!*"

"Why didn't you tell *me*?" Ron wanted to know.

"I *couldn't.* You would've tried to help me, and I knew it would have destroyed you if you couldn't, and *I* was put to death for murder," Leroy made known.

"Leroy, have you spoken to Patricia since this happened?" Chuck wanted to know.

"I talked to her right after my medical license was suspended and the look in her eyes, I'll never forget. She *actually* believed I was guilty of murdering her husband. That hurt *more* than anything I lost in the lawsuit," Leroy explained solemnly.

"Leroy, if we're right, you *will* get your life back because you *were* set up," Chuck announced. "I promise you that!"

****

Jordan walked into her house, followed by Travis, and he immediately grabbed her in a big, sultry kiss. "What're you doing?" she yelped.

"Kissing you."

Backing away, Jordan insisted, "That was *more* than a kiss."

"Was it?" he smirked, closing the door.

"Yes," she confirmed, taking off her coat. "Would you like something to drink?"

"Do you have a beer?"

"Yes, I think I do," she spoke, heading for the kitchen as he admired her shapely body in that body fitting, knee-length, rayon lavender dress while she walked away. She looked back over her shoulder and he smiled shyly, and she burst into laughter while she exited. Travis shook his head and shifted his pants to settle the bulge that was rising in his crotch. He then pulled off his coat and laid it on the chair. He looked around at the pictures of Jordan's family. He knew the older white lady and black man had to be Jordan's parents.

359

They made a handsome couple. No wonder Jordan was so beautiful. Her mother had short, curly, brown hair and her father had a low haircut with a neat mustache and beard. They looked highly distinguished. Jordan entered with two bottles of beer and handed Travis one as the telephone rang.

"Excuse me," she acknowledged, picking up the cordless phone as he nodded and sat on the couch. "Hello?"

"Hello sweetheart."

"Hi, Dad. How are you?"

"Fine and you?" he inquired.

Jordan heard her mother in the background yell, "Hi Jordan."

"Hi, Mom," Jordan called to her.

"Are you still in Greenleaf?" her father asked.

"Yes, sir."

"Do you have company?"

"Yes, Daddy, I do have company," Jordan confirmed, looking at Travis and he smiled sweetly at her.

"A *man*?" her father asked.

"Yes, Daddy. He's a man," she confirmed, sitting beside Travis, and Travis placed his hand on her exposed thigh as her dress rose. Jordan almost gasped at his touch.

"A *nice* man?"

"Yes, Daddy. He's very nice," she verified as Travis leaned over and began nibbling on her ear.

"What does he do?"

She laughed, "He's a *lawyer*."

Her father laughed also, "Good."

"I hope so," she agreed, as Travis slid his hand in the top of her dress and Jordan jumped.

"Well, honey, enjoy your evening. We just wanted to check on you."

"I'm fine," Jordan responded, and Travis looked at her and nodded and she smiled.

"Good night, honey."

"Good night," she concluded, hanging up. Then Jordan jumped off the couch and Travis tumbled over. "That was dirty."

"What was?" he questioned, smiling shyly, taking a swig of his beer.

"Torturing me while I was talking to my father!"

Standing, he teased, "Was it *torture*?" He licked his lips.

"And you know it," she charged but she wasn't smiling anymore.

Travis threw up his hands and promise, "Sorry. I'll behave." He patted the couch beside him. "Come on. Sit." She hesitated and he smiled. "Hands off! Promise!" She took a deep breath then sat beside him and took a big gulp of her beer.

Jordan knew she had to calm down. Travis was driving her insane with passion, but she couldn't let him know it.

"So, Miss Curry, do you plan to be a secretary for the rest of your life, or do you have other plans in mind?" Travis questioned, trying to take his mind off the bulge in his pants, which he knew she was aware of also.

"I don't know," she answered then took a breath. "I haven't thought much about it."

"Oh, since daddy has money, you don't have to think about it, right" he chuckled.

"It's not that."

"Then what?"

"I just haven't thought about it," she insisted. "What about you? Do you plan to ever settle down and have kids?"

"I *have* a son."

"You do?"

"Yes, his name is Malik."

"Where is he?"

"With his mother in Baltimore."

"Do you see him much?"

"Oh yeah, all the time. We're buddies," Travis confirmed. "If *I* don't call *him*, *he'll* call *me*. We speak to each other every night. He might come for Christmas."

"I'll like to meet him," Jordan remarked, and Travis focused on her. She really sounded like she wanted to meet his son. Most ladies tried to stay away from kids.

"I'd like that," he replied.

"How old is he?"

"Twelve."

"Twelve?!" she exploded. "How old are *you*?"

He laughed, "I'm thirty-two. We had him when we were in college."

"Did you love his mother?"

"No," he stated matter-of-factly. "Wanda was a pre-law student too, and she went out with me because she was mad at her boyfriend. We both got drunk, and the rest is history."

"Wow, that was *some* party."

Laughing, he concurred, "Yes, it was."

"So, do you have a good relationship with Wanda?"

"Yes, we never loved each other, so there was no drama involved. We never tried to *pretend* we loved each other either. It was just something that happened," he announced. "But we *do* respect each other."

"That's great," Jordan acknowledged. "So, do you do the child support thing and all?"

Laughing again he answered, "No, Wanda and I share Malik's expenses, and he comes and stays with me a lot when he's out of school. I pay his tuition, clothes, school supplies, and any other things his mother feels are necessary. However, she supplied the shelter when she bought her house. She's a lawyer too, so she really doesn't need money from me, but he's my son, so I do my part."

"That's nice," Jordan observed. "So, Malik goes to *private* school?"

"Yes, he's in the seventh grade."

"That's great, Travis. I like to see parents come together in the best interest of their children. It sounds like you and Wanda have an incredibly good relationship."

"We do," he replied then locked eyes with her. "But I would like to have a *better* one with *you*." He leaned forward and she met him in a kiss. "I'm crazy about you, Jordan."

"Travis, if you're talking about *sex*, it's *way* too soon."

"For *whom*?"

"For *me* and *you*," she stressed.

"Speak for yourself," he cooed, and they kissed again. Then he slid closer and pulled her in his arms so he could get a deeper kiss. Their passions soared to a burning high and Jordan pulled back. "What's wrong?"

"I'm not ready," she made known and stood.

He stood and walked behind her, "What're you afraid of?"

"Getting hurt," she admitted, and he walked in front of her. "I'm afraid of getting hurt, Travis."

He lifted her head with his finger and whispered, "I'll never hurt you."

"I know you believe that, but until you're in *love* with me, you can't say that," she hypothesized, and he took a deep breath.

"All right, Miss Curry, I'll wait," he announced. "*You're* worth it."

Chapter 36

"Ron, Toni, this is Jordan Curry," Travis introduced. "She's John's new secretary."

"How do you do?" Toni shook her hand first.

"Hi," Jordan responded.

Then Ron shook her hand, "A pleasure, Jordan."

"We met when you came to the office to see Mr. Schuster," Jordan remarked.

"Yes, I remember," Ron replied as Toni led everyone into the den. They all had to be careful not to let on that they already knew each other. Jordan and Travis had been seeing each other for over two months now and she was growing overly attached to him. She hated deceiving him, but it was her *job*. Somehow, she felt that knowing Travis's macho personality, he wouldn't take it too kindly when he found out they were all deceiving him, but that's a chance she *had* to take. Her clients came first and what was in the best interest of them was what she had to do.

"Ron, how is the case going, my man? Cause I'm working my butt off trying to do *your* job and *mine!*" Travis chuckled.

"I have a hearing before the bar association in two weeks. I don't know what they will decide," Ron explained. "Mrs. Sanders did talk her sister into not suing either the firm or me."

"Yeah, I heard she's waiting on you to defend her," Travis made known.

"Jordan, come on in the kitchen and help me fix some refreshments," Toni cut in. "They could be at this for hours." The ladies exited.

"Seems like someone has finally captured the devout bachelor," Ron teased.

Travis laughed, "She's something else."

"Do I hear the *L* word?"

"No! *Never!*" Travis burst into laughter.

"*Never* say *never,* my friend," Ron laughed with him.

****

"Toni, I don't know what to do," Jordan shared as they fixed drinks. "Travis is so *fine*. It's hard to resist him."

"Are you in love with him?" Toni asked.

Jordan pondered then answered, "Yeah, I think I am."

"You go girl!" Toni gave her a high five.

"But I don't know how *he* feels."

"Trust me, Jordan, you're *in*," Toni chuckled. "Travis has *never* looked at a woman the way he looks at you."

"Really?"

"Really," Toni insisted.

"He wants to make love to me, but I think it's too soon," Jordan shared.

"Do *you* want to?"

"Oh yes," Jordan admitted in a chuckled.

"Girl, I remember when Ron and I first made love," Toni reminisced. "I went to the brotha's house and threw myself on him. I had never done that before in my whole life. That was our *first* official date! I thought for sure I had blown it. I thought he was gonna think I was some kind of a floozy or something, but he didn't. Now, when I look back at it, that was the best decision I ever made in my entire life."

"That's sweet, but things don't always turn out like that," Jordan theorized. "And I don't think Travis is *anything* like Ron. *Travis* is a *whore*." Toni burst into laughter. "He *is*!" Jordan laughed with her.

"You might be surprised, my friend," Toni remarked. "You might be surprised."

****

Mason sat outside on the patio in the night air, looking at the stars and thinking of Brandy. The December air was chilly, but he didn't feel it. He thought of all the times he had spent with her. He thought of her smiling face. He thought of how much he loved her and wanted to see her. He wanted her back at any cost. He *needed* her back. Why wouldn't she come back? He would be going to Melissa and Simon's wedding soon, and he didn't feel like seeing anyone so happy when he was so sad. He knew that was selfish, but he couldn't help it. He loved Brandy and missed her. He wanted to feel her in his arms again and in his bed. He sniffed back tears and when Becky walked out on the patio, he didn't even notice her.

"Are you all right?" she asked, and he jerked to look at her. Then he wiped his eyes quickly.

"Yes," he responded. "Is Amy asleep?"

"Yes," she replied as she sat in the chair beside him. "Mason, why can't you love me like you love *her*?" He turned, faced his wife, and witnessed her distraught face.

Mason didn't feel like pretending any longer. He would just have to tell Becky the truth and let the chips fall where they may. "I don't know," he admitted weakly.

"I love you, Mason," Becky confessed.

"I know."

"Why hasn't that been enough for you?"

"I guess, Becky, because you tricked me into marrying you," he finally charged, and her eyes widened. "Yes, I know. I know you weren't pregnant when we were married. I can count, you know."

"Amy was late."

"Oh, stop it, Becky!" he yelled, springing to his feet. "No baby comes *two months* late! Just be honest!" She dropped her head. "Please." She got up and strolled slowly to him.

"I just loved you so much, Mason. I didn't want to lose you," she confessed. "I knew the only way you would've married me was if I was pregnant. I know I'm not pretty. You would've never married me." She sniffed. "I'm sorry."

"Did we even make love that night? I don't remember. I was drunk. Did we, Becky? Did we make love that night?"

She took a deep breath then responded, "No."

He touched her face lightly with his finger, smiled sweetly at her, and then responded, "Thank you. I just *needed* to know the truth."

"What're you going to do?"

"Nothing," he replied then kissed her lips gently. "I just needed to know the truth." He pulled her in his arms and hugged her lovingly.

****

Travis walked Jordan to her door, opened it, and handed her the key. Then he kissed her long and breathlessly. "Good night," he whispered softly.

"Aren't you coming in?"

"I better not. I don't feel too strong tonight," he chuckled. She took his hand and guided him into her house anyway, and Travis' eyes widened as his excitement grew.

He closed the door and gently pulled her into his arms and their tongues searched each other's mouth hungrily. Travis removed his black, leather jacket and let it drop to the floor, as his lips still remained glued to Jordan's. Their kisses were wet, steamy, and deep. Jordan removed her coat and attempted to throw it on the chair but missed. She didn't care because she was too much involved in making her dreams come true. Travis swept her up in his arms and carried her to the bedroom. He laid her on the bed delicately as they continued to explore the inner depths of each other's souls with their wet, hungry tongues. Travis held up long enough to yank his shirt off over his head quickly. Jordan gasped when she eyed his strong, hairy, bare chest. Then he covered her body with his again and met her desiring lips. Travis held up a little and literally tore Jordan's blouse open, exposing her lace black bra. Jordan smiled at hearing the buttons on her two-hundred-dollar silk blouse pop off, just like in the movies. As if to read her thoughts, Travis smiled and breathed, "I'll buy you another one."

"Travis," Jordan called softly.

"Yes, baby."

"I've never done this before," she confessed.

"Done what?" he asked breathlessly, mothering her neck with wet kisses.

"*This*," she stressed, and he froze.

Travis held up and looked in her clear eyes and yelped, "You're a *virgin*?"

****

Ron settled into bed with Toni and pulled her in his arms. "Chuck called while you were in the shower," Toni shared. "He wants us to go to the lake house for a meeting tomorrow night."

"We can stay here since Travis is bringing Jordan over now," Ron suggested. "It won't look too strange now."

"I told him that, but he still thinks it's better to meet at the lake house for a while."

"Okay," Ron agreed. "Did he say he had anything?"

"He said he'll update us tomorrow."

"We better solve this case soon. When I go to court in two weeks for the hearing, I've *got* to have *something*."

****

Travis held up and looked in Jordan's moist, concerned face and asked again, "You are a *virgin*?"

"You make it sound like a disease!" she chuckled. "Yes, Travis, I am a virgin." She could feel his body relax immediately. Then he rolled off her and sat on the edge of the bed. "What's wrong?"

He took a deep breath, looked back at her and asked, "And you were willing to give yourself to me?" She nodded slowly. "Why?"

369

"What'd you mean *why*!" she shrieked, sitting beside him. "I care for you." He stood and pulled on his pants. "What's wrong?"

He turned and faced her again. "Jordan, I…"

"You're not in love with me," she finished.

"It's not that. It's just that…" he started then paused. "I just don't want to mislead you."

She stood and pulled on a housecoat. "You think I'll get too clingy if I give my virginity to you?"

"I don't know what to think," he chuckled. "It's been a long time since I met a virgin."

"So, what do we do now?"

He rubbed across his twists briskly then responded, "The hell if I know."

****

Toni turned over in bed in the dark room, and Ron was missing. "Ron," she called, but he didn't answer. She rose from the bed, slipped on his pajama top, and walked out the bedroom. "Ron!"

"Yes, sweetie," he called from downstairs.

"Where are you?" Toni asked, strolling down the staircase.

"I'm right here, sweetheart," he responded at the bottom of the stairs, drinking some water.

"What's wrong?"

"I couldn't sleep. Did I wake you?" he asked, planting a kiss on her forehead.

"No, but when I woke up and you weren't there, it was weird," she confessed, following him into the kitchen.

"I'm sorry, baby. I tried not to wake you. I know you have to work in the morning," he explained, sitting at the table.

Sitting at the table also, she proclaimed, "It's gonna be all right, honey." He looked at her and smiled, touching her hand.

"I know, sweetie. Thank you for saying that," he affirmed. "I'm just ready to get my life back." He sighed deeply. "I studied and worked so hard to build my reputation. And to know that it could be stripped away in a second because of lies is a little dishearten."

"I know it is, baby, but we'll get through this *together*."

He smiled sweetly at her and checked, "Have I told you lately how much I love you?"

She returned her husband's loving smile and verified, "Every day."

****

"Look, Jordan, I care for you, but…" Travis started but was silenced by his ringing cell phone. He fished it out of his pocket and answered. "Hey, buddy."

"Hi, Dad," a tall, thin, little milk-chocolate-tan boy said on the other end with NBA pajamas on and short, neat twists in his hair. "Are you sleeping?"

"No. I'm up."

"I called your landline. You didn't answer."

"I'm not home, buddy."

"Oh, I see," Malik understood, smiling. "Who is she this time?"

"Her name is Jordan and she's very nice."

"Oh, this one has a *name*?" Malik laughed.

"Will you lay off your old man!" Travis laughed with the child.

"Is she pretty?"

"Yes, she's *very* pretty," Travis recognized, sharing a smile with Jordan.

"Can I talk to her?"

Surprised, Travis pondered, "Sure." He extended the phone to Jordan. "My son wants to talk to you."

"He does?!" Jordan yelped, and Travis nodded with a smile on his face. Jordan took the phone and spoke. "Hello."

"Hi," Malik said on the other end.

"How are you?"

"I'm well. Thank you," he answered. "I'm Malik. How are you?"

"I'm well, too. Thank you," Jordan replied feeling a little weird not knowing where this relationship was going with Travis. "I'm Jordan Curry."

"I've never heard of a girl named *Jordan*."

"There're a few of us," Jordan chuckled as Travis got up and walked into the restroom.

"Will I see you when I come to visit my dad for Christmas?"

"I hope so."

"Ask dad to text me a picture of you."

With raised eyebrows, Jordan agreed, "Okay, if you'll text me one of *you* back."

"It's a deal," Malik agreed then heard his mother call him. "Well, I gotta go. I have to go to bed."

"All right, I'll put your dad back on," Jordan said. "It was nice talking to you, Malik."

"Cool," he acknowledged, and she had to stifle a laugh as Travis reentered the room and she handed him the phone.

"Malik, what do you think?"

"I think she's nice," Malik answered as his mother called again. "Dad, I gotta go to bed. Mama's calling me."

"Okay, son," Travis replied. "How is your mom?"

"Well, you know. She's *mom*," he smirked sarcastically. "She's dating some judge now."

"Is he nice?"

"He's all right," he frowned.

"Hey, don't be so hard on your mother. Give this man a chance, okay?"

"All right," Malik agreed.

"Good," Travis concluded. "Tell your mother I said hello."

"Copy that."

"Pleasant dreams, son."

"You too, Dad."

Hanging up the phone, Travis looked at Jordan and announced, "That was *Malik*."

"He seems very nice," Jordan observed with a sweet smile. "You have to text him a picture of me."

"Oh *really?*"

"And he's going to text me a picture of him."

"So, you and Malik became buddies in five minutes," he laughed, and she laughed with him.

"He's a sweet child."

"Don't call my son *sweet*, Jordan," Travis joked, trying to look serious.

"I'm sorry," Jordan burst into laughter.

"Hum um," he groaned.

Jordan looked deep into his eyes and wanted to know, "Travis, tell me what's on your mind."

"I don't know what's on my mind," he stressed, pulling on his shirt. "Let's have lunch tomorrow, okay?"

"Sure."

He came back to the bed and sat beside her and inquired, "So, since you are a virgin, you're not on the pill or anything?"

"No, I'm not," she confirmed. "Is that a problem?"

"It might be. You were about to have sex with me. What would daddy say if his little girl ends up pregnant?"

"He'll say I hope he was worth it, and I'll say he was."

"Good for you," he admired then applauded. "But are *you* ready for a little one?"

She took a deep breath then replied, "Probably not. Why?"

"I love my son, but the next time I have a kid, I want to do it the right way. I want to be married." He paused and focused on her. "Do you feel me?"

She smiled and responded, "Yeah, I feel you."

"I better get outta here. We'll talk tomorrow."

Toni Talk   Lurma Swinney, PhD

Chapter 37

The baker took down the icing labeled with a big "3" on it and pushed number "4" and "5" down to fill the empty slots. Melissa walked in and asked, "Is the icing okay now, Liz?"

"Yes, it's fine. Making an extra two last night made all the difference. I'm getting ready to use the third one already. After the holidays, we can go back to making three again," Liz explained.

"Good," Melissa agreed. "Hurry. The counter is looking rather bare."

"All right," Liz confirmed with her plump, dark chocolate, round face.

"Hey, Liz, I do appreciate all of you offering to cater my wedding."

"We're looking forward to it," she acknowledged. "With all you have to do, that's *one* area you don't have to worry about."

"That's a relief, too," Melissa replied. "I can't believe it's almost here."

****

"Travis Bland's office. How may I help you?" Felisha answered with three more lights lit up on the telephone.

"Felisha, it's Jordan. Is Travis in?"

"No, he isn't, Jordan," she answered shortly. "Sorry, Jordan, I gotta go. It's a mad house around here today." She hung up the phone before Jordan could say anything else.

Jordan hung up and looked at four thirty on her watch. She hadn't heard from Travis all day, and they were supposed to have lunch together. She wondered if now that he knew she was a virgin, had he lost interest in her. Was he hiding from her today? She had to fight back her tears. Why do men lie so much? She didn't understand it. She hadn't realized how much she cared for him. As hard as she tried to fight it, a few tears rolled down her face anyway, and she wiped them away quickly. *She should've known better* than to get involved with someone like Travis Bland.

****

"Toni, have you found out who wrote that article yet?" Tyler asked, entering Toni's office.

"No, not yet."

He sat in front of her desk. "I wish I had my hands around his neck for publishing those hideous pictures with my name on them."

"How do you think *I* feel?" Toni leaned back in her chair. "Everyone thinks I betrayed my husband. If my reputation gets tarnished people will stop reading my column." They remained silent for a moment.

He stood and concluded, "When you find out who the dirt bag is, let *me* at him first!"

"I will, Rambo," Toni laughed, and he turned to leave. "Tyler." She called and he stopped. "You go by Ron's law firm on the way home, don't you?"

"Yeah, sometimes," he replied. "You need something?"

"Beverly's letting me use one of her cake pans, and I was wondering if you were going by there, if you could pick it up for me?"

"Sure."

"She didn't bring it today. She said someone else has it, but she'll have it by Friday. Could you swing by there Friday after work and pick it up for me?"

"Sure, Toni. Anything for you, my love," he cooed.

"Thanks, Tyler."

"I usually leave here about five. Will she still be there?"

"I'll ask her to wait for you," Toni replied. "Just bring it to work Monday. I don't need it before then."

"Okay, sweetie," he confirmed, heading for the door again. "Smooches."

"Smooches."

****

Jordan walked into her house and looked at her answering machine. The lights were not blinking so she knew she didn't have any messages. She couldn't believe Travis would let a whole day go by without even calling her. She felt so betrayed and bewildered. She dragged herself into the bathroom to take a shower. She had to meet Ron, Toni, and Chuck at the lake house, but her heart was not in it tonight. She knew she shouldn't have gotten involved with anyone while she was on a case. She never had before. She didn't know what possessed her to do so this time. She stripped and stepped under the warm, steamy water. Soon she was crying hysterically as the water soaked her body.

****

"Hi, Mom," Toni greeted, entering her mother's kitchen.

"Hi, honey," Mrs. Melton returned, receiving a kiss on the cheek from her. "How are things coming with the investigation?"

"Slow," Toni answered, dropping in a chair at the table, while her mother continued to cut up onions over a steaming pot.

"Well, just trust God. He'll see that things turn out all right, honey."

"I know," Toni agreed. "Did you take your medicine today?"

"Yes, *Mommy*," Mrs. Melton joked, and Toni laughed with her. "How is Ron?"

"Good," she replied.

"*Well*, Toni," she corrected. "My goodness, you make your living as a writer. Speak correctly."

"Yes, ma'am," she singsong sarcastically. Her mother laughed with her. "What're you cooking? It smells good."

"Beef stew," she answered. "Take some home with you, so you won't have to cook tonight."

"All right," Toni agreed. She was so happy that her mother now treated her like a daughter and Ron like a wonderful son-in-law. There *is* a God somewhere! There *must* be!

****

Bill walked into the house and Rita was sitting on the couch, looking at the television, looking frail and weak. "Hi, honey," he spoke, bending down and kissing her on the cheek.

"Hi."

"How do you feel?"

"Like I *look*," she chuckled.

"You look beautiful," he came back with, sitting beside her and gently patting her hand.

"Liar," she chuckled as the telephone rang, and Bill picked up the cordless telephone off the coffee table.

"Hello," he answered then paused. "Yes, this is Bill." Pause. "Yes." Pause. Suddenly, he burst into laughter and cheers. "Honey," he exploded to Rita. "They found a donor!" She smiled halfheartedly as he went back to the telephone. "Oh, thank you, Doctor. Yes, I'll have her there. Eight o'clock!" He hung up, thanked God then flopped beside Rita and pulled her in his arms. "Oh honey, everything is going to be all right!" He kissed her lips hard. "Everything is going to be all right!"

****

"Ron, Toni, Jordan, we found Tracie Myers, the nurse," Chuck announced.

"Have you talked to her yet?" Ron wanted to know.

"No, I don't want to spook her and make her run until we find Brandy. She's down in Myrtle Beach living *large*, so she's not going *anywhere* right now. I have a feeling someone paid her *well* to set up Leroy. I have someone keeping an eye on her until we're ready to make our move," Chuck explained.

"Chuck, did you check out the exterminator?" was Jordan's question.

"Yes," replied Chuck.

"Do you think that's necessary?" Ron inquired. "Rodney's a regular. Bev told me he came but I didn't think anything of it."

"Someone had to bug your office, Ron," Chuck added.

"But Rodney's been working for his company for years," affirmed Ron. "He's been servicing our offices before I started working there."

"He has a gambling problem," Chuck shared. "He could be bought off."

"Did you talk to him?" Toni asked.

"No," Chuck answered.

"Why not?" Toni wanted to know.

"Because he's dead?" Chuck confirmed. "Hit and run."

"What?!" Ron yelp. "Do you think he was paid off and then murdered to keep from talking?"

"It's possible," Chuck concurred.

"This is getting scary," Toni observed. "When do you plan to question the nurse?"

"I want to see the tape of the surgery and talk to a few other people first. We are going to need proof to make her confess, and I mean *hard* proof," Chuck explained. "We will need something concrete to stand on before we accuse someone of *murder!*"

****

"Jordan, you're very quiet tonight," Toni observed when Chuck had already hung up and Ron went into the kitchen to fix some more beef stew Mrs. Melton sent to him.

"Toni, I made a terrible mistake," Jordan admitted.

"What happened?" Toni asked, moving from the couch to sit on the sofa next to Jordan.

Jordan replied half-heartedly, "I was going to sleep with Travis last night, but I decided to tell him I'm a virgin and I scared him off."

"Why do you think that?"

"We were supposed to have lunch together today, and he didn't even have the decency to call and...*make up* something!" she explained then blew her nose. "He acts like I'm trying to trick him."

"That doesn't sound like Travis."

"I called his office today and Felisha was so short with me, as if she was hiding something," Jordan explained then started crying hard, and Toni pulled her in her arms. "Why do men do this, Toni? I'm falling in love with Travis and I thought he cared for me too." She cried. "I thought he was the one! Why would he hurt me like this?" Toni didn't have an answer for the sad woman. All she could do was offer her support, so she cradled weeping Jordan in her arms and let her release what she had probably been holding in all day. Ron stepped in and witnessed the scene of his wife trying to comfort their hysterical friend, so he quietly exited again.

Chapter 38

Jordan dialed a number at her desk. After a few seconds of ringing, a voice on the other end answered, "Alexis Jones."

"Alexis, could you come down here to answer the phone while I go and get something to eat?" Jordan asked.

"Sure. Where're you going?"

"To the little Chinese restaurant down the street. I'm not staying. I'm just getting take-out."

"Would you bring me some shrimp fried rice?"

"Sure," Jordan replied. "Large or small?"

"Small."

"Okay."

"Stay there. I'll be right down to give you the money."

"Don't worry about it," Jordan replied, grabbing her jacket to cover her loose-fitting tan cashmere sweater and hunter green skintight pants over three-inch heels. "Do me a favor, just call and add it to my order, please."

"Sure."

"Okay, I'm leaving."

****

"Beverly, would you get Mrs. Sanders on the phone, please?" Jamie asked over the intercom.

"*Which* Mrs. Sanders?"

"Gloria Sanders, the case Ron was working on before he left."

"Why do you want *her*? She made it perfectly clear that she wants *Ron* to defend her."

"Let *me* worry about that, please, Beverly," Jamie sarcastically remarked. "Just get her!"

"I can't do that," she refused, and he flew out of the office to confront her.

"What'd you mean, you can't do that? *You* work for *me*! I asked you to do something! Do it!" he raved.

"Let's get something perfectly clear, Jamie! I *work* for *me*!" Beverly countered. "And I will *not* be a part of some underhanded scheme you have to *steal* Ron's clients!"

"*Underhanded*?!" he snapped. "I just want to *talk* to the woman, for Christ's sakes!"

"Then you'll have to do it without *me*!"

"What is it with you, Beverly?" He calmed down. "Why don't you like me? I've never done anything to hurt you. *I* didn't fire Ron Joyner."

"I didn't say you did."

"Then what is it about me that you don't like?"

"Remember, you asked for this," she stated, and he nodded. "I don't like the way you order me around! I know you came from a school setting, but I'm *not* one of your students! I am a grown woman, and just because my paycheck isn't as heavy as yours does not mean you're any better than I am! As far as I'm concerned, my character is a *lot* more decent than yours! I don't *cheat* on my husband!" She stopped and stared at him and he remained silent.

Jamie took a deep breath and countered feebly, "Thank you for your honesty." He exhaled slowly. "I'm deeply sorry. I never meant to treat you like you were less than I am. I value your expertise."

"And *Billy* isn't any better," Beverly continued. "He looks down his nose at me, too. That's one thing I've never had to worry about with Ron. He always treated me with *respect*! *That's* the reason *I* respect *him* so much!"

He took a breath. "Beverly, could we start over?" Jamie queried humbly, and her eyes widened. "I need you. I want us to be friends. We probably won't ever be as close as Ron and you, but we can still be friends, right?"

"Sure, as long as you know where I stand," Beverly made known. "I will not compromise my integrity for you, Billy, or anyone else, so don't you *ever* ask me to do so."

"So noted," Jamie confirmed. "So, asking you to call one of Ron's clients would be *compromising* your integrity?"

"Absolutely!"

"Then I'm very sorry," he apologized, extending a hand. "Friends?" She stared at his hand long and hard. Then he tried his hand at humor and mimicked Billy Dee Williams in *Lady Sings the Blues*, "Do you want my arm to fall off?" Beverly burst into laughter, stood, and received his handshake.

****

Jordan walked into the restaurant, still thinking of Travis and how he had jilted her. She had to fight hard to keep the tears away. She had cried on Toni's shoulder and then cried herself to sleep when she got home. She still hadn't heard from him. Jordan paid for her food and the Chinese man handed her the bag and she turned to leave. When suddenly, she froze dead in her tracks. She couldn't believe her eyes. Travis, the love of her life, looking very handsome in a dark blue pinstriped suit with a light blue shirt, and dark blue necktie and handkerchief, was sitting in a back corner, all cozy with a beautiful, older, Caucasian woman, smiling as if he had no worries in the world. She wanted to turn and walk out but the pain in her heart wouldn't let her. Instead, it guided her steps and before she knew it, she was standing at Travis' table, looking down on the man who had broken her heart. At first, he didn't notice her because he was so involved in his conversation with the woman. Soon he realized someone was standing there and looked up and their eyes locked. He smiled as if they were the best of buddies as he stood and greeted, "Jordan, hi."

"You son-of-a-bitch!" she spat.

"What?" He looked puzzled.

"How could you?" she charged with rage, as uncontrollable tears soaked her distraught face. "How could you treat me like this?"

"Jordan, I..."

"Don't talk to me, Travis Bland!" she fumed.

She turned to leave, then Travis jumped up, and caught her arm. "Jordan..." he called. By Instinct, she jerked away and slapped his face.

"Don't you touch me, you two-timing, snake in the grass!" she barked then stormed out in tears.

Travis took a deep breath, focused on the woman, and offered sweetly, "Would you please excuse me?"

"Sure," she agreed. "I'm a jealous woman myself." He smiled shyly at her then ran to catch Jordan.

Travis caught up with Jordan at her car, having a hard time unlocking her car door with the remote because of her tears. "Jordan!" he called, grabbing the keys out of her hand. "Wait a minute."

She swirled around and demanded, "Give me my keys!"

"No!" he insisted. "What is wrong with you?"

"What is wrong with *me*?!" she raged. "You're the one who disappeared an entire day without a trace! I guess you're finished with me and ready to throw me away like an old shoe since you found out I'm not one of those little bimbos you're used to. Now give me my damn keys, so you can go back to your *date*!" He smiled slightly and Jordan grew even more upset. "I'm glad you think hurting me is so funny! Give me my keys!" She jerked to grab her keys and he swished them behind his back.

"Not until you calm down and listen," he declared.

"Listen to *what*, Travis? What could you possibly say that I would want to hear?"

He stared deep into her tear-soaked, light-brown eyes and confessed, "I love you."

"Ha!" she grunted. "Then why are you here with that...that little...*bimbo*?" Travis really smiled then.

"That *bimbo* is a *client*," he chuckled. "A very *wealthy* and *important* client."

"Don't lie to me, Travis. I'm not in the mood for games," she charged.

"Neither am I," he grew serious, handing her a handkerchief from his inner jacket pocket. "Have you listened to your messages?"

"What *messages*? I don't have any," she spat.

"I left you three messages yesterday. I wondered why you never returned calls."

"You left me three messages?" she pondered.

"Yes," he made known. "Phillip called me early yesterday morning and said he had already booked me a flight to Greenville. This man was accused of armed robbery and murder in a convenient store hold-up. I had to hurry to catch that flight, but I called you just before I left. I thought that you were still asleep."

"I get up early. I was probably in the shower."

"I was busy all day yesterday. I got a break about three o'clock and I called you at the office, and Alexis answered the phone and said you were gone to the bank."

"I did go to the bank, but Alexis didn't tell me you called."

"Ask her," he suggested. "Then when I returned to the hotel about nine o'clock last night, I called you again." He cocked his head with a slight smirk on his face. "And we're going to have to talk about where you were at nine o'clock at night." She smiled. She couldn't tell him that she was with Ron and Toni.

"I guess I was still at the spa," she lied.

"I left another message for you to call me," he explained. "Then I was so tired I fell asleep, and when I woke up this morning, I hopped on the plane and came back. As soon as I walked into my house about eleven, there was a message from Blake telling me to meet this client here today at noon, so then I had to rush here and be totally humiliated by the love of my life in front of a very important client! End of story!"

"Why didn't you call my cell?"

"I didn't want to disturb you in case you were busy."

"Oh, Travis, I'm sorry," Jordan proclaimed.

"And the lady has a temper," Travis chuckled, smiling sheepishly. "I'll be so glad when Ron comes back. They're trying to work me to death."

She rubbed his face where she had hit him and repeated, "I'm sorry. I thought…"

"I *know* what you thought," he finished. "Jordan, I have *never* told a woman I loved her, other than my mother, of course." He paused. "I could *never* hurt you. That's why I couldn't make love to you. I wanted to be sure before I take something so precious from you." She was crying again.

"Please forgive me?" she pleaded, and he smiled and nodded.

He gently wiped her tears with his finger and made known, "I missed you."

"I missed you too," she sniffed.

"I could tell," he whispered, and she giggled.

"I'm sorry," she repeated, and he brushed her face lightly with his finger.

"I want to kiss you," he cooed.

Looking around at the people walking by on the sidewalk, Jordan chuckled, "Here?"

"Yes, *here*," he confirmed then pulled her into his arms lovingly and met her lips with a very deep, moist, kiss. Then he hugged her close.

"I love you so much, Travis."

"I love you, too, baby," he said then kissed her again.

"Huh hum," they heard a grunt and broke apart.

"How are you, Mr. Denton?" Travis asked shyly.

"Not as well as *you*, Mr. Bland," he teased.

Travis immediately made introductions, "Jordan, this is Calvin Denton. Mr. Denton this is Jordan Curry, the love of my life." Travis' eyes locked with Jordan's and they smiled sweetly at each other.

Extending a hand to Jordan, Mr. Denton broke the trance between Travis and Jordan and greeted, "Nice to meet you, Miss Curry."

Taking his hand, Jordan replied. "Likewise, sir. Thank you."

"Your wife is already in there, Mr. Denton. I'll be right in," Travis added.

"Take your time," he offered. "Miss Curry, it was nice meeting you."

"Thank you, Mr. Denton," Jordan accepted, and then he walked into the restaurant.

"Would you like to come inside and meet Mrs. Denton?" Travis asked Jordan.

"Oh no!" she exploded. "I feel like such a fool. What she must think of me!"

"She said she's a jealous woman also, so she understood."

"No. I really gotta get back and give Alexis her food."

"Can I see you tonight?" he cooed. "I missed you so much."

"You better know it," Jordan acknowledged, and they kissed again, this time shorter. He opened the car door for her and handed her the car keys, and she hopped in. He closed her door, and she cranked the car and rolled the window down. He bent down and kissed her through the open window.

"See you tonight," he cooed. She nodded then drove off.

****

"Mason, is your article ready?" Bill asked as he sat in the conference room with Toni, Mason, Gary, and some other production staff members.

"I need to put a few final touches on it, Bill," Mason made known.

"What kind of touches?" Bill inquired. "We need it today, Mason. It's already Thursday. Those articles have to be into the print room by three."

"I'll have it today!" Mason promised.

"Is that enough time, George?" Bill focused on the short man sitting in attendance.

"If we could get it by three," George replied.

"You'll have it," Mason confirmed a little aggravated. "Or just pull up one already in the junket." Toni stared into space for a moment and didn't hear Bill talking to her.

"Toni!" Bill called again. "Are you with us?"

Shaking her head, she reacted, "Oh, I'm sorry, Bill. What were you saying?"

"Don't tell me you don't have *your* article ready either."

"I've already sent it to you," Toni shared.

"Oh, that's right. It's in the junket," Bill laughed. The junket was what Bill called his finished articles. He coined that title when he first started as the chief editor and claimed that all he was getting from the writers was junk. So, he would throw the articles in a small vault in his office, which no one had access to but him, until it was time for them to be printed. Each writer always had five articles each in the junket, and if they didn't use the oldest one on the upcoming Friday, then Bill would archive them in the history files in the attic. This allowed him to keep the articles fresh and updated. "All right, it looks like we're adjourned here." Everyone stood to leave.

"Bill, how is Rita?" George asked.

"She goes into the hospital Monday," Bill shared.

"I know you're excited," Toni added.

"Yes, I am. This is a dream come true. This is all we want for Christmas," Bill glowed.

"Tell her we'll all be praying for her," another lady made known as they left.

"Thank you. I will," Bill replied.

****

"Hi, Jordan," Jamie spoke, standing over her desk.

"Hi, Jamie," she returned.

"When are Travis and you coming back to ride?"

"I don't know. Travis is so busy lately since he's having to do *his* work *and* Ron Joyner's."

"Well, tomorrow is supposed to be a beautiful day," he added. "And the staff won't be there to bother you. I gave them time off until after Christmas."

"That was nice of you," Jordan acknowledged. "So, who's taking care of the stables?"

"Yours truly," he shared as Travis entered.

"Jamie, how are you?" Travis spoke, feeling a twinge of jealousy at Jamie's attention to Jordan.

388

"My man!" Jamie received, giving Travis a hand bump. "When did you get back?"

"Long enough to see you drooling over my baby," Travis joked, and Jordan dropped her head, snickering. Jamie's mouth dropped open.

"Oh no, man!" he exploded. "I was just wondering when you two wanted to ride again!" Travis burst into laughter.

"Just kidding, man," he laughed, and Jamie sighed a breath of relief. He didn't want to make any waves with the big dogs around here. He was the new kid on the block. Travis bent down. He and Jordan kissed.

"Hey again." Travis cooed.

"Hey," she replied.

"So, when are you coming back?" Jaime inquired as Travis stood again.

"I don't know when I'll be able to come back, but Jordan can take someone else with her if she wants to," Travis suggested.

"I wouldn't know who to take," Jordan responded.

"Take *Toni*," Travis suggested.

"I don't know her that well, honey. You've only introduced us once," Jordan made known. "Can she ride?"

"Toni Melton-Joyner can do *everything*," Travis chuckled.

"Maybe I'll call her if you think it's okay," Jordan concluded.

"Of course, I think it's okay."

"Jamie said we could go tomorrow."

"Sounds great. I'll be working late, but I could see you tomorrow night. You'll be finished by then, right?"

"Yes, we should, but Toni Melton-Joyner is a very busy woman," Jordan remarked. "She probably won't be able to come on such short notice, but I would like to ride again."

"*Call* her," Travis ordered as John Schuster walked out his office.

"I should have known my beautiful, new secretary was holding up my meeting," he announced.

"We're coming, John," Jamie spoke first. "Jordan, let me know if you're coming."

"I will," she replied, as Jamie walked into the office with John.

Touching her hand as he began walking away, Travis finalized, "See you tonight." She nodded.

****

"Hi," Toni spoke to Ron, entering their kitchen as she met him with a kiss.

"Hi," he recognized, stirring a steaming pot in a pair of warm-up pants, T-shirt, and no shoes, as she sat at the table.

"What're you cooking?"

"Chicken bog."

"Wow! Sexy. Handsome and a good cook," Toni cooed. "You would go for a pretty penny on the auction block."

He batted his eyes and cooed, "You wanna *auction* me?"

Toni got up and wrapped her arms around his waist from the rear and purred, "Never!" She kissed his back then released him. "I'm going to take a shower, honey."

"Okay, baby."

She started out the door then turned back and added, "Oh, honey, I forgot to tell you. Jordan called and asked me to go horseback riding with her tomorrow. Do we have anything planned?"

"No, honey. I don't think so," he thought, "It sounds like fun."

"So, you don't mind?"

"Of course not," he confirmed. "Who has stables...oh, *Taffy Hines*."

"Taffy Hines-*Heard*!" Toni stressed and he chuckled.

"You're getting off early enough to go, aren't you?"

"Yes, we're going at noon. Jordan said she's taking off early, too."

"Okay, cause I don't want you out there too late."

"I won't be."

390

"Maybe I could get with Travis, Simon, and a few of the guys for a poker game."

"Oh, so you're not going to miss me?" she smirked.

"I *always* miss you, my love, when you're not with me. *Always*," he stressed, and she came back, and they kissed again.

"So, if you're getting a card game for tomorrow night, maybe I'll just hang out with Jordan, and maybe call Angel, Melissa and Denise, and we can take in a movie or something."

"All right, baby."

"I know Melissa needs a break from all those wedding plans."

"I guess so," he agreed as she exited. "Hurry back. Dinner is almost ready."

****

Jordan rushed into her bedroom, looked at the answering machine, and the light was not blinking. She pushed the button and to her surprise a message came up. "Hi, baby, it's me," Travis said. "I'm gonna have to take a rain check on our lunch date. Phillip wants me to catch a plane to Greenville this morning. I'll be spending the night. I'll call you later. Bye." Jordan smiled wide. He *had* called. The next message was from her mother. "Hi, sweetheart. Call me when you get in. Love you." The last message was another one from Travis. "Hi, honey, I'm beat. I'm back at the hotel. Call me on my cell when you get in. I called you at work today and still didn't get you. I'm wondering where my baby is at nine o'clock at night. I would call your cell, but I don't want to disturb you if you're busy." He chuckled. "I'll see you tomorrow. My plane leaves at eight in the morning. Bye." There were no more messages. Jordan knew it was time to get another answering machine...or come into the twenty-first century and get voice mail. She spent a miserable night last night for no reason. He *had* called just like he said. She had believed him anyway. She supposed she just *wanted* to believe him because she loved him.

The ringing of the doorbell brought Jordan out of her daydream. On her way to the door, she pulled the door to her office shut. She didn't want Travis looking in there at all her work equipment, like cameras, guns, recorders, and such. She usually kept it locked, but she would lock it later. Right now, she wanted to see her man. She trotted to the door quickly.

Jordan opened her door in a short, satin, sexy, red nightshirt, no shoes, and her hair pulled back in a ponytail, and Travis, in a black jogging suit, gasped. "Wow!" he breathed.

"Hi."

"Hi," he replied, taking her into his arms and kissing her deeply.

"You smell good," she cooed in between kisses.

"I took a shower when I got home," he shared between kisses. "You smell good, too."

"I took a shower too," she giggled as they sat on the couch together.

****

"Honey, Ron wants to know if you want to come over and play cards tomorrow night?" Melissa asked Simon as he sat on the couch with her, rubbing her feet.

"Yeah, sure," he replied, receiving the phone from her. "Hi, Ron."

"Hi, Simon."

"Yeah, I'd love to."

"Good and tell Melissa to get a babysitter. Toni has something planned for the ladies too."

"All right," Simon agreed. "Thanks for the invite." When he hung up, he smiled, and Melissa focused on him.

"What?"

"I'm just surprised is all."

"Simon, you, Ron and Travis used to be close. I don't see why you couldn't again," Melissa noted. "And he did agree to be your best man, and Travis agreed to be a groomsman."

"Yeah, I know," he recognized. "I just thought he agreed because of *you*."

"I don't think so," she countered. "Ron is his own man."

"You know, I've missed the friendship Ron, Travis and I once shared."

"Well, maybe it's time to get it back."

"I think you're right," he concurred. "Oh, he says to get a babysitter. Toni has something planned for the women too."

"Oh okay," she acknowledged. "I can ask mom and dad. I'll just let the children spend the night with them."

"Really?" he cooed. "Maybe I better come back after the card game."

"*Next* week, darling," she indicated the wedding date, laughing, and he pouted then burst into laughter with her.

****

"I'll get us something to eat," Jordan suggested, standing.

"Can you cook?" he joked.

"I can make *sandwiches*," she giggled, and he laughed.

"I *thought* you were too pretty to know how to cook."

"That's not fair," she pouted, putting her hands on her hips, then proceeded to leave the room.

He hopped up, grabbed her from the rear, laughing and said, "Just kidding, honey." He planted a kiss on the back of her head then picked up the television remote but knocked over a glass of water. "I'll get a towel."

"Travis, I need to tell you something." He raised an eyebrow, waiting in anticipation, but before she could say another word, the telephone began to ring.

"What is it, honey?"

She looked at the caller ID and said, "It's my parents. Go and get a towel. We'll talk when I hang up." He nodded his head and left as Jordan picked up the cordless telephone. "Hello."

"Hi, honey."

"Hi, Mom," Jordan replied, leaving the den, and walking into the kitchen as he entered the bathroom in search of a towel.

"I called you last night," her mother announced. "Did you get my message?"

"I just got it, Mom," Jordan answered, turning on the stereo to play soft jazz music, and then she sat at the kitchen table.

"Are you all right?"

"Yes, Mom, I'm fine."

"Your father said you met someone."

Smiling wide, Jordan confirmed, "Yes, I have."

"Is he nice?"

"Very nice."

"Is he good looking?"

"*Very* good looking," Jordan beamed.

****

Travis didn't see a small towel in the bathroom, so he exited, calling, "Jordan." With the music on, she didn't hear him. He walked down the hall searching for a linen closet, so he opened her office door. He froze as his eyes widen when he witnessed all the expensive cameras, microphones, tape recorders, and...*guns*! "What the hell...?" he murmured to himself.

"Travis!" Jordan called and he could hear her footsteps approaching. "Mom sends her...." She froze in her tracks when she saw that he was standing at her office door, staring blankly at her equipment. He raised his head slowly and they locked eyes.

"What in the hell is all this, Jordan?" he asked, but she didn't answer. She just dropped her head. "Who are you?!"

****

"What's wrong?"

Looking down in his wife's face with her head in his lap, Ron replied, "Nothing. Why?"

"Liar!" she blurted.

"No, you didn't!" Ron laughed.

"Mr. Joyner, if you don't tell me what's on your mind, I'll have to take matters in my own hands."

"Ooh, that sounds interesting," he joked.

"What is it, honey…your job?"

Taking a deep breath, he admitted, rubbing her short, silky hair, "I'm just so sick of this mess."

"I know, baby, but it'll be over soon."

"I'm just getting a little discouraged. Jordan hasn't found anything yet. Brandy is nowhere to be found. I just want this to be over and done with, so things can get back to normal."

"I know, sweetie," Toni sympathized with her husband. "We just have to be patient. Maybe Jordan will find something soon."

****

"What the hell is all this, Jordan?" Travis snapped.

"I was going to tell you when the telephone rang," she finally answered, yanking open the door beside them and grabbing a towel. She handed it to him, and he took it slowly. His mind was still on who she was.

He took a breath, turned to her, and advised, "Tell me now!" He forgot all about the water he wasted on the table.

"I'm a private investigator. I work for Chuck Warren Investigative Firm."

"Investigator?!" he spat, and she nodded slowly. "Who're you investigating…*me*?"

"*No*, oh, *no!*" she exploded. "You were *never* a suspect!"

"Who hired you?"

She took a breath then confessed, "Ron and Toni Joyner hired my firm."

"Ron...?" his breath ran out. "*Ron* hired you?" She nodded. "But they acted as if they didn't know you."

"We had to keep my identity under wraps."

"From *me*?!"

"From *everyone!*" she stressed then took a breath. "Travis, I didn't know I was going to fall in love with you."

"Were you seeing me to get information from me?"

She blew hard with a raised eyebrow and stated, "I can't believe you would ask me that. *You* pursued *me*, Travis. *I* didn't pursue you."

"Then why didn't you tell *me*?"

"Ron and Toni are my *clients*, Travis, just like *you* have clients. You can't tell me anything about your clients and neither can I. I am bound by the *same* laws as you are when it comes to client confidentiality."

"But why didn't *Ron* tell me? We're supposed to be friends."

"Ron *is* your friend," she insisted. "He told me from the very beginning that he knew without a shadow of a doubt that you weren't involved in this mess." She paused. "Then after we started seeing each other, Ron expected *me* to tell you. But it happened so fast, Travis. I...I..." She was at a loss for words.

He dropped in a chair in a trancelike state as he murmured, "A Private Eye." Travis shook his head then looked up at Jordan. "Has our whole relationship been a lie?"

"What do you think, Travis?" she retaliated. "What do you *really* think?"

He shook his head and chuckled slightly, "I don't know anymore."

"Yes, you do!" she insisted. "I was willing to give myself to you completely." She paused. "*You* know!" He focused on her long and hard then smiled.

"Yeah, I do," he admitted, standing, and holding out his hands to her. She strolled into his arms without hesitation, and he held her tight.

"I love you, Travis."

"I love you, too…" he shared then added, *"Nancy Drew."* She burst into laughter and he laughed with her.

Chapter 39

"Hi, Tyler," Toni acknowledged, entering his office, where he had a darkroom in the back.

"Hi, gorgeous," he spoke, sitting at his desk, holding some negatives up, examining them.

"I'm leaving early. Don't forget to go by and pick up that pan for me from Beverly."

"She has it now?"

"Yes, I just talked to her."

"Okay. I won't forget," Tyler replied, putting the negatives down and focusing on her. He couldn't let this moment go without teasing her. "You're a little homemaker now since you said *I do*? Cake pans and shit?"

Toni chuckled, "What're you talking about?"

"That man's keeping you chained down to a stove now?" he laughed. "Since when did *you* start baking?"

"For your information, Mr. Know-it-All, *I'm* not baking. Melissa's employees are catering her wedding, and they need to borrow Beverly's cake pan to make a special kind of cake for the reception. Cammie said she couldn't find one locally, so she had to order one, and they were out of stock, so it won't get here until after the wedding," Toni explained. "She said she remembered talking to Beverly at *my* wedding, and Beverly said she had a cake pan like that...*satisfied*?"

"If *you* are," he answered sarcastically and Toni burst into laughter, getting up.

"We have an interview Monday, okay?"

"In town?"

"Yeah, at a nursing home. I have a complaint that the residents there are not being treated fairly."

"What time?"

"Nine or ten. No set time. They'll be there all day."

"Cool."

Heading for the door, Toni called back, "I'm outta here, handsome."

"You're *leaving*?"

"Yeah, I'm going horseback riding," Toni shared then stopped, turned to him again, and announced. "Didn't I tell you?"

"No," he flatly stated. "Well, all right, *Elizabeth Taylor*!"

Toni laughed, "Good one, Tyler. See you Monday."

"Solid."

****

"Hi, Beverly," Jordan spoke, entering the office.

Beverly stopped typing, smiled and responded, "Hi, Jordan. How are things with Travis?"

"Very good," Jordan replied, smiling wide.

"I can see that," Beverly jeered. "You're glowing."

"Am I?"

"Yeah."

"What can I say, I'm in love," Jordan chuckled.

"That's great," Beverly shared her joy. "Travis's good people."

"Thank you, Beverly."

"So, what brings you this way?"

"I was wondering if Jamie was here."

"*Jamie*?!" Beverly spat. "What do you want with *him*?"

"Toni and I are going to his stables today to ride."

"You mean his *wife's* stables!" Beverly corrected and Jordan giggled slightly. "No, he isn't here. He left a few hours ago, and I bet you anything that *Felisha* left with him. They're going for a little morning rendezvous if you know what I mean."

Jordan laughed, "You're still not getting along with Jamie?"

"Yeah, we get along just *fine*, as long as he stays outta *my* way, and I sure as heck will stay outta *his*," Beverly stated matter-of-factly, and Jordan couldn't help but laugh.

"Will you just tell him that I'm going to pick up Toni and we're going to head on out there?"

"Sure, honey."

"Have a good weekend, Beverly," Jordan concluded, turning to leave, and almost bumped into Jamie, carrying a bakery box in his hand.

"Hi, Jordan," he acknowledged. "You're leaving?"

"Yeah, I was just telling Beverly that I'm going to pick up Toni and we're going to head on out to the stables," Jordan explained.

"Okay, great," he replied. "Hey, how about a cake square?" he offered, opening the box.

"No thank you," Jordan answered then turned to leave. "See you, Beverly."

"Okay, honey," Beverly finalized.

"Beverly, I didn't know Ron Joyner's sister owned a bakery," Jamie announced, holding out the open box to Beverly.

"Yes, Melissa has had that shop a while. She and her husband opened it before he died."

"Yes, I heard. I've been going there for years, but I didn't know she was Ron's sister," he made known. "Please join me." He picked up a cake square and bit into it.

Beverly picked one up also and accepted, "Thank you."

"You're welcome," he responded. "Didn't I hear something about she's marrying Simon Kennedy?"

"Yeah, next Saturday."

"It's a small world."

"Yes, it is," Beverly agreed.

"Here, take all of these. Some of the girls here might want some," he suggested, placing the box on her desk.

"Thank you," she accepted. "I'll let them know they're here."

"You're welcome," he responded. "Is Billy back from court yet?"

"He's out of court. He went home early. He wasn't feeling well."

"Well, the flu is going around."

"Yeah, I know."

He headed for his office asking, "Any important calls I need to return?"

Toni Talk   Lurma Swinney, PhD

"Your wife," Beverly responded sweetly, and she noticed that he momentarily froze. The dirty rat just finished screwing Felisha and now had to face his wife. "She said it was important for you to call her back as soon as possible."

"I will. Thank you, Beverly," he acknowledged then exited into his office. Beverly had to admit that although she didn't care much for Jamie, he *was* trying to get along with her. She could, at least, do the same and meet him half-way. *Half*!

****

Ron was sitting at his computer when the telephone began to ring. "Hello," he answered quickly.

"Ron, we found Brandy Sears," Chuck blurted out. "I'm going to see her."

"Where is she?"

"In a small town called Burnsville."

"That's about thirty minutes from here."

"Yeah," Chuck confirmed. "You wanna come?"

"Oh yeah," Ron replied.

"Stay there. I'll pick you up," Chuck advised.

"You're coming *here*?"

"Yeah."

"But coming here is out of your way. I can meet you."

"I'm in Greenleaf already."

"You *are*?"

"Yeah, I had to check something out at the hospital," Chuck explained. "I also had the police pick up Tracie Myers today."

"You *did*?"

"Yeah."

"I thought you wanted more evidence."

"And I got it. I'll explain when I get there."

"I'll be waiting."

402

****

"It's so beautiful out here," Toni admired, smiling wide as she and Jordan trotted slowly on their horses after having a vigorous ride.

"It sure is," Jordan agreed. "Want to stop and let the horses rest a while?"

"Yeah, that'll be good," she agreed, then stopped. Jordan stopped with her, and they hopped off their horses, and sat on the scenic green grass under the tree.

"Do Ron and you ride much?"

"Oh no. Ron hates it."

"Really?"

Laughing, Toni continued, "Ron said he doesn't like those big eyes looking at him." Jordan laughed with her.

"Travis loves to ride," Jordan added.

"Speaking of Travis. What's up with you two?"

"You were right, Toni."

"About what?"

"About *Travis*!" Jordan chuckled. "You told me to give Travis time to explain what happened."

"And did he?"

"Yes, it was my fault, at least my *answering machine*. Travis called me three times that day, and I didn't get his messages because the lights weren't blinking on my answering machine."

"That's good," Toni acknowledged. "I knew there had to be a reason Travis didn't call."

"You were right," Jordan replied then added.

"And about the other thing."

"The sex?" she asked, and Toni nodded. "I think he's afraid to have sex with me, but that's okay. I'm a little afraid myself."

"There's no hurry. You have the rest of your life."

"That's true," Jordan agreed. "Also, Travis found out about *me*."

With widened eyes, Toni asked, "How?"

"He was looking for a towel and walked into my office. I forgot to lock the door."

"Was he very upset?"

"At first, but he understood that Ron and you are *clients* just like *his* clients and deserve the same confidentiality."

"Well, that's good."

"I let him know that he was *never* a suspect."

"Good," Toni agreed.

"Travis is so sweet, Toni," Jordan beamed. "I don't know how I got so lucky."

"You're nice too, Jordan."

"Thanks, Toni."

Looking at her watch, Toni observed, "It's almost four o'clock. We better head back if we want to meet the girls for a night out on the town."

"All right," Jordan agreed as they stood. Jordan jumped on her horse and yelled, "Race you back." She took off, laughing hysterically.

"Hey, not fair!" Toni chuckled, mounting her horse also and charging after her.

****

"You're just getting back from court?" Felisha asked Travis as he entered the office, handsomely dressed in a three-piece brown suit and shoes, silk tan shirt with a matching necktie and handkerchief.

"Yeah, and I'm beat."

"You don't look beat. You look nice."

"Thank you," he accepted then focused on her again. "Felisha, Jordan said she called the other day when I was in Greenville."

"Jordan?"

"Yes, Jordan Curry, John's secretary."

"Oh yeah," she remembered. "I was so busy. It was a mad house that day."

"Listen, Felisha, whenever Jordan calls, it's okay to tell her where I am."

"Really?"

"Yes."

"Are you seeing her?"

Smiling wide, he confided, "Yes, I am."

"Well, good for you. Congratulations."

"For what?"

"For finally finding a woman you can run *to* instead of *from*!" she laughed, and he laughed with her.

"I wasn't that bad, was I?"

"Wasn't that *bad*?!" Felisha exploded. "I used to spend more time juggling your women around than any other job here."

"I'm sorry," he understood. "But now, those days are over."

"This sounds serious."

Travis thought for a moment then came back with, "I guess it is."

****

"This looks like it," Chuck said to Ron as he pulled his Ivory Cadillac Seville into the yard of a small but neat gray, frame house, sitting back off the main house on a little dirt road.

Looking at Google map on his cell phone, Ron agreed, "Yes, this is it."

They both exited the car and walked to the door. Chuck rang the doorbell, but they didn't hear any movement on the inside of the house. He then banged profusely on the wooden door. Soon the door opened slowly, and Brandy was standing there in blue jeans and a red cashmere sweater, with her hair pulled back in a ponytail. "Hello, Brandy," Ron spoke first.

"Hi," she whispered slowly. "What can I do for you?"

"You can start by letting us in," Chuck spoke firmly. "It's rather cold out here." She pondered for a while then unlocked the screen and let them in.

Chuck and Ron looked around the small house. Although it was small, it was neat and clean. "You may sit if you like," she offered.

"Thank you," they said together.

"Brandy, this is Chuck Warren," Ron spoke as they sat in opposite chairs and she sat on the couch, focusing on them. "Toni and I hired his investigative firm to help us find out who set us up." She lowered her head and stared at the floor, confirming their suspicions. "Brandy, we know *what* you did, but we don't know *why* you did it? Could you shed some light on this for us please?"

She took a deep breath then announced quietly, "I had to."

"Why?" was Chuck's question.

"Because my brother told me to," she answered.

"Why would your brother want to destroy my family?"

"Because he hates you."

"Why? What have I ever done to him? I don't even know your brother," Ron wanted to know.

"Brandy, please talk to us," Chuck added.

Ron took a deep breath then added, "Brandy, why does your brother want to destroy my family?"

She held her head up and looked squarely into Ron's eyes and stated, "Because you're...*our* family too!"

****

Beverly glanced at four forty-five PM on the clock. It was time for her to go. Neither Jamie nor Billy was back yet, but that wasn't unusual. Sometimes they went straight home instead of coming back to the office after a long day of negotiations outside of the office. She put the cake pan on her desk. Tyler would be coming by to get it soon. She was ready for her weekend. This week seemed extremely long for some reason. She walked into Jamie and Billy's office. She sometimes had to shut down their computers before she left. Beverly began her ritual. One of the computers wouldn't close for some reason. She figured it was frozen from setting idly most of the day. She went about trying to close it with the control, alt, delete buttons, but to her surprise a document popped up on the screen. Beverly froze solid. There was Toni's phony article, which had cost Ron his job, staring at her on the computer screen!

"What the..." she started but was cut short by a hand covering her mouth and nose with a moist cloth. She gasped for air but couldn't find any. Soon she collapsed and was drag back into her office and into the supply closet. The door was then locked from the outside with her key which was then dropped back into her purse. The purse was then placed into her desk drawer.

****

"What're you talking about?" Ron asked Brandy. "What do you mean, *we're* family?!"

Brandy took a deep breath then shared, "Your father had an affair with my mother and produced my brother."

"*You're* my sister?!" Ron exploded.

"No, but my *brother* is *your* brother," she explained. "My mother later married my father and had me."

"Who *is* your mother?"

"Annie Sears."

"That name doesn't sound familiar," Ron pondered.

"My mother was your father's mistress for years."

"But what does this have to do with why you set Toni and Ron up?" Chuck wanted to know.

"It wasn't *me*. It was my *brother*," she stressed. "I was helping my brother to right a wrong."

"What *wrong*?" Ron countered.

"The wrong of your father not living up to his responsibility," she answered. "My brother and I went through hell all our lives while you and your siblings had *everything*!"

407

Ron dropped his head. He couldn't believe what he was hearing, and Chuck's heart went out to him. Ron finally found his voice again and asked weakly, "Did your brother, Traci Myers, and you set up my brother, Leroy?"

"Yes," she admitted. "I was a candy striper in the hospital, and I supplied Tracie with a list of Dr. Joyner's patients. She took it from there."

"So, you killed an innocent man just to set up Leroy?" Chuck made known.

Brandy's eyes widened as she stood and insisted, "*I* didn't kill anyone! Tracie looked over the chart! She said the man was dying, so she didn't have to do anything but make it seem like Dr. Joyner killed him. We didn't kill anybody!"

"The man wasn't dying," Chuck reassured her. "It was a routine procedure. Your brother and Tracie *killed* him."

"No!" she exploded. "No! They said the man died on his own!"

"They lied!" Chuck insisted. "Tracie made sure the man received an overdose of meds. That's what killed him."

Brandy couldn't believe it. She flopped on the chair again. "They lied to me," she stated softly. "But it had to have been *Tracie*. My *brother* isn't a *murderer*."

"Your brother had to have known. Tracie Myers was paid a lot of money to do what she did, enough to *retire*," Chuck added.

"I didn't know," Brandy insisted, wiping a few tears. "Honestly, I didn't."

"You've got to turn yourself in, Brandy, to clear all of these people," Chuck spoke, and she looked up at him with sad eyes. "The police have already picked up Tracie Myers, but I haven't talked to her yet. Whether you cooperate or not, all of you are going down! I guarantee you that!" She locked eyes with Chuck, and then she nodded slowly.

"Of course, I'll come back," she sniffed, getting up.

"Where can we find your brother?" Chuck inquired. "Tracie was alone when they picked her up."

She looked at Ron and revealed, "He works at your law firm." Ron's eyes widened.

408

"We don't have anyone named Sears working there, and he couldn't have used a fake name because everyone is checked out before they're hired."

"He isn't a Sears. That's *my* father's name. My brother uses my mother's maiden name because she wasn't married when she had him," Brandy explained.

"Who is he?" Ron wanted to know.

****

"How was your ride, ladies?"

"It was great," Toni answered, smiling wide as she dismounted her horse after Jordan.

"Good," Jamie replied. "You ladies are simply glowing." He began securing the horses into the stable while Jordan and Toni helped him to put up the saddles and other equipment. "So, Toni, how is the job coming?"

"Great," Toni acknowledged.

"No more phony articles floating around?" he added.

"I hope not," Toni confirmed, and Jordan's eyes widened as she grew attentive.

"Well, I'm sure you have some good ones left in the junket," he chuckled, and Toni froze. How did he know about the junket? She didn't respond, but Jordan noticed her expression. He was about two stalls away from them and Jordan put her finger over her mouth to tell Toni not to speak and motioned with the other hand for her to head towards the door. They both started in that direction and as soon as they made it there, Jamie leaped in front of the door, blocking their exit.

"Leaving so soon, ladies?" he sarcastically jeered.

"We have dinner plans," Jordan answered, trying to stay calm.

"Sorry to detain you," he announced smugly.

"*Detain* us?" Toni inquired.

Whipping out a forty-five-caliber pistol, he stressed, "Yes, *detain* you." He motioned for them to walk away from the door just as Toni's cell phone began to ring. "I wouldn't answer that if I were you, Mrs. Melton-Joyner!"

****

"Toni's not answering her cell phone," Ron made known, hanging up as Chuck drove as fast as he could, with Brandy in the back seat.

Ron couldn't believe what was happening. Toni was at the stables with a madman. Jamie Heard had seemed so nice and sincere. He couldn't believe that was the man who had tried to destroy his family, and what was worse, *he* was the one who recommended the job to the man. Jamie, his *brother*! This was just too much to swallow all at once. "How long is it going to take to get there?" Ron asked Chuck.

"Not long," Chuck replied. "Don't worry. He has no reason to hurt Toni and Jordan. And Jordan's pretty resourceful. She can handle a little punk like Jamie Heard."

"I hope you're right," Ron responded.

"My brother isn't a murderer!" Brandy insisted. "I told you, it had to have been Tracie!"

"Yeah, right!" Ron sarcastically replied. "Hurry, Chuck!"

****

Tyler walked into Beverly's office a little later than he thought he would be and looked around. He didn't see Beverly, and he assumed she couldn't wait and left. He saw the cake pan on her desk. "Oh, she left it," he said aloud then picked it up and started for the door. He stopped when he heard a pounding. He turned to listen and heard it again. Then he heard a faraway voice, but he couldn't

410

make out what it was saying. Tyler walked back into the office to observe. He noticed that the pounding was coming from the closet. He rushed over there and called, "Beverly?!"

"Tyler?" Beverly called. He pressed his ear close to the door.

"Yes, it's me. Where's the key?"

"I don't know where he put it. It might be in the desk drawer," she called back. "Hurry, Tyler!"

Tyler rushed to the desk and found Beverly's purse and found some keys. He ran back to the closet and tried several of them. The fourth one worked, and he yanked open the door, and Beverly exhaled deeply. "Thank God!" she exploded.

"What happened?" Tyler asked.

She grabbed his arm and blasted, "Come on! I'll explain on the way!"

"On the way where?" Tyler countered, following her.

"On the way to Taffy Hines' stables. Jamie Heard locked me in there. I saw his reflection in the computer monitor just before he knocked me out with chloroform or something," she explained. "Toni and Jordan are out there. They might be in trouble."

"Shouldn't we call the police and Ron?"

"We'll call Ron on the way! I don't want to call the police yet. I might be wrong. But we'll call Dr. Joyner just in case someone gets hurt," she insisted, running out the door as Tyler followed her.

"Ron's brother?"

"Yes," Beverly confirmed as they waited for the elevator.

"I thought he didn't practice medicine anymore."

"He doesn't, but I rather call him for a false alarm than anybody else," she explained, hopping on the elevator.

"This sounds heavy. I better take my camera."

****

"So, you're the one who helped Brandy set us up?" Toni queried.

"No! *Brandy* helped *me*!" he announced proudly as he stood beside Jordan at a safe distance while she tied Toni's hands to the back of a chair. He then inspected it by yanking on it and felt good that it was secure. "Sit down!" he ordered Jordan to a chair beside Toni. She sat slowly.

"Why?" Toni wanted to know.

"Why what?" he remained smug as he tied Jordan's hands behind the chair like she had tied Toni's.

"Why did you set us up?" Toni asked. "We don't even *know* you."

"Because he's getting back at my father," Ron stated, entering the stable door, and Jamie jerked up to look at him.

****

Tyler positioned himself on a ladder at a top window of the stable so he could get a good view. He put on his high-powered lenses so he could get close-up shots. Beverly sat on the bottom of the ladder and watched the occurrence in the stable from a lower window. When she arrived with Tyler, she was about to enter the stables when she spotted Ron and Chuck, and Chuck insisted that she stayed out of sight.

****

"Getting back at your *father*? For *what*?" Toni requested.

"Because Jamie is my father's illegitimate son," Ron announced.

"I'm glad you're here, bro," Jamie acknowledged, smiling sarcastically, pointing the gun at Ron. "I've never been invited to a family reunion."

"We didn't know about you," Ron stated. "If we had, we…"

412

"Would've *what*?" Jamie spat. "Welcomed me with open arms?"

"Yes," Ron insisted, ignoring his sarcasm.

"I doubt that," Jamie sneered.

"Tracie Myers has been apprehended. It's over, Jamie," Ron continued. "We know about the overdose she gave Hank Timmons and made it look like negligence on Leroy's part."

"Touché!" Jamie sneered sarcastically. "My sister and I will be long gone before they start to look for us."

"We also know about the exterminator you paid to plant that bug in my office, and then you killed him to tie up loose ends," Ron continued.

"He was a loser!" Jamie spat.

"Jamie," Brandy yelled, entering, and his eyes widened.

"Brandy, what the hell are *you* doing here?" Jamie blasted.

"They found me," she shared. "Jamie, tell Ron you didn't kill anyone… that it was all *Tracie's* doing!" Jamie just stared at his baby sister as tears ran down her face. "Tell him, Jamie. Tell him you're not a murderer!"

"Brandy, get over here!" he demanded, and she slowly strolled to him. "Haven't I always taken care of you?" She nodded. "Then don't cry and don't worry about a thing. I will continue to take care of you."

"Jamie, what happened at the hospital?" Brandy asked as Leroy entered, followed by his father and all eyes focused on them.

"Well, if it ain't daddy dearest!" Jamie barked.

"Ron, Beverly called and said you might need me," Leroy spoke. "What's going on?"

Ron took a deep breath then announced, "Leroy, Dad, this is Jamie Heard."

"Jamie?!" Mr. Joyner exploded.

"So, you *do* remember me?" Jamie snarled.

"Of course, I do," Mr. Joyner replied. "But what are you doing? Why are you holding everyone hostage?"

"Dad, Jamie said he's your son," Ron spoke up and Mr. Joyner's eyebrows lifted.

"My *son*?!" he repeated.

"And you know it, old man!" Jamie spat. "You used my mother for years, and then when she had me, you dropped her like a hot potato."

Mr. Joyner took a deep breath and responded, "Jamie, that is not true. I asked your mother if I was your father, and she said no."

"You liar!" Jamie yelled. "You broke her heart! Then she married that…that…*pervert*!"

"My *dad*?" Brandy whispered.

"He wasn't your father, Brandy! He was a maniac!" Jamie raged through clenched teeth.

"I don't remember him," Brandy replied. "He left when I was still a baby."

"He didn't *leave*!" Jamie yelled. "I *killed* the son-of-a-bitch!" Everyone froze at Jamie's confession. "I was nine years old, and he came into my room one night and…." He couldn't finish. Tears were running down his face as he looked at Brandy. "Mother helped me bury him in the woods, and we never talked about it again. Everyone thought he abandoned us."

"Oh, Jamie, you *did* kill that man in the hospital?" Brandy breathed with tears streaming down her face which drew Leroy's attention.

"What man in the hospital?" he inquired.

"Mr. Timmons," answered Ron. "Leroy, you didn't kill him. Tracie Myers and Jamie did."

"Tracie?!" Leroy exploded. "She was one of the best surgical nurses on my team. Why would she do that?"

"For *money*! What else?!" Jamie spat. "She was a greedy little slut! I paid her well. Of course, I had to marry a rich old broad to do it though, but it was worth it."

"Why was destroying my life worth it?!" Leroy demanded.

"Because *he*…," Jamie yelled, pointing a finger at Mr. Joyner, and added, "abandoned me when I needed him." He focused on Mr. Joyner. "You could've helped us, but your *family* was too important to you." He paused and wiped his tears. "You quit coming around when I was about six. It destroyed my mother. She started drinking, and then she married the first creep that came around. We lived in hell those two and a half years when he was there, until I

414

had enough." He paused again. "I had to make you pay for leaving us."

"Jamie, who told you I was your father?" Mr. Joyner asked.

"My *mother*," he sniffed. "She said you knew but you didn't *want* to know."

"I'm sorry, son, I guess I didn't," Mr. Joyner admitted. "But please give me a chance to make it right."

"It's too late for that!" Jamie spat.

"It's *never* too late," Mr. Joyner insisted.

"It *is* for *that*," Jamie sniffed again.

"What're you going to do with us?" Jordan asked.

Jamie stared long and hard at her then replied noticeably light heartedly, "Oh, I'm sorry. I didn't tell you, did I?" Everyone remained silent. "I'm going to *kill* you! *All* of you!"

****

Travis sat on the couch and dialed Jordan's number again. He wondered if she was still out at the stables. He called Ron and Toni's house again. Ron had invited everyone over for a card game tonight and he wasn't there. It was almost six o'clock. He wondered where everyone was. He called the bakery and Melissa answered the telephone. "Melissa, it's Travis."

"Hi, Travis."

"Hi," he spoke. "I'm trying to track down Ron. Have you seen him?"

"No, but Simon is supposed to join you guys tonight for some R and R."

"Yeah, I know," he pondered. "And you're going out with the ladies, right?"

"That's right."

"It's almost six o'clock and it's not like Ron to be late. He said to meet him at his house between six-thirty and seven," Travis explained.

"Did you try his cell phone?"

"Yes, but he's not answering."

"Melissa," Liz called. "It's busy out here, so I'm going to go ahead and fix the last batch."

"Hold on, Travis," she said then focused on Liz. "Do we have enough icing?"

"Oh, yeah. We still have number five."

"Okay," Melissa replied then went back to the phone. "I'm back, Travis."

"Sure."

"That *is* strange for Ron to disappear without calling you, knowing he has a get-together tonight," Melissa observed. "Travis, call me if you hear anything, and I'll tell Simon not to go until he hears from you."

"All right, honey. Later," Travis finalized then hung up. "Where in the hell is everybody?"

****

"Jamie, you can't kill all these people," Brandy insisted.

"Brandy, be quiet!" he demanded. "Go to the car and wait for me!"

"No, I won't let you kill these people!" Brandy repeated as tears started flowing heavily now. "You're all I have, Jamie. Please don't do this. I love you. You're my big brother. You've always taken care of me. Let's just go and get on a plane to Mexico like we planned."

"I can't do that, Brandy," he maintained. "They *have to* pay."

"Jamie, let it go, please," she pleaded with him.

"No!" he yelled. "If he had lived up to his responsibility, none of this would've happened. You and I would've had a good childhood just like his *precious* children!" He looked at Mr. Joyner again. "Your precious Melissa is going to get hers, too."

"What're you talking about?" Ron asked.

"After today, *five* is going to be her lucky number," Jamie announced proudly.

"Did you do something to Melissa's food?" Ron gasped.

"No, just the icing in number five," Jamie bragged. "Don't worry. Her husband will be around to defend her after all her customers...*die*!"

"Die?!" Toni gasped.

"No, Jamie, you can't!" Brandy added in distress.

"Brandy, let me handle this!" he insisted.

"But you can't kill Melissa's customers!" Brandy pleaded. "They're innocent people. Jamie, think about what you're doing. Your brothers and sisters didn't know about you. They're innocent!"

"They knew! They *all* knew, and now they're all going to die!" Jamie raged, lifting his gun to aim.

****

Becky and Amy entered the family room and Mason was sitting on the couch staring into space. "Hi, Daddy!" Amy exploded on his lap, and he swooped her up.

"Hi, Princess," he accepted, smiling wide. "You're getting heavy."

"You're home early," Becky observed.

"Yeah, I guess I am," he replied nonchalantly then focused on Amy. "Where've you been, kitten?"

"Grandpa's ranch," she beamed.

"Ooh, did you feed the horses?" Mason shared her enthusiasm.

"Yeah," she yelped then focused on her bag. "Want to see what I bought, Daddy?"

"Sure, honey," he agreed, and she jumped off his lap, opened her bag and pulled out a little pink Barbie doll makeup case. "You're wearing *makeup* now?" Mason chuckled.

"It's just play-play," she made known.

417

"It won't hurt her face," Becky confirmed then looked around. "Is Cecilia still here?"

"No, I told her she could go early," Mason revealed. "She cooked though."

"Oh, okay."

Mason bent over in Amy's little face and asked, "Honey, want to run up to your room so mommy and daddy can talk a little?" Becky expressed her surprise openly with her facial frown.

"Okay, Daddy," she agreed. She met Mason with a quick kiss on the lips then skipped out with her toys.

Becky focused on her husband then sat in a chair across from him. She asked cautiously, "What is it?"

He took a deep breath then announced, "Becky, neither of us is happy. I think it's time to be candor. I think it's time we talked about a separation and maybe even a divorce."

****

Just as Jamie's gun went off, Brandy jumped to him yelling, "No, Jamie!" Jordan noticed that the gun was moving towards Toni, so she quickly rocked her chair over, throwing herself in front of Toni, knocking them both to the floor; as Chuck burst into the stables, loading Jamie with bullets, followed by three policemen.

Beverly took a deep breath then walked away dialing on her cell phone. "Come on, Melissa, answer," Beverly snapped. There was no answer, so she called an information service to get Simon's number.

"Hello, Simon Kennedy," he answered.

"Oh, thank God," Beverly breathed. "Simon, this is Beverly, Ron's secretary."

"Hi, Beverly."

"Simon, listen carefully. Run next door to Melissa's Bakery and tell her *not* to use the icing in container number five."

"What is this all about, Beverly?"

"I don't have time to explain. Just go and stop her from using the icing in container number five. It's poisonous!"

"My God!" Simon exploded, dropping the phone, and dashing out.

****

Ron ran to Toni and Jordan as Brandy dropped to the floor next to Jamie's bloody body. Ron didn't know who was shot, Jordan or Toni. It seemed like blood was everywhere. "Toni!" he called as he witnessed that she was buried underneath both Jordan and Jordan's chair on the floor.

"It's Jordan, Ron. She's been shot!" Toni screamed. While he untied her hands, Beverly rushed in, followed by Tyler, and she started untying Jordan's hands.

Toni moved out of the chair and Ron pulled her away and Toni positioned Jordan's head on her lap. "Jordan," she called, and she opened her eyes slowly.

"Toni," she squeezed out. "Now, do you believe I gotcha back, newspaperwoman?"

Toni smiled lovingly at her, then Jordan's head dropped to the side, and she closed her eyes. "Hold on, Jordan. The ambulance is on the way," Toni exploded.

Leroy observed Jordan's state then announced, "She's not going to make it that long." Ron and Toni simultaneously jerked to focus on him.

"Leroy, please, do something," Toni pleaded, and he just stared.

"Please, Leroy," Ron added.

"I don't know if I can," Leroy replied. "My hands may not be as steady as they once were."

"It's like riding a bike is what you once told me," Ron smirked then smiled at his brother. Leroy pondered momentarily then jumped down to Jordan's body.

"Ronnie, my bag is in dad's car," he announced, leaping into action as Toni moved from under Jordan while Ron flew out the door.

Brandy screamed hysterically, sitting on the floor, cradling Jamie's body in her arms. Mr. Joyner walked to her slowly and sat beside her. Then he gently pulled her in his arms. "He was all I had," she cried uncontrollably, laying her head in Mr. Joyner's chest. "My brother was all I had!"

****

"Mason, you can't be serious!" Becky exploded, trying to keep her voice low.

"Becky, you know you're not happy."

She jumped up, ran and sat beside him on the couch and declared, "I love you. I know you're going through some type of crisis right now, but I'm patient. Whenever you want to talk about it, honey, I'm here for you."

He stressed, "Becky, this is not a *temporary* crisis! I'm just not happy and you know it."

"But we can work through this."

"Work through what? We've been working through it for over *seven years*. It's not getting any better."

She pondered for a while as tears began to roll down her face. "Is it Brandy?"

Mason took a deep breath and answered, "No."

"Toni?"

Shaking his head, chuckling slightly, Mason replied nonchalantly again, "No."

"Then what is it?"

"I've told you. I'm not happy."

"Are you still seeing Brandy?"

"I don't even know where she is," he admitted and her eyes widened, so he explained. "Brandy left *The Herald* a while ago. I haven't heard from her since."

"She left?"

"Yes."

"Then if it isn't Brandy, then why do you want a divorce?"

"Becky, I've told you, it has nothing to do with *anyone* but *you* and *me*," he insisted. He took a deep breath. "When we got married, we said it would be temporary. You knew I didn't love you. You told me you were pregnant, so I did the honorable thing. I just can't see spending the rest of my life unhappy like this."

"Brandy made you happy?'

"Why are you still talking about *Brandy*? I'm trying to tell you how I feel. Brandy has *nothing* to do with this."

"But you do still love her, don't you?"

Mason took another deep and concentrated breath then confessed, "Yes, I do." Becky lowered her head and wept even harder. "I don't want to hurt you. I respect you too much for that, but I can't lie to you anymore."

Becky leaped up and insisted, "Then go, Mason!" He was surprised and she knew it. "You're right. I'm tired of fighting for our marriage *alone*. You're not happy because you've *never* given us a chance!"

"I've never given our marriage a chance because you've never given *me* a chance. A chance to get to know you. A chance to love you before you tricked me into marrying you!"

"I just loved you so much."

"But you knew I was involved with Toni at the time, and Toni and I were building on something very special until you lied."

"Then go to her, Mason. Just choose which one you want, *Toni* or *Brandy* or *whoever*!" she snapped, and he just stared at her. Then he slowly shook his head.

"This has nothing to do with either Toni *or* Brandy and you know it," he insisted. "You lied to me. You tricked me into a marriage you knew I didn't want! You didn't even *consider* my feelings!"

"I *did* consider your feelings. I thought I could make you happy!"

"But you couldn't, not with me feeling so trapped," he explained. "Maybe if you had given us a chance to get to know each other, things would've been different. I needed *time* to fall in love with you, but you didn't give me that option!"

"I'm sorry!" she yelled throwing her hands up in the air. "I'm sorry for *living*!"

"And I'm sorry, too, that I couldn't be the kind of husband you deserve. But I do thank you for finally telling me the truth about the baby." He went to her and took her hand. "I care for you, Becky, but it has never been *love*. I need to be happy again, and I believe you need the same. You can't possibly be happy with a man who doesn't love you. You'll find someone. You are a very caring and loving woman. Don't sell yourself short."

****

Simon exploded into the bakery like a madman as two customers were leaving. He stopped them at the door and Melissa looked at him. "Simon, what is it?"

"Please wait one moment," he told the two ladies, as he looked at Melissa and whispered. "Lock the door." She did so right away then he took her hand and dashed into the back.

"Simon, you're scaring me. What is it?"

"Have you used the icing in container number five yet?"

"Yes, we just used it."

"Where are the bake goods you used it on?" he asked as Liz started to walk pass them with a tray full of cake squares.

"Wait, Liz," he demanded.

"Simon, we have customers waiting," Melissa protested.

"Is this the icing from container number five?" he asked Liz.

"Yes, why?"

"Have you used it on any other bake goods, other than these?"

"Yes, I just put some in the case."

"Would you go and get them, please?" he instructed, and she looked at Melissa, and she nodded. Liz put the tray down and walked out.

"Is something wrong with my icing, Simon?" Melissa questioned.

He took a deep breath then admitted, "It's been poisoned, sweetheart." He had to catch Melissa for she felt her legs give way. He helped her to a chair as Liz brought the tray of cake squares back. "Are you all right, honey?"

"Poisoned?" Melissa blurted out, and he nodded.

He looked at Liz and blew hard, praying silently as he asked very cautiously, "Are these all you used from container number five?"

"Yes," she answered.

"Are any missing?" he inquired cautiously.

She counted them and answered, "No." Simon breathed again.

"Thank God," he said, blowing hard. "Are you absolutely sure?"

"Yes, I just put them out," she confirmed.

"And are you sure the counter help didn't get any from this tray and refill it with another tray?"

"No, we don't do that here," she answered shortly.

"I'm not trying to offend you, Liz. You do a great job, but the icing in container number five has been poisoned."

"Poisoned?!" Liz gasped.

"Simon, how?" Melissa asked, finding her strength.

"I don't know the details yet, but Beverly, Ron's secretary called and told me."

"Why didn't she call *me*?" Melissa wanted to know.

"I don't know. Check your phone," he suggested, and Melissa checked the phone and found that it was partially hung up.

"Oh, I must've done that when I talked to Travis," Melissa stated. She took a deep breath then fell into Simon's arms. "Thank you, baby."

"You're welcome," he accepted then focused on Liz, still standing there. "Liz, don't throw any of that away. We might need it for evidence." She nodded then walked away.

"Oh, my customers!" Melissa yelled. She grabbed a few wrapped Christmas ornaments off a table, which she kept for unexpected guests and dashed to the door.

"Ladies, I'm sorry to keep you waiting," she announced. The bakery was now full, with six people waiting to leave. She handed each one of them a wrapped ornament. "Merry Christmas." The women beamed with excitement, thanking her as she opened the door to let them out.

Simon joined Melissa at the door. "Call Ron and see what the hell is going on," he suggested.

Part Five

One Week Later

Chapter 40

Melissa was glowing as she strolled down the isle of the church on her son's arm, smiling brightly at Simon, her future, her strength, her love. Simon thought Melissa was the most beautiful woman he had ever seen in his life in her ivory colored, lace embroidered wedding gown with the ivory, sheer veil hanging over her beautiful face, and her hair flowing loosely in dangling curls around her happy face. Melissa's heart seemed to do a double take as she spotted her husband to be, standing so tall and handsome in his ivory tuxedo.

Ron watched his sister approach as he stood beside her groom and felt a warm feeling inside that she had found someone to love, someone whom her children also adored. She was so torn up after her husband's death, and at one time, he thought she would never recover, but seeing her today, he knew without a shadow of a doubt, that there is a God. Toni and Denise stood together in sequined rainbow gowns, with baby breaths encircling their heads like crowns, across from him. Ron looked at his stunning wife, smiled lovingly at her, and she returned it. Toni could never get used to looking at her handsome husband without a twinge of passionate warmth. She wondered if that feeling would last forever. People always said it wouldn't, but she was out to prove them wrong. She desired her husband just as much now as she did the first night that they were intimate. Travis stood beside Leroy, the other groomsman, and smiled sweetly at Jordan, who occupied a space in the wedding party as a bridesmaid with another friend of Melissa's. They had also worn rainbow-colored gowns as well, but they didn't have a pink sheer scarf around theirs.

Little Alexandria served as the flower girl, walking slightly ahead of her mother, smiling very brightly, in an ivory-colored, lace gown, and a crown of baby breath adorning her head.

Mr. and Mrs. Joyner sat on the front row of pews with Simon's parents as they watched the happy union. Mr. and Mrs. Kennedy were distinguished looking people. They approved of Melissa right from the start. They had to admit that they were a little reluctant when they learned that she had two kids. Children can be a strain on a new marriage. However, after they met Keith and Alexandria, they had no more doubts. The children were simply wonderful, and they loved and accepted Simon like their own father.

Bill sent his regrets because Rita was recuperating from the bone marrow transplant, but he was overjoyed that the doctors expected her to have a complete recovery.

Angel and David sat together holding hands, remembering their own wedding. Their boys were staying with David's parents for a couple of days, and they were enjoying each other immensely. He was relieved that she had cut out all that talk about having another baby. He was selfish and didn't want to share her with a new baby right now.

Mason sat in the audience alone, and he couldn't tell you when the preacher announced the happy couple husband and wife. His mind wasn't on the wedding. It was on Brandy. He couldn't believe that Brandy had used him just to get to know about Toni, to destroy her. Toni is his friend. How could Brandy have done that to her? Although he knew Brandy deserved just what she was getting, he must admit that it was killing him to know that she was locked up behind bars, awaiting her trial. He wanted to pay her bail so badly, but he didn't want it to appear that he was betraying Toni and Ron. Mason was now living in his downtown penthouse alone, and it felt good to finally take a stand to end his farce of a marriage. He had already started divorce proceedings and to his surprise, Becky wasn't making it hard for him. They had agreed that she would keep the mansion in the country, the beach house, the Mercedes, and the Porsche, and he would keep the penthouse, the lake house, his Lamborghini, and Escalade. They never shared a bank account, so he would keep his money and she would keep hers. He would pay all of Amy's expenses, something *he* had insisted on doing. When Mason came back to reality the preacher was announcing the happy couple husband and wife.

****

"Ron, do you have a minute, honey?" Toni asked, entering the sunroom where he sat, looking over some papers.

"Yeah, babe, what's up?" he acknowledged, sitting back on the couch while removing his reading glasses to give her his undivided attention.

"What're you doing?"

"Just looking over Mrs. Sanders' case. We go to trial next week," he announced.

"Okay. I could come back later."

"No," he countered, sitting up now, and reaching out to her. She took his hand and sat beside him with a manila folder in her hands. "What's up?"

"I've finished my article and I wanted you to take a look at it."

"Honey, I'm sure it's fine."

Extending the folder to him, she revealed, "I had to name people, and I wanted you to read it before I submitted it. I wouldn't want to dishonor your family or you. If you're uncomfortable with it, I'll table it...*forever!*"

"Toni, I appreciate that, but if *you* don't tell the story, someone else will, and I'd rather my family were at your mercy than anyone else's."

"Still, I want you to read it," she suggested. "Even if you agree to print it, you might want to change some things."

"*You're* the journalist, not *me*. Whatever you write, I'm sure it will be fine."

"Thanks, but I still want you to read it."

He looked at the folder she had handed him then asked, "*Now?*"

"Please."

Nodding slowly, he agreed, "Okay."

"I'll leave you alone until you finish," she announced, and he nodded, then she left.

Ron sat back on the couch, put his reading glasses back on and opened the folder slowly. He took a deep breath and began:

Hey! Hey! Hey! America!

 Is loyalty dead? Is family value dead? Is honesty dead? Is justice dead? I'm going to attempt to answer these questions today, and when I finish, maybe you, too, will be able to answer them as well.

 Today, I'm going to talk about my own personal relationships. No, I don't have an interview with a well deserving person. I only have my life over the past few months. So today, America, let's talk about me, my family, and the things that touched our lives recently.

 Three months ago, my character, my reputation, and my marriage were attacked by an article in my column that stated that my husband, Attorney Ron Joyner, revealed some confidential information to me about a client. I'm here to set the record straight. I know a lot of you have been waiting for me to respond to that article, but I was in no position to respond... until now. I thank God that my loyal fans knew that article was not written in either my style or my voice. For those of you who believed it was my writing style, I would like to let you know that I do not write articles that would cause a teenaged girl to want to end her life. I would not write articles that would cause my husband to be suspended from his job with a multimillion-dollar lawsuit hanging over his head and an investigation that could end his career. That article was written by someone else and pushed through the printing press without my knowledge for one reason and one reason only: to destroy my husband while using me as the fall guy.

 Who would do such a thing? Believe it or not, a family member! Unbeknownst to my husband and his family, there was an illegitimate son born to his father and his past mistress. This son's bitterness turned into rage and then to murder. Jamie Heard was a lonely, disturb young man, who had a successful career, but his rage kept him from enjoying the fruits of his labor because he felt he had a score to settle: a score to settle with his biological father whom he thought had abandoned him, not realizing that his father was unaware of his connection to Jamie. Jamie decided to begin his vendetta with his father's children, starting with the eldest, Dr. Leroy Joyner. It didn't matter to Jamie that in Dr. Joyner's capacity, in order to destroy him, someone had to die, and that's exactly what happened. The victim was Mr. Hank Timmons. Jamie solicited the help of an ambitious nurse named Tracie Myers to help in his dirty deed to set up Dr. Joyner. When Mr. Timmons died, Dr. Joyner was sued and lost everything, including his wife and two children. Jamie also had the help of a baby sister, Brandy Sears, whom he cared for all her life, so she thought she owed him her loyalty. However, Brandy Sears didn't know anyone would die, but Jamie and Tracie knew. They knew!

Next, Jamie targeted the only other son of his biological father, Attorney Ron Joyner, my husband. By that time, Jamie had married the rich and powerful Taffy Hines and used her money to pay off Tracie. He planted Brandy into The Weekly Herald, where my office is housed, while Jamie took up shop in Ron's place of employment, Schuster, Collins, and Ballentine Law Firm. Jamie found out about the secret that Mrs. Gloria Sanders had shared with Ron by using an exterminator to plant a bug on Ron's office, but later murdered the man to tie up loose ends. Jamie wrote the incriminating article, and Brandy, being an employee of The Weekly Herald, pushed it right on through to the printing press.

Unfortunately, Jamie wasn't finished yet. He also tried his hand at destroying his father's oldest daughter, Melissa Washington-Kennedy, but failed. Jamie's life ended at his wife's stables when he held five people at gunpoint with the intent of murdering again, including my husband and me, but the police and Chuck Warren of Warren Investigative Firm arrived and ended Jamie's rage and torment. Now, we are all trying to get our lives back in order. Dr. Joyner has partitioned the court for the reinstatement of his medical license, Ron is practicing law again, and I am moving forward!

Is loyalty dead? Nurse Tracie Myers proved it wasn't... if the price is right. Is family value dead? Brandy Sears proved it wasn't when she risked her freedom to repay her brother for his loyalty to her when they were motherless at childhood. Is honesty dead? Jamie proved that it was, but you, my fans, proved that it wasn't when you believed in me. Is justice dead? Jamie is no longer alive and both

Brandy and Tracie are incarcerated, awaiting their trials. I'll let you be the judge.

So, the next time you decide to be unfaithful to your spouse, stop, think, and think again! Is the price too high? I think it is. Tell me what you think!

Until next time, America, be happy, be healthy, and be blessed!
Toni Melton-Joyner

Ron looked at the powerful pictures Tyler had taken at the stables. He had captured the entire event as it unfolded. No wonder Toni trusted him so much. He was hugely talented. Ron closed the folder and stared into space. Then he stood, walked into the bedroom where Toni was lying on the bed, looking at the television. She sat up when he entered. He handed her the folder and she just stared at him. He took a deep breath then stated, "Print it."

"Are you sure?"

"I'm sure."

Chapter 41

"You're famous, girlfriend," a rough-looking lady announced calmly, in the roomful of orange-jumpsuit-dressed ladies looking at television in the recreation room of the county jail, as she threw a copy of *The Weekly Herald* in Brandy's lap. Brandy picked the magazine up slowly and read Toni's article. She was pleased that Toni didn't make her out to be some kind of a monster, but rather a victimized loving sister, which she was. She had no idea what her brother was capable of. She was happy to hear from her lawyer that Tracie had confessed and admitted that Brandy knew nothing about the murder at the hospital. That was something Jamie and Tracie had decided to do, without sharing that bit of information with her.

"Listen up, ladies!" a guard entered, announcing. "Some of you have visitors!" As she called the names, Brandy tuned her out. She knew she didn't have any visitors because the only family she had was dead. Besides, she had been locked up a little over a week and no one came to see her but her lawyer who was a public defender. She had no money to hire a decent one. She had thought about selling her car to pay for one but decided against it. Her house and car were the only things she had to remember her sweet Mason, and she wasn't letting them go for *anything*. She wondered how he was doing. She hoped he realized that she really did love him with all her heart. Maybe one day he would forgive her.

"Hey, Sears, you too!" the guard yelled, intruding Brandy's thoughts, as the other ladies filed out the door.

"I have a visitor?" she asked softly, and the lady nodded. She thought that it must be her lawyer. She hoped he had good news. Although she realized whatever the jury decided, she still would be looking at two years in jail. The DA had dropped the murder charge against her after Tracie's statement; that didn't change the fact that she *had* conspired with her brother to ruin people's lives.

Brandy fell in line behind the other ladies and another guard trailed behind her. She was in a minimal security city jail. There were no longtime prisoners or deadly women. They were all there

433

for minor things, such as getting in fistfights, writing bad checks, shoplifting, and so on.

Brandy walked into the open room slowly, searching for her lawyer's face while the other women joined their families at individual small tables. She didn't see him, but her heart seemed to skip a beat when she spotted Mason standing there, looking so tall and handsome with his dark, bronzed skin, tailor-made, grayish-blue pinstriped, two-piece suit, expensive shoes, Rolex watch, and groomed dark brown, wavy hair. He looked so out of place. The women and their visitors all gasped when they spotted him. Whispers soared through the room, as they speculated whom he was there to see. Then Brandy strolled over to him slowly.

Mason smiled slightly and greeted weakly, "Hi."

Brandy's heart seemed to melt. She felt so ashamed and so heartbroken at seeing the pain in his eyes and hearing the hurt in his voice. She finally found her voice and whispered very throaty, "What're you doing here?"

"To see you," he disclosed then motioned for her to sit at a nearby table. She sat slowly and he joined her on the opposite side, staring deep into her eyes. Mason's heart went out to Brandy. He hated to see her in a place like this. With all she'd gone through, she still looked extremely beautiful, even in bland clothes, unruly hair, and no make-up. "How are you?"

"Fine, I guess," she chuckled. "Considering."

He smiled with her then took a deep breath and added, "You look well."

Brushing her straight, lifeless hair out of her sad face with her hand, she accepted, "Thanks." There was a long, uncomfortable silence between them. "Mason, I don't know what to say to you."

"That makes two of us," he admitted then took a deep breath. "But you can start by telling me if what we shared was all a lie."

"No!" she answered quickly, trying to keep her voice low. "No, it wasn't."

"So, you didn't just *use* me to get to Toni?"

"No, I didn't need to," she shared. "Mason, I fell in love with you the moment I laid eyes on you. And the first time we made love, I knew you were just having an extramarital affair with me, but I didn't care because I loved you. I wouldn't have slept with you if I hadn't."

"Then why, Brandy? Why did you do it? Why did you try to destroy my friends?"

****

"Hello, Mrs. Kennedy," Simon addressed, smiling wide, focusing on Melissa in his arms as they lay in bed.

She shared his wide smile and responded, "Hi, Mr. Kennedy." They met in a sweet kiss.

"Are you hungry?"

"No," she answered, snuggling up even closer in his arms.

Melissa was so nervous last night when she and Simon were intimate for the first time. She hadn't been with a man since the death of her husband, and she wasn't sure if she could satisfy one anymore. Simon soon made her feel so relax and so confidant. He took his time with her and made her realize that they had the rest of their lives together. She loved him so much. He kissed her again.

Simon didn't know it was possible to be this happy. And with *one* woman! Melissa was *everything* he had ever wanted. He thought that no *one* woman could completely satisfy him...until Melissa. She was smart, intelligent, and *so* sexy. She satisfied every part of him, and he would spend the rest of his life showing her just how important she was to him. They kissed again. He slid on her. Melissa welcomed her new husband lovingly. He was smothering her face and neck with kisses and she was moaning aloud now. She knew this was *their* time together. Once they returned to their jobs, her children, and their families, *then* she would share him, but not right now. This was their last day in Belize together, so they had to savor every moment. "I love you, Mrs. Kennedy," Simon whispered while nibbling on her ear.

"I love you," Melissa echoed, basking in his ever so gentle arms.

****

"Toni, your article was brilliant," Mrs. Melton admired at the dinner table as Toni and Ron joined her for dinner Sunday afternoon.

"Thank you, Mom."

"Ron, how are your parents?"

"They're coping," Ron answered. "It's hard, but I think they're going to make it."

"Good."

"And your brother?"

"We filed for his reinstatement, but it takes a while for the paperwork to go through."

"Well, we'll keep praying that everything goes well for him."

"Thank you, Mama Effie. I appreciate that," Ron accepted.

"Oh, and congratulations on getting the Sanders' case."

"Thank you."

"That poor woman has gone through so much," Mrs. Melton added.

"Yes, she has," agreed Ron.

"Are you going back to your law firm?"

"I don't know," he replied. "They didn't stick by me when everything happened, and I don't know if I want to work with people like that. I'll make a decision after I finish Mrs. Sanders' case."

"And our phone is ringing off the hook for Ron to represent them," Toni added.

"Well, maybe you should try solo for a while," Mrs. Melton suggested.

"I'm weighing all options," Ron shared as Toni's cell phone began to ring.

"Excuse me," Toni stated, getting up. She pulled her cell phone out, walking away.

"This food is delicious, Mama Effie," Ron admired.

"Thank you, son," she accepted. "I *do* enjoy cooking." Toni came back to the table with a blank stare on her face.

"Honey, what is it?" inquired Ron.

"That was Tyler. Rita Hurley just died."

****

"I had no other choice," Brandy finally answered.

"We *always* have choices, Brandy."

She took a deep breath and countered, "Well, *I* didn't." She took another breath. "Mason, you couldn't possibly understand. You grew up with loving parents and a *lot* of money. I don't expect you to understand my life and what I went through."

"Try me, Brandy," he pleaded. "I *want* to understand."

She took a long and concentrated sigh and began, "When I was a little girl, all I remember about my mother was that she drank a lot. She was drunk more than she was sober. She was a waitress at some truck stop restaurant, and whenever she got off work, she would come home with either a bottle, a truck driver, or both. I was nine years old when she finally drank herself to death. I never understood why she was like that because the pictures I saw of her younger days, she was beautiful. The night that my brother was killed, it was finally revealed to me. My mother simply *could not* live with the fact that she and Jamie had covered up my father's murder."

"Who murdered him?'

"My brother."

"Jamie?!" he shrieked, and she nodded.

"He sexually abused Jamie," she added weakly. "And that changed Jamie's whole life. I really wish people would just stop and think about what they're doing to children before they violate their little innocent bodies." She paused. "I often wondered why Jamie always seemed to feel he needed so many women. I guess he was just trying to prove to himself that he wasn't gay because he had been molested by a man." She paused and wiped a few falling tears.

Mason reached in his inside pocket and extended a handkerchief. "Thank you." She wiped her tears, took a deep breath then continued, "When my mother died, Social Services Child Welfare Department took me. Jamie wanted to keep me, but they wouldn't let him because he was underage. Since he was seventeen, he didn't have to go with them, so he stayed at the house. He was already working part-time at a grocery store, so he was able to take care of himself." She paused again. "The first house I was placed in, I was raped by the man of the house." Mason's eyes widened and she continued, "I went to Jamie's school the next day, found him, and told him what had happened to me. He promised me that would *never* happen to me again." Her tears were flowing heavy now and she had to stop again to regain composure. Finally, she went on, "Jamie took me home with him, and it took them six months to realize that the foster parents didn't have me anymore. They were still collecting the money for me. Then they said I ran away. By then, Jamie was already eighteen and he filed adoption papers to get me legally. Social Services didn't try to stop him because I told them what had happened to me, and they didn't want us to go public with that. So, Jamie adopted me, and he dedicated his life to me. He made sure I had food to eat even when he didn't have any. Many days I saw my brother go to bed without eating, and he would say he wasn't hungry." She looked up in his caring eyes. "Mason, you've never had to worry about where your next meal was coming from."

"No, I haven't," he admitted breathlessly.

"When Jamie started college, he used to help me with homework and spend time with me. Sometimes, I would wake up late at night to use the restroom, and he would be studying. My brother made so many sacrifices for me." She paused to blow her nose. "Then one day Jamie realized that God had given him a gift. He was good looking, and he could get women, a *lot* of women. He started dating older women and they would do *anything* for him, such as buy food for us, pay our utility bills, and more. One lady he became involved with was a pageant consultant and she started entering me in beauty pageants. I won a few, and the pageants' scholarships became an opportunity for me to pay my way through college. When I was in my senior year of college, Jamie came to me and told me who his father was, and he said that it was time to get even with the bastard. He said our lives would have been a lot different if the son-of-a-bitch had lived up to his responsibility. He said we would start with the man's most precious commodity: his *children*." She paused and sniffed. "Mason, I know you can't understand this, but my brother meant the world to me. He was the only person I knew that really loved me. I couldn't let him down."

"What happened to the man who raped you?"

"They found him dead in an alley a year later," she shared. "He was beaten to death."

"Jamie?"

She hunched her shoulders slightly and admitted, "I guess so, but I never asked him, and he never volunteered to tell me and that was fine with me."

He stared deep into Brandy's sad eyes and replied quietly, "You've had a hard life."

"Please don't hate me," she cried. "I love you so much. That was *never* a lie. You and Jamie are the only two people in this world that I knew genuinely loved me. I could handle any punishment they give me, but I couldn't handle your hating me."

He placed his hand on hers, stared deeply into her sad, tear-filled eyes and replied softly, "I could *never* hate you, Brandy. *Never!*" She burst into tears and he jumped up and pulled her in his arms.

"No touching!" the guard yelled then focused on Mason. "Oh, I'm sorry, Mr. Whittaker. I didn't know it was you," he added then walked away.

"Now that Jamie's dead, I have *no one!*"

"You have *me*." he made known, holding her close. "You will *always* have *me*." He held back and focused on Brandy's sad face, and then he surprised her by planting a sweet kiss on her lips. Everybody watched them in amazement, but Mason and Brandy didn't care. It felt so good for her to be in his arms again; and he wanted time to freeze with her there. "I love you, Brandy," he whispered in her ear. She burst into tears again as he held her close.

****

Jordan, Travis, and Malik were playing basketball in the back of Travis's house. Travis was playing against both of them and beating them. "All right, I need one more basket," he bragged to them as he took the ball out. Jordan and Malik huddled up together and Travis wondered what they were planning. "Come on, it's too late for that!" He laughed.

"Come on, we're ready," Jordan called back as she and Malik got into position.

As soon as Travis dribbled the ball in, Jordan jumped on his back, knocking the ball out of his hands and Malik grabbed it and scored a basket. "We won!" Malik yelled.

"No, you didn't," Travis protested in laughter as Jordan and Malik high fived each other. "Y'all cheated!"

"We won!" echoed Jordan, laughing hysterically with Malik.

"You still have about three more baskets to get!" added Travis.

"Face it, Dad. We won!" Malik laughed as he and Jordan cheered.

"I don't believe it!" Travis continued to laugh. "This is a conspiracy!" He jumped towards Malik, and the child took off running in the house, laughing hysterically. Then Travis focused on Jordan, but he noticed that she had stopped laughing and was bending over, holding her stomach. He rushed to her. "Jordan, baby, what's wrong?"

"I don't feel well," she replied. "I guess it's too much excitement."

"Maybe you started too early after the gunshot wound."

"Maybe."

"Come on. Let's go in the house and I'll fix you something to eat."

****

Toni felt numb as she and Ron entered their home after leaving Bill and his children. They were all so sad. Rita had been doing so well when, suddenly, she took a turn for the worse. Toni didn't know what to say to Bill. They had always been like second parents to her. Why did this have to happen the day before Christmas? It's a good thing their children were home though.

"Are you all right?" Ron asked Toni.

She blew hard then answered, "Not really." He pulled her in his arms and let her cry. She had tried to be brave for Bill and his children, but she couldn't hold back her tears any longer. Her husband held her close as she released all her hurt.

****

"Hello, Ernest Parker here."

"Mr. Parker, this is Mason Whittaker," he announced in his cell phone.

"Hello, Mr. Whittaker," the short man acknowledged. "How are you?"

"Okay, thanks," Mason answered.

"What can I do for you?"

"You're representing Brandy Sears, correct?"

"Yes, I am."

"How much is her bail?"

"Fifty thousand dollars."

"Where can I meet you to arrange it?"

"Mr. Whittaker, Miss Sears is scheduled to go before the judge next week for her sentencing since she has already pled guilty. And since it's Christmas Eve, I don't think we could possibly get a judge to…"

"Mr. Parker, I want Brandy out of jail *today*. Do you hear me? *Today*! Now you tell me what I have to do to make that happen, or I'll be finding her another lawyer *today*!"

****

"Ooh, Miss *Thang*, you're full of surprises," a lady jeered to Brandy as the women sat in the television room after visiting hours. "You're Mason Whittaker's woman?"

"*Mason Whittaker*?!" another lady exploded.

"Yeah, they were all into each other out there!" the first lady replied.

"I don't believe it," another lady chimed in. "If you're *Mason Whittaker's* woman, what in the hell are you doing in *here*?"

"I'm not Mason's woman," Brandy finally defended.

"I saw you two out there," the first lady added. "Come on, you can tell us. We won't tell anyone. We know Mason Whittaker is *married* and you don't want to hurt him, but we won't tell! Come on. Give us the 411. How is he in *bed*?"

"Girl, you know a white boy ain't got nothing in that department," another woman added, and Brandy smiled.

"I bet Mason Whittaker do," the first lady remarked. "Come on, give us the scoop."

"There is no scoop," Brandy insisted.

"Then why were you *kissing* him?"

"You were *kissing Mason Whittaker*?!" another lady shrieked.

"Um hum," the first lady answered. "And one of those *French* kisses, too. Not just a little peck on the cheek."

"So why don't he get your black ass outta here?" another lady asked.

"Cause those rich men can use yore ass, and as soon as you get in trouble, that's all folks!" another lady added.

"Okay, Mason and I *did* have a brief affair, but it was over long before I came here," Brandy admitted.

"How was he in bed?" the first lady sneered.

"I don't kiss and tell," Brandy teased.

"Come on, honey, tell us!" interjected another lady. "How *big* is that *thang*?"

"Let's just say, some brothas would be *very* jealous!" Brandy chuckled and the ladies burst into a roar of oohs and ahs.

"Ooh, that man can lay his pants on my bedpost any day!" the first lady gleamed.

"Ah, *any* man can lay their pants on your bedpost any day, slut!" another lady cackled, and the first lady shoved her in laughter.

"Did he buy you stuff?" the first lady inquired.

"Rich men are stingy as hell!" a lady with a gruff voice declared.

"Not Mason," Brandy added. "He was generous to a fault." There were more oohs and ahs.

"Then why don't he get yore black ass outta here?" the lady with the gruff voice added.

"Sears!" the guard yelled, and Brandy stood. "Somebody out there likes you, girl. You just made bail!" The ladies roared with wild excitement, and the guard didn't have a clue.

****

Toni opened her front door, and Mason was standing there. "Hi," he spoke.

"Hi, Mason. I guess you've heard?" she recognized, taking his hand, and guiding him into the house.

"Heard what?" he asked puzzled as she closed the door.

She blew her nose and shared, "Rita passed away. Didn't you hear?"

"No!" he exploded. "When?"

"Earlier today," she shared as Ron entered.

"I haven't been home much today," Mason made known.

"Hi, Mason."

"Hi, Ron," he accepted as they shook hands.

"Come in," Ron offered, and Mason followed him into the den with Toni trailing behind.

"How is Bill?" Mason asked as he sat on the chair while Ron and Toni shared the couch.

443

"Not too good," Toni answered. "We were there earlier."

"Are the kids home with Bill?" Mason inquired.

"Yes, they're home," Toni answered.

"That's good," he replied.

Toni took a deep breath then admitted, "I'm sorry, Mason, I didn't give you time to say why you came over."

"It's okay," he responded. "You're upset."

"Go ahead. I'm all right," she proclaimed.

"Mason, would you like something to drink?" Ron offered.

"No, thank you, Ron," he rejected. "I'm fine." He took a deep breath. "I came to ask you both a favor. I didn't know Rita had died."

"What is it?" Toni inquired puzzled.

"I saw Brandy today. I have her lawyer working on getting her released on bail," he started then stopped and sighed deeply. "Brandy's sentencing is set for next week. I know that usually just before sentencing, the judge will ask the victims if they have anything to say." He paused as Toni and Ron shared a glance. "I was wondering if you could speak on Brandy's behalf?" There was an uncomfortable silence, but Mason continued anyway, "When Brandy's mother died, she was only nine years old. She was placed into a foster home where she was sexually assaulted." Toni gasped.

"I didn't know," she exclaimed.

"I didn't either," Mason went on. "Brandy's brother, Jamie, took care of her." He went on to explain everything that Brandy had shared with him. Ron noticed Toni cringing, so he took her hand. Mason finished, "So, I'm asking you to help *her*...if not for *her*, for *me*." Mason paused and locked eyes with Toni. "I love her." He paused. "I know I'm asking a lot, but I would be eternally grateful if you would try to help her."

Toni focused on her husband and noticed him taking a deep and frustrated breath, and then she focused back on Mason. "I don't know what to say, Mason," she started slowly. "Brandy and Jamie almost destroyed us."

"I know, but it wasn't *Brandy*. It was *Jamie*," Mason made known.

"With *Brandy's* help," added Ron.

444

"Yes, I understand that, but you also said it was *Brandy* who intervened to stop Jamie from killing everyone that day in the stables," Mason remembered. "All I'm asking you to do is to *think* about it." He looked at his watch then stood. "I've got to go and pick her up, but *please* think about it."

****

Mr. Joyner joined his wife in the den as she stared at the sparkling, gleaming Christmas Tree. "A penny for your thoughts," he suggested, sitting beside her on the sofa.

She exhaled deeply and recalled, "I was just thinking how things can change in an instant."

"How so?"

"Ron called and said Bill Hurley's wife died."

"And right at Christmas. That's a shame."

"Yes, it is," she agreed then focused on her husband. "Did you love her, Tim?"

"Who?"

"Annie Heard?"

"No," he answered quickly, and he knew his wife was still waiting on more. "Joyce, I was young and dumb. I know that's no excuse, but I had faults. But I worked through them, and we've never been happier."

"Are there anymore out there, Tim?"

"Any more what…children?"

"Yes, *yours*?"

"No," he insisted. "And I still don't think Jamie was mine."

"Are there any that *might* be yours out there?"

"No, Joyce. I promise. There are no more children out there that could *possibly* be mine."

"I hope not because the next time, they might succeed in destroying our family."

****

Brandy strolled slowly out the door of the jail and focused on Mason standing there waiting for her. By the time she had changed and was released, it was twelve thirty AM. She smiled at him and he returned it. "Thank you, Mason," she finally said.

"Merry Christmas," he reciprocated, extending a single red rose to her. She ran into his arms and they kissed lovingly.

"I love you so much," she declared.

"Then you'll spend the rest of your life showing it," he suggested, and she jerked back and looked in his eyes, searching for clarification. "Becky and I are separated and getting a divorce." Brandy's mouth dropped open.

"You're kidding!" she exploded, and he shook his head.

"I love you, Brandy, and it was time to bury that dead horse that Becky and I called a marriage."

"Oh, Mason!" she shrieked, exploding into his arms again in a long, passionate kiss.

"Let's go home."

****

"Mom!" Keith shrieked as Melissa and Simon walked through the door of Simon's parent's house. He jumped to run in his mother's arms, followed by Alexandria, who jumped into Simon's arms and he picked her up. Simon's parents had wanted the children to stay with them while they were on their honeymoon to get to know them.

"What're you two doing up so late?" Melissa laughed.

"We were waiting for *you*," Keith admitted, and he hugged Simon.

"But we weren't supposed to get back until *tomorrow*," Simon added.

"We knew you wouldn't let us spend Christmas without you," added Alexandria and they laughed.

"That's exactly what they told us," Mrs. Kennedy confirmed.

"You're ready to go home?" inquired Melissa.

"I guess so," Keith answered nonchalantly.

"Well, looks like we could've stayed another day," Melissa laughed.

"We had a ball," added Mr. Kennedy.

"Thank you so much," Melissa acknowledged.

"No. Thank *you*," Mrs. Kennedy countered. "They're marvelous kids."

"What did you bring us, Dad?" Keith asked and Simon froze as his eyes locked with Melissa's and she smiled sweetly. He couldn't believe that Keith had just called him dad. He felt his eyes moisten.

Finding his voice, Simon chuckled, "We'll let Santa Clause bring it."

"Ah," Keith grumbled in laughter. "Come on, Allie. Let's get our stuff."

"I'll help you," Mrs. Kennedy added, rushing after them.

"I'll get you two some hot chocolate," Mr. Kennedy offered as he exited into the kitchen.

Simon and Melissa faced each other, and their lips met lovingly. "This is the second greatest moment of my life; hearing Keith call me dad."

"What's the first?"

"When I married you," he cooed

"Oh, honey," she purred. "That is so sweet." They met each other with another gentle kiss.

****

Brandy sat in a bathtub full of bubbles, relaxing and enjoying her house. She didn't think she would see her house again for at least two years. She laid her head back and thought how lucky she was to have a man like Mason fall in love with her. "Would you like some company?" he asked, invading her thoughts.

"Absolutely," she beamed. Then he undressed and stepped into the bathtub behind her and pulled her in his arms. She laid her head back in his chest and melted in his arms as he hugged her close.

"How do you feel?"

"I feel *great*."

"Good."

"It must be nice to have so much money."

"Why?" he asked. "The old cliché is right you know. Money *can't* buy happiness."

"But it can buy *respect*," she added. "Look at the way the guard backed down when you hugged me at the jail when he saw that it was you. And who could've gotten me out of jail on *Christmas Eve* but someone rich like you?" she explained.

"Brandy, being rich isn't all you think."

"Well, I'd much rather be rich and unhappy than poor and unhappy," she chuckled.

"Well now, you're rich *and* happy," he stressed, extending his hand in front of her with the biggest most beautiful diamond ring Brandy had ever seen in her life. She jerked around to face him, and he smiled. "Will you marry me?"

"Mason…" her breath ran out.

"Is that a yes?" he probed.

"Mason, I might be going to jail next week."

"Then I'll wait for you."

"I couldn't ask you to do that."

"*You're* not asking. I'm telling you! I *will* wait!"

She took a deep breath and proclaimed, "I love you so much, but I don't know if we could make a marriage work. We come from two entirely different worlds."

"What are you saying, Brandy, that I'm good enough to *sleep* with but not to marry?"

"Of course not!" she exploded. "I just don't want to embarrass you."

"You could *never* embarrass me."

448

"You say that *now*, but what about when we're out in public? Mason, you're *famous*! People are going to talk."

"Then *let* them!" he insisted. "Brandy, I love you. I have never loved anyone the way I love you. I don't want to lose you. I don't want to keep *sleeping* with you and then having to go home. I want us to be together, *forever*." He kissed her lips. "Will you marry me?"

"Can we wait until my sentencing next week?"

"No."

"Why not?"

"Don't you trust me?"

"Yes, but…"

"No buts. *Will…you…marry…me?*"

She smiled wide then concluded, "Yes! Oh yes, Mason! I will!" She exploded in his arms. They hugged and kissed lovingly.

****

"What do you think?" Toni asked Ron as she joined him in bed.

"About Brandy?" he searched, and she nodded, sliding into his arms. "I think we need to think about this long and hard before we stick our necks out for a girl who deliberately tried to ruin our lives."

"She did try to *save* us in the end."

"Are you saying you want to help her?"

"Mason is a friend," Toni made known. "I remember when I first started at *The Herald*, Mason went out of his way to help me."

"That's because he thought he was gonna get a taste of this brown sugar," Ron laughed.

"Oh, no you didn't!" Toni exploded, jumping up in a sitting position, facing him.

"Don't deny it," Ron continued to laugh. "You know you and Mason had a thing going!"

"Are you jealous," Toni teased.

"Of course," he joked, pulling her down on him. "Just like you were when you saw *Vickie*." He planted a kiss on her lips.

"Yes, but you and Vickie were *lovers*. Mason and I *weren't*."

"Maybe you and Mason weren't *physical* lovers, but I bet you were *emotional* lovers."

"What's that supposed to mean, that I was in love with *Mason*?!" she exploded.

"*Were* you?"

"No!" Toni yelped again. "We went out a few times. That's all! You're beginning to sound like *Becky*!"

"Come on, honey, tell the truth. You and Mason were a *lot* more than just friends."

"Why do you think that?"

"I don't know. Just a feeling."

"I told you Mason and I went out a few times."

"You did *more* than *just* go out, Toni. You and Mason were starting something heavy at one time."

"That depends on what you mean by *heavy*," she declared. "We never fell in love with each other."

"No, baby, I didn't say you fell in love with him. I'm simply saying that you were *more* than just friends."

"Ron, that's been so long ago, I don't even remember. All I know is that Mason and I are friends *now*. He helped me a lot in getting my career started."

"And you want to help him *now*?"

"I guess so."

"Then what're you going to do?" Ron asked. "Are you going to speak for Brandy or not?"

Part Six

Seven Years Earlier

Chapter 42

"Mason, meet our newest journalist, Miss Toni Melton," Bill introduced as Mason entered his office where Toni stood to greet him. "Toni, this is Mason Whittaker."

Extending a hand, Mason greeted, "Hi, Toni."

"Hi, Mason," she replied, taking the lead from him that they were already on a first name basis.

"I love the article you did on Mercy Hospital," Mason added.

"Thank you," she accepted graciously.

Toni's hair was in a long, silky wrap, hanging about an inch below her shoulders, with neatly cut bangs outlining her perfect teeth and pretty, pecan tan face. Mason was attracted to her right from the start.

"Let me know if you need any help," he offered.

"Thank you," she accepted, then chuckled. "I just might take you up on that."

"Please do," he continued.

Toni thought she had never seen a man so attractive as Mason Whittaker. He was so good looking with his dark brown wavy hair hanging a little short of his shoulders and his stylish designer wind suit, which she knew was expensive. Mason Whittaker had money and he reeked of it. She figured him to be a spoiled little rich boy, always crying to daddy if things didn't go exactly his way.

"All right, now that the formalities are over, let's have a seat and get down to work," Bill interjected, breaking the immediate chemistry between his lead columnists.

****

"Toni, what is this?!" Mason exploded into her small office, waving some papers.

Looking up from her desk, Toni asked, "What?"

"This article you wrote."

"What about it?" she wanted to know, standing to meet him.

"It has no flavor."

"*Flavor?*"

"Where is the depth? The passion? *Your* voice? All you did was cite details. Honey, writing a column is a lot different from writing an article in the newspaper."

"It *is?*"

"Sure, it is," he confirmed, showing her the paper. "Look here. You said she was scared. Scared how? Was she petrified, shivering, nervous, what? And why was she scared?"

Her perfume was driving him wild, and he felt an immediate sensation coming on, so he flopped down in a chair and patted the other one for her to join him. She sat in the chair next to him and leaned toward him. That wasn't helping. He had to get out of there. This woman was gorgeous, and she was driving him insane. If he didn't leave soon, he would do something stupid like kiss her, and probably get his face slapped.

"Do you see what I mean?"

"I think so," she understood. "I'll work on it."

"Pull out all those notes from journalism class that you thought you would *never* need again," he laughed, and she laughed with him. Soon their eyes locked, and he took the plunge and leaned forward and planted a feather kiss on her lips. To his surprise, she kissed back.

"Would you like to have dinner tonight?" he inquired breathlessly.

"Sure," she accepted, finding it difficult to find her voice. Mason Whittaker was so sexy; she could barely contain herself.

"I'll pick you up at seven," he finalized then stood.

"All right," she complied, standing also. They kissed again then he handed her the papers and left.

****

Toni and Mason sat on the couch in her den kissing passionately. He began unbuttoning her blouse and she stopped him. "What's wrong?" he breathed. "I'm crazy about you. I thought you knew that."

"That's not it," she admitted. "I'm just not ready yet."

He chuckled, "We're both single and over twenty-one. I won't hurt you."

"That's not it," she answered then stood, and he stood with her.

"Then what?"

"I'm just not ready."

"You don't have anything against *white boys*, do you?" he probed.

"No, I've dated white boys before."

"Good," he acknowledged then lifted her chin with his finger. "I want to make love to you, Toni. I promise I won't hurt you."

"I believe you, Mason. It's just that everything is moving so fast. I'm just not ready right now. Please understand."

He took a deep breath then stated, "I do. I understand." He confirmed. "Still friends?"

"Oh yes," she concurred.

****

"Toni, you're killing me!" Mason exploded as they sat on the couch in his office.

"What?"

"Look at the structure in this article. You're still not sharing yourself with your audience. This is *crap!*"

"Hey, hey, hey, you don't have to get nasty!" Toni blurted out.

"I'm sorry, honey. It's just that writing is a passion for me, and when I see a talent like yours being wasted on junk like this, I can't stand it!" he shared then patted her face lovingly. "Forgive me? I didn't mean to be so brutal." She pouted and he planted a kiss on her lips and cooed, "Please." She smiled and he smiled with her, pulling her in his arms.

****

"Are you going to make the deadline, Toni?" Bill asked while Mason and Toni shared his office.

"I think so," she answered weakly, gazing at Mason.

"You *think* so?!" Bill exploded then remained firm. "I need an article, Toni, and quick!"

"She'll have it," Mason interjected.

"Are you sure?" Bill was concerned.

"I'm sure," Mason went out on a limb. "You have my word."

****

Mason entered Toni's apartment and she immediately handed him some papers. "Hello to you, too, Toni," he greeted sarcastically.

"Hi," she recognized, receiving a kiss from him.

"You're finished?" he asked, and she nodded.

Mason sat on the couch and opened the folder. "Hey! Hey! Hey! America?" he read with widen eyes.

"*My* voice," Toni countered.

"I like it," he stated then smiled.

He sat back and read her article silently while she fidgeted nervously, staring out the window. When he took a deep breath, she knew he was finished so she turned to face him. He closed the folder, stood, and went to her. She held her breath awaiting his response, as he handed the folder back to her. "Brilliant!" he announced then smiled.

"Really?" she exploded in smiles.

"Really," he repeated, and she grabbed him, laughing hysterically.

"Thank you, Mason! I owe it all to you!" she chanted as they held each other tight.

"You did it, not me," he made known.

"Let's go out and celebrate," she suggested. "My treat."

Grabbing her around the waist and pulling her close, he cooed, "Why can't we celebrate *here*?" He kissed her deep and almost took her breath away.

"*Friends* remember?" she insisted, breaking away from him.

"No, I *don't* remember *that*," he chuckled as she grabbed her purse and opened the door.

"Come on!"

"Hey, wait a minute," he stopped her. "I need to ask you something."

"What?" she turned back to face him.

"My parents are throwing a fund-raiser campaign dinner for some dude who's running for senator. Would you like to come with me?"

"Sure, when?"

"Saturday."

"*Saturday*?"

"Yeah, is that a problem?"

"Angel and I are going to the beach Saturday."

"What's she going to do with her baby?"

"She has a husband, Mason," Toni sarcastically replied. "She needs the break, and we planned it over a month ago."

"You sure you can't get out of it?"

"I'm sorry," she cooed. "Maybe next time."

****

Mason dragged into Toni's office and flopped in a chair. She looked up from her desk and smiled. "Mason, what's wrong?"

"Toni, I did something so *stupid* Saturday."

"What?"

"And it's all *your* fault."

"*My* fault!" she giggled. "Why? What happened?"

"I was bored stiff at that fund raiser dinner my parents threw, and I kept drinking. You know I'm not used to alcohol and before I knew it, I was *feeling no pain.*"

"Did someone take you home?"

"Yes," he confirmed then focused on her. "Becky Ward, the Mayor's daughter." He paused. "When I woke up Sunday morning, she was in my bed."

"You *slept* with her?" Toni inquired strongly.

"I don't remember. I was drunk."

"What did *she* say?"

He took a deep breath then admitted, "She said we did, but I honestly don't remember having sex with her." Toni just stared at him. "She's not even *pretty*. I can't believe I did that."

"Well, it's over, Mason. Move on," Toni suggested.

"With *you*?"

"What?"

"I want us to be *more* than friends, Toni. Will this affect our relationship?"

"Mason, we don't *have* a relationship. We're *just* friends!" she stressed, and he stood and walked behind her desk. He pulled her up gently.

"You know that isn't true. We're *more* than *just* friends."

"Then why would you sleep with Becky Ward?"

"I told you, I was drunk. I don't even remember it."

"That doesn't excuse it, but at least you're honest. You didn't have to tell me."

"I will always be honest with you. You don't have to ever worry about that," he shared then kissed her. "So, I'm going to have to build your trust again, right?"

"Maybe," she smirked.

"What?"

"I like to see a rich boy squirm."

"That's cold, Toni," he laughed. "*Cold.*"

****

Mason opened the door to his penthouse in boxers only, and Toni exploded in excitement, "Mason, *five* magazines just picked me up."

"That's great, honey," he smiled with her.

"Go put on some clothes and let's go and celebrate!" she raved.

"You're on your way, Miss Melton!" he shared her enthusiasm, going close to her. He kissed her lips smoothly.

"I owe it all to you," she sobered, and they kissed again.

He took her in his arms and kissed her deeply; she welcomed the affection. Then Mason swept her up in his arms and carried her into the bedroom. He placed her feet on the floor as their lips still entwined in kisses. He unbuttoned her blouse and let it drop to the floor. Then he unclasped her red lace bra and dropped it with the blouse, exposing her perfectly rounded, brown breasts. Mason gasped when he saw them. They were so perfect. He held down and tantalized her ear with his tongue, and Toni moaned with pleasure. He unbuttoned her blue jeans, and she wiggled out of them with his help, exposing her red lace panties. Mason bent down and pulled her panties off slowly, trailing every inch of her thighs and legs with soft, tender kisses. Then he slipped out of his boxers and Toni gasped. He laid her on the bed gently. He covered her soft, smooth body with his as they kissed hungrily. He lifted her legs and wrapped them around his hips. He wanted to savor this moment. He had been wanting her for so long. It all seemed like a dream, but it was actually happening. She was actually giving herself to him, and he would cherish this moment.

Toni thought to herself how much she wanted Mason. He had been so patient with her. She was now ready to surrender her love to him.

Just when he was ready to consummate their love, the telephone rang, and they froze momentarily, but he knew the answering machine would pick it up, so he didn't dare stop what he was doing. She arched to receive him.

Suddenly a voice invaded their worlds with, "Mason, it's Becky. Please call me as soon as possible. I'm pregnant! We're going to have a baby." Mason froze and so did Toni. He couldn't believe what he had just heard. How could she be pregnant? They were only together once, and he didn't even remember it! Becky's announcement had drained all the desire from their bodies and Mason felt Toni stiffen underneath him. He took a deep breath then rolled off and landed beside her.

"She can't be," he finally announced.

Getting up, Toni added, "But she *is*."

"Toni, please don't go," he begged, getting up with her.

"Call Becky, Mason. She needs you now."

"This can't be happening!" he insisted as she got dressed.

"But it *is*," she countered, and he grabbed her hand.

"Things don't have to change between us."

"They *already* have," she made known. "We should've just remained friends anyway like we agreed to do."

"No!" Mason yelped. "I never agreed to that. I want *more* than that for us."

"But that's all we can be, especially now that Becky's carrying your child."

"I don't know that it's mine. I mean, she couldn't have been a virgin! What kind of woman sleeps with a man the first night she meets him?!"

"Don't try to justify it!" Toni demanded, staring into his eyes. "Stand up and be a man!"

He took a deep breath then explored, "Are you angry with me?"

"No," she admitted. "I would've been if you hadn't told me about Becky, but you did. So, I have no reason to be angry with you."

"We can still be friends, right?"

"Absolutely. We'll always be friends," she confirmed. They met with a sweet kiss. "I'll see you tomorrow at the office."

Part Seven

Back to the Present

Monday, December 28th

Chapter 43

When the judge entered, Brandy looked back at Mason, and they shared a smile. Then she glanced at Ron, Toni, Melissa, Simon, and the rest of the Joyner family sitting together, ready to crucify her. She felt so ashamed for the part she played in trying to destroy them. Although she was deeply sorry, she knew they would never believe it.

The judged looked over the papers, then he looked up, and announced, "Before I pass sentence, is there anyone in the Joyner family here today who would like to make a statement?"

Ron squeezed Toni's hand lovingly, then she stood, and announced, "Yes, your honor, I would."

"Come forward and for the record, Mrs. Melton-Joyner, state your name and your connection to this case," the judge acknowledged.

Brandy sighed deeply. She knew her goose was cooked now. She knew Toni hated her, and she didn't blame her. Toni had a lot of clout in this town. The judge had even called her by name. She knew Toni was there to *bury* her. She'd see Mason in two years if she were lucky.

Toni walked to the podium in the middle of the floor and leaned forward in the microphone. "My name is Toni Melton-Joyner. I was a victim in this case. It was my article that Miss Brandy Sears replaced with a phony, detrimental one." She paused to gather her thoughts.

"Continue, Mrs. Melton-Joyner," the judge urged.

Toni cleared her throat and spoke, "When that article was released, and I knew I hadn't written it, I was angry and hurt. I felt betrayed. My marriage was challenged because my husband had lost his job, about to lose his license to practice law, and was facing a multimillion-dollar lawsuit. Needless to say, but our lives were in shambles. When we found who had tried to destroy us, I felt hatred and contempt for Brandy Sears and her brother, Jamie Heard." She paused and took a deep breath. "Then, with the help of a good friend, Ron and I realized that we weren't the only victims. *Brandy Sears* was also a victim, a victim of love and loyalty for her brother.

She was a young girl who was left motherless at an early age, and it was her brother, Jamie, who took care of her, sacrificed for her, and made her into the wonderful woman she is today."

Tears were rolling down Brandy's face as she listened to Toni. "Although Jamie was an evil person, *Brandy* is not. In the end, her good sense intervened, and she tried desperately to stop him, but his rage was unstoppable. Yes, Brandy helped Jamie to a certain extent, but even *she* didn't know what her brother was capable of at the time. Yes, Brandy and Jamie almost ruined my husband, his family and me, but we survived. It was terrible what she did for her brother, but she felt obligated and justified to help him because after all, he had been there for her all her life, protecting her and shielding her from any hurt, harm, or danger." Toni paused briefly.

"Brandy felt she owed her brother, and who wouldn't feel the same way as she did? I commend her for her loyalty and commitment. She must've felt he was all she had." Brandy cried hard and her lawyer gave her a handkerchief from his inner pocket. It was as if Toni knew her inner thoughts; how she felt, and she was happy to know that someone understood.

"Your honor, I speak on behalf of my entire Joyner family when I plead to you to give Brandy Sears back her life. She's suffered enough. Her brother is now dead and cannot have any more influence over her. Even if he were still alive, I believe in my heart that Brandy Sears' strings have been cut from him. Let her go on with her life. She has a brilliant mind, a man who loves her unconditionally, and friends who will help her through this difficult time of bereavement." She focused on Brandy. "We forgive you, Brandy. We *will* support you." Toni focused back on the judge. "That's all I have to say, your honor. Thank you for this time." She took her seat again and Ron took her hand lovingly.

The judge took a deep breath, cleared his throat and stated, "Mrs. Melton-Joyner, I have heard your plea. I commend your family and you for your stance in this matter. Mr. Joyner, you better hope your wife never decides to become a lawyer and go up against you in court." He chuckled and Ron smiled with him. Then the judge sobered. "Brandy Sears, I came in here with every intention of imposing the maximum penalty by law that I could give you for the part you played in your fraudulent acts against the Joyner family, but hearing Mrs. Melton-Joyner's plea, I must say that I have had to rethink my position." He took a deep breath. "Miss Sears, would you care to make a statement before I pass sentence?"

Brandy stood slowly, cleared her throat, and said weakly, "Your honor, I would just like to apologize to Toni, Ron, and their family for what my brother and I did." She cleared her throat again and focused on the Joyner family, and Mason dropped his head slowly to hold back his own tears. "I'm deeply sorry. If I could undo it, I would." Then she took her seat again.

The judge paused then ordered, "Will the defendant please rise?" Brandy and her lawyer stood. "Brandy Sears, you have pled guilty of the crime of fraud and malice. Are you ready for your sentence?"

"Yes, sir, your honor," Brandy answered shakily with a trembling voice.

Mason held his breath with her as the judge announced, "Brandy Sears, for being found guilty of the crime in which you are accused, by the authority invested in me by the state of South Carolina, I hereby sentence you to six months of probation." Brandy's mouth dropped open as she placed her hand over it. "You are to report to your probation officer once a week for the duration of your probation. If you violate your probation, you will be apprehended and housed at the Greenleaf County Women's Correctional facility for the duration of your sentence. Miss Sears, do you understand the terms of your probation?"

"Yes, sir, your honor," Brandy squeezed out of trembling lips as her lawyer put his arm around her shoulder.

Immediately after the judge dismissed court, Mason rushed over to Brandy, grabbing her in his arms. "Mason, I can't believe it," she cried. "I don't have to go to jail."

"No, you don't, sweetheart," he concurred, smiling wide, and then kissed her lips deeply. They made their way to Toni and Ron before they left the courtroom.

"Saying thank you doesn't seem to be enough," Brandy announced to them as Mason held her hand.

"You're welcome," Toni accepted then hugged Brandy lovingly.

"Thank you! Thank you!" Brandy chanted in between tears in Toni's ear as they embraced.

****

Jordan, Travis, and Malik played Monopoly on the kitchen table. Every time Malik won, he would stand up, shout, and do a little dance. Jordan got such a kick out of the child's enthusiasm. He was a super kid. The telephone began to ring as Malik just won the game, and he was shouting his victory. Travis picked it up, still laughing at his son. "Hello?" he answered.

"Hi, Travis," Malik's mother said on the other end.

"Hi, Wanda," Travis giggled. "Why didn't you warn me that this child was so good at Monopoly?"

"That's his favorite game," she confirmed. Wanda was an average looking woman, no frills about her at all. She was rather short and hippy, but it looked good on her. She wasn't a pretty woman by any stretch of the imagination, but she was classy. Her hair was pulled back in a neat add-on ponytail, and her dark business suit fit her curves to perfection.

"Now you tell me," Travis continued to laugh. "Malik, your mother." Malik ran to the phone and Travis handed it to him.

"Hi, Mom."

"Hi, honey, are you having a good time?"

"Yeah. Jordan's cool," he snickered, walking out the room with the cordless phone.

"I'm *cool*," Jordan chuckled, and Travis laughed with her.

"I think so," Travis acknowledged, meeting her with a kiss. "How do you feel?"

"I feel fine. Thank you," she acknowledged as Malik ran back into the den with them.

"Now, what can I beat you guys at next?!" he yelped.

"Let's do something else first, buddy," Travis suggested, and Malik handed him a small box.

"What're you two up to?" Jordan wanted to know.

Travis stood and knelt in front of Jordan while Malik smiled wide, and Jordan gasped. "I love you, Jordan." He opened the box and exposed a beautiful, sparkling diamond ring. "Will you marry me?" She focused on Malik who was trying hard to contain his excitement and then back on Travis. "Well?"

"Yes!" she exploded, and Malik cheered as Travis pushed the ring on her trembling finger.

"I love you," he breathed then kissed her lips softly.

"I love you," she replied with tears rolling down her face as Malik joined them in a group hug.

****

"Toni, you got a minute?" Mason asked, entering her office.

"Sure," she answered. "I didn't think you would be in today. I thought you and Brandy would be celebrating."

"I have to finish my column, but I'm leaving early."

"Yeah, me too," she joined as he sat in front of her desk. "So, what's up?"

"I just wanted to thank you personally for helping Brandy today."

"You're welcome."

"Toni, do you remember what we were doing when Becky told me she was pregnant?" Mason asked shyly and Toni chuckled.

"How could I forget?"

"I didn't say it to embarrass you; I just want to make a point."

"And that is?"

"That night when Becky called, you and I were taking our friendship to another level."

Toni cleared her throat, feeling a little embarrassed and solicited, "Is there a point to this story, Mason?"

He laughed, "Yes, there is. I promise." He sobered and added, "I cared for you; you know that, right?"

"Yes, and I cared for you, or we wouldn't have gone that far."

"And, by the way, Becky finally admitted to me that she and I didn't have sex that night. I was too drunk even if I wanted to."

"You're kidding!"

"I kid you not!" he teased. "She was just out to get me, and it worked."

"That's terrible."

"Yes, it is," he concurred. "But after that night when Becky called and you and I never did get together again, I always blamed her for us not hooking up. I felt trapped in a loveless marriage, and I didn't know how to get out without hurting my daughter." He paused. "But I always held on to the idea of what would've happened between *us* if Becky hadn't called that night. You and I probably would've been married by now."

Chuckling, Toni observed, "I don't know about *married*! We're too much alike!"

"Yes, we are," he agreed. "It wasn't until *today* that I realized why fate had it that you and I never slept together. I know I wanted to, and I felt that you did too for a while."

"You're right, I did…until you got married."

"And I blamed Becky for that, so I couldn't love her. I *resented* her," he went on. "But today, I realized that I didn't *lose* a lover that night, I *gained* a friend…a *true* friend, and I am eternally grateful for that." He paused again and stood, and Toni stood to meet him. "Toni, I didn't know what love was until I met Brandy. She satisfies every desire in me. Now, I know what you and Ron have together. It's a love like no other. And today, you gave me my life back when you gave Brandy back to me. I didn't want this day to end until I let you know just how much I appreciate what you did and how much I value our friendship. You put your personal feelings aside to help Brandy because of your friendship with *me*." He paused. "Thank you."

"You're welcome, Mason."

"I'll never forget what you did today," he declared then pulled her in his arms. "I love you, Toni."

"I love you, too, Mason," she concurred as Angel entered.

"Oh, excuse me," she hesitantly spoke, and they broke apart as she started to leave.

"Angel, don't leave. I'm going," Mason made known, and she stopped.

"So, when is the wedding?" Toni asked.

"What wedding?" Angel exploded.

"Mason and Brandy," Toni answered.

"We can't decide until my divorce is final, but you'll be the first to know," he shared then planted a soft kiss on Toni's lips. "Bye."

"Bye."

"See you, Angel," he called as he left.

"See you," Angel responded then focused on Toni, and smiled wide. "Well, do I need to call Ron and report this?"

"Report what?"

"That you're *kissing* Mason Whittaker?"

"You're crazy!" Toni yelped. "Mason and I are *just* friends."

"Are you sure?" Angel teased.

She took a breath and confirmed very definitively, "*Positive!*"

Part Eight

Four Months Later

April

Chapter 44

"Mom!" Toni called, entering her mother's house.

"In the den," she heard her mother call back.

Toni walked in the direction of her mother's voice and entered the den, where her mother was on a step ladder, hanging curtains. "Hi, Mom," she spoke.

"Hi, honey," Mrs. Melton replied. "How are you?"

"I'm good...I mean *well*," Toni answered, and automatically started giving her mother a hand.

"You're not working today?"

"I left early."

"You're not sick, are you, honey?"

"Oh no! I just finished my column early, so I left."

"Oh, all right," Mrs. Melton understood. "How is Ron?"

"He's fine," Toni shared. "He's working hard on the Sanders' case right now."

"I thought that case was over."

"Not yet. I think Ron will do his summation tomorrow."

"From what I hear, he put on a brilliant defense."

"I think so," Toni chuckled. "He should have. I haven't seen much of him these past few weeks. He's been working until the wee hours of the night."

"At the *office*?!" she exploded.

"No, Mom," Toni laughed. "In his *home* office."

"Oh," Mrs. Melton laughed with her. "How are all the newlyweds?"

"Who? Jordan and Travis; or Mason and Brandy; or Melissa and Simon?"

"All."

"Well, let's see," Toni pondered. "Jordan and Travis have been married for four months now and Jordan just found out that she is pregnant. Mason and Brandy have been married for three months now and Brandy is about two months pregnant. I don't know if Melissa and Simon want children or not."

"Wow, everybody seems to be doing great," Mrs. Melton observed as Toni helped her down off the ladder. "Now, when are you and Ron trying again?"

"I don't know. We haven't talked about it."

Her mother chuckled, "Don't wait too long. You're not getting any younger, girlfriend."

****

"Hello, everyone," Ron spoke as he took a seat in the conference room between Travis and Carol, and everyone greeted him back.

"Everyone is here," John announced, looking around at the two other partners, Travis, Ron, Carol, Thomas, Billy, and Katie. "We can start now."

"Mr. Schuster, you remember you said that I could leave a little early today. My babysitter has a doctor's appointment today," Katie reminded him.

"Yes, Katie, this meeting shouldn't take very long," John responded.

"How is the little one, Katie?" Carol inquired.

"Fine," Katie answered, smiling wide. "Growing like a weed."

Focusing on Travis, Carol added, "And Jordan, Travis? How is she?"

"Doing great," Travis made known.

"I never thought anyone would tame *you*!" Carol laughed.

"That goes to show, love conquers all," Travis laughed with her.

"Tell Jordan we said hello, Travis," Blake added. "She did a super job while Katie was gone."

"Yes, she did," added Phillip. "If she ever wants to come back, I'm sure we could find a place for her."

"Thank you. I appreciate that," Travis acknowledged. "But Jordan's going to be too busy with the baby to take on a fulltime job."

"I understand," John added then focused on Ron who seemed a million miles from all of them. "Ron, are you all right?"

He looked up, smiled slightly, took a deep breath, and replied, "Yeah, I'm fine."

"Ron, we would like to announce while everyone is here that we're going ahead with our plans to make you a full partner, effective immediately," John spoke, and the room exploded with applause as everyone stood up, focusing on Ron, who remained speechless.

When the room was silent again, Blake continued, "We don't know of anyone who deserves it more than you."

"Here! Here!" Travis cheered and Ron nodded his acknowledgement to his friend.

"I don't know what to say," Ron finally spoke then cleared his throat. "I take that back. Yes, I do." He cleared his throat again then stood. "John, Blake, Phillip, I appreciate the vote of confidence, but it's a little late." All eyes widened in surprise, focusing on Ron. "When that article was published in Toni's column back in September, there were only *two* people in this firm who believed in me, *Travis* and *Beverly*."

"Ron, it's not that we didn't believe in you. It's just that…," Phillip started but Ron cut him off.

"Let me finish please, Phillip," Ron interjected. "I have been with this firm longer than anyone other than the partners, and for you to just dismiss me like you did was painful. I didn't even have a trial. You decided upon yourselves that I was guilty. Therefore, I'm going to have to turn down that partnership. Being partners with someone means that they have your back, no matter what, and *you…didn't* have mine when I needed you." He paused. "The only reason I'm here now is to defend Mrs. Sanders. She hired the firm and she insisted on *my* representation, and I wouldn't do anything to harm either this firm or my client. But after this case is over tomorrow, I will be leaving this firm." He handed John a paper. "My resignation, sir."

475

"Can't we discuss this, Ron?" was Blake's question.

"The only discussion I need to have right now is with my wife because she's the only one whose opinion in which I give a damn." He paused. "My summation will be in the morning and I won't be back." He looked around the room and smiled slightly. "Have a nice day." Then Ron walked out, and Travis jumped up to follow him.

****

Becky opened the door and Mason was standing there exposing all thirty-twos. He looked so good in that deep, bone colored, casual suit that she wanted to just grab him and never let him go. Although he was now married to Brandy and having a child with her, Becky still loved him. "Hi, Mason," she spoke, opening the door. "Come in."

"Hi," he responded, coming in. "Where's Amy?"

"Upstairs doing her homework."

"Is anything wrong?"

"No, why?"

"Because you called and asked to see me," he acknowledged, following her into the family room.

"I just needed to ask you something," she pondered, putting out her cigarette then sitting. He sat across from her.

"What is it?"

"I would like for you to take Amy home with you for the rest of the week. I'm going on a cruise."

He beamed, "That's great! When are you leaving?"

"I'm flying to Florida in the morning, and then I'm going on a seven-day cruise to a few islands."

"By *yourself?*"

"Yes, I need to get away for a while."

"Are you all right?"

"Not really, but I *will* be," she shared, wiping her tears quickly. "I promised myself I wouldn't do this." He got up and moved on the couch beside her.

"What is it, Becky?"

"What do you think, Mason?! My husband leaves me for a younger, more beautiful woman, and my daughter loves that woman more than she loves me!"

"That's not true."

"It *is* true. All Amy ever talks about is Brandy this and Brandy that. Brandy is so beautiful. Brandy is so smart. Amy *idolizes* your new wife."

"That's because Brandy and Amy both love pageants, and since Brandy is coaching Amy and she has won a few titles, they just connected," Mason explained. "That's all. Amy could never love *anyone* more than *you*."

"Mason, face it, Amy would rather be with Brandy and you than with me," she wiped her tears with her hand again, and Mason handed her some tissues from the table.

"I'm sorry you feel this way, but Amy is a *child*. She doesn't think anything about it when she talks about Brandy. She doesn't know she's hurting you."

"Nevertheless, it *does* hurt," she admitted. "And the funny thing is that I don't blame Amy. I'm unhappy and she knows it."

"I'm sorry, Becky," Mason apologized. "I never meant to hurt you."

"I know that," she confirmed then blew her nose, and looked into his sparkling, brown eyes and inquired faintly, "Are you finally happy, Mason?"

Mason took a deep breath then answered, "Yes, Becky, I am."

She dropped her head and returned, "I know you are. I'm sorry I couldn't put that gleam in your eyes."

"It had nothing to do with you. I was just not ready to be a husband and a father when we got married."

"Because I lied?"

"I guess so."

"If I could take it back, I would."

"I know, Becky," he made known. "I know."

"It still hurts, Mason," she wept. "I love you so much, and it hurts like hell to see you with another woman."

"I'm sorry."

Standing, she snapped, "Quit saying that!"

"Saying what?"

"You're *sorry*," she insisted, and he stood with her.

"But *I* am. I'm sorry that you're so unhappy."

"And *you're* so happy," she finished.

"Well…*yes*," he acknowledged shyly.

"I'm glad you are," she made known then took a deep breath. "I've just got to get away for a while. You don't think Brandy would mind Amy staying with you a few days, do you?"

"Oh no!" Mason exploded. "She'll love it."

"When is the baby due?"

"Amy told you about the baby?"

She exploded in laughter, "That's an *understatement*! Amy's probably more excited about that baby than either Brandy or you!" Mason laughed with her.

"It's due in November."

"Hoping for a *boy*?"

"You know it!" he chuckled.

Becky sobered and took a deep breath and admired, "You're simply glowing, Mason. Happiness can do that, you know."

"Well, I'm *certainly* happy," Mason chuckled again.

Becky snickered also, "You're too damn honest!" He laughed with her. "Go and get your child and get the hell outta here!"

****

"Hi, honey," Toni greeted, entering Ron's home office where he sat in pale green silk pajamas.

"Hi, baby," he acknowledged, looking up, removing his reading eyeglasses, and meeting her with a quick kiss.

478

"You're home early."

"Yeah, I told John, Blake, and Phillip what they could do with their partnership and…"

"So, they finally offered you the partnership again?!" she squeaked.

"Yeah."

"And you told them to take that job and shove it?!" she laughed.

"Something like that," he laughed with her, and she dropped on his lap, hugging him around the neck, planting a kiss on his lips.

"I'm so proud of you."

"Thank you, Mrs. Joyner," he accepted and kissed her again. "Excuse me, Mrs. *Melton*-Joyner!"

"Mrs. *Joyner* will do just fine," she cooed then met him with another kiss. "You smell good." He started nibbling at her ear.

"So do you," he replied, bathing her neck with tender kisses.

"Um, I thought the honeymoon was over."

"It's *never* going to be over," he declared then kissed her deeply. He started unbuttoning her blouse while massaging her chest with soft feather kisses. "Why would you think that?"

"Well, we went from making love every day to none at all for weeks now," she chuckled, and he jerked back and looked at her.

"Oh, honey, I'm sorry," he proclaimed. "I was so wrapped up in this case, I guess I neglected you."

"It's okay."

"No, it's not okay."

"I understand, baby," she added. "I know how important this case is to you." He held her head up with his finger to look her squarely in the eyes.

He stressed very sternly, "*Nothing* is more important than *you. Nothing!*"

"That's sweet, honey," she accepted.

"It's true," he emphasized. "And the next time, help a brotha out!" he teased. "Tell me when I'm falling back on my duties. I'm not a mind reader, you know."

Laughing, she agreed, "Okay, I will."

479

"Good," he cooed. "Now let's go to bed. I've been neglecting my beautiful wife long enough."

"You're ready to go to *sleep*?"

He smiled shyly, winked, and cooed, "Who said anything about *sleeping*?"

Toni singsong, "Oh, I remember *you*!"

****

"Brandy!" Mason called.

"In the nursery, honey," she called back, and he followed the direction of her voice.

When he entered the room that they were making into a nursery, Brandy was sitting in a rocking chair, putting some curtains through a rod. "Hi, honey." He spoke, bending, and meeting her with a kiss.

"Hi, sweetheart," she cooed. "How was your day?"

"Great," he beamed. "I have a surprise for you."

"Really?"

Amy jumped into the room with her arms outstretched and yelled, "Ta dah!"

"Amy!" Brandy exploded, springing up and meeting the child with a hug. "This is a pleasant surprise."

"I'm staying until next Sunday," Amy made known with a big smile caressing her cute little face.

"Next Sunday!" Brandy blasted in smiles. "That's great! What're we gonna do?"

"Can I help you decorate the baby's room?" Amy asked.

"Sure," Brandy replied. "But I'm sure we can think of more than that to do for a full week!"

"You can help me with my dance routine! The Little Miss Greenleaf Pageant is coming up soon, you know."

"It's a deal," Brandy agreed as Amy started helping her with the curtains while they talked and giggled. Mason stood back and

480

smiled. It felt so good to see his two favorite girls getting along so well.

He tugged Amy's ponytail and said, "I'll go and get your things, honey."

"Okay, Daddy," she answered, but kept right on talking to Brandy about the upcoming pageant.

****

"Are you hungry?" Toni asked Ron as they snuggled in bed.

"Starved," he replied then kissed her moist forehead.

"It's too late to cook. I'll order something for delivery," she suggested, getting up.

"Okay," he groaned, patting her nude behind.

"What would you like?"

He focused on his wife's bare behind and cooed, *"You."*

****

"Hi," Travis addressed, hugging Jordan from the rear as she stood over the stove, stirring a pot.

"Hi," she purred, laying her head back in his chest.

"How are you two?" he asked, placing his hand on her stomach.

"We're good," she answered, turning around in his arms, and they ended in a long kiss. "Are you hungry?"

"Yeah, what's for dinner?" he inquired, moving to the table, and sitting.

"Beef stew."

"Wow, you're getting pretty good at this domestic stuff," he chuckled. "You might not want to go back to work after the baby comes."

"Don't even try it, Travis!" she insisted. "I'm *going* back to work."

"But why, honey? I make enough money to take care of us."

"It has nothing to do with money, Travis. I *like* working," she stressed. "I thought we had this all settled."

"All right! All right!" he agreed, throwing his hands in the air. "I hear ya!" She just stared at him. She knew this conversation about her going back to work was *not* over and so did he.

Chapter 45

Toni tipped into the courtroom just as Mr. Lowery, the assistant DA was standing to give his summation. She focused on Ron looking so handsome and confident as he sat on one side of Mrs. Sanders while Travis sat on her other side. Ron glanced back slowly as if he knew someone was looking at him, focused on her, and they shared a smile. Then, he focused his attention back to Mr. Lowery who was approaching the jury.

"Ladies and gentlemen of the jury, you might think you have a hard task at hand, but in actuality, you don't," he started. "You might be saying to yourselves, how can I send a devoted mother either to jail for the rest of her life or to her death, when she has a daughter to nurture back to health after a terrible ordeal?" He paused. "The truth of the matter, ladies and gentlemen, is that you have *no* choice. It is your *duty* to uphold the law no matter how justified you feel Mrs. Sanders' actions were." He paused again and strolled to Mrs. Sanders and stared at her, eye to eye, and expressed sympathy for her. "It's a terrible thing to witness your child being violated. No parent should ever have to endure that." Ron felt Mrs. Sanders cringe and he placed his hand on hers to calm her. "But by the same token, *no* parent has the right to take the law in his or her own hands either."

He walked back to the jury. "If we allow parents to vindicate their children's wrong doers then we might as well throw out the laws that we fight so hard to uphold. Oh yes, I know the defense is throwing fancy words at you like *temporarily insane*, but she *wasn't* insane when she confessed to the police right after she picked up a gun and shot her defenseless husband, one, two, three, four...*five* times. She knew *exactly* what she had done and *so...do...we*." He paused again for emphasis. "Mrs. Sanders was *wrong* in murdering her husband. *You* know it, *I* know it, and *she* knows it." He paused and stared the jury in the eyes one by one then ended with, "So, ladies and gentlemen, I employ you to *do...your...jobs*. Don't let this murderer go free, no matter how sorry you feel for her. The fact is that Mrs. Gloria Sanders *murdered* her husband *in...cold...blood*.

These facts are undisputed. It is *your* duty to come back with a verdict of *guilty*!" He stared at the jury long and hard. "Thank you." He took his seat slowly.

****

"Amy, are you ready, honey?" Brandy called, standing at the door in a deep purple wind suit and sneakers with her hair pulled back in a ponytail.

"Coming, Brandy!" Amy yelled from upstairs, as she charged down in a pink and white wind suit and sneakers. Her hair had one single cornrow braid down the back. "You feel good enough to go?"

"Of course, sweetie. I feel...*well*...enough," Brandy corrected Amy's grammar, touching the child's nose and she smiled. "We're going to pick you a dress that will knock the socks off those judges."

"You think I really have a chance at being Little Miss Greenleaf?"

"You have more than a chance," Brandy stressed. "We'll work on your dance routine when we come back, okay?"

"Okay," Amy agreed, smiling wide, opening the door. "Then, when we find *me* a dress, we can buy the *baby* some stuff."

"It's a deal," Brandy agreed, following her out the door. Brandy couldn't believe how Amy had taken to her. She thanked God every day that she didn't have to deal with the resentment some stepparents have to go through with stepchildren. She was also happy that Becky hadn't tried to poison Amy's mind against her. After all, she *did* have reason. She *was* sleeping with the woman's husband. Brandy took a deep breath. She didn't know life could be so sweet. She loved helping Amy prepare for pageants, and Amy was a real natural. She had won a few pageants and was getting comfortable on stage. Brandy also knew that Amy had won a couple of the pageants because she was a *Whittaker*, not because she was the best, but she would *never* share that with Amy.

Brandy and Amy jumped into her Lexus and she drove to the end of the driveway, and before she knew it, a car swerved out of nowhere and slammed into them. They screamed at the top of their lungs.

****

Ron remained seated behind the desk in the courtroom, focusing on the jury, and then he began softly, "Ladies and gentlemen of the jury, Mr. Lowery is right. Your job isn't hard at all today." The door opened and he paused as Mrs. Whittington, Mrs. Sanders' sister, entered with a distraught Priscilla, Mrs. Sanders' teenaged daughter. All eyes fell on them as they took their seats. Mrs. Sanders smiled at Priscilla and the girl returned her mother's smile lovingly. Ron took a deep breath. He was glad Mrs. Whittington had brought Priscilla. The jury needed to not only *hear* about the little girl, but to *see* her as well.

Ron stood and continued, "Ladies and gentlemen, your job isn't hard because I believe you want justice just as much as we do." He paused. "Let's examine those facts for a moment that Mr. Lowery shared with you: Mrs. Sanders *did* confess to the police that she shot her husband, but the officer who took her statement admitted *himself*, on the witness stand, that she was incoherent, as if she were in a trance of some sort. The psychologist testified that Mrs. Sanders' mental state was borderline comatose at the time that he examined her, right after her husband's death. Mrs. Sanders' friends, relatives, co-workers, church affiliates, sorority sisters, and even her ex-husband all testified that Gloria Sanders is the nicest and most sympathetic woman they know." He paused. "Now, what would drive a church going, mild-tempered, moral woman like Gloria Sanders to snap and take a life?" He paused while they pondered the question. "*One* thing…she was pushed beyond her limits. The psychologist testified that we *all* have a breaking point, whether we want to admit it or not. That day, Gloria Sanders reached *hers*!"

****

Mason tore into the hospital and to the receptionist's desk. "Hi, I'm Mason Whittaker. My wife and daughter were brought here after an accident!"

"Yes, Mr. Whittaker," the lady acknowledged, smiling slightly. "I'll take you to them."

He focused on her and asked with a wavering tone, "Are they all right?"

Leading him down the hall she replied, "Yes, I think so." He breathed a sigh of relief for the first time.

When Mason walked into the emergency room and spotted Brandy, conscience, looking as beautiful as ever, he was so happy, tears swelled up in his eyes. He ran to her and grabbed her in his arms as the nurse walked out. "Oh, God, I was so scared." He confessed, holding her in his arms lovingly.

"We're all right," she confirmed.

Suddenly, he held back, sniffed, and stared into her eyes as he asked softly, "And the baby?"

"Fine," Brandy acknowledged, and he pulled her back into his arms.

"I've never been so scared in my whole life." He cradled her, and Brandy never felt so loved by *anyone*. She knew Jamie loved her, but he had used that love in the end to manipulate her. Mason, on the other hand, loved her unconditionally. He finally held back, took some tissues from the table beside her bed and wiped his tears away. "Where is Amy?"

"Next door."

"Let me go and check on her. I'll be back," he promised, and she nodded, then he grabbed her again and kissed her deep. "I love you so much."

"I love you too," she made known before he left.

Mason walked into Amy's room and she was sitting up in bed talking to a nurse about the beauty pageant, with pride and arrogance heavily reaping her tone. Mason couldn't help but to smile. She was nothing like her mother. Becky was always so insecure with her looks, and Amy was *too* secure with hers. "Daddy!" she exploded when she saw him.

"Hi, Princess," he spoke, rushing to her, and taking her into his arms. "How are you?"

"I'm fine," she confirmed. "How is Brandy?"

"She's good," he shared, releasing her then turning to the nurse. "I see she's talking your head off."

Smiling, the lady said, "I don't mind, Mr. Whittaker."

"Is the baby okay, too?" Amy blurted out.

"The baby is fine," he concurred.

"Good," Amy responded. "I don't know how we missed that car. He was coming straight at us, but Brandy backed up so fast, he only bumped us softly."

Mason felt a new sensation in his heart as he whispered, "Thank you, God."

"Daddy, when can we go? Brandy and I still have to get my dress!" Amy continued and Mason burst into laughter.

****

"Let's take a trip down memory lane for a moment," Ron continued, focusing on the jury. "Mrs. Gloria Sanders had the perfect home, the perfect job, the perfect daughter, and the perfect husband, or so she thought." He stopped for a moment. "Mrs. Sanders worked hard to give her husband and daughter a beautiful home that they could cherish. After the divorce from her first husband, she never thought she would find true love again. Then this well-educated, successful man comes into her life, and she felt there was another chance for her to achieve happiness. She had finally found a man who would love her and take care of her daughter and herself." Priscilla started weeping softly, and her aunt pulled the child in her arms. Ron hated to put her through this ugly mess again, but he *had* to. She needed her mother. "That Saturday morning was a normal morning in the household. Mrs. Sanders went to her sorority meeting, as usual; her husband went fishing, as usual; her daughter went to a friend's house, as usual. There was nothing unusual about that day." He paused. "Then Mrs. Sanders' arrived at her meeting and found it to be cancelled, due to an emergency, so she returned home." He focused on the jury as Simon entered silently and sat beside Toni. He and Toni shared a smile.

"Come with me, ladies and gentlemen, to 835 Brookdale Lane on that Saturday morning that changed many lives forever." He paused. "When Mrs. Sanders arrived home, she noticed her husband's car in the driveway. She didn't think much about it because he would sometimes ride with someone else. She knew her daughter was at a friend's house, and if her husband were home, they could have some quality time together." Tears ran down Mrs. Sanders' cheeks as she listened to Ron invading her life. "She walked upstairs to her bedroom, but her husband was not there. Then she heard noises coming from her daughter's room and she headed in that direction. Just before she opened the door, she heard her daughter's faint cry, telling someone that he was hurting her. Begging, pleading with him to please stop. Can you hear her? Can you hear the cries of that innocent little child, begging for mercy and pleading not to be violated?" Ron's voice cracked as he felt her pain. The three ladies in the jury were all wiping their tears by now, and the nine men were fighting to contain theirs.

"We are *parents*! We're supposed to *protect* our children. We're supposed to shield them from any hurt, harm, or danger." He paused and added weakly, "Where was that little girl's protection that Saturday morning? Can you feel the hurt and anger of her mother as she opened that door and came face to face with every parent's worst nightmare? Her daughter wasn't just being violated by just *anyone*. No, not a *stranger*, not a long-lost uncle, not even a family friend." He paused and sniffed his own tears back. "It was the *man* of the house. The *provider*! The *protector*!" The room was silent as he breathed. "Now, who will protect our children when their protector is the violator?"

Ron paused and dropped his head. There wasn't a dry eye in the courtroom as Priscilla cried hysterically in her aunt's arms. Mrs.

Sanders turned and motioned for her sister to take her child out, and she did so immediately. Then Ron turned back to the jury and took a deep breath. "Ladies and gentlemen, that was Mrs. Gloria Sanders' breaking point. She no longer felt the security of a perfect home and family she had worked so hard to build. She looked in her daughter's sad eyes and all she saw was pleading, hurt, and pain. Why had this happened to her? Her mother couldn't explain it. Then Mrs. Sanders left the room, feeling totally defeated, but instead of her husband doing the decent thing and leaving the house to give her time to focus and calm down, he chose to follow her; a woman he had just betrayed, defeated, emotionally brutalized. He *chose* to *confront* her and *follow* her into their bedroom to *explain*. What could he explain?" Ron stopped again and stared at the jury. "From that point on, Mrs. Sanders was not responsible for her actions. She doesn't even remember taking the gun out of the drawer. Her body was on autopilot. All she remembered was hearing her daughter scream and looking at her husband's bloody body on the floor." He paused and walked away from the jury. "It's scary, ladies and gentlemen, but we all have one. We all have a *breaking point*, and that Saturday morning, Gloria Sanders reached hers."

He paused once more and returned to the jury where almost all of them had their heads hung low. "I want to ask you one question." His next question was slow and deliberate as he asked, "If *any parent* had walked in on a man violating his or her innocent little girl's body and hearing the little girl beg for mercy, what would *that parent* have done?" The members of the jury all jerked their heads up at the same time to face him. Ron eyed the jury head on and repeated weakly, "*What...would...a parent...do?*" He locked eyes with each member of the jury then added, almost in a whisper, "Parents really don't know if they haven't been faced with that decision yet. Until that Saturday morning, Gloria Sanders hadn't either. Until that Saturday morning, if you had asked Mrs. Sanders if she could take a life, she probably would've laughed in your face." He paused again to let the jury ponder then concluded, emphasizing each word. "*I hope and pray* that *no other parent is ever faced with that kind of reality.*"

****

"I guess this is my seat," a medium-height, dark complexioned, distinguished looking man said taking a seat beside Becky at the lunch table aboard the cruise ship. She smiled politely at him and he returned it. Becky was dazzling after visiting the salon on the ship and letting them have their way with her. They took her dull, lifeless, straight red hair, cut the front into layers of bangs, and layered the rest down her back with soft wavy curls. She had never had a permanent in her whole life until today. They showed her how to apply just enough make up to conceal the flaws in her face, including the freckles. She looked and felt greater than she had in years. Noticing that they were the only two at the table, he added, "I guess everyone else is at the gambling tables." He chuckled slightly and Becky just smiled dryly at him. "Joseph Waverly," he introduced, extending a hand to her. "But my friends call me Joey."

Receiving his handshake, Becky followed, "Rebecca Whittaker, but my friends call me Becky."

"I hope *I* become a friend," he flirted, smiling shyly. Her eyes widened as she turned a crimson red. She wasn't used to men paying her compliments.

"What may I get you to drink, sir?" The waiter was there immediately.

Focusing on Becky, Joey asked, "Is that tea good?"

"Yes, *very*," she answered.

"Tea it is then," he came back with to the waiter.

"Yes, sir," the waiter acknowledged then exited.

"Are you enjoying your cruise?" Joey asked.

"Yes, I am," she answered shortly, taking a sip of tea.

"I know a beautiful woman like you isn't sailing alone. Where is Mr. Whittaker?"

"With the newer, younger, and improved Mrs. Whittaker," she chuckled.

"Sorry," he laughed with her. "So is the former Mrs. Waverly, or should I say Mrs. *Toi Davidson*. He was her personal trainer." They laughed together and it felt good for Becky to laugh.

"And the bad thing about Brandy is that my daughter *adores* her."

"Is she nice?"

"Unfortunately, *yes*!" She burst into laughter. "And that just makes it harder for me to hate her."

Laughing with her he contributed, "And my girls think Mr. Toi Davidson is a *Mr. Universe* contender. The little snot nose kid, still wet behind the ears."

"How old is Toi?" She continued to laugh with him.

"Twenty-four," he added. "And Sonja's thirty-nine. I thought she was out of her cotton-picking mind!"

"I think Brandy is about that age also," Becky continued to laugh.

"Maybe we should get Toi and Brandy together, and then we can get our spouses back."

"That wouldn't work," she laughed. "Brandy is pregnant, and if she left Mason, I still couldn't get him because he would probably have a heart attack and die!" They both burst into laughter.

Still laughing, he added, "And Sonja would have a heart attack if Mr. *Hunk* dumped her as well!" The waiter returned and stared blankly at Becky and Joey having such a good time laughing, and they caught each other's gaze then burst into laughter again. Becky didn't know when she had had such a good and relaxing time before. They finally sobered and focused on the waiter.

"May I take your order, sir?" he asked.

Looking at Becky, Joey inquired, "What're you having?"

"The veal."

"Same for me," he said to the waiter.

"Very well," the waiter acknowledged then walked off.

"So, is Brandy a tall, blue-eyed, dumb blonde too?" Joey focused back on Becky.

"Quite the contrary. She's a tall, brown eyed, dumb brunette," Becky laughed again. "She's African American."

"Really?"

"Yes, and *gorgeous*," Becky added. "She's an ex-beauty queen, and now she has my daughter all wrapped up into pageants, and Amy thinks the sun rises and sets on *beautiful* Brandy."

"It's hard when you feel your children are on the side of the enemy, isn't it?" he acknowledged, and she nodded. "Toi is a body builder and my daughters, being teenagers, think he's the greatest thing since...*padded bras*." They laughed again. "You said your husband's name is Mason?"

"Yeah, do you know him?"

"Mason Whittaker of *Mason on the Move*?"

"One in the same," she confirmed. "And Mason just *moved* right on the hell outta my life." They burst into laughter again.

"The man must be *nuts* to leave a beautiful, intelligent woman like you."

"Thank you," Becky accepted, focusing on this charming man. She wasn't used to men calling her beautiful. She liked it.

"Where do you live, Becky?"

"South Carolina and you?"

"Atlanta," he answered. "We're not too far away."

"From what?"

His eyes locked with hers as he replied, "From each other." She smiled sweetly at him and he returned her smile.

"What do you do in Atlanta?" she finally asked after finding her voice.

"I'm an investment broker," he answered. "And you?"

"Before I married Mason, I used to help my father on his ranch, but after I married Mason, I didn't work for seven years. Now, I'm helping my father at the ranch again."

"Did you miss it?"

"Oh yes. I don't know why I ever stopped because Mason sure as hell never cared what I did." She shook her head with a slight smile. "It's great being back," she added. "Do you ride?"

"A little."

"Then you'll have to come and visit sometimes so you can ride. We have a very impressive stable."

"I'd like that," he accepted. "I'd like that very much." Suddenly, she realized that she had just invited a total stranger to her home, and she felt embarrassed. But who cares? She had to get on with her life.

****

Ron, Toni, Simon, and Mrs. Sanders sat in the courtroom's café sipping on coffee. "How long do you think it will take for them to reach a verdict?" Mrs. Sanders wanted to know.

"It's hard to say," Ron replied.

"I'm ready to know, one way or another," she added. "I'm tired of living my life in limbo."

"I know it's hard," Ron sympathized. "Hopefully, it won't take too long."

"I've got to get back to the office," Simon made known, standing. "Ron, that was an excellent summation."

"Thank you, Simon," Ron accepted as his cell phone began to ring.

While he answered it, Toni focused on Simon, "How are Melissa and the kids?"

"Doing great," he answered.

"I haven't talked to her in a while," Toni continued. "She taught me how to cook, you know."

"No, I didn't know that," Simon acknowledged as Ron hung up his cell phone.

"What is it, honey?" Toni solicited as Travis walked towards them.

Ron focused on Mrs. Sanders and announced, "That was Beverly. The jury has reached a verdict."

****

Mason walked into the huge sunroom where Brandy was sitting, looking at the television. "Are you all right, honey?" he asked.

"Yes, I'm fine," she confirmed as he sat beside her on the couch. "What's Amy doing?"

"Playing with Cynthia in her room."

"Cynthia?"

"Yeah, the little girl from next door."

"Oh yeah. They're so quiet I forgot she was here."

"She's still talking about buying that dress." He laughed.

"I'll take her tomorrow," Brandy acknowledged.

"Honey, I was thinking," he said, turning to face her. "Why don't I hire you a driver."

"A driver?!" she exploded.

"Yes, so you won't have to worry about fighting traffic in your condition."

Taking a deep breath Brandy insisted, "Honey, I don't need a driver. I can drive."

"Baby, I know you can drive. This isn't about that."

"Then what is it about?" She was growing angry, and he knew it. "It was just an accident, Mason. We all have them, including *professional* drivers!"

"I just want to do all I can to protect you."

"And I appreciate it, but I'm perfectly capable of driving my own car!"

"Okay! Okay!" he surrendered, throwing his hands up in the air. "I was just trying to help. Don't bite my head off!"

Brandy took a deep breath then explained, "Mason, I didn't grow up rich like you. I don't believe in wasting money."

"It's not a waste to get you a driver, honey."

"Yes, it is, when I'm capable of *driving* myself!"

"Okay, I won't mention it again."

She knew he was only looking out for her well-being, so she softened, "Mason, I love you for even thinking enough of me to consider that, but trust me, I don't need a driver."

"I would do *anything* for you, sweetheart. You know that."

"Yes, I do," she concurred. "But…"

"But what?"

"Rich people are different from poor."

He chuckled, "We're all *people*, Brandy!"

"But you think differently from us," she continued. "You can buy almost anything you want at any given time. I'm not used to that."

"Then *get* used to it, honey. My money is also your money now."

"Mason, people will never look at me like they do you."

"And why is that Brandy? You're my *wife*!"

"But I wasn't *born* rich," she insisted. "Do you remember when I told you that the house I was living in was not for sale?" He nodded. "I knew it because I tried to buy it, and she wouldn't sell it to me. Then *you* just bought it with no problems."

"Yes, honey, but...."

"And...," she cut him off, "When I was in jail, the rule was absolutely *no* touching and as I mentioned before, when the guard started to break us up and saw who you were, he not only looked the other way, but he also *apologized* for interrupting."

"Brandy, what do you want me to do, apologize for being rich?"

"No, I want you to realize that *I'm* not."

"But you are *now*."

"Then give me time to adjust. Don't throw all the luxuries on me all at once. This house for instance. I would have been perfectly happy for us to live in my little ranch house, but you had to have a mansion," she explained. "Don't get me wrong, I'm not downing you because you're used to having nice things above and beyond the rest of us, but just give me time to adjust, please."

"I hear you, honey," he gave in. "I never meant to offend you."

"I know," she admitted. "You just want the best for me, and I appreciate that." She sighed deeply. "When I was in jail the women wanted to know how you treated me, and I had to let them know that you're very generous."

"They asked about *me*?"

"Oh yeah. They think you're pretty hot...." she shared then burst into laughter and added, "for a *white* dude!"

"Oh, no you didn't," he burst into laughter with her, pulling her in his arms.

"*I* think you're pretty hot, too," she sobered then met his lips in a deep kiss.

"Glad to hear it," he cooed between kisses. "Did the doctor give you a complete bill of health?"

"Um hum," she murmured between sultry kisses.

"Let's go upstairs," he purred, nibbling on her ear.

"What about Amy?"

"We can lock the door. She and Cynthia are playing."

"Are you sure?"

He stood and pulled her up gently into his arms and murmured, "Oh yeah, I'm sure." Brandy burst into laughter and Mason swished her up in his arms. She wrapped her arms around his neck, massaging it with tender kisses as he proceeded towards the stairs.

Suddenly Amy exploded into the room, with Cynthia trailing behind, blurting out, "Daddy, will you take us to the movies?"

Brandy jumped down and giggled as she tried to stand in front of Mason to conceal the bulge in his pants. "*Now*, Princess?!" he exploded.

"Yeah. Cynthia's mom said it's okay," Amy added then focused on her stepmother. "Brandy, pleaseee!"

Brandy glanced back at Mason and smiled, and then she looked at Amy, saying, "Sure, honey."

"Let's go and get ready!" Amy blurted to Cynthia. The two of them turned to leave.

"What time does it start?" Mason called before they were out of earshot.

"Seven," Amy yelled back and then the girls disappeared.

Mason turned Brandy around by the shoulders, planted a kiss on her lips and said, "Children! We can't live with them..."

"...And we can't live without them." Brandy finished and they simultaneously burst into laughter.

****

"Madam Foreperson, have you reached a verdict yet?"

"Yes, sir, Your Honor," the lady stood and announced.

"Bailiff," the judge instructed, and the man walked over to her, took the paper, and handed it to the judge. The judge read it and handed it back to the bailiff. He handed it back to the foreperson. "Will the defendant please rise," the judge ordered. Ron and Travis stood with a shaking Mrs. Sanders. "Madam Foreperson, what is your verdict?"

The lady focused on the paper and read, "In the case of the state of South Carolina verses Mrs. Gloria Sanders in the charge of murder in the first degree, we the jury find the defendant..." You could hear a pin drop as she finished, "...not guilty!"

The courtroom roared with chatter as Ron breathed a deep sigh of relief. Mrs. Sanders grabbed him and hugged him tight. "Thank you! Thank you," she chanted in his ear as tears rolled down her face.

"You are welcome," Ron accepted.

"You believed in me from the very beginning when no one else did, including *myself*," she continued. "I'll never forget you." He pulled her in his arms again and hugged her close.

The judge silenced the courtroom long enough to release Mrs. Sanders, thank the jury, and adjourn court. Mrs. Sanders' family ran to her. They all hugged tight as they walked out of the courtroom. Toni made her way over to Ron and Travis, and Ron put his arm around her waist. "Congratulations," she beamed.

"Thank you," he replied then planted a kiss on her lips.

"You did a hellava job, Ron!" Travis admired, shaking Ron's hand.

"Thank you, buddy."

"Congratulations, Counselor," the assistant DA offered, extending a hand.

"Thank you," Ron accepted graciously, and then the man walked away with his staff.

****

"Angel, what happened to Ricky's arm?" David asked, entering the kitchen where she was putting the dishes on the table.

"He sprang it sliding down the stairs," she answered, receiving a kiss from him.

"Is it bad?"

"No, not really."

"You don't seem concerned," he observed, sitting at the table.

"He's a *boy,* honey. He's going to get hurt sometimes."

Smiling, he reflected, "You're so level-headed." He pulled her down in his lap and she turned and straddled his lap. They kissed long and passionate. "You remember when you used to give me lap dances?" She giggled.

"You still remember that?"

"Of course, I do," he laughed with her. "You were so sexy, you used to have me so excited even before we could get in bed."

"Sometimes, we didn't make it to the bedroom."

"Un hum," he moaned, nibbling at her ear.

"Hey! What do you mean *were* sexy?!"

"You know what I mean," he remarked, kissing her again.

"Do you want a lap dance now, baby?" she cooed.

"Um hum," he murmured, still nibbling on her ear, as she rolled her hips around on his lap. She felt his body respond immediately and she smiled. It was nice that she could still turn her husband on.

"Daddy, Sammie hit me!" Ricky exploded in with a cast on his arm. David dropped his head on her shoulder, and Angel giggled, planted a kiss on his forehead and stood.

"I'll be there in a minute, Ricky," David made known, and Ricky ran out. He took a deep breath and stood. "And you want to have *another* one?!" She giggled, patting his behind as he exited.

****

Toni laid, cuddled up in Ron's arms in bed. "Ron," she called softly.

"Um hum," he moaned with his eyes still closed, holding her close.

"Are you ready to try to have another baby?" she asked cautiously, and Ron's eyes popped open, but he didn't answer. "Ron?"

"I heard you, honey. I was just caught off guard."

"Why?"

"I didn't know you were thinking about having another baby."

"Well, are you ready?"

"If you are, sweetheart, I am."

She held up and supported her body on one elbow over him to looked in his attentive, hazel eyes. "I want to know what *you* think."

"Toni, *I* want what's best for *you*," he shared. "I would love for us to have a baby, but I want it to be what *you* want." He rubbed her cheek lightly with the back of his fingers. "Are you ready?"

Toni took a deep breath then confirmed, "Yeah. I am." He smiled and kissed her lips. Then he held up, took the remaining pack of birth control pills off the table, and dropped them into the wastepaper basket beside the bed. Toni smiled wide, falling on him in a long, captivating kiss.

Chapter 46

Becky opened the door for Mason and Amy, and he almost lost his breath. He had never seen her look so attractive. Her hair was shorter and in waves of silky, shiny, stylish curls instead of straight and lifeless. Her skin was radiant and darker and not pale and drab. He didn't even see her freckles. Her makeup was flawless. She wore a pair of rayon navy pants with a navy and white silk blouse with three-inch navy heels. Becky never wore either tight-fitting clothes or heels. Mason was speechless.

"Mom, you look pretty!" Amy exploded into her arms.

"Thank you, sweetie," Becky accepted, hugging her daughter. "I missed you."

"I missed you, too," Amy shared. "What did you bring me?"

"A lot of stuff. They're on your bed," Becky laughed.

"All right!" Amy exploded, charging up the stairs.

Finally finding his voice, Mason admired, "You *do* look great, Becky."

Smiling, she accepted, "Thank you, Mason."

"So, getting away really agreed with you?"

"Yes, it did. I don't remember when I've had such a wonderful time."

"I'm glad."

"How is Brandy?"

"Great," he replied then added, "Brandy and Amy were in a car accident, but they didn't get hurt."

"Thank God."

Staring at her, Mason recognized, "I just can't get over how different you look."

"*Better*, I hope."

"Oh yeah," he chuckled.

"I needed to make a change, so I did," she made known. "I realized I couldn't go on living my life in the past."

"Good for you."

"And I *met* someone."

With widen eyes Mason inquired, "You *did*?!"

"Yes, he's from Atlanta. He's an investment broker. We both went through similar circumstances, so we hit it off very well."

"Great," Mason approved then decided to tease. "So, when are you going to *Atlanta*?"

"In two weeks," she answered, surprising him, and she saw his shock by his raised eyebrows.

"Wow! Is this the same Becky who left a little over a week ago?" he laughed, and she laughed with him.

"No!" she announced proudly. "This Becky is a *lot* better!"

Part Nine

October

Chapter 47

"Ready, Ron?" the man asked, sitting on the edge of the roof as Ron, Toni, Travis, Jordan, Angel, David, Melissa, Simon, Denise, Barry, Mr. and Mrs. Joyner, Beverly and her husband, Jordan's parents, Mrs. Melton, Mr. Melton, and Juanita stood on the ground looking at the two-story brick building.

"Ready, Gordon," Ron called. "Let it rip!"

The man uncovered the neon sign and it flashed, *Joyner, Bland, and Kennedy, Attorneys at Law*. Everyone applauded as they hugged and kissed with enthusiasm. Then Ron, Travis, and Simon took hold of the huge scissors and together, they cut the ribbon in front of the entrance. Everyone cheered again. Ron, Travis, and Simon led everyone into their new building for the grand tour. Beverly showed off her desk first, right in the front entrance.

"Beverly, you think you can handle *three* lawyers?" Toni asked smiling.

"Oh yeah!" Beverly shrieked. "They know me!"

"We *sure* do," Ron agreed, throwing his arm around Beverly's shoulder, and pulling her close.

The tour went on to Ron's, Travis's, and Simon's large offices, fully furnished with the finest, expensive furnishings, each with an attached restroom. Ron's office was decorated in brown and beige, Travis's in black and gold, and Simon's in gray and marble. They took the elevator up to the second floor with the huge conference rooms and more restrooms.

"And we have our own investigative staff," Travis announced as they walked into Jordan's office, also upstairs, equipped with a basinet for the upcoming baby in the ivory and turquoise surroundings. Everyone oohed and ahed as Travis planted a kiss on Jordan's lips. They had finally come to an agreement about her working status. This was an arrangement that suited both of them. Travis' mother would be the standby babysitter when needed.

The tour ended back downstairs in the large break room area that included a fully staffed kitchen and dining room, with a catered five-course meal by Melissa's staff. They all sat to eat while being served by Melissa's staff in style.

"So, Ron, how are you going to get cases?" Denise asked, taking a bite of her chicken. "You're going to advertise?"

"Girl, we already have about twenty cases," Beverly made known, sipping her tea.

"Really?" Denise countered surprised.

"Yeah," Ron answered, taking a bite of his macaroni and cheese. "That's why Simon and Melissa can't go on the cruise with us. We need someone here to hold down the fort."

"Yeah, but you'll make it up to us later," Melissa acknowledged, taking a forkful of collard greens and rice.

"You better know it," added Travis, chewing profusely.

"This food is delicious," Mr. Joyner added, followed by praises from the rest of the group.

****

Leroy walked out of ER, pulling off his surgical mask with another doctor. "Like riding a bike, huh, Leroy?" the lady doctor admired, pulling off her mask also.

Smiling wide, he recognized, "Something like that."

"That was some terrific job you did in there," she added.

"Thank you, Donna," he responded. "I couldn't have done it without you."

"Liar," she laughed, and he laughed with her. Then he stopped and faced her.

"You know, when everyone thought I had killed Mr. Timmons, you were the only one who I felt really believed in my innocence. There were a few who testified on my behalf, but *you* really believed in me. I don't want another day to pass by without telling you how much I appreciate you," he explained.

"You're very welcome, Leroy," the almond tan, plain-looking lady replied, shaking her short curls vigorously after removing her cap. "I never had any doubts. I know what a fine surgeon you are. You wouldn't have made the kind of mistakes they were claiming."

"I appreciate it."

"It's okay."

"Are you seeing anyone?" he asked, surprising her and himself.

"No, I'm not," she answered after a short hesitation.

"Would you like to have dinner with me tonight?"

Smiling wide, she answered, "I'd love to."

"Great," he accepted. Leroy knew it was time for him to get on with his life. He knew getting his wife back was impossible, since she had now remarried. He knew in his heart that he didn't love her anymore anyway. "I'm going by to see my kids right now. Is around eight good for you?"

"That's fine," she beamed. Dr. Donna Bellows had always had a major crush on Leroy but fought hard to contain it because he was married. Now, this was like a dream coming true for her. She kind of sensed that Leroy liked beautiful women and she was far from beautiful, but wow! Life is wonderful!

"I'll see you then," he finalized, and she nodded. He touched her arm lightly and walked away, and she proceeded in the opposite direction.

Leroy headed towards the doctor's lounge to pull off the surgical attire. It felt so good to him that his children had agreed to see him. They even acted as if they looked forward to it. He had hurt them so badly, and he was glad he was finally getting his life back in order.

People who say what they would *never* do have never hit rock bottom. When the one woman you love unconditionally looks you in your face and calls you a murderer, you don't know how you would react. He didn't know either until it happened to him. He didn't even want to *live* anymore. That's the reason he started the drinking. He *wanted* to die. He just didn't want to put a gun to his head, so he did it slowly. He was willing to give up his wife, children, everything for Patricia Timmons, and she had hurt him beyond his wildest imagination. She wouldn't even talk to him or see him. He never in a million years thought he would end up a drunk without a purpose until it happened to him. Although he had quit the booze cold turkey, he still attended AA meetings faithfully. He never wanted to repeat that part of his life. He had let down a lot of people, and he would spend the rest of his life trying to regain their trust. The courts had restored all his assets back to him. He was now in a nice condo, driving a Mercedes Benz again, money in the bank, *and* his career back. Life was grand!

Leroy was so deep in thought; he turned the corner quickly and almost collided with another person. "Oh, excuse me," he apologized then focused on the person and froze.

"Hi, Leroy," the tall, caramel-tan lady replied, adorned in a stylish, two-piece, burnt-orange business suit and her hair in shoulder-length, micro-braids, holding a beautiful vase of flowers.

Leroy took a deep breath as his heart fluttered profusely and he squeezed out quietly, "Hello, Patricia."

****

"So, how was lunch?" Mason asked Angel, entering the office.

"Great! I hated to come back," she remarked.

"Is Toni back?"

"Yeah, she's here," she said as he proceeded into Toni's office.

"Hi," he addressed, entering her office.

"Hi. How is Brandy?" Toni replied, standing to meet him.

"Hating herself," he laughed. "She's not used to being so fat."

Laughing with him, she countered, sitting on the edge of her desk to face him, "She'll get over it. When is the baby due?"

"In about seven weeks."

"Excited?"

"Oh yeah!"

"Have you decided on a name for him yet?"

"Not yet," he shared. "Just between you and me, I think Brandy wants to name him after her brother."

"Jamie?!" Toni exploded and he nodded. She chuckled. "As long as he doesn't turn out like Jamie."

"Tell me about it," he laughed with her. "So, when are you leaving?"

"Sunday."

"Well, I'm out of here. I probably won't see you again before you leave, so have a good time."

"Thank you. We will," she accepted, standing, and receiving a loving hug from him. "Tell Brandy not to have that baby before we get back. It's no fun having a shower when the baby's already here."

He laughed, "I'll tell her." She walked out with him as he left her office.

Mason focused on Angel and concluded, "See you, gorgeous." She held up briefly and smiled as he left. Toni focused on her friend looking frustrated.

"Anything wrong?"

"I can't find your article for Friday!" Angel answered. "And you won't be here to do another one. What're we going to do?"

"Don't panic," Toni urged. "I'm sure it's here somewhere." Toni walked to Angel's desk. "Have you sent it to Bill yet?"

"I don't know."

"Call him and see."

"I called. I couldn't get him."

Looking at her watch, Toni offered, "It's five fifteen. His secretary is already gone. I'll run down there and see if he's still here." Angel nodded as she left.

"I'll keep looking."

****

"You look great, Leroy," Patricia finally broke the uncomfortable silence.

"Thank you. So do you," he recognized, trying to settle the knot in his heart.

"Congratulations on getting your job back."

He smiled slightly, and then corrected sarcastically, "It wasn't *just* my job I needed back. It was my *life*!"

"Well, you seem to have bounced back well."

"After almost eight years I would say it was well overdue."

"I guess so," she concurred then took a deep breath. "Leroy, I don't know what to say to you. I'm so sorry for everything."

"So am I, Patricia," he reflected. "So am I."

"I came to see a friend," she made known. "But later, could we have dinner or something? I would love to sit and talk for a while." She paused. "I never stopped loving you."

He chuckled, "How could you love a *murderer*?"

"I really didn't believe you had killed Hank, Leroy. I just felt so guilty. I needed *someone* to blame."

"And *I* was it?"

"I'm sorry," she explained. "Like I told you before, Hank had that heart attack when I told him I wanted a divorce. I just felt that it was my fault."

"It wasn't your fault. Hank's heart would've eventually stopped without the shock of facing a divorce. It came from all the fatty foods he'd eaten all his life."

"I know that now," she understood. "So, what about tonight? I've been wanting to call you, but I didn't know what to say." She paused. "Could we please have dinner tonight and see if we could get this relationship back on track? I mean if you still feel the same way about me as I do you."

Leroy heard the words he had prayed to hear from Patricia for almost eight years now. And, at this point in his life, he realized that he had gone through hell and back...*without* her! And he really didn't *need* her anymore. She had cured him of that. What's more, although he still cared for her, he knew he didn't *want* her anymore. She had deserted him when he needed her most, and he could never trust her again. Leroy cleared his throat and proclaimed softly, "I'm sorry, Patricia, I'm moving my life forward now. I can't go back."

"I promise you, Leroy, if you would just give me a chance, I will prove to you that you can trust me again. I have been absolutely *miserable* without you," she pleaded.

"And what about *me*, Patricia? I needed you eight years ago, and you threw me out to the wolves and abandoned me. How could I *ever* trust you again," he explained as tears rolled down her face. "I prayed, night after night, that you would come and rescue me, or at least tell me that you believed in me, but you never did." He paused and sniffed back his own tears. "I want *everything* in my life back...except *us!*" He paused and she dropped her head. "I'm sorry. We will *never be* again." He stared at her long and hard then started to leave. "Goodbye." When she looked up, he was out of sight. She fell against the wall and surrendered to hysterical tears.

****

Toni walked into Bill's office. She saw his suit jacket on the back of his chair and his briefcase on the desk, so she knew he was still there. "Bill!" she called, but there was no answer.

Toni took a deep breath, went to his computer, and opened the folder with her name on it. She searched for the article. They were listed by dates. She noticed that two articles had the same dates so she opened one up, thinking Angel might have mixed them up. She began reading, and as she read her eyes widened. She gasped as she heard a voice say, "I had no choice." She jerked up and looked in Bill's face.

"Why, Bill? I thought of you like a father," she squeezed out. "Why would you try to destroy me?"

"I never meant to destroy you," he made known.

"But this article is the same one that Jamie Heard wrote," she observed then focused on him. "You *did* authorize it!" He dropped his head, and Toni took a deep breath and dropped her head in her hand. She couldn't stop the tears from flowing. He moved closer to her.

511

"I'm sorry, Toni," he squeezed out. "I never meant to hurt you...or Ron. You are like a daughter to me."

She sniffed and asked, "Then why? Why did you do it?" She moved from behind his desk.

"I had no choice," he insisted, moving behind the desk, and sitting.

"We *all* have choices, Bill," Toni stressed, sitting in front of his desk.

"Rita was sick for a long time," he explained. "Her medical bills were astronomical. The insurance ran out, and I started using our savings. She needed treatments. *Expensive* treatments! After our savings were used up, I started cashing in insurance policies, stocks, bonds, anything I could get money from." He paused. "Pretty soon there was nothing left. Once when Rita was in the hospital, I met this nurse who said she knew someone I could get a loan from, and I could pay him back at my own pace."

"Tracie Myers?"

"Yes," he continued. "So, she introduced me to Jamie Heard." He stopped and took a deep breath. "I borrowed money from him so Rita could get one of her surgeries. Then, years later, he came to me and said it was time for me to pay him back, but I found out that he didn't want money. He wanted me to let that article go through. He said if I didn't, he had people who could make my children and grandchildren disappear...*forever.*"

Toni dropped her head again. She couldn't believe what she was hearing. The man she trusted with her life had betrayed her, and she *could* understand why. She focused on him and inquired softly, "Bill, why didn't you come to *me*? I would've gladly given you any amount of money you needed."

"Silly pride," he answered. "But if I had known what kind of person Jamie Heard was, I would've gone to *anyone* other than him. Hindsight is always twenty-twenty. And after all that, Rita still died." Toni remained silent for a moment.

"So, what part did Brandy play in all of this?" Toni asked, looking up at him. "Did you and Brandy conspire against me?"

"No, I didn't even know Brandy was Jamie's sister. He just told me to leave the article out and it would be picked up. I found out later that she was the one who picked it up. I don't think she even knew I was involved. I think she thought Jamie had arranged it some other way. Initially, Jamie planted himself into Ron's law firm to plan something, but Brandy came to work here by pure coincidence. Jamie Heard didn't even know you were seeing Ron when Brandy started here. It started out as being just a job for her," he explained. "I'm so sorry, Toni. I wanted to tell you so badly, but I was ashamed."

"Bill, I understand," she finally replied. "If I knew Ron was in trouble, I would do just about anything to help him." Bill burst into tears, and Toni jumped up, moved around his desk, and pulled him in her arms. "It's okay. It's over!"

****

"Are you ready to go?" Travis asked Jordan as he entered her office.

"Yes," she answered. "You know, there's something I don't understand."

"What's that?"

"Ron has some pretty sisters. You and Ron were so close all your lives. Why weren't *you* interested in Melissa or Denise?"

"Me?" he exploded in laughter. "Melissa and Denise were like my *sisters*. Besides, *Simon* had his eyes set on Melissa even when we were in school, but she didn't know he existed. All she saw were *Ron's* friends." He continued to laugh. "And *Denise*, she's a trip. God bless Barry." She laughed with him.

"I just wondered."

"It's funny, but I never thought of either Melissa or Denise as love interests, and they would probably laugh if anyone mentioned *me* to them."

****

513

Toni's cell phone began ringing just as she and Bill were releasing their embrace. They both sniffed and wiped their tears then she answered her phone. "Yeah, Angel."

"Toni, did you find it?" Angel blurted out.

"Hold on," Toni said then focused on Bill. "Bill, did Angel send you my article for next week?"

"Yes, I have it."

Toni went back to the phone and shared, "Angel, he has it."

"Thank God," Angel breathed. "Are you all right?"

"Yeah. I'm fine. I'll see you Sunday."

"What time does our flight leave for Miami?"

"Twelve noon."

"Okay. We'll be there," Angel finalized. "Bye."

"Bye," Toni concluded then hung up, and then she focused on Bill. "Are you all right?"

"Yes, I am for the first time in a long time," he shared.

"I'll see you when I get back next week, okay?" Toni made known and he nodded. She turned to leave.

"Toni!" Bill called and she stopped and turned to face him. "I love you; you do know that don't you?"

"Yes, Bill, I do," she concurred. "Don't worry. You have a great weekend."

"I had planned on telling you one day. I even have a confession already written on my computer in my personal folder."

"It's okay, Bill, *really*," she insisted. "I understand why you did it. I *really* do."

"You are such a good person. Rita loved you too."

"I know, and I loved her, and I will *continue* to love you."

"Do you forgive me?"

"Yes, of course, I do," she acknowledged then went back to him and hugged him again. "I do, Bill. I really and truly do." He pulled her close and Toni felt his love pour out to her. Then soon he released her, and she proceeded towards the door. "I'll see you when I get back." He nodded as the door opened from the outside.

"Oh, Mr. Hurley, Mrs. Melton-Joyner, I didn't know anyone was still here," the security guard announced.

"I was just leaving," Toni made known.

"I'll walk you to your car," he suggested.

"Thank you, but I have to go back to my office first."

"It's okay. I'll walk with you," he insisted.

"Thank you," she accepted then focused back on Bill. "I'll call you tomorrow." He nodded.

"Mr. Hurley, I'll come back and check on you after I walk Mrs. Melton-Joyner out to her car," the security guard promised, and Bill nodded.

Toni walked out with the man as he talked about his grandchildren. Suddenly, they heard a loud sound from Bill's office, and Toni froze. Then she dashed back and opened the door to witness Bill, lying on the floor, soaking in his own blood with a gun in his hand. Toni burst into tears as she ran to his body. The security guard grabbed his cell phone to call 911.

Chapter 48

Toni was still numb from Bill's early morning funeral as she sat on the plane in first class beside Ron. Travis, Jordan, Angel, and David didn't know what to say to her. They understood her pain, but they just remained speechless. Every now and then, Ron would see a tear trickle down her face, and he would pull her in his arms. He hoped the cruise would help her deal with her friend's suicide.

****

Becky sat across the table from Joey in Atlanta, in the expensive, fancy French restaurant having an exquisite dinner. They had been seeing quiet a lot of each other these last few months and she didn't know anyone else could make her feel so alive and happy after Mason, but she was wrong. She never felt beautiful enough for Mason, but Joey accepted her for who she was, and he seemed to love who she was, and she liked that. She even stopped smoking and her body never felt better.

"How is your food?" Joey asked.

"Delicious," she answered.

"You're beautiful, Becky," Joey admired, staring deep into her eyes. Her hair was pulled back into a French twist with ringlets dangling around her face. She felt and looked great.

"Thank you, Joey," she accepted. Mason had met him on one of his trips to South Carolina and Mason seemed to like him. They hit it off well. Not that it mattered, but she was happy because Mason wouldn't make a fuss about Amy spending time with the two of them.

Joey took Becky's hand and declared, "I love you, Becky." Becky was speechless. She felt the same way about him, but it was so nice hearing a man actually say that he loved her and *meant* it.

"I love you too, Joey," she breathed, then they leaned across the table and kissed lightly.

"Will you marry me?" he asked without hesitation and she froze as he stared into her deep blue eyes, awaiting an answer.

"Yes," she finally responded, after finding her voice. "Yes." She laughed and cried at the same time. Joey jumped up and leaped around the table, grabbed her up and pulled her in a close embrace. With all the people in the restaurant, Becky and Joey could only feel each other's presence. All of Becky's proper upbringing went flying out the window as she kissed and caressed the man of her future in the middle of the floor.

****

"Mrs. Joyner, what seems to be the problem?" the ship doctor asked Toni as she sat on the examining room table.

"I guess it's motion sickness. I need something to settle my stomach."

"Let me examine you first, okay?" he suggested, and she nodded. "Have you been stressed out lately?"

"A little. I lost a very dear friend to suicide just before this trip."

"I'm sorry," he sympathized. "Please lie down."

"Doctor, if you find something wrong with me other than motion sickness, please be discreet in telling me. I don't want to ruin my husband's trip. And we'll deal with whatever it is when we get back."

"Certainly, Mrs. Joyner," he agreed. "By the way, I love your column."

"Thank you."

****

"Dad, what're you doing here?" Mason asked, walking into his father's office at the magazine.

"Just helping Gary to get in place to take over as the chief editor," Mr. Whittaker replied in his stern, sophisticated voice.

"What does mom say about you're working?"

"What she always says," he chuckled. "So, what else is new?" They laughed together. "How is your beautiful wife?"

"Great," Mason answered, smiling.

"When is the blessed event?"

"In about six weeks."

"Good. We can hardly wait to see our first grandson," Mr. Whittaker replied. "How is Becky? Amy says she's seeing someone."

"Yeah. A man from Atlanta. He's genuinely nice."

"Then you approve?"

"Oh yes."

"Good, I like to see people getting along when they get divorced...for the *children's* sake."

"I agree."

****

"Toni Melton!" a lady shrieked. Toni looked up from her dinner and smiled slightly. "I *heard* you were on this cruise. I wanted to talk to you."

"Hello...," Toni searched for a name.

"Cookie Walker."

"*The* Cookie Walker!" Toni exploded, standing. "Of WPOW television station?"

"That's me," the lady acknowledged.

"It's nice to meet you," Toni greeted. "I'm sorry I didn't recognize you."

"It's okay. It's so good to finally meet you."

Pointing to Ron, Toni introduced, "My husband, Ron Joyner."

"How do you do?" the lady extended her greeting with an outstretched hand.

"How do you do?" Ron accepted, standing, and shaking her hand.

"Please, don't get up," she chuckled, and he sat again.

"Our friends," Toni continued the introductions. "Travis and Jordan Bland; David and Angel Scott." They extended greetings to the classy lady.

The lady focused back on Toni and added, "I would love to talk to you about your own television news magazine show." The group exploded in excitement.

"A *television* show?" Toni repeated.

"Yes, as you know, we carry *Veronica Live*. You've been a guest on her show. We would love to bring *Toni Talk* to television," the lady announced.

"That's very flattering," Toni expressed.

"I know you'll have to think about it," she hypothesized. "So just see me sometime during the cruise, or...," she handed Toni a business card, "give me a call when you get back."

"I..."

"Don't answer yet. Think about it," she insisted then focused on the others. "Enjoy your cruise." Then she walked off and Toni sat again.

"My own television show," Toni repeated.

"Honey, that sounds like a great opportunity," Ron shared her enthusiasm. "Congratulations." He kissed her cheek.

"Thank you," Toni replied.

"That's great," Jordan added.

"This is big news," chimed in Travis.

"We're going on *television*," Angel exploded.

"*We*?!" inquired David.

"Of course. I'm Toni's assistant," Angel giggled. "Where she goes, *I* go!"

Toni laughed with her and said, "I hate to burst everyone's bubble, but I'm not taking the job."

"Why not, honey?" Ron wanted to know.

"A television show is a lot of work and a lot of hours," Toni explained. "With my column I can do that at home if I choose to do so, but a *television* show, I'll have to *be* there."

"You sound like you're planning to work at home," Angel asked Toni.

"I am for a while," she confirmed.

"Honey, you've got to go on with your life," Ron suggested. "I know Bill meant a lot to you, but don't stop *your* life because he chose to stop *his*."

"I'm not *stopping* my life, honey," Toni made known.

"Then what's all this talk about working at home and not wanting to do the television show?" Ron questioned.

"Because that's hard work for a woman who's trying to change diapers and fix bottles," Toni shared then smiled. Ron's eyes stretched and she nodded. "We're pregnant."

"Honey, why didn't you tell me?" he glowed.

"I just found out myself," she made known, and before she could say anything else, Ron had jumped up, pulled her up, and was spinning her around.

"We're going to have a baby!" he exploded, and everyone was looking at them now. He finally put her down and pulled her in his arms in a long passionate kiss. "I love you."

"I love you," she said to her husband as their friends jumped up to get in their hugs. It was truly a celebration for them as they sailed the merry seas.

The End

Thank you for reading my book.

Please read my other books:

Consequences, a novel of friendship that is centered around three lifelong friends: Cecily, a pediatrician who became involved with organized crime when she paid her way through medical school as a call-girl, which becomes a living nightmare for her; Lillian, a housewife turned alcoholic, who fights hard and steady for her husband, who has a philandering desire for Cecily; and Trudy, a wild and spirited fashion model, who finds comfort in the arms of Cecily's ex-pimp, turning to food at her heartbreak, achieving obesity and a failing career.

Sister Lucy: depicts church leaders in their fallible lives, their chaotic entanglements, and their struggles with temptations. The novel opens with a mystery that would lead to a "spiritual conclusion." Not everything is peachy with the ministers and preachers of the St. John Fellowship Community Church. Beyond the sermons and the hymns, they are stuck in illicit affairs, spiritual crises, and lies. Sister Lucy Davis, one of the ministers, sings like an angel but her heart cries out with guilt and discontent, as she struggles to reassess her faith and to find her way out of dead-end relationships. Unknown to Lucy, her misadventures are pushing her into danger. At one point, Lucy scans the mess in her life, wondering what the heck happened to that church-going woman who was always ready to extend a helping hand. Lucy Davis' latest boyfriend is none other than Reverend Clyde Mitchell, a charismatic leader who finds pleasure in the beds of all women except his wife's. Rev. Mitchell's son Kip, a handsome detective, struggles to be faithful to the ideals of his religion but covets Lucy. Minister Samantha Marsh further complicates matters by plotting to ensnare Kip.

Sister Lucy II (Kip & Lucy): a continuous novel about the struggles, triumphs, victories, obstacles, and faith of the saved and the not so saved. It is centered around the handsome and charming Pastor Kip Mitchell and his lovely wife Lucy, as they continue their lives together in love and happiness, with trouble lurking behind every nook and cranny. Kip and Lucy quickly find out that the devil doesn't have new tricks, just new people. Dr. Robin Bonner has set her sights on Kip. She sets her traps carefully for him as she tries desperately to hide from a tormenting past, while etching a place in the heart of Dr. Julius Hammond. Just as Dr. Bonner feels that she is making progress with snaring Kip, a long-time buried truth is revealed that could change all their lives.

Single Mom: A novel of trials, tribulation and faith as told through the eyes of a single mom. Carla David was a mother of three, living a dream life with Brandon, the man of her dreams. Until one day, without either forewarning or expectation, he tells her that he doesn't want to be married anymore. To say Carla was either shocked or bewildered would be a drastic understatement, because she had neither education nor gainful employment and is in dire fear of what to do next. Carla soon learns that Brandon had been harboring a secret, which jolts her into reality that she is a single mom, and she does not have time to wallow in pity, but pick herself up, step up to the plate, and take care of her children. What Carla does will not only inspire single moms everywhere, but it will encourage them as well, as they witness her transformation growing from a weak, self-pity married woman to a strong, vibrant single mom who will put herself in harm's way to protect her children at any cost.

Soon to be released: *Forgotten Memories*: What would you do if you woke up one morning not remembering who you were? That is what happened to famous artist, Vinny Perkins. She had a great life, a wonderful husband, a supportive friend, and a caring family, but she woke up one morning not remembering any of them. Not only did Vinny have to worry about not remembering anything, but she also had to worry about who and why someone was desperately trying to kill her. *Forgotten Memories* will appeal to mystery buffs everywhere, as they ride with Vinny on her journey to remember the unknown while danger is lurking on every side, as she tries to continue her life with her scheduled art show. Vinny doesn't know what she witnessed before her almost fatal accident that took her memories away, but she does know that she must regain an ounce of recognition before someone succeeds in killing her. *Forgotten Memories* takes you through the mysterious, mind bobbling, twists and turns of a woman running out of time to remember her past to save her life in the present.

THANK YOU FOR YOUR SUPPORT.

About the Author:

Lurma Swinney, PhD

Dr. Lurma Swinney is a native of South Carolina. Her passion is writing. She is a Christian and credits God for everything good in her life. Dr. Swinney started writing at a young age but did not become serious about writing until she became an adult. Dr. Swinney has worked in schools throughout South Carolina and New Jersey. She earned her Ph.D. from Capella University in Minneapolis, Minnesota. Dr. Swinney is a member of Alpha Kappa Alpha Sorority Incorporated. She writes to inspire, educate, and encourage all people. Please visit her website at sdpublishinghouse.com. You may also email her at swinney@sdpublishinghouse.com.

Thank you for your support.

CPSIA information can be obtained
at www.ICGtesting.com
Printed in the USA
BVHW070954060421
604322BV00006B/8